Urania
The Story of a Young Woman's Love

&

The Novella
of Giulia Camposanpiero and Thesibaldo Vitaliani

by

Giulia Bigolina

Medieval and Renaissance Texts and Studies

Volume 262

AL MAGNIFICO, ET ECCELLENTE DOTTOR DI LEGGI, IL. S. BARTOLOMEO SALVATICO.

GIVLIA BIGOLINA.

E si potesse, ualoroso, et nobilissimo Giouine, misurare à pieno tutti gli humani affetti con qualche esteriore operatione, io non dubito che molti i quali si dimostrano essere suiscerati amanti, misurandoli si scoprirebbono che poco ò nulla amano; et all'incontro molti altri, de' quali alcuni per poco sapere, et alcuni perche lor manca l'ardir di manifestarsi pare che amino poco; nondimeno chi ben misurar gli potesse, esser fedeli, et suiscera tissimi amanti si conoscerebbono. Et qllo, che de gli amanti io dico, medesimamente d'ogni

Trivulziana 88, folio 1r
Reproduced by the kind permission of the
Archivio Storico Civico e Biblioteca Trivulziana.

The Villa Bigolin at Selvazzano.

URANIA
The Story of a Young Woman's Love

&

THE NOVELLA
OF GIULIA CAMPOSANPIERO AND
THESIBALDO VITALIANI

by

Giulia Bigolina

edited and translated by

Christopher Nissen

Arizona Center for Medieval and Renaissance Studies
Tempe, Arizona
2004

*A grant from Northern Illinois University
has assisted with meeting the publication costs of this volume.*

*Dust jacket image: "The Judgment of Paris" by Paolo Veronese.
Courtesy of the Samek Art Gallery, Bucknell University, Lewisburg, PA.*

© Copyright 2004
Arizona Board of Regents for Arizona State University

Library of Congress Cataloging-in-Publication Data
Bigolina, Giulia, d. 1569.
 [Urania, nella quale si contiene l'amore d'una giovane di tal nome. English]
 Urania, the story of a young woman's love : the novella of Giulia Camposanpiero and Tesibaldo Vitaliani / by Giulia Bigolina ; edited and translated by Christopher Nissen.
  p. cm. — (Medieval and Renaissance Texts and Studies ; v. 262)
 Includes bibliographical references and index.
 ISBN 0-86698-305-8 (alk. paper)
  1. Nissen, Christopher. II. Title. III. Medieval & Renaissance Texts & Studies (Series) ; v. 262.

PQ4610.B58U7313 2004
853'.4—dc22   2004052922

This book is made to last.
It is set in Bembo,
smythe-sewn and printed on acid-free paper
to library specifications.

Printed in the United States of America

Contents

Acknowledgements	ix
Introduction	
1. Giulia Bigolina and Sixteenth-Century Padua	1
2. The Discovery of Bigolina's Works and her Place in the Canon	20
3. *Urania, The Story of a Young Woman's Love*	29
4. "The Novella of Giulia Camposanpiero and Thesibaldo Vitaliani"	42
5. *Urania*: Text and Translation	50
6. "La novella di Giulia Camposanpiero et di Thesibaldo Vitaliani": Text and Translation	53
Urania, The Story of a Young Woman's Love	56
"The Novella of Giulia Camposanpiero and Thesibaldo Vitaliani"	291
Works Cited	323
Index	333

Acknowledgements

My search for Giulia Bigolina has taken many years, since that day in August 1996 when I first read her work in Borromeo's *Notizia di Novellieri italiani* in the Marciana Library of Venice. Throughout this time I have received much essential aid and advice from a great many people. First and foremost I wish to thank the Research and Artistry Committee of the Graduate School of Northern Illinois University, as well as the Gladys Krieble Delmas Foundation, for the two grants which made it possible for me to travel to the libraries and archives of Padua and other cities of the Veneto, as well as to Milan, the Vatican, Besançon, and Paris.

Among the many librarians and archivists who were helpful to me, I acknowledge especially Lavinia Prosdocimi and Pietro Gnan of the University of Padua Library, Emilia Veronese and Luciana Rea of the University of Padua Archives, Adriano Zattarin of the State Archive of Padua, and Monsignor Claudio Bellinati of the Biblioteca Capitolare. I also wish to thank the many scholars who gave me indispensable advice during the course of my research and the preparation of this edition, among them Renzo Bragantini, Francesco Piovan, Elda Martelozzo Forin, Vincenzo Mancini, Gloria Allaire, Deanna Shemek, Maria Bendinelli Predelli, Dennis McAuliffe, Enrique Fernandez, Sheila Cavanaugh, Robert Buranello, Leslie S. B. MacCoull, Elisabetta Manetti, Patrizia Bettella, and Giorgio Padoan. A number of art historians came to my rescue in a field in which I still have much to learn, and of these I am especially grateful to Mary Quinlan, Judith Testa, Rosanne Dwyer, Lia R. Markey, David M. Stone, and Catherine Hess. Antoinette Brazouski very kindly reviewed my Latin translations, and I am indebted to Ruggero Stefanini for his invaluable

ACKNOWLEDGEMENTS

philological advice. Giovanni Spani and Marika Mies of the University of Padua assisted me in my research during those times I was unable to come to their city, and I extend special thanks to them.

I must also thank the staff of the Newberry Library Center for Renaissance Studies for allowing me to participate in the 2001 Summer Institute in the Italian Archival Sciences, where I was able to consult with Franca Petrucci Nardelli and Armando Petrucci on numerous paleographical and editorial matters relating to this book. Finally, although mere words hardly seem sufficient, I must acknowledge my tremendous debt to Rossella Consiglio of the State Archive of Padua for all of her help, advice and unflagging support. This book is dedicated to her.

Introduction

1. GIULIA BIGOLINA AND SIXTEENTH-CENTURY PADUA

In 1560 the Paduan priest and historian Bernardino Scardeone published a history of his city in Latin, which also included biographies of many distinguished Paduan citizens. He devoted an entire section, "De Claris Mulieribus Patavinis," to women, and it is here that we find the only scholarly assessment of the works of Giulia Bigolina to have been written while she was still alive:

> ... remarkable elegance, charm and grace of speech, as well as exceptional knowledge of the Tuscan tongue, all greatly exalt Giulia Bigolina. In whatever time she has free from the work of Pallas [i.e., domestic tasks], this woman strives mightily to secure for herself the perpetual immortality of her name; and she plainly demonstrates, by means of her innate ability, that skill in poetry is the same in women as it is in men. For she writes in a language that is rhythmical and fluent, very elegantly rendered in the vernacular, so that in this kind of style she cannot rightly envy any writer, either ancient or modern. Up to now she has written many things worth reading, which are truly esteemed by all readers with great applause, and which are perused with the greatest delight. Foremost among them are certain comedies or tales in Boccaccio's style, which nevertheless maintain at all times matronly propriety. These tales are characterized by distinguished subject matter, marvelous artistry, varied outcomes, and unexpected conclusions. Granted, love is discussed in these stories, and the passions of lovers have their place therein; nonetheless, all these things are treated here so chastely and modestly that these stories make suitable reading for any honest matron. For they do not reveal the slightest trace of lewdness, apart from the persistent afflictions, fallacious hopes, and long-

Introduction

lasting servitude of those youths who are more mad than loving. All her works are very virtuously told, well furnished with proverbs and good judgments, and suited to their subject matter. For this reason these tales can easily induce the reader to embrace virtue and turn away from vices.[1]

Although this fleeting glimpse tells us next to nothing about Bigolina's life, and little enough about her works, it is still quite substantial compared to other contemporary assessments. A few other sixteenth-century critical references to her are known, all written after Bigolina's death circa 1569, and they say far less than Scardeone. Ercole Marescotti (also known as "Filogenio") included her name on a list of celebrated women poets which he published in Fermo in 1589 (*Dell'eccellenza della donna*, 171). In that same year Bigolina appeared in Luigi Contarini's *Il vago e dilettevole giardino*, again on a list of prominent women writers (392). Contarini arranges all of his famous women under various descriptive headings, calling them "Dotta" [learned], "Casta" [chaste], "Lussuriosa" [wanton], "Animosa" [daring], and the like. Bigolina's group, which includes Vittoria Colonna, Veronica

---

[1] "... ita nunc Juliam Bigolinam facundia singularis, lepor, gratiaque sermonis, & eximia Etruscae linguae peritia vehementer extollit: cui quantum per otium ab opere Palladio vacare contingit, magnopere annititur ad perpetuam nominis immortalitatem sibi parandam: quando quidem poeticam facultatem, non aliam in viris quam in foeminis esse suo ingenio manifeste demonstrat. Scribit enim & rhytmica & soluta oratione, idiomate vernaculo elegantissime, ut in eo genere dictionis, nemini veterum aut recentium scriptorum invidere possit. Scripsit hactenus complurima lectu dignissima, quae sane à cunctis legentibus magno applausu probantur, & summa delectatione leguntur: & in primis quasdam comoedias seu fabulas, ad Boccacii morem (servato tamen ubique matronali decoro) insigni argumento, artificio mirabili, eventu vario, & exitu inexpectato. In quibus licet de amore tractetur, & intermisceantur amantium affectus: ita tamen & pudice, & modeste omnia, ut quamlibet honestam matronam decere possit: quod nihil prorsus oleat impudici: neque aliud sapiat, praeterquam assiduas afflictiones, fallaces spes, & inanes cogitationes, & perduram amentium potius quam amantium juvenum servitutem: omnia sane honeste dicta, verbis & sententiis instructa, & rebus accommodata: utpote quale, & lectorem ad amplectendam virtutem allicere, & à vitiis deterrere facile possint": B. Scardeone, *Historiae de Urbis Patavii* . . . (1560; repr. Bologna: Forni, 1979), 418–19. The translation is mine, as are all translations from Latin or Italian which follow. For the tendency of sixteenth-century scholars to refer to novellas as "comoedias" [comedies] see Enzo Esposito's introduction to his edition of Ser Giovanni Fiorentino's *Pecorone* (Ravenna: Longo, 1974), viii n. 3. Esposito finds it curious that Michele Poccianti characterized the *Pecorone's* novellas thus in 1589, but it would seem that the use of this term reflects the novella's conspicuous absence from the standard genre types of the classical literary tradition.

Introduction

Gambara (here mistakenly called "Vittoria" also), Laura Battifero, Laura Terracina, and others, appears under the heading "Virtuose" [virtuous ones], which would seem to echo Scardeone's appraisal of her. Then in 1594 Theodor Zwinger described the most prominent members of a number of distinguished Paduan families, including the Bigolini, for which he mentions only two persons, one of them "Iulia, eruditione clara, & vernacula poesi, nostra aetate" ["Giulia, outstanding in erudition and vernacular literature, of our own time" (*Methodus Apodemica*, 283)]. Of these critics, only Scardeone took note of Bigolina's most distinguished contribution to the literature of her age: her vernacular fiction in prose.

Scardeone's emphasis on the moral content of Bigolina's works reflects much more than mere clerical bias. It reveals as well the uniqueness of his subject's choice of genre. One of the central paradoxes of the late medieval and Renaissance Italian novella, as founded and shaped by Giovanni Boccaccio in the fourteenth century, lies in the peculiar associations between women and the novella text, associations which are not so apparent in any other literary genre. When Boccaccio declared in his *Decameron* that his novella collection was intended primarily for the consumption of women, and then went on to pretend that the majority of the tales in that collection were recounted by women in a fictionalized garden setting, he established a set of expectations which prevails in many subsequent *novellieri*, especially those written after the late fifteenth century (*Decameron*, ed. Branca, 1: 8–10). Renaissance novellas and novella collections often emphasize the role of women as narrators, readers, or characters within the tales.

And yet a paradox persists, for no matter how much Italian women might see themselves reflected within the various facets of the novella tradition, there was one role in which they almost never participated: that of writer. More Italian women took to writing in the sixteenth century than in any previous era, but nearly all of them gained fame as poets, not as writers of prose fiction, and especially not as writers of novellas "ad Boccacii morem." This choice was clearly a risky one for a literate woman of the time, as Scardeone's words bear witness. Ever since Boccaccio's age the novella had acquired a questionable reputation in some circles, as the literary form in which such sexual improprieties as fornication and adultery might most easily be depicted. Boccaccio himself had, at a certain point in his life, expressed reservations about women reading his *Decameron*.[2] Therefore Scardeone felt he had to take special pains to preserve the image of a novella writer who happened to belong to a respectable noble family, even at the

---

[2] Francesco Bruni, *Boccaccio. L'invenzione della letteratura mezzana* (Bologna: Il Mulino, 1990), 44, 261.

INTRODUCTION

expense of a more thorough treatment of her literary efforts. In describing her as he does, he inadvertently takes note of her greatest claim to fame, as the first Italian woman ever to gain recognition in the realm of prose fiction.[3]

No story of Bigolina's was published in her lifetime, and for centuries her work has languished in the shadowy margins of the Italian literary canon. Reliable biographical information regarding her has not been preserved in any critical study, either during or after the sixteenth century, but a few facts can be found in the State Archive of Padua and other places. The Bigolini, or Bigolin, had originally come to Padua from Treviso in the fifteenth century and eventually attained noble status in their adopted city. By the sixteenth century they were a noteworthy family with members who had distinguished themselves in such endeavors as warfare, writing, and jurisprudence.[4] It was frequently a custom of the time to refer to women of important Veneto families by the feminine form of their surname, and in Giulia's case she seems to have always preferred to call herself Bigolina in legal documents, even after her marriage. This is the name by which she has been known ever since.

The year of Bigolina's birth cannot be known with certainty, but two documents in the Padua Archive help us establish a rough time frame for it. In one, dated 1543, we are told that her father Girolamo Bigolin had received a dowry from Bigolina's mother Alvisa (Aldovisa) Barbo Soncin in 1516, while in another we find Bigolina already married to a certain Bartolomeo Vicomercato in 1534.[5] Thus she was likely born after 1516, but probably not much past 1520, even if we take into consideration the young age at which girls of the time were typically married. In 1527 Girolamo is referred to as being already deceased (ASP AN

---

[3] For a discussion of the problems facing Italian women who wished to write novellas or other works perceived as employing " 'realist' erotic language," especially in the period before 1580, see Virginia Cox, "Fiction, 1560–1650," in *A History of Women's Writing in Italy*, ed. L. Panizza and S. Wood (Cambridge: Cambridge University Press, 2000), 52–64, here 53.

[4] For the origins and famous members of the Bigolini family see V. Mancini, *Lambert Sustris a Padova: La Villa Bigolin a Selvazzano* (Selvazzano: Centro culturale, 1993), 53–55, and G. Wiel Marin, "Antiche vicende di Santa Croce Bigolina," *Padova e la sua provincia* 2 (1969): 2–4, here 2. For Alessandro Bigolin, famed as a defender of the Venetian Republic during the War of the League of Cambrai, see Scardeone, *Historiae*, 400. For a family tree of the Bigolini, including Giulia, see Mancini, *La Villa Bigolin*, 148.

[5] Archivio di Stato di Padova, *Archivio notarile* (hereafter cited in text as ASP AN) 4839, fol. 697r, and ASP AN 4830, fol. 827r.

INTRODUCTION

4839, fols. 696v–698r). Alvisa appears frequently in archival documents and was still alive at least as late as 1554 (ASP AN 5216, fol. 484r).

The records of the University of Padua tell us that Vicomercato, a native of Crema, was a law student in 1533.[6] The university has no record of his taking a degree, and no archival document mentions any professional title for him, so it would seem that he abandoned his university studies at some point, perhaps in order to marry into the distinguished Bigolin family. A document of 1542 indicates he was still alive in that year, but by 1554 another calls Giulia a widow (ASP AN 5208, fols. 246r–247v; 5216, fol. 484r). The Padua Archive has two lists of the fields and houses that were included in Bigolina's dowry possessions, and they tell us she owned a great deal of land outside of Padua, some of it bordering the even more substantial holdings of her brother Socrate. The first list, dated 30 May 1561, bears the heading "Beni stabili, li quali possedo io Giulia Bigolina di mia dote" [Real estate which I, Giulia Bigolina, possess as part of my dowry].[7] The second list, immediately following the first in the document, is dated 21 March 1569 and was witnessed by Bigolina's son Silvio Vicomercato. By this time Bigolina is clearly deceased: "Siano aggiunti alla prima pollizza della q. (i.e., *quondam*) M. Giulia Bigolina campi tre arativi ..." [Let three arable fields be added to the first list of the late Lady Giulia Bigolina ... (*Estimo* fol. 141r–v)]. It is quite possible that Bigolina had died not long before the date of this second list, since her death could have necessitated a fairly prompt reassessment of her holdings. In any case, we may conclude that the author's life span may be placed sometime between the years 1516 and 1569, and that she could not have been much past the age of fifty when she died.

To the best of my knowledge, Bigolina's only holographic document in the Padua Archives is her will, dated 27 June 1563 (ASP AN 829, fols. 64r–66r). There can be no doubt that this will was written in Bigolina's own hand, for this fact is attested not only by the notary's Latin preface ("... infrascriptum testamentum manu propria scriptum infrascriptae dominae testatricis ...": fol. 64r), but also by Bigolina herself in her introductory statement:

Conoscendo io Giulia Bigolina quanto questa nostra humana vita è fragile, et caduca, et come spesse volte aviene che un' il quale un giorno vive sano,

---

[6] E. M. Forin, *Acta Graduum Academicorum Gymnasii Patavini 1501–1550* (Padua: Antenore, 1982), 296.

[7] See Archivio di Stato di Padova, *Estimo 1518*, Polizze della città, busta 34, fols. 142r–143v.

Introduction

et allegro, l'altro sequente vien tratto alla sepoltura, ne si truova maggior' insania ne'l mondo quanto è quella di tale che a cio spesse volte non pensa, ne si puo dir che vi pensino quelli i quali nella matura etade si lasciano a non pensata Morte cogliere senza haver di sè, et di l'haver suo doppo di sè ordinato, et disposto, ond'io per non cadere in tale errore, et per lasciar pace, et concordia doppo me tra quelli ch'hanno ad esser miei heredi, o che aspetino da me gratitudine alcuna, o percio deliberato mentre io son per la Iddio gratia sana dell'inteletto quantunque non molto de'l corpo di ordinare, et disporre l'ultima mia volonta qui sopra questa carta de mia man propria . . . (ASP AN 829, fol. 65r)

[I, Giulia Bigolina, am aware of how frail and transitory is this human life of ours, and how it often happens that a person might one day live in health and joy, yet the next be taken to the grave. There is no greater insanity in the world than that of the person who does not often think about this; nor can it be said that those who are advanced in years, yet allow themselves to be taken by death all unawares, without having arranged for the disposition of themselves and of their goods, are thinking about this. Therefore, in order not to fall into this error, and in order to leave peace and concord after my demise among those who will have to be my heirs, or those who expect any sign of gratitude from me, I have decided, while I am by the grace of God of sound mind, even if not so healthy in body, to draw up my final will here on this paper, in my own hand . . .]

This will, three folios in length and written in a very neat and precise hand, is rather more introspective than the norm. It would seem to be the work of someone who took her literary ambitions seriously, and indeed its occasionally didactic tone might remind the reader of certain passages in *Urania*. We may glean from it a few more facts about Bigolina's life. As we know from her second list of dowry holdings, she did not have long to live when she wrote this, and indeed it would seem that in 1563 she was already in ill health. In subsequent paragraphs she mentions three children: Silvio, almost certainly the first-born since he was her principal heir and the recipient of the bulk of her lands and goods (fol. 66r), Ottavio, who was a priest associated with the church of the Eremitani in Padua (fol. 65v), and Gabriela, a nun in the convent of San Bernardino (fol. 65v; and she is also mentioned in ASP AN 5216 cited above, fol. 485r). It was sometimes the case in this period that the offspring of landowning families of modest wealth who were not principal heirs ended up in holy orders, so that the families would not have to

INTRODUCTION

subdivide the patrimony or provide dowries, and this might well have been the case here. Bigolina did grant Ottavio some arable fields, with the understanding that upon his death they would go to Silvio or his heirs, while Gabriela was to receive only a few items of clothing and a stipend of twelve ducats a year (fols. 65v–66r). Bigolina also left some household items to her servant Vendramina, of whom she was apparently quite fond, and provisions for a pension for her sister Maria.

Bigolina's remarkably precise instructions regarding her funeral and the disposition of her body after death reveal a few more things about her character and the circumstances of her life. She wished her body to be washed and dressed in the habit of a nun of St. Clare, then watched over by nuns or by other "good persons" for forty hours before burial if she were to die in one of the cooler seasons, but only for thirty hours if she were to die in the summer. Bigolina takes a rather severe tone in stipulating this, evidently out of fear of being buried alive, for she says that if these instructions are not strictly followed then her heirs will be liable to pay fifty ducats to the poor orphans ("... et siano ubligati a questo sotto pena contrafacendo di pagar duccati 50 alli poveri orfani," fol. 65r). She then continues:

> Io voglio doppo il termine de l'hore 30, over 40, senza alcuna funeral pompa con duoi soli Preti della Parrochia, con 4 torze di peso d'una lira l'una, portate da 4 Monache di San Bernardino sia condotto detto mio corpo nella Chiesa di detto San Bernardino, et ivi in una delle Sepolture delle Monache sia sepolto, però prima avisando le mie fraglie, cioè IHS, et san Giovanni della Morte, et altre, se in altre in quel tempo mi ritrovasse (*sic*), et sia sodisfato ogni mio debito qual con esse in quel tempo io mi ritrovassi havere, et sia da dette mie fraglie com'è usanza accompagnata alla Sepoltura, et harrei piacere se cio piacera al mio herede d'esser similmente accompagnata alla sepoltura da gl'orfani cantanti le letanie, ma a cio non lo stringo. Et se per caso il R.^{do} Padre Maestro Ottavio mio Figliuolo (come ha piu volte detto) fosse pur disposto di voler il mio corpo nella sua Chiesa de gli heremitani non gli sia da 'l mio herede quanto a questo interdetto, ma nel resto sia adimpita tutta la mia volonta ... (ASP AN 829, fols. 65r–v)

[I wish, at the end of the thirty or forty hours, that my aforementioned body be borne to the church of the aforementioned San Bernardino without any funeral pomp, accompanied only by two parish priests and four candles of one *lira* weight each, carried by four nuns of San Bernardino; there I wish it to be placed in one of the tombs of the nuns. However, first I wish that my confraternities, that is IHS (Jesus) and San Giovanni

7

Introduction

della Morte, as well as any others that I might have joined by that time, be informed, and that all the debts that I might have to them be paid. As is customary, I wish to be accompanied to my burial site by these confraternities, and I would also like it if my heir will allow some orphans to sing litanies as they follow me to my grave, but I will not compel him to do this. And if by chance my son the reverend father Ottavio is still willing (as he has often said) to allow my body to be placed in his church of the Eremitani, let my heir have no objection to it; but in all else let things be done according to my will.]

In the Veneto, the term *fraglia* refers to a guild or confraternity; those with a religious orientation were typically involved in charitable work with orphans or the destitute. Her two references to orphans in the document reveal that Bigolina was particularly sympathetic to them.

Although this document provides us with clues concerning the whereabouts of Bigolina's grave, it still seems likely it will never be found: the church of the Eremitani in Padua was famously damaged by an Allied bomb in 1944 (along with several frescoes by Mantegna) and has since been rebuilt, whereas the church of San Bernardino no longer exists.

It is not known when Bigolina started to write, and there exists no indication that she ever sought to publish her works. The first datable reference to one of her literary works appears in Pietro Aretino's last letter to her in 1549, thanking her for a sonnet she had sent him. She emerges as a public figure in the late 1540s, when she may have been around thirty years old; the earliest possible reference to her appears in a short encomiastic poem in octaves by Giovanni Maria Masenetti, called *Il divino oracolo in lode dei nuovi sposi del 1548 e di tutte le belle gentildonne padovane* [The Divine Oracle, in Praise of the Newlyweds of 1548 and all the Lovely Paduan Noblewomen]. This work was published in pamphlet form in Venice that same year. The poem recounts a dream vision on the part of the first-person narrator, who sees a triumphal procession of famous women led by Venus, including many of the most prominent women of Padua. Masenetti devotes a whole octave to Gerolama Bigolina, a woman of the Papafava family who had married Giulia's cousin Dioclide. Subsequently he sees two more women who appear to be "dee del sommo choro" ["goddesses of the highest chorus"], one of whom is also named Bigolina (*Divino oracolo*, fol. 23r). In his study of the frescoes in the Bigolin family's villa at the town of Selvazzano outside of Padua, which belonged to Dioclide Bigolin in the mid-sixteenth century, Vincenzo Mancini asserts that this must be none other than the author Giulia Bigolina herself, and indeed

INTRODUCTION

her prominence in the clan would likely have assured her a place in a local encomium of this sort (*La Villa Bigolin*, 132 n. 30). Although Masenetti says that Gerolama is "dottata d'eloquenza alta, e divina" ["endowed with high and divine eloquence" (*Divino oracolo*, fol. 22v)] he makes no such claim in the case of the second Bigolina, which would seem to indicate that her writings had not made much of an impression at this point.

About a year later Bigolina managed, apparently through her own efforts, to catch the attention of Pietro Aretino, one of the greatest personalities of her time and long a resident of nearby Venice. In 1550 the fifth book of Aretino's letters was published, including among them three which he had written to Bigolina (letters 338, 339, and 353). The first two are dated September 1549 and the third is dated October of that same year. Each of Aretino's letters responds to something which Bigolina had sent to him, in a series of correspondences which Bigolina seems to have initiated. In letter 338, addressed to "Madonna Giulia Big.," Aretino thanks her for a letter she had sent him, a letter which he says he shared with his friend, the artist Titian:

> Se mai mi fur care lettere, carissima èmmi stata quella, che di suo pugno istesso mi ha datto in man propria la vostra cameriera gentile. Era meco, quando ch'ella mi comparse innanzi, Tiziano; quel Pittor dico, che quanto la fama è famoso; il cui soprano ispirito per esser tutt'uno col mio, nel sentirmi leggere ciò che per mera cortesia mi scrivete, se ne compiacque non altrimenti che se a lui ciò che a me tocca toccasse, e ben vero, che in le cotante laude attribuitemi, stemmo così tra noi un poco insieme sospesi, risolvendoci poi a metterle a conto più tosto de la bontà di voi, che al merito di me ... (Aretino, *Lettere*, ed. Procaccioli, 5: 261)

> [If ever letters were dear to me, most dear was the one that your kind chambermaid delivered to me with her own hand. When she appeared to me, Titian was with me; I mean that painter who is as famous as fame itself. His most excellent soul was one with mine as he listened to me reading the things which you write to me through simple courtesy. He took as much pleasure from it as he would have if the kindness you show me had been meant for him. Indeed, we were uncertain for a time how to regard the great praise you bestowed upon me; eventually we decided to attribute it more to your kindness than to any merit of mine ...]

Although Aretino did publish some of the letters he had received from other

Introduction

correspondents in his *Lettere scritte a Pietro Aretino* (1551), he did not include Bigolina's among them so we cannot know its contents. For his part Aretino, as the Western world's first great publicist, seems to imagine that Bigolina would like nothing so much as to be made better known, through his own efforts:

> ... Imperochè una mente grata, e di fervor' piena, in cambio di quello che dar non può, se stesso dona. Sì che in luogo di ciò che non sono, pigliate me proprio; sodisfacendone il nome vostro in l'onore che la mia penna s'ingegnarà di fargli in memoria. Benchè il di lei calamo più che altro è bastante a redurlo in isquilla, sonante in gloria di sè medesimo, ne i Templi di tutti i secoli. Sì che bisogna ch'io pensi di essercitarmi in servirvi, e non in celebrarvi. Ma perchè nulla in simil arte io non vaglio, è forza che adopri, in vece di i piedi, la lingua, confessando l'obligo ch'io tengo a l'amore filialmente portatomi da voi, Giulia madonna, perch'altro che amorevolezza non vi sentite nel petto e ne l'anima. Per il che l'umanità di che vediamvi composta, se ne congratula con la Natura, che tale vi ha fatta quale le sue caritadi vorrebbero che ci nascesse ciascuna. Che se ciò fusse, la vertù, e non il vizio; la moderanza, e non la superbia; l'onestà, e non la lascivia, predominaria il sesso che honorate con le gentilezze, adornate con i costumi, e alluminate con le osservanze ... (Aretino, *Lettere*, ed. Procaccioli, 5: 261–62)

> [... a spirit which is grateful and brimming with fervor gives itself in place of that which it cannot give. Therefore, take me in the place of those things which I am not, and let your name be satisfied with the honor with which my pen will find ways to memorialize it, even though my pen's inkwell is sufficient in itself to make your name a trumpet peal, resounding in its own glory, in the temples of the ages. It might be necessary that I consider serving you rather than celebrating you; but since I am not good at such things, I am forced to employ my tongue rather than my feet. I confess that I feel obliged to you, on account of the filial love which you, Lady Giulia, have shown me; for you feel nothing but love in your heart and soul. On this account, the human kindness which we see you are made of is conjubilant with Nature; for Nature has fashioned you in just the way that she, in her benevolence, would wish to create every woman born. If every woman were so, then virtue instead of vice, moderation instead of haughtiness, and chastity instead of lasciviousness would predominate in that sex which you honor with kindness, adorn with manners and illuminate with reverence ...]

Introduction

Aretino answers praise with praise, ever mindful, as Scardeone would be later, of preserving Bigolina's good name. In fact, any man of the time would have to take such pains if he wished to sound supportive of a highborn woman who dared aspire to create a public persona for herself; and so Aretino calls her love for him "filial," and makes a point of emphasizing her virtues. He pompously claims he will make her name "a trumpet peal," but seemingly for nothing more than her kindness and good manners. If Aretino knew anything about her creative writings, or if she made any mention of them herself, his letter gives no clue.

Bigolina seems to have greatly desired to stay in Aretino's good graces by one means or another, for later that same month she sent him something very different: a serving girl, to look after his household and his young daughters. This time Aretino's response, in letter 339, was less charitable, for the girl was too young and immature for Aretino's needs, as he states in his characteristically blunt way:

> La Vilanella da la benignità vostra mandatami è più bisognosa che altri lei governi, che atta ella a governar altri. Certo la sua cera farebbe un torto grande al guardare Agnelle, caso che si mettesse a intertener bambine. (Aretino, *Lettere*, ed. Procaccioli, 5: 262)
>
> [The country girl whom, in your kindness, you have sent to me has more need of being looked after herself than she is capable of looking after others. Certainly her mien would do great wrong to the herding of lambs, were she to begin spending time with little girls.]

Aretino goes on to speculate that perhaps his friend Titian might find a place for this girl in his own household; while for his own part he requires girls between the ages of fourteen and eighteen, "and not too unattractive, inasmuch as where beauty resides, good may also be found" ("e di vista iscoparicente non troppo; imperochè dove è il bello, è quasi sempre il buono ancora," Aretino, *Lettere*, ed. Procaccioli, 5: 262).

It is surprising that Bigolina came to choose such a gesture, especially given Aretino's vast reputation for lechery and her own clearly stated love of feminine virtue. She might not have been aware of Aretino's tendency to sexually exploit his female household servants, even if Aretino did not take great pains to conceal it himself in his various writings.[8] However, it is not unreasonable to imagine that Bigolina had heard of Aretino's interest in maids from the Paduan lawyer Fran-

---

[8] J. Cleugh, *The Divine Aretino* (New York: Stein and Day, 1966), 153–54.

INTRODUCTION

cesco Macassola, who corresponded often with Aretino. In a letter dated April 1548, which appears in Book IV of his *Lettere* (published 1550), Aretino thanks Macassola for recommending a loyal serving maid to him at a time when Aretino was having a crisis in his household staff (Aretino, *Lettere*, ed. Procaccioli, 4: 276–77). It is clear from such correspondences that Aretino took the problem of finding reliable serving women quite seriously, although once more one cannot help having suspicions regarding his motives. In this letter to Macassola, for instance, he indicates that he would prefer the woman to be not only trustworthy but also attractive; for if she is, "... io sono un Re picciolino" ["I am a little king" (Aretino, *Lettere*, ed. Procaccioli, 4: 277)]. Although no direct link can be demonstrated between Macassola and Bigolina, she was clearly quite familiar with the community of Paduan jurists and students of law, in whose circles she and her family had moved for quite some time. Apart from the fact that her uncle Antonio Maria Soncin possessed a law degree, and her husband Vicomercato had studied law in Padua, her dedication and introduction to *Urania* show she was on very familiar terms with Bartolomeo Salvatico, a jurist who also studied law at the University of Padua.[9] From her place at the fringes of this community of Paduan legal professionals, Bigolina might well have had occasion to hear accounts of Macassola's dealings with Aretino.

In any event, Aretino published a third letter to Bigolina, dated October 1549, in order to thank her for yet another gesture on her part; this time it was the sonnet, no longer extant, which she had written in praise of him:

Bigolina Graziosissima, egli è certo che chi vol farsi riputazione dove non è, mandici in suo scambio la fama. Questo dico in proposito del parermi d'averne qualche poco ancor io, poi che solo per conoscermi voi in bocca di lei, vi sete mossa a scrivermi in laude un così vivo, un così nuovo, e un così chiaro sonetto. Benchè a ciò havvi spinto più tosto la bontà che il giudizio; e per non dilettarvi meno di ben dire che di ben fare, ciò avete esseguito ... (Aretino, *Lettere*, ed. Procaccioli, 5: 276)

[Most gracious Bigolina: it is certainly true that those who have not yet made a name for themselves must send forth fame in the place of the reputation they wish to gain. I say this because it seems I must still be rather famous myself, for you only know me on account of my fame, and yet

---

[9] On Antonio Soncin's law career see Scardeone, *Historiae*, 251, and Mancini, *La Villa Bigolin*, 132 n. 20. For Salvatico's later career as a successful jurist, see G. Vedova, *Biografia degli scrittori padovani* (Padua: Minerva, 1832), 197–98.

INTRODUCTION

you have taken it upon yourself to write so lively, original, and brilliant a sonnet in praise of me. Kindness has moved you in this, rather than good judgment; nonetheless, you have done it in order that you might take as much delight in good words as you have in good deeds . . .]

However, Aretino's words of praise and gratitude are tempered somewhat by the ambivalent conclusion to the letter:

. . . vado pensando in lo qual modo, o in che via, possa mostrarmivi grato, non pure inverso l'onore, ch'io conseguo in grazia de i vostri versi, ma circa il desiderio che infiammavi talmente l'animo, che d'altro non si strugge in più ansia, che del vedermi in presenzia. Io nel ciò sentire e non gloriarmene fuor di modo, biasimo la mia natura modesta, in la maniera che ho già laudato il suo non esser superba. Imperochè cotal sorte di vertù non mi lascia gustare se non in parte il piacere che provarei in le viscere se altiero omo pur fussi. Ma se ogni sterile saluto d'una minima serva fammi suo, come è da stimare che l'affezzione portatami da voi, Donna egregia, mi abbi fatto vostro? Ecco ch'io, poi che altro non ho che lo ingegno, che di quello darovvi tributo al bel nome, onde ala generosità vostra nobile non succederà mai d'aver cagione di pentirsi de la benivolenzia di cui mi fate, perch'io la riconosca, dignissimo. D'Ottobre in Vinezia. M.D.XLIX. (Aretino, *Lettere*, ed. Procaccioli, 5: 276–77)

[. . . I am wondering how I might show you my gratitude, not only for the honor I have gained through your verses, but also for your desire to meet me in person, a desire which so burns your soul that it has nearly become an impatient longing. I hear of this desire, yet I do not glory in it too much, and for this I blame my modest nature; and in the same fashion I have praised my own nature for not being overly proud. Virtue of this sort does not permit me to indulge excessively in the visceral pleasures I would feel if I were an arrogant man. But if any little chambermaid can make me hers through an insignificant word of greeting, how am I to regard the fact that I have been made yours by the affection that you, a woman of substance, have shown me? Well then, I will employ my wit, the only thing I have, to pay tribute to your lovely name. In this way your noble generosity will never have cause to regret the benevolent gesture whereby you make me fit to recognize it; and by causing me to acknowledge that gesture, you have conferred great dignity upon me. October, in Venice, 1549.]

Introduction

The hint that her interest in Aretino bordered on the obsessive, as well as the comparison between her words of greeting and those of "any little chambermaid," could not have encouraged Bigolina much in her efforts to be taken seriously by the great man, especially in view of his comments in his previous letters concerning fame and household servants. In any case, after this brief exchange Aretino published no further correspondences with Bigolina.

However, Aretino was not the only distinguished figure with whom Bigolina was acquainted. She also made an impression on the Venetian mathematician Francesco Barozzi (1537–1604), who lectured in Padua in 1559 and published his highly regarded *Cosmografia tolemaica* in 1585.[10] Late in life he gathered his correspondences with noteworthy acquaintances over the years, with the aim of publishing them; and among these is a letter from Giulia Bigolina. Barozzi's copy of his epistolary collection, now in the Bibliothèque Nationale de France in Paris, bears a note on the flyleaf saying he had edited and copied the letters "in modo che si può stampare" (so that it can be printed); but no edition of the letters ever appeared. Most of the letters bear dates which range from 1555 to 1588, following no clear chronological order. Unfortunately Bigolina's letter, which appears near the end of fol. 25v, is undated. It reads as follows:

Al Mag.^{co} Ill. Franc.° Barozzi
Si suol dire che un spirito cortese, et gentile con le frequentate sue natural cortesie è cagione che mille rispettosi saliscono al lodevole grado della discretione, et mille discreti traboccano nello precipitoso pelago della presontione, come al presente sarà per aventura di me intravenuto che essendosi V. M.ª degnato usarmi tanta cortesia d'invitarmi con la propria persona alla sua Comedia, tratta dalla grande sua cortesia sarò fatta audace, ò forse presontuosa à chiederle in gratia che si degni farmi favore di due bolettini l'uno per mio fig.^{lo} et l'altro per un mio Nepote, accio possino anchor loro participare del diletto, che s'havrà nel udire la Comedia di V.M; et se quella mi concederà cotal gratia le ne restarò doppiamente in particolare obbligata, et alla buona gratia di V.M. inchinevolmente mi racc.^{do}.
Di Casa
                      Di V.M. Humile Serva
                           Giulia Bigolina

---

[10] See "Barozzi Francesco," *Dizionario biografico degli italiani*, 56 vols. (Rome: Istituto della Enciclopedia fondata da Giovanni Treccani, 1960–), 6: 495–99.

Introduction

[To the Magnificent and Illustrious Francesco Barozzi:
It is customary to say that a kind and courteous soul, through frequent use of its innate courtesies, causes a thousand respectful souls to rise to the praiseworthy realm of discretion; yet it may also cause a thousand discreet ones to spill over into the perilous sea of presumption. This last may have just happened in my own case, for inasmuch as Your Magnificence has deigned to show me such courtesy as to personally invite me to his comedy, I find that his great courtesy has so emboldened me (or perhaps made me so presumptuous) that I wish to ask him to please do me the favor of giving me two tickets, one for my son and another for a nephew of mine, so that they too might share in the delight of hearing Your Magnificence's comedy. If he grants me such a favor I will be doubly and particularly obliged to him. I humbly commend myself to the good graces of Your Magnificence.
writing from her home,

Your Magnificence's humble servant,
Giulia Bigolina]

Bigolina's rhetorically elegant letter to Barozzi requesting extra tickets to see a play[11] tells us a great deal about her status in the intellectual life of the Republic of Venice during this period, if one looks at the epistolary collection as a whole. Barozzi's twenty-three letters include twenty-one individually named correspondents, among them such luminaries as the Jesuit mathematician Christopher Clavius (who was a member of Pope Gregory XIII's committee to reform the Julian calendar),[12] the Archbishop of Crete Pietro Lando, the rhetorician Benedetto Bembo, the intellectual firebrand Paolo Sarpi, Cardinal Camillo Paleotto, various medical doctors, doctors of law, ambassadors to Crete, mathematicians reviewing Barozzi's draft of the *Cosmografia*, and others. Barozzi also includes several of his mathematics lectures, prepared in Latin for an audience at the University of Padua. Not only is Bigolina the only female letter writer included here, but she is also the only correspondent whose letter deals with mundane, non-professional matters; for Barozzi, unlike Aretino, seems to have been particularly disposed to collect only letters of great pitch and moment. Barozzi's inclusion of this letter must be seen as

---

[11] No comedy is listed among Barozzi's works, either published or unpublished (*Dizionario biografico* 6: 497–98).
[12] See U. Baldini, "Clavius, Christopher," in *Encyclopedia of the Renaissance*, ed. P. F. Grendler, 6 vols. (New York: Scribner, 1999), 2: 17–18.

15

Introduction

one more clear indication that Bigolina had come to be regarded a personage of some repute in the culture of the Venetian Republic at this time, fit to join a company of illustrious professional men.

Bigolina also finds an exalted place in a poem in octaves by the Paduan author Angelo Leonico, printed in Venice in 1553. In the concluding tenth canto of this work, a version of the story of Troilus and Cressida (*L'amore di Troilio, et Griseida, ove si tratta in buona parte la guerra di Troia*), Leonico makes use of the common topos of the "return to port," wherein the conclusion of the poet's labors is compared to the safe and happy end of a long sea voyage, with friends and supporters lining the shore to give welcome, as in Canto 46 of Ludovico Ariosto's *Orlando Furioso*. Here Leonico's authorial persona sees a large group of women to whom he says he owes a great debt (octave 3), among them Catherine de' Medici and distinguished members of the Strozzi and Fregoso families. Bigolina receives special attention as the crowning glory of the fifth octave:

> De la fronde Febea incoronata
> Ecco la dotta Giulia Bigolina,
> E dopo lei seguia molta brigata,
> D'huomini, e donne verso la marina,
> Che tutti meco de la mia tornata
> Fan festa . . . (fol. 54r)

> [Crowned with the leaves of Phoebus
> Here comes the learned Giulia Bigolina;
> And after her followed a great crowd
> Of men and women approaching the shore,
> Who are all rejoicing at my safe return . . .]

As Marisa Milani has noted, Bigolina is the only woman mentioned by Leonico who achieved renown not merely because of a lofty family name, but rather through her own creative efforts.[13] For Leonico, she is clearly a writer of distinction by this time in her career: called "dotta" and wearing a crown of laurel leaves, she is set at the head of the group of celebrants whom she leads, a group which even includes men. Surely her writing endeavors must have been well

---

[13] M. Milani, introduction to Angelo Leonico, *Il soldato*, in *Quaderni veneti* 13 (Ravenna: Longo, 1991), 7–28, here 15 n. 18.

Introduction

under way by this time, and her reputation in Padua quite well established for her to merit such a description.

Bigolina is depicted in one other contemporary text. She makes a rather extensive appearance as an interlocutor in an unpublished dialogue entitled *A ragionar d'amore*, which today exists in a single manuscript in the municipal library of Besançon. It was written by Mario Melechini, an otherwise unknown Paduan, who states in his introduction that this is the first thing he has ever written (fol. 3v). No other work has been ascribed to him, and the name Melechini is not attested in any list of Paduan families. Nevertheless he dedicated the work to a man of some renown, Charles Perrenot de Granvelle (1531–1567), abbot of Faverney and brother of the famous cardinal Antoine Perrenot de Granvelle, advisor to Philip II of Spain. The manuscript of *A ragionar d'amore* is undated, but internal evidence suggests it was written around 1554.[14]

This dialogue situates Bigolina fully as a participant in those literary debates on the nature of love which were immensely popular at this time, and which are reflected as well in *Urania* itself. In this work she is shown to be an authority on the subject of love, just as her alter-ego Urania makes herself out to be in Bigolina's romance. The main participants in the dialogue are Carlo Perenotto and Antonio Coraro, who meet on a street in Padua and begin to debate on the nature and definition of love. Coraro is not a known figure; the text establishes him as a Paduan but he is no more attested in the documents of that city than the author Melechini. "Perenotto," on the other hand, is none other than Charles Perrenot himself, a native of Besançon who is said to be residing in Padua at this time, probably as a student and evidently well before he was forced into holy orders by family pressure and his powerful brother.[15] Perenotto and Coraro discuss love in

---

[14] Melechini's list of the greatest women of Padua mentions "le due speronelle, che sono maritate nelli Papafava" (fol. 15r: "the two little Speroni women who are married in the Papafava family"). Both Lucietta and Diamante Speroni, daughters of Sperone Speroni, married Papafava men, but because of Diamante's husband's untimely death, the condition described above only lasted for the brief period 1554–1555. This provides a fairly precise date for Melechini's text. See M. R. Loi and M. Pozzi, introduction to Sperone Speroni, *Lettere familiari*, 2 vols. (Alessandria: Edizioni dell'Orso, 1993–1994), 1: 21.

[15] On Charles Perrenot, a man of romantic bent who longed to be freed from his holy orders in order to marry, see C. Duvernoy, *Notice sur les maisons de Granvelle et de St. Mauris-Montbarre, dans le comté de Bourgogne* (Besançon: Proudhon, 1839), 6, and A. Castan, *Catalogue général des manuscrits des bibliothèques publiques de France*, 32: *Besançon* (Paris: Plon, 1897), 354. Melechini depicts him as young and in love; he was twenty-three in 1554. The likelihood that he was a student in Padua is borne out by the fact that his brother

Introduction

terms largely borrowed, at times verbatim, from the enormously influential *Dialoghi d'amore* of Leone Ebreo. Deciding they need a wise woman to listen to their debate and provide commentary, they fall to discussing the relative merits of various Paduan women of leading families in an effort to choose the best one (fols. 15r–17r). Coraro promotes Diamante Sperona, the daughter of one of Padua's most famous citizens, the humanist Sperone Speroni, and also speaks highly of Laura Sperona Brazola, who was Speroni's niece. Perenotto, for his part, champions Giulia Bigolina, and in time Coraro comes to accept her as long as she will do little more than listen (fol. 55r). The two men walk to Bigolina's house where she greets them warmly, then agrees to participate in the discussion, after first humbly claiming to lack the qualities they require: "... sarete venuti con gran sete à un pozzo senza acqua ..." ["you have probably come with great thirst to a waterless well" (fol. 56r)]. Her role in the dialogue is in fact essentially passive, but at times she is made to quote Leone and influence the course of the debate in fairly substantial ways (fols. 58v, 60r). It might be said that she participates more in this dialogue than do the female characters in Bembo's *Asolani*, but far less than many a female interlocutor in other love dialogues of the time.[16] Moreover, she is scarcely allowed to act as a final authority in these matters, the way her own character Urania does. Although Bigolina's efforts at writing are never alluded to, in championing her Perenotto makes reference not only to her "bel spirito" [lovely spirit] but also to her "soave suo parlare" [sweet way of speaking], which would indicate she had acquired some reputation as a rhetorician (fol. 11r). When they conclude their debate and bid her farewell, Coraro says he is certain she must now have to busy herself with domestic chores, since she is a woman (fol. 102v), and this reminds us of Scardeone's claim that Bigolina had to find time off from household tasks in order to write ("cui quantum per otium ab opere Palladio vacare contingit"). At the end of the dialogue it becomes clear once more that Melechini's purpose has been not only to discuss the nature of love, but also to identify the best woman in Padua to participate in the discussion. Coraro's final declaration shows that he now finds Perenotto's choice was fully justified:

Antoine is known to have attended the University of Padua, suggesting a family tradition (see W. Keller, "Antoine Perrenot de Granvelle," in *New Catholic Encyclopedia*, 6: 695–96).

[16] See R. Buranello, "Figura Meretricis: Tullia d'Aragona in Sperone Speroni's *Dialogo d'amore*," *Spunti e ricerche* 15 (2000): 53–67, here 54, for a discussion of the role of women in Cinquecento love dialogues. Sperone Speroni's innovative role for the interlocutor Tullia d'Aragona in his *Dialogo d'amore* (published in 1542) might have inspired Melechini in the creation of his character Bigolina.

Introduction

Certamente c'hoggi, habbiam' havuto una felice giornata, per essere stato noi nella contemplatione di cosi eccellente Donna. Veramente à quanto scorgo, non habbiamo detto cosa se non buonissima, di che molto felici siamo stati; essendo stata questa ad udirne; dalla quale alcuna cosa habbiamo sentito ragionare, per la quale certamente essa si mostra molto di sapere. (fol. 104r)

[Certainly we have had a pleasant day today, having been in the company of so excellent a woman. As far as I can see, we have truly not said anything that was not most worthy, and for that we have been very glad, with this woman there to hear us; and we have heard her reasonings, by which she shows that she knows a great deal.]

One other figure of these times needs to be taken into account: Ferrante Sanseverino, Prince of Salerno (1507–1568), to whom Bigolina's interest in the city of Salerno, so evident in *Urania*, might well be ascribed. This man was celebrated during his reign for his love of learning and the arts, and although it is specifically known that he fostered an association between the universities of Padua and Salerno, Bigolina certainly had a more direct opportunity to see him, and perhaps even make his acquaintance, during the Prince's rather dramatic visit to her city.[17] In 1551 Ferrante ran afoul of the Spanish viceroy of Naples, Pedro de Toledo, and after becoming wounded in an assassination attempt, was forced to flee Salerno with his entourage.[18] Late that year he was in Venice, but soon thereafter he went to Padua to have his wound treated by the medical doctors of the university (Carucci, *Ferrante Sanseverino*, 45). Given that his flight and troubles with both the viceroy and Emperor Charles V had become an Italian *cause célèbre*, it is easy to imagine that his arrival, with all his retainers and his well-known love of pomp, constituted an event of no small importance for the Paduan upper classes. While in Padua the prince was summoned to Innsbruck to explain his case to the emperor, but when he tried to negotiate for his personal safety the negotiations broke down and in 1552 Ferrante thought it best to declare himself a rebel, renouncing

---

[17] On Ferrante's links to the University of Padua, see F. Piovan, "La condotta allo Studio di Salerno di Matteo Macigni e Paolo da Lion (1543)," *Quaderni per la storia dell'Università di Padova* 32 (1999): 99–111, here 99.

[18] R. Colapietra, *I Sanseverino di Salerno* (Salerno: Laveglio, 1985), 211; C. Carucci, *D. Ferrante Sanseverino, Principe di Salerno* (Salerno: Stabilimento Tipografico Nazionale, 1899), 41–43.

INTRODUCTION

both his principate and his properties (Carucci, *Ferrante Sanseverino*, 45–47). Ultimately he fled to France under the viceroy's sentence of death, and there he was to end his days, the last of a distinguished line. Although no firm connection between the prince and Bigolina can be established, it would seem evident that this visit made quite an impression on her. Not only did she dedicate one of her stories, "Panfilo," to the prince, but she also set much of the action of *Urania* in Salerno, and made a prince of Salerno (called Giufredi, a name not attested in either Colapietra's or Carucci's histories of the family) one of *Urania*'s central characters. Moreover, it can be demonstrated that *Urania* was written in or shortly after 1552, the very year the ill-starred prince was in the Veneto. Bigolina dedicated the work to Bartolomeo Salvatico and referred to him as "dottore di legge" [doctor of law], while repeatedly stressing his youth. Salvatico (1533–1603), who eventually became a distinguished jurist, is known to have received his law degree from the University of Padua in 1552, when he was about nineteen years old.[19] The dramatic arrival of a suffering, exiled prince, famously fond of literature and loudly protesting his innocence on the European stage, coinciding with the graduation of a virtuous young man whom Bigolina admired greatly: these seem to have been the factors which directly prompted her to write *Urania*.

There is no evidence that Bigolina ever left the environs of her native city during her lifetime, and this would be normal enough for a married woman and mother of her social background. Nonetheless, she did manage to make the acquaintance of such luminaries as Aretino and Barozzi, and quite possibly Charles Perrenot de Granvelle, Scardeone, and Ferrante Sanseverino as well. As the respectful words of Scardeone, Melechini, Masenetti, and Leonico attest, her writings earned her a place of considerable importance in the intellectual and artistic life of mid-sixteenth-century Padua.

2. THE DISCOVERY OF BIGOLINA'S WORKS AND HER PLACE IN THE CANON

After the time of Scardeone, Contarini, Marescotti, and Zwinger, Bigolina often appears in catalogues of illustrious women or Paduan authors. In 1609 the cleric Pietro Paolo di Ribera said she had no peer in her own time in the composition

---

[19] E. Veronese and E. Dalla Francesca, eds., *Acta Graduum Academicorum Gymnasii Patavini 1551–1561* (Rome: Antenore, 2001), 79.

Introduction

of "Favole, Comedie, e cose amorose" [fables, comedies and amorous things], citing as his source a "trustworthy Paduan gentleman" (*Donne Illustre antiche & moderne* [Venice: Deuchino, 1609], 287). In 1620 Francesco Agostino Della Chiesa offered further praise; however, except for his statement that Bigolina was as distinguished in verse as in prose, everything he says is paraphrased from Scardeone, and he reveals no more firsthand knowledge of her works than does Ribera (*Theatro delle donne letterate* [Mondovì: Gislandi, 1620], 171–72). A few years later, in 1639, the scholar Jacopo Filippo Tomasini (1595–1654) published a list in Latin of the contents of his personal library, including therein the first scholarly reference to one of Bigolina's specific texts:

> Iuliae Bigolinae Cl. M. (i. e. Clarae Mulieris) Fabula de Pamphilo Etrusco Idiomate Principi Salernitano inscripta. ch. 4 (Tomasini, *Bibliothecae Patavinae Manuscriptae* . . . , 126)

> [The story of Panfilo, in the Tuscan vernacular, dedicated to the Prince of Salerno, by the illustrious woman Giulia Bigolina. Paper, in quartos.]

Unfortunately, the manuscript to which Tomasini refers remains lost, and the current state and whereabouts of Tomasini's library are not known. Moreover, no other copy of the "Story of Panfilo" has ever been mentioned by subsequent scholars.

One of the most intriguing of these early references to Bigolina appears in Luca Assarino's *Raguagli del regno d'amore Cipro*, first published in 1646. Here, in "Raguaglio IX," Bigolina is mentioned as one of three women writers engaged as secretaries by the court of Cyprus, charged with the task of opening and deciphering coded letters received by the court at a time when a plot against the freedom of women has been uncovered (*Raguagli*, 46–50). Once more Bigolina is depicted as a wise and learned woman who is especially capable of lecturing on the finer points of love: when one of the letters is found to contain Boccaccio's declaration of desire for the daughter of the King of Naples, Assarino has Bigolina hold forth for several pages on the topic of men of humble birth who fall in love with women of much higher social status. Although Assarino was a novelist, he was especially known as an historian; nonetheless the *Raguagli* must not be read as an historical work, inasmuch as it provides little more than a series of anecdotes and pronouncements by famous figures concerning love and Cyprus as the home of Venus. No dates are provided for this supposed event, and even though a court of the Kingdom of Cyprus was indeed maintained by the Venetian Republic at Asolo during the sixteenth century (writ large in Bembo's love dialogue *Gli*

Introduction

Asolani), Assarino does not make any direct association with that place here. In any event, the other women with whom Bigolina is said to be working are both writers of pastoral dramas who flourished later than Bigolina: Maddalena Campiglia (1553–1595), and Barbara Torelli Benedetti, whose *Partenia* was completed in 1587.[20] Thus it would seem that Assarino is primarily bent on embellishing Bigolina's traditional portrait, already established by Melechini and Bigolina herself in the pages of *Urania*, as a learned and eloquent woman who had much to teach on the subject of love.

In the eighteenth century a considerable number of antiquarians took to cataloguing and assessing Cinquecento authors and texts. In 1741 Francesco Saverio Quadrio published this commentary on Bigolina:

> Costei maravigliosamente s'innalzò colla molta cognizione della Toscana Lingua, e colle pulite Opere, che in prosa, e in verso pubblicò alla luce; e fu forse figliuola di quel Bigolini, di cui esta nell'Ambrosiana un'Operetta MS. in prosa, intitolata, *Sogno Faceto sopra le Scarpe di Aldo Manuzio*; ed è il Codice Q. 115. (*Della storia e della ragion di ogni poesia*, 2: 271)

> [She raised herself to marvelous heights with her great knowledge of the Tuscan language, and with her very polished works, which she published in prose and in verse; and perhaps she was the daughter of that Bigolini whose little manuscript work in prose, called *Facetious Dream Concerning Aldus Manutius' Shoes*, can be found in the Ambrosiana Library; it is Codex Q. 115.]

Apart from the fact that Quadrio cannot substantiate his speculation about Bigolina's relationship to the author of the Ambrosiana manuscript, he was also quite alone in imagining that Bigolina ever succeeded in publishing anything during her lifetime, either in prose or in verse. A few years later Conte Giammaria Mazzuchelli offered a more thorough and sober assessment of Bigolina, noting that she flourished in the mid-sixteenth century, and was a poet who earned the praise of Pietro Aretino for a sonnet that she had sent him. Mazzuchelli is the first scholar to take note of the three letters to Bigolina which Aretino published in Book V of his *Lettere*. He also made some effort to describe and catalogue her known

---

[20] Cox, "Fiction, 1560–1650," 55.

Introduction

works. After listing the judgments of previous critics, and declaring that he knows of no printed works by Bigolina, despite Quadrio's claim, he says this:

> C'è noto bensì, che una sua Operetta intitolata: *Urania*, nella quale prese a descrivere gli amori di Una Giovine così chiamata, esisteva a penna in 4. già alcuni anni in Verona nella Libreria Saibante, e che una sua Novella d'un certo Panfilo Toscano da lei indirizzata al Principe di Salerno, fu già tra' MSS. di Jacopo Filippo Tomasini (*Bibliothecae Patavinae Manuscriptae* p. 128) in un Codice cartaceo in 4. (*Scrittori d'Italia*, 2: 1222)

> [However it is known that a small work of hers entitled *Urania*, in which she undertook to describe the love affairs of a young woman by that name, existed for many years in the form of a quarto manuscript in the Saibante Library of Verona. It is also known that a novella of hers, telling of a certain Tuscan named Panfilo, and addressed to the Prince of Salerno, was once in the manuscript collection of Jacopo Filippo Tomasini (*Bibliothecae Patavinae Manuscriptae* p. 128) in a paper codex in quartos.][21]

Mazzuchelli could not say much about the two Bigolina works he had heard about, but it does seem that he thought that they were essentially quite different, for he used differing terms to describe them. Although he called the "Panfilo" story a novella, in an effort to approximate Tomasini's Latin term *fabula*, he employed Bigolina's own term, *operetta*, to describe the very long and amply developed *Urania*. Nonetheless, Mazzuchelli demonstrates little or no direct knowledge of Bigolina's works, and provides no clear idea of the extent of her literary output. It would remain the task of another eighteenth-century scholar, the Paduan Anton Maria Borromeo, to produce a more comprehensive census of Bigolina's manuscripts, and to finally publish one of her stories, "La novella di Giulia Camposanpiero e di Tesibaldo Vitaliani," more than two hundred years after her time.

Borromeo's *Notizia di Novellieri italiani* appeared in 1794, and included specific references to the whereabouts of two manuscripts containing two of Bigolina's narratives, "La novella di Giulia Camposanpiero e di Tesibaldo Vitaliani," and *Urania*. After indicating that he had made copies of these two narratives, both of which he calls "novelle," Borromeo says this about the author:

---

[21] I disagree with Mazzuchelli's reading of Tomasini's adjective "etrusco," which he has modifying "Pamphilo" (therefore he refers to Panfilo as a Tuscan). I am convinced it was meant to modify the noun "idiomate."

INTRODUCTION

Questa Gentildonna Padovana, poco conosciuta da' nostri, e meno dagli stranieri, scrisse molte eleganti Novelle ad imitazione del Boccaccio, come si ha dallo Storico Scardeone, le quali non hanno mai veduta la luce. La prima delle due riferite si conserva nella copiosa Libreria del Sig. Co. Giovanni Cav. de Lazara, Gentilhuomo, che per le sue cognizioni, e pel genio alle belle arti onora la nostra Città; e di questa per sua gentilezza mi permise di trarne copia. L'altra assai lunga intitolata *Urania* ho potuto fare trascrivere in Verona dalla Biblioteca del Sig. Marchese Saibante. Una terza delle *Avventure di Pamfilo* indiritta al Principe di Salerno era posseduta da Monsig. Tommasini (sic) che la registra tra suoi MSS. Teodoro Zuingero, che ha potuto conoscere in Padova questa Gentildonna, la chiama in un suo libro *eruditione claram, & vernacula poesi*: e invero ch'Essa si esercitasse nella volgar Poesia lo abbiamo ancora da Pietro Aretino, che le indirizza alcune Lettere, e in una rende grazie d'un Sonetto, che gli aveva mandato ...

Ora io credo di far cosa grata agli eruditi perchè abbiano un Saggio dello stile di questa Egregia Donna, pubblicando la Prima delle suddette Novelle. Sarà questa la terza in ordine, nel fine del Libro. (*Notizia*, 6–7)

[This Paduan lady, little known to our compatriots and even less among foreigners, wrote many elegant novellas in imitation of Boccaccio, as the historian Scardeone describes; these have never been published. The first of the two referred to above is kept in the copious library of Count Giovanni, Cavalier de Lazara, a gentleman who honors our city through his knowledge and fondness for the fine arts; he has kindly permitted me to make a copy of it. I have managed to have a copy made of the other one in Verona, in the library of the Marquis Saibante; it is very long and bears the title *Urania*. A third one, called *The Adventures of Pamfilo* and dedicated to the Prince of Salerno, was once in the possession of Monsignor Tomasini, who lists it among his manuscripts. Theodor Zwinger, who was able to make the acquaintance of this lady in Padua, refers to her in one of his books as "outstanding in her erudition and in her vernacular literature." Indeed, we also have it on the authority of Pietro Aretino that she wrote vernacular poetry, inasmuch as he addresses some letters to her, and in one of them thanks her for a sonnet which she had sent him ...

I believe I am doing a great service to scholars by publishing the first of the novellas mentioned above, and by providing them with an example of this distinguished woman's literary style. This novella must be the third in the sequence, appearing at the end of the book ...]

Introduction

Borromeo had found and transcribed two of Bigolina's stories, but knew nothing of the whereabouts of the third which Tomasini had so briefly described in 1639. He is the first scholar ever to make reference to "La novella di Giulia Camposanpiero," and no other titles of Bigolina narratives, besides the three he mentions, are known today. The fate of the "Panfilo" manuscript was as unclear to him as it is to us now, although we may yet hope this work will turn up some time in the future.

After Borromeo, readers at last had a published text of Bigolina's to consult, as well as some idea of the nature and quantity of her surviving works. Borromeo's edition may well have led the scholar Melchiorre Cesarotti to make his claim that Bigolina, among women, was as great a writer in prose as Gaspara Stampa was in verse, although he does not cite a source for his brief description of her (*Opere* [Pisa: Capurro, 1813] 29: 415–16). One critic in the early nineteenth century, Bartolommeo Gamba, did read the original *Urania* manuscript and pass some judgment upon it; in fact, Borromeo and Gamba, along with the Trivulziana cataloguer Giulio Porro, are the only scholars before the late twentieth century to show any firsthand knowledge of *Urania*. Even though Gamba's works reveal that he was generally quite drawn to Renaissance women authors (he had a collection of their letters, and also compiled a list of illustrious Veneto women of the sixteenth century), he clearly was not impressed by this one: "Questo è forse il Codice Originale che fu dato dalla Bigolina medesima a Bartolommeo Salvatico Dottore di Leggi, cui la lunga e nojosa Novella è indirizzata" ["This is perhaps the original codex that was given by Bigolina herself to Bartolommeo Salvatico, Doctor of Law, to whom the long and boring novella is addressed"]: *Novellieri, materiali biografici* 4: 73–74].[22] Gamba goes on to describe the cover of the codex, which he saw either in Verona before 1811 or in Milan where it was taken thereafter, noting that it includes Salvatico's monogram, an indication that it was likely the very copy Bigolina sent to the young man. The rest of his description of her is taken verbatim from Borromeo's *Notizia di Novellieri italiani*.

Later nineteenth-century scholars, such as Giuseppe Vedova, Pietro Leopoldo Ferri, Napoleone Pietrucci, and Giambattista Passano, all took some pains to keep

---

[22] For Gamba's interest in Renaissance women, see Bassano del Grappa, Biblioteca Civica, MS. 30 B 11, *Gamba autografi* vol. 1 ("Lettere familiari di valorose donne italiane del secolo XVI") and vol. 2 ("Galleria delle donne più illustre delle provincie venete"). Gamba does not mention Bigolina in either of these manuscripts. In a reference to Bigolina in print Gamba maintains a neutral tone and does not call *Urania* boring (see Gamba, *Delle novelle italiane in prosa* [Florence: Tipografia all'insegna di Dante, 1835], 87).

INTRODUCTION

Bigolina's memory alive in their various catalogues of novella writers, famous Paduans, or distinguished women.[23] By and large, however they do little more than repeat the assessments of Borromeo and his predecessors. None of these writers did any original research on Bigolina's manuscripts, although Passano does provide useful bibliographical information concerning a pair of nineteenth-century reprints of Borromeo's edition of "La novella di Giulia Camposanpiero."[24] In 1884 Giulio Porro published a catalogue of the manuscripts in the Trivulziana Library which included the first printed description of the *Urania* codex; like Gamba, Porro was inclined to think the book was Bigolina's own autograph on account of the presence of Salvatico's initials on the leather cover (*Trivulziana*, 31).

Toward the end of the nineteenth century a few critics began to analyze Bigolina's relationship to the other authors of her time. Emilio Lovarini, writing in the 1890s, was perhaps the first, although his assessment, crippled as it was by lack of information, is inaccurate: he lists Bigolina as one of the precursors of the Paduan playwright Ruzante in the production of literature dealing with Paduan country life.[25] Apart from the fact that Bigolina patently does not describe Paduan country life in either of her surviving works, she was also not likely to have been much of an influence on Ruzante, who died in 1542. Lovarini does not explain how he arrived at these conclusions, yet they did not go unnoticed, since another critic, Ludovico Frati, repeated Lovarini's statement in an article in 1892.[26] Around the same time Giuseppe Rua, an early editor of Straparola's novella collection *Piacevoli notti*, noted that Bigolina shared Straparola's inclination to append poetic riddles to her tales, inasmuch as such a poem appears at the end of "La novella di Giulia Camposanpiero"; moreover, Bigolina's frame story indicates that riddles appeared at the conclusions of the other novellas, now lost, which were recounted in the same collection.[27]

---

[23] Vedova, *Biografia degli scrittori padovani*, 112–13; P. L. Ferri, *Biblioteca femminile italiana* (Padua: Crescini, 1842), 68–69; N. Pietrucci, *Delle illustri donne padovane* (Padua: Bianchi, 1853), 21; and G. Passano, *Novellieri italiani in prosa*, 2nd ed., 2 vols. (Turin: Paravia, 1878), 2: 88–89.

[24] See Pietro Piranesi, *Novelle tratte dai più celebri Autori antichi e moderni* (Paris: Barrois, 1823) and *Nuova scelta di Novelle, tratte dai più celebri autori antichi e moderni* (Paris: Baudry, 1852).

[25] See Emilio Lovarini, *Studi sul Ruzzante e la letteratura padovana* (Padua: Antenore, 1965), 225 n. 1.

[26] L. Frati, "Un egloga rusticale del 1508," *Giornale storico della letteratura italiana* 20 (1892): 186–209, here 186.

[27] G. Rua, "Intorno alle *Piacevoli notti* dello Straparola," *Giornale storico della letteratura italiana* 15 (1890): 111–51, here 140.

INTRODUCTION

In the twentieth century critical interest in Bigolina declined, and her manuscripts were more neglected than ever. In 1941 Maria Bandini Buti included her in her book *Poetesse e scrittrici*, but not only did she base her analysis almost entirely on what Scardeone, Quadrio, Mazzuchelli, and Borromeo had already written, she also gave herself over to some rather irresponsible speculation. Since Quadrio had imagined (entirely without justification, as it appears) that Bigolina was the daughter of the mysterious Bigolini whose name is attached to the *Sogno faceto sopra le scarpe di Aldo Manuzio* in the Ambrosiana Library, Buti asserts that Bigolina was trained as a writer by her father ("gli studi di lei furono diretti dal padre, anch'egli scrittore": *Poetesse e scrittrici* [Rome: Tosi, 1941], 96). As has been mentioned, documents in the Paduan State Archives indicate that Bigolina's actual father, Girolamo Bigolin, was already dead in 1527, when Bigolina could not have been much more than ten years old. In all fairness, Buti was not the first to repeat Quadrio's notion, for Pietrucci does it as well (*Illustri donne padovane*, 21), but only Buti went on to assume that Bigolina was trained by her father. In any event Buti also has the incorrect impression that Aretino praised Bigolina for her novellas, even though he never mentioned them in any of his three letters. As in the case of all the scholars of the nineteenth century, Buti imagines that the *Urania* manuscript was still in the Saibante collection in Verona because that was where Borromeo had seen it in 1794. No one but Porro, writing in 1884, ever took note of the manuscript's transfer to the Trivulziana Library in 1811.

In 1948 Michele De Filippis published a study of Italian literary riddles which includes a description of the one Bigolina appended to "La novella di Giulia Camposanpiero." De Filippis, a student of Straparola, doubtless found her by following Rua's exiguous trail, and says nothing more than what he could derive from Borromeo. Nonetheless his account of her, the first in English, includes a complete synopsis of "Giulia Camposanpiero" along with an interpretation of her concluding sonnet-riddle.[28]

De Filippis was to provide virtually the final word on Bigolina until the present day,[29] and in the second half of the twentieth century her works fell out of critical favor for many years. Paolo Procaccioli's anthology of Aretino's letters, which appeared in 1991, does include one of those to Bigolina, but Procaccioli's note on her says very little and cites only Scardeone as a source (Aretino, *Lettere*, 2: 1107). Procaccioli says still less about Bigolina in the notes to Volume 5 of his

---

[28] M. De Filippis, *The Literary Riddle in Italy to the End of the Sixteenth Century* (Berkeley: University of California Press, 1948), 87–88.

[29] As this edition was going to press, a first edition of *Urania* appeared: G. Bigolina, *Urania*, ed. V. Finucci, Biblioteca del Cinquecento 104 (Rome: Bulzoni, 2002).

Introduction

complete edition of Aretino's letters, published in 2000 (Aretino, *Lettere* 5: 539). Even in Padua today her name is scarcely known to librarians and scholars, and the only public memorial to her is a tiny street, Via Giulia Bigolino (*sic*), in the Sant'Osvaldo district outside the walls. Two published catalogues of Paduan streets, which are readily available in libraries and bookstores, reveal the extent of local misinformation regarding Bigolina. In his 1972 catalogue Giovanni Saggiori claimed to know precisely her dates of birth and death, although his source for this information remains a mystery: he said she lived from 1563 to 1623 and cites only two of the less useful sources, Quadrio and Cesarotti, neither of whom ever claimed to know when she lived.[30] However, Saggiori's claims are nowhere near as damaging as those of Giuseppe Toffanin jr., whose book *Le strade di Padova* (Rome: Newton and Compton, 1998) draws on Saggiori's misinformation, then provides an unfair moral judgment:

> Padovana (1563–1623), autrice di novelle ad imitazione del Boccaccio, rimaste inedite. Il Cesarotti, audacemente, raffrontò il valore della Bigolino nella prosa a quello di Gaspara Stampa nella poesia.
>
> Fu in corrispondenza con Pietro Aretino, il quale in una lettera la ringrazia per un sonetto; il che porterebbe a sollevare seri dubbi sulla moralità della nostra scrittrice. (*Le strade di Padova*, 76–77)

> [Paduan [1563–1623], author of novellas in imitation of Boccaccio, which remain unpublished. Cesarotti boldly compared Bigolina's worth in prose to that of Gaspara Stampa in poetry.
>
> She corresponded with Pietro Aretino, who in a letter thanks her for a sonnet; this would lead one to raise serious doubts concerning our author's morality.]

Toffanin, whose pronouncement on Bigolina is the last of the twentieth century, has provided a pretty coffee-table book which doubtless graces many homes in Bigolina's native city. Evidently he imagined that since she was a Renaissance woman who wrote she must have been a courtesan, and yet he would never have reached such a conclusion if he had troubled to read either her surviving works, suffused as they are with a love of virtue, or indeed Aretino's letters to her. Moreover, he accepts and repeats Saggiori's dates, only to imagine that an author said

---

[30] G. Saggiori, *Padova nella storia delle sue strade* (Padua: Piazzon, 1972).

INTRODUCTION

to have been born in 1563 could have corresponded with Aretino, who died in 1556.[31]

3. *URANIA: THE STORY OF A YOUNG WOMAN'S LOVE*

The years 1550–1553 witnessed a variety of new developments and a resurgence of interest in the Italian novella collection, especially in the Veneto region, and it is precisely in this time period, as I have noted, that *Urania* came into being.[32] Indeed, without even knowing that 1552, the year that Salvatico received his law degree, was the work's *terminus post quem*, Borromeo was ready to postulate a place in such a collection for *Urania*, for he imagined that all three of Bigolina's known prose narratives, including the lost "Panfilo," must have been part of the same novella collection with frame story to which "La novella di Giulia Camposanpiero et di Thesibaldo Vitaliani" quite plainly belongs. Speaking of "Giulia Camposanpiero" he wrote, "Sarà questa la terza in ordine, nel fine del Libro" ["This novella must be the third in the sequence, appearing at the end of the book"]: Borromeo, *Notizia*, 7)]. This would constitute a neat way of organizing Bigolina's oeuvre if it could be demonstrated, but unfortunately the evidence suggests otherwise. Tomasini's enigmatic manuscript description tells us only two things about "Panfilo": that it is in Italian ("Etrusco idiomate") and that it is dedicated to the Prince of Salerno ("Principi Salernitano inscripta"). Not much information to be sure, but at least the second fact serves as a probable indication that this story was not meant to be part of the same *novelliere* as "Giulia Camposanpiero," since the latter work does not have a dedication of its own. At times Renaissance novella writers, such as Masuccio Salernitano and Matteo Bandello, did provide rubrics addressed to

---

[31] Prior to this, Toffanin had also erroneously concluded that Bigolina had married a certain Iacopo Leoni, even though the documents in the Padua State Archive affirm that she married Bartolomeo Vicomercato. See Toffanin's introduction to Carlo Leoni, *Cronaca segreta de' miei tempi* (Padua: Rebellato, 1976), 6.

[32] On the popularity of the novella collection in Venetian territory during this period see G. Auzzas, "La narrativa veneta nella prima metà del cinquecento," in *Storia della cultura veneta*, ed. G. Arnaldi and M. Pastore Stocchi, 6 vols. (Vicenza: Neri Pozza, 1976–1986), 3: 99–138, here 119–33; M. Guglielminetti, introduction to *Il tesoro della novella italiana: I secoli XIII–XVI* (Milan: Mondadori, 1986), xxxvii; and D. Pirovano, introduction to G. F. Straparola, *Le piacevoli notti*, 2 vols. (Rome: Salerno, 2000), 1: x–xi.

INTRODUCTION

illustrious individuals for each novella within their collections, but Bigolina does not seem to have had this inclination. The proem and conclusion of "Giulia Camposanpiero," with their references to a *brigata* of tale-tellers under the tutelage of a "queen," La Cavaliera Conte, quite plainly fit the mold of the novella collection with fictional frame story, a type exemplified first and foremost by Boccaccio's *Decameron* and later, in Bigolina's own time and region, by such works as Parabosco's *I diporti* and Straparola's *Le piacevoli notti*. Collections of this type typically do not provide individual dedications to the tales, and *Urania*, which bears a dedication to Bartolomeo Salvatico, does not appear in any way to be part of the larger work meant to contain "Giulia Camposanpiero." *Urania's* proem, quite independent in itself, bears no resemblance to the story framing the "Giulia Camposanpiero" narrative, with its happy *brigata* of tale-tellers encamped on the hill of Mirabello.[33] Therefore we may conclude, on the basis of the evidence we have, that Bigolina's three known prose narratives, "Panfilo," "Giulia Camposanpiero," and *Urania*, were not meant to be part of a larger work, even if the frame story of "Giulia Camposanpiero" refers to other novellas that were originally meant to accompany it.

In any case, *Urania* should not even be considered a novella, the judgments of earlier writers notwithstanding. Only three scholars, Borromeo, Gamba, and Porro, are known to have examined this work before the present day, and all of them referred to it as a novella, perhaps because Scardeone had placed such emphasis on Bigolina's link with the novella tradition. But it is important to note that Bigolina herself dispenses with genre definitions in this case, preferring to call what she has written an *operetta*, a "little work." On the other hand, she clearly labels "Giulia Camposanpiero" a novella (292, 318). *Urania* is a much longer, more complex, and more ambitious narrative than "Giulia Camposanpiero," and this fact, coupled with the allegorical proem in the first person, place this work more in the realm of the prose romance than the novella.

In the Italian literature of the late Middle Ages and Renaissance the line between novella and prose romance was often blurred, and many narratives transcend easy categorization. Boccaccio's *Decameron* contains many stories which some critics have been inclined to call "romance novellas" (*novelle romanzi*), not so much because of their length but because they share certain motifs with classical and medieval romances, i.e. emphasis on amorous content, on the separations and wanderings of lovers, on the vagaries of fortune which in turn lead to triumphant

---

[33] On the tendency toward realism and geographical precision in Veneto frame stories, which is also revealed in Bigolina's works, see Auzzas, "La narrativa veneta," 129.

Introduction

reunions and recognition scenes, etc.[34] Such novellas appear often in the second and third days of the *Decameron*, wherein fortune is a prevailing theme, and all of the aforementioned motifs can be found in *Urania*. In a certain sense, if we disregard the allegorical proem and the extended didactic sequences of the second and third chapters, the story of Urania in its basic outline can be said to resemble many of Boccaccio's tales of love and fortune. Nonetheless, we cannot disregard that proem and the didactic sequences. These things, along with the story's length, division into chapters, and much else, bespeak the author's clear allegiance to a very different narrative style, that of the prose romance.

After its first flowering in certain works of Boccaccio, such as the *Filocolo* and the *Elegia di Madonna Fiammetta*, the Italian prose romance nearly disappeared from view for a time, and through much of the fifteenth century it is difficult to find works to which the term might be applied. By the end of the century, however, the prose *romanzo d'amore* experienced something of a renaissance, and re-emerged in three quite disparate works: Francesco Colonna's *Hypnerotomachia Poliphili*, Iacopo Caviceo's *Libro del Peregrino*, and Iacopo Sannazaro's *Arcadia*. Colonna's and Sannazaro's works are the best known today, although only Sannazaro's is frequently read, since the *Hypnerotomachia*, a baffling and linguistically arcane work, is far better remembered for Aldus Manutius' 1499 illustrated edition than as an actual literary text. The *Hypnerotomachia* and the *Arcadia* each follow separate trends in their depictions of unreal, otherworldly settings, the one an allegorical-didactic dream vision, the other a combination of poetry and prose in a setting meant to evoke the ancient Greek pastoral tradition. Both tell of love stories in the first person, although in each case the tenuous plot is nearly lost beneath the weight of extraneous, digressive material.

---

[34] For a definition of the *novella-romanzo* in the context of the narrative categories of the *Decameron*, see M. Baratto, *Realtà e stile nel Decameron* (Rome: Riuniti, 1984), 129, and G. Guglielmi, "Una novella non esemplare del *Decameron*," *Forum italicum* 14 (1980): 32–55, here 33. P. Zumthor (*Towards a Medieval Poetics*, trans. P. Bennett [Minneapolis: University of Minnesota Press, 1992]) also provides useful perspectives on this phenomenon (285–334). In the context of ancient romances, B. E. Perry (*The Ancient Romances* [Berkeley: University of California Press, 1967]) provides a broad definition of the genre which, in the main, fits *Urania* quite well: "... an extended narrative published apart by itself which relates — primarily or wholly for the sake of entertainment or spiritual edification, and for its own sake as a story, rather than for the purpose of instruction in history, science, or philosophical theory — adventures or experiences of one or more individuals in their private capacities and from the viewpoint of their private interests and emotions" (*The Ancient Romances*, 44–45).

INTRODUCTION

The love story is much more the central focus of the least known of these early novels, Caviceo's *Libro del Peregrino*, which was written in the late Quattrocento and printed in Parma in 1508. This work was quite popular, seeing no fewer than nineteen new Italian editions by the middle of the Cinquecento, as well as translations into French and Spanish,[35] and the trend it inaugurated leads more surely to Bigolina's *Urania* than either the *Hypnerotomachia* or the *Arcadia*. The book begins with the author falling asleep and dreaming that he sees a ghost, Peregrino, who will recount to him in three lengthy books the story of his great love for Ginevra, a love which in time will lead to Peregrino's demise. The setting is no longer the distant past, as in Boccaccio's *Filocolo*, nor is it Sannazaro's pastoral heterocosm, nor Colonna's allegorical dream landscape. Instead the narrative takes place in the real Italian cities of Caviceo's own time, even if the text abounds with Greek names and incongruous references to classical culture. The lesson on love which Peregrino provides in this long book is resolutely negative: Peregrino stumbles from one misadventure and misfortune to another in his obsessive attempts to spend time with his beloved, and even though they eventually marry, Ginevra dies soon afterward in childbirth, and the wretched Peregrino quickly follows her, becoming the text's admonitory ghost. Although the book abounds with elements derived from the ancient Greek romances, elements such as the separation and wandering of the lovers, the character of the true friend who accompanies the protagonist on his wanderings, temporary imprisonments, dramatic trials and last-minute rescues from execution, and so on, Caviceo carefully avoids the "happily ever after" ending which typically characterizes the ancient novels of Longus, Achilles Tatius, Chariton, and others, preferring to recount his lovers' demise as a sort of exemplum of the dangers of erotic love.

Despite its popularity, the *Libro del Peregrino* did not inspire many other writers to produce similar works. As has often been noted, Italian authors of the early modern period always showed a far greater predilection for romances in verse than in prose, while their preferred vehicle for prose fiction was the novella.[36] Only a tiny handful of prose romances are known from the Cinquecento, and by and large they attracted little attention, even though Italian translations of some of the

---

[35] For a discussion of the popularity of this work in the Cinquecento see A. Albertazzi, *Romanzieri e romanzi del Cinquecento e del Seicento* (Bologna: Zanichelli, 1891), 10–11; and L. Vignali, introduction to I. Caviceo, *Il Peregrino* (Rome: La Fenice, 1993), xiii–xiv.

[36] On the paucity of early modern Italian prose romances see Albertazzi, *Romanzieri e romanzi del Cinquecento e del Seicento*, 3–6; G. Raya, *Storia dei generi italiani: Il romanzo* (Milan: Vallardi, 1950), 77–78 and 91; and Auzzas, "La narrativa veneta," 133–34.

Introduction

ancient and Byzantine romances were beginning to circulate at this time. Niccolò Franco's ponderous *Philena* (956 pages) was published just once in 1547, bearing an anti-erotic message similar to that of the *Libro del Peregrino*. Ludovico Corfino's *Istoria di Phileto veronese*, a much shorter work closer in tone and structure to the old Greek novels, was also written in this period, and in Bigolina's own region, but it could not have had a great deal of influence on other authors because it was not published until 1899.

These works, sparse though they may be, form the literary tradition to which *Urania* belongs. Although Bigolina's romance does not appear to have been directly inspired by any specific romance that preceded it, it does contain numerous motifs which had become standard in the genre, such as a proem describing a supernatural visitation, characters who conduct debates on love doctrine (*questioni d'amore*), the inclusion within the text of letters written by characters, extensive laments on the cruelty of love, descriptions of journeys, portentous dreams, and the like.

Nonetheless, it must be noted that Bigolina makes a considerable effort to do something new with this style of writing. She avoids the extreme length of many of the older Italian romances, which tended to let their plots suffocate under the weight of numerous erudite digressions and subplots. Her plot is more linear, and thus more novella-like, than any other Renaissance Italian prose romance save Corfino's *Historia di Phileto veronese*. Her lack of emphasis on the trappings of classical culture (she does not call churches "temples," for instance, or have characters in contemporary Italy invoke pagan gods, as is evident in such works as Boccaccio's *Fiammetta* and *Il Libro del Peregrino*) also serves to link her more closely to the novella tradition. It is perhaps significant that the only work of prose fiction that appears to have had any direct influence on her is not a romance at all, but a novella collection, *Le piacevoli notti* of Giovan Francesco Straparola, which attained great popularity after it was first published in Venice in 1550.[37] It is interesting to note that Bigolina seems quite drawn to Straparola's supernatural motifs of fairies and magical objects, even though she is careful to maintain an air of verisimilitude throughout *Urania*: after the allegorical proem, all traces of the supernatural disappear, save in Fabio's dream and in the false and outlandish report of the Duchess of Calabria's old counselor, who invents a meeting with a fairy in order to explain the supposedly magical powers of a rose garland he wishes to bestow

---

[37] Book I of *Le piacevoli notti* appeared in 1550, Book II in 1553. Bigolina's works show several direct links to Book I (see note 47 below, *Urania* note 60, and "Giulia Camposanpiero," note 13).

INTRODUCTION

upon the Prince of Salerno. Such verisimilitude was typical of most Cinquecento prose romances, in which the supernatural is largely confined to dream sequences (i.e. Peregrino's descent into hell in Caviceo's book), and was also a hallmark of contemporary novella collections, Straparola's being exceptional in this regard.[38] Not only is the account of the fairy in *Urania* a fabulous lie, but Bigolina also takes pains to explain that the actual origin of the rose garland is exotic, yet hardly supernatural: it was made from a rose bush in the Duchess's garden, which had come from far away and had certain remarkable properties which are never described as explicitly magical.

In short, *Urania* is too substantial to be a novella, yet it is clearly the creation of someone who had been nurtured in the novella tradition. Despite its length, digressions, and didactic sequences, it reflects a novella-like linearity of plot. It is broken into chapters and contains a variety of episodes and subplots, but ultimately all of these are pointed toward a single grand resolution, which the reader reaches far more quickly (and with far fewer distractions) than in most other prose romances of Bigolina's time. The characteristics which make such books as *Il libro del Peregrino* and *Philena* scarcely readable today cannot be ascribed to *Urania*.

Bigolina's description of the origin of the story of *Urania* constitutes yet another innovation, for she avoids any reference to fictive oral narration, long a commonplace of both the prose romance and novella traditions. Novella authors usually follow two courses: either they create fictional frame stories which describe the recounting of the stories of the collection by an individual or a group of storytellers, or they declare they are merely repeating stories they have heard from someone else. Matteo Bandello often describes the precise time and place where he heard a story, or the person from whom he heard it, while Giovanni Sercambi pretends he himself is the sole tale-teller in the frame story of his *novelliere*; for his part, Franco Sacchetti claims he is merely collecting stories he has heard, or else recounting things which he witnessed or which occurred to him in his own life.[39] For centuries, novella authors presented themselves as mere compilers of

---

[38] On verisimilitude in the novella, see R. J. Clements and J. Gibaldi, *Anatomy of the Novella: The European Tale Collection from Boccaccio and Chaucer to Cervantes* (New York: New York University Press, 1977), 16–19, and B. Porcelli, *La novella del Cinquecento* (Bari: Laterza, 1973), 9–10. For Peregrino's voyage to hell see I. Caviceo, *Il Peregrino*, ed. Vignali, 244–59. For a Straparola story involving the gift of a magic object from a grateful fairy see *Le piacevoli notti*, ed. Piranesi, 5.1.

[39] See F. Sacchetti, *Il Trecentonovelle*, ed. A. Lanza (Florence: Sansoni, 1984), 1, and G. Sercambi, *Il Novelliere*, ed. L. Rossi, 3 vols. (Rome: Salerno, 1974), 1: 10–12. Bandello's *novelliere* contains many references to oral sources, but on occasion he describes in detail

INTRODUCTION

true events which they had seen or heard from others, and no one did this more conspicuously than Boccaccio himself when he pretended not to have been the actual writer of the *Decameron*'s stories (1: 469; 2: 1258). This tendency is even reflected in the great single novellas of the sixteenth century which lack frame stories, such as Luigi Da Porto's story of Romeo and Giulietta, or Niccolò Machiavelli's *favola* of Belfagor.[40] An oral source, either real or imagined, had long been a defining characteristic of the early Italian novella, and indeed Bigolina herself adheres to this tradition in the frame story of "Giulia Camposanpiero." A similar tendency predominates in the prose *romanzo d'amore*, going all the way back to Boccaccio: in nearly all cases the narration is in the first person, with the lover recounting experiences which supposedly actually happened to him (or to her, as in the case of the *Fiammetta*, the only Italian prose romance with a female protagonist before *Urania*). The principal exception is the *Filocolo*, wherein much subtler autobiographical elements are inserted within a third-person retelling of the old French story of Floire and Blanchefleur.

However, Bigolina rejects all pretense of orality in *Urania*, as well as any hint of an external, historical origin for her tale. Instead, her authorial persona boldly claims that she has made the whole story up, inspired by a stern lecture from an allegorical being who has suddenly appeared in her room. With this scene, similar to the allegorical visitations which serve to give direction to the author's creative processes in such didactic works as Boethius's *Consolation of Philosophy*, Boccaccio's *The Fates of Illustrious Men*, and Christine de Pizan's *The Book of the City of Ladies*,[41] Bigolina dispenses with the traditional narrative models for novella collections and romances alike, and journeys into literary territory that is unique for the Italian prose fiction of her time. Her impassioned defense of women likewise serves to associate *Urania* with a different literary category, closer to Boccaccio's *Famous Women (De Claris Mulieribus)* than to his *Filocolo* or *Fiammetta*. Indeed,

---

gatherings of tale-tellers, as in a typical framing narrative, who recount stories which he transcribes; see for instance the proem to novella 2:36 (in *Tutte le opere*, ed. F. Flora, 2 vols. [Milan: Mondadori, 1966], 1: 1023–25).

[40] M. Ciccuto, ed., *Novelle italiane: Il Cinquecento* (Milan: Garzanti, 1982), 25 and 95–97.

[41] See Boethius, *The Consolation of Philosophy*, trans. V. E. Watts (New York: Penguin, 1981), 1 pr. 1 (35–36); G. Boccaccio, *The Fates of Illustrious Men (De casibus virorum illustrium)*, trans. and abridged L. B. Hall (New York: Ungar, 1965), 1 (2–3) and 8 (202– 7); and Christine de Pizan, *The Book of the City of Ladies*, trans. R. Brown-Grant (London: Penguin, 1999), 1.2 (7–8). As in *Urania*, these allegorical figures (or in Boccaccio's case, a vision of Petrarch) come to reprove the author for some misguided notion.

35

INTRODUCTION

Bigolina's book reveals in at least one place the direct influence of Christine de Pizan's own defense of women, the *Book of the City of Ladies*: when Urania praises the great deeds of Judith, Esther, the Sabine women, and Veturia, she is following precisely the same subject matter, in the same sequence, as Christine's chapters 2.31–34 (see *Urania* translation 151, notes 38–41).

Urania's two parts, Bigolina's proem and the story of Urania herself, are neatly conjoined because they both share two of the work's predominant themes: the consequences of bad judgment and women's search for a safe mode of self-display. A linking factor between these two lies in the motif of the portraiture of women which permeates both sections.[42] In the proem Bigolina's authorial persona learns that her decision to have herself painted as a token of remembrance is a mistake, for her true portrait can only be found in the artistic creations of her own imagination; this she learns from a macrocephalic, one-eyed little man who is the very allegory of Judgment. She then spontaneously conceives of the story of Urania, in which we find a protagonist who already understands that the works of poetry and prose which she has sent to her faithless lover Fabio are her true portraits; indeed Fabio's new love object, a woman who is prettier but less virtuous than Urania, might provide paintings of herself as tokens of remembrance, but nothing as genuine and heartfelt as what Urania has written to him. The long letter to Fabio which Urania composes at the beginning of the work smolders with a barely restrained anger, as she tries to make him see that her greater virtue and loyalty far outweigh any of the gifts her more attractive rival might provide. Once she has vented her feelings in this letter, her task throughout the rest of the story will be to ride across Italy disguised as a man, demonstrating to all she meets, and ultimately to Fabio himself, the truth of her situation, which she expresses best in the course of the oration which she delivers to five young men in a wood near Naples:

> Et conchiudiamo ancora potersi beato chiamar quell'huomo, al quale da' Cieli fu dato in sorte, che valorosa donna gli fosse compagna. (154)

> [And let us also conclude that any man may call himself blessed, if by chance the heavens have given him an excellent woman as a consort.]

---

[42] On the subject of Bigolina's motif of portraiture see C. Nissen, "Subjects, Objects, Authors: The Portraiture of Women in Giulia Bigolina's *Urania*," *Italian Culture* 18 (2000): 15–31.

Introduction

The central task of this work is to define and depict, indeed provide a portrait in words of, this "valorosa donna," the ideal woman who does not need to resort to posing for a painting as a means of self-expression. Later on, to underscore this point, Bigolina gives us a subplot concerning a woman, the widowed Duchess of Calabria, who stands not only as an antithesis to the ideal Urania, but also as a fictional counterpart to Bigolina's initially confused authorial persona who must be taught a lesson in good judgment. After falling in love with the Prince of Salerno through his painted portrait, the Duchess allows herself to be swayed by the misguided arguments of her advisor and consents to pose for a portrait of her own, as a means to winning the heart of the Prince himself. The Duchess not only does the very thing that Bigolina managed to avoid doing, she overdoes it, posing seminude as Venus in an unscrupulous artist's version of the Judgment of Paris. This decision, leading to the Duchess's final ignominious downfall at the book's conclusion, shows the dangers which Bigolina regarded as inherent in such failed modes of self-display. Urania, whose name links her to the Platonic Celestial Venus (Οὐρανία, "the Heavenly One"), makes all of her decisions in the context of her personal ideal of the highest feminine virtue, whereas the divinely beautiful Duchess assumes the role of the Carnal Venus, engaged in an act which Renaissance scholars regarded as one of the supreme moments of bad judgment in ancient history, i.e. receiving the golden apple of discord (meant for whichever goddess could prove herself the fairest) from Paris; this in turn led to the fall and ruin of Troy.[43] The fact that Paris did this in order to receive in marriage the world's most beautiful woman only serves to clinch the argument. The antithesis between Urania and the Duchess is further enhanced by the aspect they have in common:

---

[43] For the distinction between the heavenly and vulgar Venuses as interpreted by the most influential Renaissance neo-Platonist, see M. Ficino, *Commentary on Plato's Symposium on Love*, trans. S. Jayne, 2nd rev. ed. (Dallas: Spring Publications, 1985), 2.7, 6.5, 6.7 (53–54, 113, 115–18). Long before Lady Mary Wroth's own prose romance *Urania* (published in 1621), Bigolina had already thought to apply the name to a virtuous romance heroine; in her turn, Bigolina might have been inspired by a letter which Giuseppe Betussi had appended to his *Il Raverta* in the 1540s, praising the poet and composer Luigi Cassola for his book about love which also bore the name *Urania* (149). Cassola's book was never published, and I have not been able to locate any manuscript containing it. For another Italian romance heroine named Urania see F. Passero, *Urania, overo la costante donna* (Naples: Roncagliolo, 1616). Passero's work, a verse romance intended to be read as Christian allegory, does not appear to owe any debt to Bigolina. For the Judgment of Paris see also H. D. Brumble, *Classical Myths and Legends in the Middle Ages and Renaissance* (Westport, CT: Greenwood Press, 1998), 258–61.

Introduction

that is, each must make a fateful decision while in the throes of depression and the anguish caused by lost or unrequited love; under such conditions, Urania demonstrates repeatedly her capacity to make wise choices, while the Duchess most manifestly does not. Bigolina makes use of a similar pairing of contrasting female characters in "Giulia Camposanpiero," where we find the virtuous and wise Giulia juxtaposed with the immoral and misguided Odolarica; and just as in *Urania*, these antithetical women inhabit separate lines of plot, never meeting or having much to do with each other in the story. Bigolina prefers not to put virtue and lack of virtue in direct conflict with each other, but rather to let each exist, emblematically and exemplarily, in its own separate realm and sphere of action. There is no final "showdown" between them.

Urania is Bigolina's vehicle for the expression of her love doctrine, which is supremely rational, moralistic, and even practical. In her two extended didactic passages (coming on the heels of the equally extended and didactic letter to Fabio), Urania expounds first on the hard-headed, practical realities a woman must face in choosing a lover on the one hand, and then, in the second case, on the injustice of male misogynistic attitudes. Throughout the story Bigolina presents us with a series of failed female types, such as the Duchess, Clorina, and Emilia, but also with portraits of the highest womanly virtue in Urania and the Prince's "wise maiden." Both of Bigolina's surviving narratives describe a fantasy world in which women are shown as relatively free to make their own choices in life, without social and familial constraints. Urania, who disappears from her home and family for an extended period without having her honor called into question, may stand as a case in point. In such a world, Bigolina seems to be saying, a truly virtuous woman can always be trusted to choose wisely, and thus demonstrate her worth as a "valorosa donna" to the man she loves. Presiding over these choices is Bigolina's tutelary deity, the one-eyed, huge-headed homunculus she calls "Judgment."

This emphasis on characters' choices and motivations allows Bigolina to create characters who resist simplistic moral definitions. The Duchess is not a stereotypical one-dimensional temptress, but rather a chaste widow of nineteen inclined to live a life of virtue, upon whom Love plays a cruel trick: "Therefore it was Love's desire to overwhelm and punish this gentle lady, who had been leading a happy life up to this point, and inflict great harm upon her, as an example to others" (187). Her principal fault lies in trusting the advice of a seemingly wise old man who acts as her counselor, and who has never previously led her astray. The Prince likewise resists simplistic categorization as an idealized benevolent ruler, for, despite his constant worrying that he might be viewed as something less than just and impartial, the strange sentence he imposes is engineered not only to save his

INTRODUCTION

beloved Fabio, but also to bring about the death of Menandro, whom he despises.[44] Clorina, for her part, is hardly meant to be seen as an admirable character, yet when she is forced to choose between her two suitors Fabio and Menandro, with the life of one of them hanging in the balance, she takes time to explain her choice in terms which are at once both rational and merciful. It is worth noting that the episode in Ariosto's *Orlando Furioso* upon which Bigolina apparently models Clorina's choice is much less ethically complicated, for when Ariosto's Doralice is required to select a husband from her rival suitors Rodomonte and Mandricardo it is not in the context of a crime or a sentence of death, and she is not made to explain her choice, or indeed say much of anything (27.102–107).

Bigolina is consistently interested in practical solutions to the problems of love, especially as they relate to women. When Fabio abandons her, Urania is seized by a grief so overwhelming that she expects to die, and yet her first thoughts concern solutions to the crisis that will preserve both her honor and her sanity: "Therefore she resolved to flee Salerno without delay, dressed as a man, and wander the world until such a time as the great suffering and considerable discomfort that she would undergo along the way might free her heart from its excessive, indeed insane, love for Fabio: only thus could she prove merciful to herself" (89). Here Bigolina is following a topos common in the medieval and Renaissance romance and lyric traditions, that of the depressed lover's flight from society; however, in its most typical form the lover (usually male) does not display so much rational premeditation. In his *Asolani*, Pietro Bembo says a miserable lover who seeks to lose himself in nature does so only as a desperate measure to make his beloved happier; once in isolation, he desires nothing more than to weep and wallow in unhappiness (1.27). Petrarch, in poem 35 of the *Canzoniere*, is primarily interested in fleeing the prying eyes of common people who would not understand his suffering. In the most extreme cases, the rejected romantic hero becomes a sort of wild man, living in a primitive, even mindless state until rescued by others, as exemplified by such characters as Chrétien de Troyes' Yvain, Tristan, and Ariosto's Orlando.[45] Urania clearly descends from this type of romance character, and

---

[44] Bigolina's Prince bears some resemblance to the ruler of Ferrara in Caviceo's *Libro del Peregrino*, who must also decide guilt and impose a morally troubling sentence of death in an extended trial episode (ed. Vignali, 41–74).

[45] See Chrétien de Troyes, *Complete Romances*, trans. and ed. D. Staines (Bloomington: Indiana University Press, 1990), 216–19; *Le roman de Tristan en prose*, ed. R. L. Curtis, 3 vols. (Cambridge: D. S. Breiser, 1985), 3: 173 (871); and L. Ariosto, *Orlando Furioso*, ed. M. Turchi, 2 vols. (Milan: Garzanti, 1984), 23.111–36 (2: 632–38). For a study of the motif of the romance hero mad for love, with emphasis on Tristan as depicted in the *Tristano*

might well stand as the best example of a female equivalent to them, but there are considerable differences.⁴⁶ Bigolina is careful not to let her character wallow uselessly in her grief for long, despite her initial tears and laments. Nor does Urania have the luxury of living like a beast in nature, tearing off her clothes and uprooting trees in order to show her distress, as Orlando does; for she is a woman, and must act more sensibly, adhering to the all-important ideals of feminine virtue, if she is to be accepted and respected by the readers of her time. The male disguise allows her to do this without risk to her honor, and she scrupulously maintains this illusion throughout her long series of adventures.

In time, Urania discovers new uses for her disguise: originally it was merely a ruse to allow her to indulge in her solitude unmolested, but subsequently she finds it also grants her the opportunity to do useful work as a teacher, because she is able to communicate her doctrines of virtue and the worth of women to groups of young lovers who are convinced she is a man. It allows her to indulge in the didactic purpose which, as the conclusion of the proem makes plain, is central to the work as a whole. By the end of her adventure, this "anti-Orlando" has turned her original aimless wandering into a resolute plan of action. Riding into Salerno on the very day Fabio is to be executed, she employs a second, very different male disguise to tame and kiss the Prince's bestial Wild Woman, an emblem of the female "wildness" and lack of virtue which she has consistently rejected within herself.⁴⁷ With Fabio free and his hand in marriage won, Urania has now solved the

---

Panciatichiano, see M. J. Heijkant, "Tristan Pilosus: La folie de l'héros dans le Tristano Panciatichiano," in *Tristan-Tristant: Mélanges Danielle Buschinger*, ed. P. Crépin and W. Spiewok (Greifswald: Reineke, 1996), 231–42.

⁴⁶ Bigolina's depiction of Urania's aimless ride also owes much to a similar episode in Ariosto's *Orlando Furioso*, wherein Bradamante allows her horse to wander while she is consumed with sad and jealous thoughts of her lover Ruggiero (32.61–64 [2: 878–79]).

⁴⁷ For the implications of the motif of male disguise in both of Bigolina's works see C. Nissen, "The Motif of the Woman in Male Disguise from Boccaccio to Bigolina," in *The Italian Novella*, ed. G. Allaire (New York: Routledge, 2003), 201–17. For a Paduan comedy replete with women disguised as men, which might have inspired Bigolina (the ride of Ginevra and Ghita in disguise parallels to some extent that of Urania and Emilia), see Ruzante's *L'Anconitana*. On the phenomenon of the Wild Man or Wild Woman in Renaissance literature, see R. Bartra, *The Artificial Savage: Modern Myths of the Wild Man*, trans. C. Follett (Ann Arbor: University of Michigan Press, 1997), 53–92. See also J. Vitullo, *The Chivalric Epic in Medieval Italy* (Gainesville: University Press of Florida, 2000), 51–61 for the motif in medieval Italian chivalric epics, and Heijkant, "Tristan Pilosus," 240–42 for the notion that Tristan is depicted as a Wild Man in the *Tristano Panciatichiano*. Straparola's influence seems apparent here, as well: Wild Men appear in *Le piacevoli notti* 4.1

Introduction

crisis which had originally led her to self-imposed exile, and proved that action is far more useful to the "valorosa donna" than inaction. But she has not yet finished her tour-de-force of guile in disguise. In her final speech before the Prince's assembled court, Urania uses that same male persona to bring about her final triumph, for it allows her to prompt Fabio to admit the very thing she has been yearning to express to him, ever since she wrote him her impassioned letter: that she is the best of all women, the only one he ever should have wanted. Once she has achieved this, her work is done, and at last she doffs the male disguise she has worn almost from the very beginning of the tale, ready to return to her proper place in society, now as Fabio's wife.

It is obviously difficult to know how to place *Urania* within Bigolina's oeuvre, since so little of it survives. Nonetheless, it has the look and feel of a *magnum opus*, an elaborate and heartfelt expression of the author's beliefs and world view. In the book as a whole, but most specifically in her didactic passages, Bigolina stresses two main points in conjunction with an appeal for reform of social attitudes: first, that love of virtue should dominate all other concerns in the choice of a mate, and second, that women should be respected by men, and allowed to participate in the arts to the extent their talents will allow. These two ideas are components of her primary philosophical vision, that love is the focal point of all human experience, and it should never be communicated through mere simulacra, but rather through an awareness of one's own creative potential. In the proem Bigolina defines her task in personal, autobiographical terms: how can she find a means to express the depths of her love to Salvatico so that her memory will live on within him after she is dead? Her response is clear: she must realize her own potential, and create a work of art which will continue to speak with her voice after her demise; and thus at the proem's conclusion she hopes for a "doppia vita," a double life in a work of art, to be lived in Salvatico's mind. This, conjoined with her character Urania's heartfelt appeal for greater participation of women in the arts, suggests that Bigolina is also yearning for the "double life" of the artist who is remembered by posterity, who lives forever through the reproduction and dissemination of her work.

---

and 5.1 (in the former, the Princess Costanza captures a satyr and delivers him to the king while disguised as a man). See also note 60 in this translation of *Urania*. Bigolina's interest in Wild Men might also have been inspired by an artistic representation: a fresco by Lambert Sustris in the Villa Bigolin at Selvazzano includes a pair of them depicted as satyrs (see Mancini, *La Villa Bigolin*, cover and plate 74). I am indebted to Renzo Bragantini for his suggestion that Bigolina's wild woman (la Femina Salvatica) might well be a pun on the name Bartolomeo Salvatico.

INTRODUCTION

4. "LA NOVELLA DI GIULIA CAMPOSANPIERO ET DI THESIBALDO VITALIANI"

Borromeo is the first to mention this work, which he says he transcribed from a manuscript which Giovanni de Lazara kept in his personal collection (Borromeo, *Notizia*, 6). One manuscript containing the story is known to exist today, BP 1451 VIII in the Biblioteca Civica in Padua. The library card catalogue describes this manuscript as being of the eighteenth century, but it is quite plainly of the sixteenth, and might well be the one from which Borromeo made his copy. After the Cavaliere De Lazara's death in 1833 his library was taken intact to the municipal library of Lendinara, a town near Rovigo, but later it was redistributed to several other places, among them the Biblioteca Civica. Although the manuscript does not bear Bigolina's name, Borromeo might well have been able to infer her authorship through the novella's stylistic and thematic resemblance to *Urania*.[48]

BP 1451 VIII is written in a different hand from that of Bigolina's only other known sixteenth-century manuscript, Trivulziana 88. Trivulziana 88 is a handsomely bound presentation copy, almost certainly the work of a professional copyist and written in elegant italic script with floral designs and historiated initials, whereas the "Giulia Camposanpiero" manuscript, in a simpler and less elegant form of italic, is written in a cursory fashion without embellishments. It would appear that neither manuscript is an autograph, since their hands do not resemble that of Bigolina's will (ASP AN 829), which, as I have noted, is certainly holographic. Little evidence exists to provide a date for "Giulia Camposanpiero," and there is no clue to indicate whether this novella preceded or followed *Urania*. However, it was surely written after 1550, since it shows even clearer signs of the influence of Straparola's *Le piacevoli notti* than does *Urania*. These signs include echoes of Straparola's novella 3.4 in Thesibaldo's joust scene (see "Giulia Camposanpiero" translation, note 13), as well as the sonnet-riddle which Bigolina places at the end of her novella, following a convention established in Straparola's

---

[48] Borromeo might also have had this information from the Cavaliere himself, who was a distant relative of the author. The De Lazara family had married into the Bigolin family in the seventeenth century (for Giulia de Lazara's marriage to Dioclide Bigolin, great-grandson of Bigolina's cousin Dioclide, see the stemma in Mancini, *La Villa Bigolin*, 148). Thus it is possible that the manuscript had been kept by successive generations of the family as an heirloom before ending up in the Cavaliere's book collection. See the description of BP 1451 VIII, below, for evidence that the manuscript once bore a different cover, which might also have included Bigolina's name in Borromeo's time.

Introduction

work.[49] Only one contemporary historical figure is mentioned in "Giulia Camposanpiero," but her exact identity is not made clear. In her proem Bigolina's authorial persona addresses a gathering of tale-tellers who have met at Mirabello, one of the less prominent of the Euganean Hills about twelve kilometers southwest of Padua, near the town of Torreglia. Following a tradition established in the *Decameron* frame story, the group is led by a "queen" whom Bigolina calls Signora Cavaliera Conte, and at whose command she must recount her novella. The Conte family was one of the most distinguished of the Paduan nobility in this period, but it is not immediately clear which of its members Bigolina had in mind. Sperone Speroni wrote a number of letters to the Cavaliere Paolo de' Conti, whose son Alberto married his daughter Giulia Sperona, and in some of these letters he makes reference to Paolo's wife Bianca, calling her "la signora Cavaliera." Speroni addressed a letter to her as late as 1559, shortly after the marriage of their offspring (Loi and Pozzi, ed., *Lettere familiari*, 2: 98, 100). But Masenetti's poem *Il divino oracolo* (1548), which has been cited above for its reference to a Bigolina who is most likely Giulia, also contains an octave describing yet another illustrious Cavaliera Conte:

> Appresso v'aggiongea la CAVALIERA
> Co'l dolce sguardo, e col benigno aspetto:
> Che piu ch'Amor nei cuor mortali impera.
> Hor sculpita in quest'alma, hor in quel petto.
> La CONTE dico; d'ogni gratia intiera
> (con somma leggiadria) nido, e ricetto.
> Lustrata del bel nome LUCIETTA
> Per ch'in noi luce appar vera, e perfetta. (25v)

> [Then there approached the CAVALIERA
> with the sweet look, and the benign aspect:
> more than love, she rules in mortal hearts.
> Now she is sculpted in this soul, now in that breast.
> The CONTE, I mean; she is the refuge and nesting place,
> with greatest elegance, of every complete grace.

---

[49] For Straparola's influence on authors of literary riddles see De Filippis, *The Literary Riddle in Italy*, 30–71. De Filippis notes that the literary riddle in Renaissance Italy can be traced back to the works of Angiolo Cenni, who preceded Straparola; however, Straparola was the first to add such poems to novellas (8–9).

INTRODUCTION

She shines with the lovely name LUCIETTA
because she appears as a true and perfect light in us.]

This Cavaliera Lucietta Conte, who "rules in mortal hearts," might well be Bigolina's queen at Mirabello. Her place in the family is not entirely clear: the only Lucietta Conte whom Speroni mentions is his granddaughter, the daughter of Giulia and Alberto, born in 1574 (Loi and Pozzi, ed., *Lettere familiari*, 1: 305). In his history of the Conte family, Luigi-Ignazio Grotto degli Erri does not mention any famous Conte women of this period (*Cenni storici sulle famiglie di Padova* [Padua: Minerva, 1842], 25–55). In any event, even if the date of her composition is uncertain, in this passage Bigolina reveals a familiarity with some great lady of this family, a family which by 1558 was linked to that of the humanist Speroni.

In the sixteenth century there was a considerable vogue for literary works depicting a group of tale-tellers or discussants who, while happily ensconced in some pleasant setting for an extended period of time, entertain one another with stories, poems, or debates on various topics. What Boccaccio had begun in the *Decameron* and other works reached new heights early in Bigolina's century in such works as Castiglione's *Book of the Courtier* and Bembo's *Asolani*. As has been noted, novella collections with frame stories flourished in the Veneto in the mid-Cinquecento, and it would appear Bigolina set out to make her own contribution to the genre with "Giulia Camposanpiero." It is unclear whether she succeeded in writing a complete novella collection which has subsequently become mostly lost, or merely planned one and failed to finish it. However, the frame story she gives us does indicate that "Giulia Camposanpiero" was meant to be the last novella in the work, recounted after all the others in the company have had their turns to tell a story. "Certainly if I try to disobey the commands of the Cavaliera," says Bigolina's authorial persona in her proem, "each one of you will be justified in concluding that I alone, out of so many in this charming company, have dared to break our rules of pleasant entertainment ..." (293). And in the conclusion she says, "Gracious women and valorous men, this is the novella, or rather the historical account which I, like the others, have attempted to recount to you" (319). Further on she indicates that she hopes her riddle will be as good as those which all the others have already recited. These declarations appear to have led Borromeo to conclude that "Giulia Camposanpiero" would be the final narrative in Bigolina's collection, a collection which, as we have noted, he imagined must have also held "Panfilo" and *Urania*.[50] In any case Bigolina's frame story begins very much *in medias res*,

---

[50] The Biblioteca Municipale of Bassano has many letters from Borromeo to his pub-

INTRODUCTION

without the traditional proem explaining who the members of the group are, and without a description of the events that brought the group together and led its members to select the Cavaliera Conte as their queen. There is no indication how many days the *brigata* has been at Mirabello, nor how many stories were supposed to have been recounted up to this point. Moreover, we have no idea what title, if any, the author meant to give to the work as a whole. Basically Bigolina has left us only a fragment of a novella collection, but it is a fragment providing numerous indicators that it was meant to contain the typical elements of the genre.

The usual third-person frame narration is lacking as well, so we cannot tell if Bigolina's character is meant to be Bigolina herself or someone else speaking in the first person. The speaker is plainly a woman, but otherwise her identity is a mystery. In the conclusion she makes reference to her husband's presence in the group, certainly a rarity in most novella collection frame stories, although perhaps not in those written by women. To the best of my knowledge, the only other appearance of a husband and wife as tale-tellers in the same *novelliere* frame story is found in Marguerite de Navarre's *Heptaméron*, first published in 1559, which includes Hircan as Marguerite's husband Henri d'Albret and Parlemente representing Marguerite herself.[51] In Bigolina's case the reference is fleeting, serving only to depict the authorial persona and her husband as outsiders who have audaciously joined a group of their social or intellectual superiors: "It is clearly necessary that I conclude that you will have every right to decide that both my husband and I have shown great audacity in joining with such high intellects as all of you have" (319).

Audacity is, in fact, one of the main motifs of both this story and its frame. Although it was quite normal for Renaissance authors to begin their works with a *captatio benevolentiae*, the old classical topos of affected modesty, Bigolina carries this tendency to remarkable lengths in both her introduction and conclusion to this tale. Fiora Bassanese has shown us how Renaissance women typically belittled themselves in their writings for their putative lack of eloquence, and for the deficiencies that one might perceive in their intellectual formation.[52] Training in the

---

lisher Remondini, including one written in 1793 which mentions Bigolina (see *Epistolario Remondini* 1166–1182, vol. 6, letter 1169). However, this letter does not describe any other sources for Borromeo's supposition concerning the structure and contents of Bigolina's novella collection.

[51] For Michel François' identification of Marguerite's *devisants* see Marguerite de Navarre, *Heptaméron*, ed. François (Paris: Garnier, 1967), 447 nn. 12–16.

[52] F. A. Bassanese, "Selling the Self; or, the Epistolary Production of Renaissance Courtesans," in *Italian Women Writers from the Renaissance to the Present: Revising the Canon*, ed. M. O. Marotti (University Park, PA: Pennsylvania State University Press, 1996), 69–82,

Introduction

rules of rhetoric, which was considered so essential for Renaissance writers, was routinely denied to women. Women therefore often allude to a transgression implicit in the act of writing, an appropriation of language which is not normally their own (Bassanese, "Selling the Self," 78). Bigolina does something similar here when she has her tale-teller protest that she has been asked to exceed her powers, even though she knows she must obey her queen:

> But what am I to do? Certainly if I try to disobey the commands of the Cavaliera, each one of you will be justified in concluding that I alone, out of so many in this charming company, have dared to break our rules of pleasant entertainment; and nothing could ever occur that would disturb me more, now or at any other time.
>
> It is my right and proper duty to see if I am able, given the weakness of my faculties, to piece this together, this thing which is not just a novella, but an historical account. (293)

She fears she will not be equal to this task as narrator, the more so since it is no mere novella that she will recount (which might be understood to be safer intellectual ground for a woman), but history, which is customarily the domain of male writers. As I have had occasion to note, the Cinquecento novella typically sought to establish a closer relationship with the facts of history than did novellas of earlier periods, but something more subtle than this trend is at work here. The speaker plainly pretends to doubt her powers on the basis that she is a woman:

> Then let this be pleasing to you, gracious ladies ... that so weighty an undertaking overwhelms my foolish resistance, so that I, a woman little accustomed to such things, can receive great benefit from the favor shown to me by each of you; and wherever my wit is found lacking, your favor may make up for it and fill with me with confidence. In this way it may be that I will easily be able to accomplish so difficult a task. (293–295)

On the most superficial level of the text, this voice is merely that of a fictional tale-teller who has been asked to recount a story in a frame-story setting. It is impossible, however, not to hear as well the voice of the writer of the book herself,

---

here 70–71. Indeed, audacity on the part of women might be said to be one of Bigolina's most pervasive themes, appearing not only in both of her works of fiction, but even in her only surviving letter (see Introduction, 14–15).

INTRODUCTION

a certain "donna mal'usa a questo" ["a woman little accustomed to such things"], whose task it is to create a unique work of literature. Certain notions pervade this frame-story fragment: notions of rhetorical propriety, of defiance of authority, of the powers of women, of the consequences of moral transgressions which might threaten the unity of purpose of the social group. These notions set the stage for the narrative which follows, the story of a woman who dares to defy social conventions to claim the man she loves.

Having claimed that this is more *istoria* than *novella*, Bigolina must now be careful to set her narrative in history. She begins with the assertion that the events she will describe occurred over two hundred years previously, in the days when Padua was a republic, between the tyranny of Ezzelino da Romano in the thirteenth century and the dominance of the Carrara family in the fourteenth. After she has professed so many doubts in her own powers it is interesting to note the extent to which Bigolina fails in this task of accurately recounting historical events. Although the historical period she describes lasted from 1259 to 1318, with the specific action of her tale apparently set around 1311, she mistakenly places in her narrative the Holy Roman Emperor Sigismund, who reigned 1410–1433, as well as his contemporary Pope Eugenius IV, who reigned 1431–1447.[53] In the midst of this confusion, however, certain episodes in Bigolina's narrative reveal that she must have been inspired by a few precisely identifiable historical events. At the beginning of her narrative she refers to a victory of the Paduans over Can Grande della Scala, the lord of Verona. The most likely inspiration for this episode was the successful revolt in June 1311 of the Paduans against the forces of the Holy Roman Empire, which had taken power in the city with Can Grande's help (Cappelletti, *Storia di Padova*, 1: 198–99). In that same year the pre-humanist poet Albertino Mussato, a famous figure in Paduan history, was chosen to serve among the ambassadors sent to Milan to represent the city at the coronation of the emperor Henry VII (Scardeone, *Historiae*, 260; Cappelletti, *Storia di Padova*, 1: 203–4). Both Scardeone and Cappelletti stress Mussato's eloquence and rhetorical skill on this occasion, as well as in other similar episodes. Therefore it is not unreasonable to imagine that Mussato might have served at least in part as Bigolina's model for her character Thesibaldo Vitaliani, the learned orator who is sent to Bologna to use his great eloquence on Padua's behalf at the coronation of the Emperor Sigismund.

---

[53] For a comment on the inaccuracy of Bigolina's historical account see Borromeo, *Notizia*, 126. For a history of Padua in the period between the fall of Ezzelino da Romano and the rise of the Carrara see G. Cappelletti, *Storia di Padova dalla sua origine sino al presente*, 2 vols. (Padua: Sacchetto, 1874), 1: 173–212.

INTRODUCTION

Fassini mentions another relevant episode, this time set in the correct city: in 1310 the Paduan Republic sent a group of ambassadors to Bologna to speak with the papal legate Arnaldo about the position the city should take with regard to the imminent arrival in Italy of Henry VII for his coronation, and among these ambassadors was a certain Palamede de' Vitaliani, of whom little else is known (in *Cenni storici*, 317). It would surely seem Bigolina has this period in the history of her city primarily in mind, even if she has replaced Henry VII, the Emperor so bent on conquering Padua, with the more benevolent Sigismund who reigned over a hundred years later. Her desire to place Eugenius IV in her narrative might be explained at least in part by pride in her family origins, since it is known that one of her mother's more famous ancestors, Ludovico Barbo, Abbot of Santa Giustina in Padua and later Bishop of Treviso, was named envoy to the Council of Basel by that pope in 1432.[54]

The narrator's audacity in the proem is matched by the audacity of the strong and capable character Giulia, who, perhaps not by accident, bears the same name as the author herself. She alone, of all the women of Padua, succeeds in winning the love of the supposedly unattainable Thesibaldo Vitaliani, a young man who is not only phenomenally handsome and graceful, but also highly skilled in arms and letters, the two qualities most useful for "la vita cittadinesca," the life of a citizen in an Italian city-state. Thesibaldo is not only a citizen of the first rank, but also, as Bigolina takes pains to tell us, an object of fascination for all the ladies of the town, especially those who are not yet married. However, Thesibaldo has sworn never to marry, and rejects all those women who offer themselves to him. As in *Urania*, Bigolina is pleased to create a world in which women themselves are seen to make such offers, without apparent consideration for their families' wishes. When Giulia finds herself dancing with Thesibaldo at a party, she addresses him quite forthrightly:

> Therefore she became bold, and ventured to tell him that he should consent to show his skill at the joust on her behalf. Vitaliano had no keen reasoning to refuse her. Indeed, convinced by her arguments and overwhelmed, he promised to satisfy her desire, and affirmed that he owed her satisfaction in even greater matters. (297)

The term "overwhelmed" does not completely do justice to the Italian "violentato," which suggests that Thesibaldo has been violently assaulted, even violated,

---

[54] J. W. Stieber, *Pope Eugenius IV* (Leiden: Brill, 1978), 17 n. 17.

INTRODUCTION

by Giulia's bid. Further on we are shown how Thesibaldo himself regards this remarkable event which will change his life. We are told that Giulia wins Thesibaldo by combining male and female attributes: her "bellezza" [beauty] succeeds because it is accompanied by "una viril dispostezza" [a manly disposition] which he cannot resist. Thus he finds himself riding out to joust, his identity hidden under white armor which displays his new motto TU SOLA PUOI ["you alone are able"; (299)]. After days of fighting, he bests every other knight in the field. After this the two marry in secret, then just as secretly consummate the marriage. Bigolina does not always fully explain her characters' motivations, and in this case we are never told why such secrecy is necessary, but it clearly reflects even greater boldness on the part of her protagonist Giulia. Thus Thesibaldo is forced to recognize Giulia as a most excellent woman, the only woman for him; and as in the case of *Urania*, the plot culminates with a moment of decision on the part of the male protagonist who must choose the right lover. Like Fabio, Thesibaldo is faced with an offer of love from another woman, one who is extremely attractive and well connected: Odolarica, the daughter of the Holy Roman Emperor himself. Since his marriage to Giulia has been kept secret he could easily accept the Emperor's offer of Odolarica's hand, but he refuses and stays with the one extraordinary woman who has managed to win his heart, the woman who combines manly strength with the highest feminine virtue.

Bigolina's authorial persona has declared that she will take a considerable risk and recount events which we are meant to regard as historical; she will therefore tread on difficult rhetorical ground. Meanwhile her counterpart, the fictional Giulia of fourteenth-century Padua, sets a rather different, though equally bold, task for herself: dispensing with modesty, she will dare to conquer the man who has conquered all others, the man who even scorns the company of women. The word "ardire" (to dare) appears in both contexts, and Giulia Camposanpiero succeeds because she is not only "bella," but also "artifiziosa" (clever), endowed with a certain "viril dispostezza." The underlying topos here is classical: Thesibaldo is modelled on the type of Hippolytus of Greek legend, the son of Theseus who offended Aphrodite by refusing to fall in love with any woman. Nearer to Bigolina's own time the type reappears to some extent in the Troilo of Boccaccio's *Filostrato*, and even more plainly in the scornful Iulio of Politian's *Stanze*, who would much rather devote himself to hunting and the manly sports than look at the nymphs who yearn for him. In the old topos divine intervention is always required to bring about a change in the static condition, either by causing Phaedra to fall tragically in love with Hippolytus, or, in the context of the Renaissance revival of

INTRODUCTION

mythological topoi,[55] by causing Politian's Iulio to dedicate himself to the nymph Simonetta. Here Bigolina has, to use one of her favorite terms, dared to do something rather different. Dispensing with references to the machinations of the gods, as is fitting in a work purporting to concern history, she creates a character who can overcome the haughty "man's man" solely through her own abilities. Thesibaldo's new motto TU SOLA PUOI would seem to be emblematic for both Giulia Camposanpiero and Giulia Bigolina: if the former can win the unwinnable man, arrange a secret marriage and thereby change her state through sexual triumph from "donzella" [maid] to completely fulfilled "donna" [woman], so too can the latter, "donna mal'usa a questo," be the one who succeeds in properly recounting the tale. Bigolina emphasizes a similarly subtle association between the values and abilities of the authorial persona and those of the female protagonist in *Urania*, wherein Urania's actions reflect what the narrator has learned about portraiture and self-expression in the allegorical proem. This tendency to allow for an interpenetration of ethical messages between authorial persona and narrative protagonist, which is a feature of both of Bigolina's surviving works, constitutes one of her most remarkable literary traits, and one for which she especially deserves to be remembered.

5. *URANIA:*
TEXT AND TRANSLATION

The manuscript Trivulziana 88, preserved in the Trivulziana Library in Milan, is a leather-bound paper codex in quartos, containing only *Urania*. As Gamba and Porro both noted, it seems to be a presentation copy because the brush-gilded impressions on the cover include Bartolomeo Salvatico's initials; therefore the copy must be the very one given to him by the author. Everything, from the binding to the script and decorations, bespeaks a lavish copy meant to be a gift. The neat italic handwriting, set in perfectly ordered text blocks, looks to be that of a professional scribe.

The codex measures 210 x 150 x 30 cm. It has a leather cover glued to pasteboard, with five raised bands around the spine. The gilded title VRANIA appears on the cover, above Salvatico's initials, set within a decorative floral frame. Two blank and numberless folios precede the 176 folios of text, and two more blank

---

[55] For Hippolytus in Renaissance interpretations see Brumble, *Classical Myths and Legends*, 170–71.

Introduction

folios are included at the end. All of the folios are without visible watermarks. The text begins at fol. 1r, with the title in Roman square capitals: AL MAGNIFICO, ET ECCELLENTE DOTTOR DI LEGGI, IL. S. BARTOLOMEO SALVATICO . . . It ends on fol. 176r with the words ". . . et Menãdro cõ la sua Clorina lungamente, et felicemẽte uissero."

There are two illustrations, historiated initials showing mythological figures in the same style as Giolito's very popular contemporary editions of Petrarch's works. These include an historiated S on fol. 1r at the beginning of the proem, which appears to depict Semele being visited by Jupiter, and an N historiated with a drawing of Neptune on fol. 22r, where the story of Urania begins. These two folios also have decorative floral designs and titles in precisely drawn Roman square capitals. The five chapter breaks are indicated by floral designs, and the new chapters begin with large unadorned initials.

The first references to this manuscript are those of Mazzuchelli and Borromeo in the eighteenth century, cited above. Both of them state that the manuscript was in the private library of the Marchese Giambattista Saibante in Verona. A note inserted in the codex mentions that it was sold in Venice to the Marchese Trivulzio in 1811 by the abbot Alvise Celotti, who had originally planned to publish it with a dedication to Trivulzio. The codex has been in the Trivulziana ever since. The copy which Borromeo says Saibante allowed him to make of the manuscript is most likely the one which exists in the Vatican Library today, known as Patetta 358. A note on fol. 1r of Patetta 358 indicates that it was copied directly from the Saibante manuscript, and the style is clearly that of Borromeo's age. This manuscript is an almost perfect reproduction of the original, and reflects only minimal editorial efforts, such as corrections of misspellings and some slight changes in punctuation. No effort was made to emend the original's two lacunae.

I have prepared my Italian text directly from Trivulziana 88, with a number of editorial changes intended to make the text more accessible to the modern reader. These include the creation of paragraphs and the addition of quotation marks, as well as capitalizations according to modern norms. Titles of rulers and nobility are capitalized, as they consistently are in the manuscript. Chapter breaks have been numbered. I have also corrected misspellings, as indicated in the footnotes, and expanded standard abbreviations such as *cagiõ* for *cagione*, *mõdo* for *mondo*, *V.E.* for *Vostra Eccellenza*, and the like. Accent marks have been removed from six monosyllabic words on which they often or consistently appear: *à, ò, ì, fù, fà, sò*. Conversely, I have added accent marks to a number of words: *ne* (negative particle), *se* (pronoun), *giu, piu, cosi, perche, benche, impercio, da* (verb), *accio, si* (adverb), *glie (egli è)*, as well as to the text's spelling of the second person plural of the present tense of the verb *essere* (*sete*). I have added apostrophes to the following

51

INTRODUCTION

words to match modern usage: *de'*, *di'*, *mo'*, *que'*, and *e'* (a pronoun which frequently appears in this manuscript in the place of the definite article *i* in masculine plural possessive constructions: *e' suoi*). Aside from these changes, I have not modernized the orthography. Prepositions which in modern Italian would be conjoined with definite articles are not modified in this transcription, for example *pe' 'l, a i, a gli, de gli*, etc. I have also followed the manuscript in separating pronouns which would be combined in one word in modern Italian, such as *glie l'*. Certain adverbs or conjunctions which are compounds in modern Italian often appear in this manuscript as two separate words, and I have left them this way in the printed text (*poi che, vie più, se ben, o pure, a pena*, etc.). The modern form *cioè*, consisting of the combination of the pronoun *ciò* and the verb *è*, has been written out as separate words when it appears so in the manuscript. Dialect variants, which are rare in this text, and a few difficult words are indicated in the notes.

The manuscript's two lacunae appear to be due to the copyist's skipping a single line of text in the original draft. They are indicated in both text and translation by three periods enclosed by brackets, as well as by footnotes.

I have made some changes in the manuscript's punctuation as an aid to the modern reader. By and large, colons have been turned into full stops, along with some semicolons which appear to mark sentence breaks. In some places I have added or removed commas in order to facilitate the reading of Bigolina's sentences, which are typically constructed of a long series of clauses separated by commas or semicolons. Overall, however, I have made as few changes in her punctuation as possible in order to preserve the rhythm of her narrative style.

In my English translation, I have consistently broken Bigolina's long sentences into a series of smaller ones to make her prose style more palatable to the modern reader, and have sometimes substituted characters' names for pronouns when necessary, in order to make her meaning clearer. All paragraph breaks match those which I have created in the Italian text. Since Bigolina writes in highly polished, rhetorically elegant prose, without colloquialisms or anything hinting of "low style," I have endeavored to preserve this tone in my English vocabulary and sentence structure. The only time I have taken any real liberties with Bigolina's literal meaning is in the subtitle to the work, "The Story of a Young Woman's Love," which is not intended to be a direct translation of the original "Nella quale contiene l'amore d'una giovane di tale nome" ["in which is contained the love of a young woman by that name"]. My aim has consistently been to create a text which accurately reflects the intentions and meaning of the author, yet is clear, pleasant to read, and easy to understand.

INTRODUCTION

6. "LA NOVELLA DI GIULIA CAMPOSANPIERO ET DI THESIBALDO VITALIANI": TEXT AND TRANSLATION

As I have indicated, this novella survives today in two forms, the sixteenth-century manuscript BP 1451 VIII of the Biblioteca Civica in Padua, and the published version edited by Borromeo which was likely based on the Civica manuscript. I have prepared my text directly from BP 1451 VIII, which varies somewhat from Borromeo's edition. Borromeo modernized the manuscript's spelling and punctuation according to eighteenth-century norms, and also made a few more substantial changes, at times leaving out words or even whole phrases. I have shown these more substantial changes in the notes. Since the changes which Borromeo makes can be attributed to either scribal errors or the editorial norms of his time, I do not see any evidence that Borromeo consulted a manuscript which contained a version of this work other than that preserved in BP 1451 VIII.

BP 1451 VIII consists of eleven paper folios in quartos measuring 20 x 14.5 cm. The cover, on which nothing is written save a call number, consists of a sheet of modern lined notebook paper folded around the folios and sewn in place with a single length of thread up the spine, in makeshift fashion, with a gathering between folios 6 and 7. Holes in the folios indicate the manuscript was probably once bound in a different way, with an original cover which has now been lost. No watermarks appear on any of the folios, which have been cut down from larger-sized sheets along the bottom and right edges. The text begins on fol. 1r, with the title written in Roman square capitals: "NOVELLA DI GIULIA CAMPO SAN PIERO ET DI THESIBALDO VITALIANI RACCONTATA NELLO AMENISSIMO LVOGO DI MIRABELLO . . ." The text concludes on fol. 8v: ". . . com'i vuī sapeste ben esporre." Three blank folios are included after the end of the text. Along with the title and Thesibaldo's motto "tu sola puoi," the initials of the work's four sections (introduction, novella text, conclusion, and final sonnet) are also in unadorned Roman capitals, while the rest of the text is in italics. Inelegant looping designs, perhaps meant to evoke floral drawings similar to those in Trivulziana 88, occur at the end of the last three sections. At the top of folios 5r, 7r, and 8r the symbols .yõ.xõ. are visible, possibly an abbreviation of the Greek spelling of the name Jesus Christ. Bigolina's name does not appear anywhere within this manuscript.

Neither of the sixteenth-century manuscripts of Bigolina's works contains many grammatical or orthographical forms suggestive of Paduan dialect. Nonetheless, there are considerable differences of spelling between the two, and the hands are clearly quite distinct. Double consonants, which are uncommon in Veneto

Introduction

dialects, occur in odd words in BP 1451 VIII: for example *stragge, propponimento, raggione, raggionando, proppalerebbe, condittioni, pallo, sallire, caggione, riccamate, fatte* (for *fate*); such forms do not occur in Trivulziana 88. Spellings such as *puoco, anchora, schola, schalle* (for *scale*) appear in BP 1451 VIII but not in Trivulziana 88. Forms of the verb *ritrovare*, which occur often in both manuscripts, contain a *u* only in the Civica manuscript (*ritruovare*). Third person plural endings of first conjugation verbs in the past absolute tense are written as *-arono* or *-orono* in Trivulziana 88, but consistently as *-orno* in BP 1451 VIII. The use of accent marks in this manuscript follows that of Trivulziana 88 in all particulars save in the case of the word *ma*, which is accented in the Civica manuscript but not in Trivulziana 88. A few spellings reflecting Paduan dialect pronunciation do occur in the Civica manuscript, such as *Padoa* for *Padova* and *doi* for *due*. Trivulziana 88 is quite plainly a presentation copy written by a professional scribe, whereas the Civica manuscript appears to have been prepared in a simpler, more casual fashion. As I have noted, the handwriting of BP 1451 VIII differs to some extent from that of Bigolina's autographic will in the State Archive of Padua (ASP AN 829).

I have prepared this text according to the same norms I established for the transcription of *Urania*. I have retained all of the manuscript's original spellings, such as the names Thesibaldo and Thiso (spelled Tesibaldo and Tiso in Borromeo's edition), with the exception of the name Camposanpiero which I have changed from three separate words to one as in modern usage. As in the case of Trivulziana 88, I have created paragraphs and added quotation marks to this text. I have also expanded abbreviations, modernized accent marks, added apostrophes, and changed capitalizations according to the patterns I established for the transcription of *Urania*. Prepositions, conjunctions, adverbs, and pronouns which are compounds in modern Italian are left separate here, as they appear in the manuscript. The title *imperadore* (emperor), usually abbreviated in this manuscript to *imp.*, has been expanded to the full form and capitalized in keeping with the capitalizations of titles of rulers in the transcription of the *Urania* text.

URANIA

The Story of a Young Woman's Love

AL MAGNIFICO, ET ECCELLENTE DOTTOR DI LEGGI, IL. S. BARTOLOMEO SALVATICO

GIULIA BIGOLINA

Se si potessero, valoroso et nobilissimo giovine, misurare a pieno tutti gli humani affetti con qualche esteriore operatione, io non dubito che molti i quali si dimostrano essere sviscerati amanti, misurandoli si scoprirebbono che poco o nulla amano; et all'incontro molti altri, de' quali alcuni per poco sapere, et alcuni perchè lor manca l'ardir di manifestarsi pare che amino poco; nondimeno chi ben misurar gli potesse, esser fedeli et svisceratissimi amanti si conoscerebbono. Et quello, che de gli amanti io dico medesimamente d'ogni qualità d'amicitia voglio dire: et di qui nasce un non conosciuto grandissimo errore, che tali vengono da alcuni in sommo prezzati, che se quelli potessero gli loro affetti ben misurare, non gli guardarebbono a pena. Et molti altri poi, i quali sono poco considerati, et meno prezzati, se misurati fossero, in sommo grado d'honore sarebbon tenuti; per la qual cosa a me pare, che non poco quelli fanno ingiuria a sè stessi, che si conoscono esser veri amanti, o perfetti amici, et mancano di far tutte quelle operationi, che possono bastare a far (quanto si può) manifesta la perfettion de' lor cuori; che se tutti quei che ben amano così facessero, gli veri da i finti si conoscerebbono tosto; imperciò che non potendo i finti continovar lungamente nelle amorevoli operationi, a pena lo incominciato guado harrebon segnato, che stanchi di più seguirlo se ne tornerebbono a dietro; et così ogni vero assai tosto aperto et manifesto sarebbe.

Et questo, che io ho detto non per altro l'ho detto eccetto che per risvegliar la memoria in voi gentilissimo giovine; et raccordarvi come tra il numero de'

TO MR. BARTOLOMEO SALVATICO,
MAGNIFICENT AND EXCELLENT
DOCTOR OF LAW

GIULIA BIGOLINA

If one could, O talented and most noble young man, measure in full all human affection through outward deeds, I do not doubt that many who claim to be fervent lovers would be shown, once tested, to love little or not at all. On the other hand, many others seem to love but little, either because they have little experience, or because they lack the courage to reveal their feelings; nonetheless, these people would be known as the most fervent and faithful lovers, if anyone were to test them thoroughly. What I have said regarding lovers goes for any type of friendship as well, and from this arises an unrecognized, yet very grave error. Some people esteem certain others very greatly, and yet if they could measure the affections of those they esteem so much, they would scarcely glance at them. By the same token, many others who are given little consideration, and who are esteemed even less, would be held in the highest honor if they were tested. Therefore it seems to me that those who are regarded as true lovers or perfect friends, and yet are found wanting when it comes to those acts which are necessary to show the perfection of their hearts, do no small injury to themselves. If all those who love in a proper fashion performed such acts, one would quickly be able to tell the true lovers from the false, inasmuch as the false would not long be able to pursue the tasks of love, and would turn back from the ford without crossing, too exhausted to continue. By such means, every true lover would be very quickly revealed.

 I have said all this for no other reason than to rekindle your memory, most kind young man, and remind you that you can count me, along with yourself,

pochi, che hoggidì veri amici si trovino al mondo potete me con voi medesimo connumerare; che essendomi la prima volta, che io vi conobbi, et che mi fu il sommo vostro valor manifesto, nelle rare, anzi singolari vostre virtudi infinitamente compiacciuta. Per la qualcosa tutta d'honesto amore m'accesi, nacque in me parimente quel desiderio che io ho detto, di farvi aperto con convenevoli operationi il grande mio affetto. Onde io voglio dire, che se quale ho potuto, che non già dirò quali sono i meriti vostri, o il mio desiderio. Mi son sempre ingegnata di farvi questo mio honesto affetto conoscere, non è chi meglio di voi stesso lo sappia; poi che come sapete da indi in qua, che io vi conobbi, mai son mancata hora con amorevoli lettere, et hor con diverse sorti di rime di visitarvi sovente. Et se alcuno dicesse, che tali mie operationi assai deboli stromenti son state, per far creder a voi che d'infinito merito sète, che in me tanta perfettione di affetto si trovi, che meritevole me faccia d'esser presso di voi in grande consideratione tenuta; et io a ciò gli rispondo che d'avantaggio circa alcune parti io confessarei quanto ei dicesse esser vero, ma da un'altra parte ben poi vorrei sostenerli, che un nobile, et valorosissimo cuore, quale è il vostro, assai più prezza una osservatione, et uno amorevole affetto, il quale con tutto il cuore offerto gli viene, quantunque di tanta perfettione non fosse, che altro affetto, et osservatione non prezzarebbe, i quali di vie maggior perfettione assai, non con tutto il cuore, ma con parte di quello offerti gli venissero: imperciochè havendo all'atto della volontade rispetto, assai più vale un picciolo tutto, che una grandissima parte.

Hor dunque tra me stessa più volte considerando come giamai son mancata con tutte le deboli forze mie di farvi manifesto, quanto con l'affetto del mio cuore honestamente et perfettamente vi amo, et con ogni mio sapere vi osservo. Parevami che solamente una operatione da fare, per sodisfare al debito mio con esso voi mi mancasse: et ciò era di lasciar qualche raccordanza di me medesima presso di voi, acciò che quando io più viva non fosse, non vi uscisse fuori della memoria il grande et puro amore co'l quale vivendo vi havevo amato. Et mentre più volte pensando, et ripensando n'andavo intorno a quello, che io havesse potuto operare, acciò che di me qualche raccordanza vi rimanesse, sovennemi come quegli antichi heroi, i quali contanti maravigliosi fatti fecero al mondo, la maggior parte di loro lasciarono dopo morte le loro imagini tale in marmo, tale in bronzo, tale in oro, et tale in altro metallo sculpite; et ciò credomi che facessero acciò che i loro popoli, a i quali havevano assai giovato, et da i quali mentre che vissero furono amati di cuore. Così mirando le loro imagini venissero a tenir viva quella memoria in sè stessi, che de' ricevuti beneficij con i loro signori gli facean debitori; et che perciò così morti come erano, fossero medesimamente ancora amati da quelli. Ond'io da que' tali pigliando argomento pareva a me che verun'altra più propria operatione,

Urania: The Story of a Young Woman's Love

among those few true friends who can be found nowadays in the world. The first time I met you, your great worth became evident to me, and I was infinitely pleased with your rare, indeed singular virtues. This caused me to burn with virtuous love for you; moreover there was born in me that desire, which I have just described, to make my great affection known to you through appropriate deeds. So I wish to say, inasmuch as it has been within my power (and I will not speak of your fine qualities, nor of my desire), I have always endeavored to make this honest affection known to you, and no one knows this better than you yourself. As you are aware, ever since I met you I have never failed to visit you often, sometimes with loving letters, and sometimes with poetry of various styles. Someone might say that these efforts of mine have been very weak instruments for making you, who are of the very greatest worth, believe that there is so much perfect affection in me, or that I deserve to be held in high regard by you. To this I respond that to some extent I would confess this is true, and yet on the other hand I would assert that a noble and most worthy heart, like yours, appreciates much more a word or an amorous sentiment that is heartfelt, even if lacking in perfection, than another word or sentiment which is offered halfheartedly, however more perfect it may be. With regard to acts of the will, a tiny whole is worth much more than a very great part.

Therefore I have often thought to myself how I have thus far failed, on account of my weak powers, to show you the perfect, chaste, and heartfelt love I bear you, and to let you know I revere you completely. It seemed to me that there was only one thing left to do, to satisfy the debt I owe you: I must leave you some remembrance of myself, so that when I will no longer be living, you will not forget the great and pure love I bore you in life. While pondering at great length how best to do this, I remembered how the ancient heroes, who had done so many marvelous deeds in the world, often left their images sculpted in marble, bronze, gold, or other metals after they were gone. I believe they did this so that the people whom they had served so well, and who had loved them so much while they lived, could look upon their images and thereby keep their memory alive. The people and their leaders had received so much benefit from these heroes, and owed them so much; therefore they loved them still, even after they were gone. Thus it seemed to me, according to the example these men

non harrei potuta fare, per lasciar dopo la mia morte, viva in voi di me la memoria, come era la imagine di me stessa lasciarvi. Ma non essendo a fatto il lume della ragione in me estinto, il quale pur mi lasciava discernere come al sesso, nè al grado, et meno alla bassezza delle operationi mie non convenevasi che in scoltura (sola convenevole a gran personaggi) io mi vi lasciassi, deliberai la imagine mia lasciarvi in pittura; et solamente mancavami a deliberare il modo, nel quale pingere io mi facessi.

Et mentre un giorno, il quale tutta sola nella camera mia rinchiusami su, et giù per quella passeggiando n'andava, et pur sopra il modo pensando, nel quale più appropriato a dimostrarvi la osservanza, et amor che io vi porto havesse potuto farmi depingere, ecco che per la gonna di dietro assai forte mi sento tirare. Onde io, che certo sapevo non ritrovarsi alcuna persona nella camera meco, mi sentì da un grande spavento percuotere il cuore, pur rivolgendomi in dietro per chiarirmi da cui così forte io venivo per la gonna tirata, veggio che uno et assai contrafatto homicciuolo minore che esser non si dice un pigmeo era quello, che tale effetto faceva. Era questo homicciuolo ignudo del tutto, et haveva una così grande testa, che bastevole quasi sarebbe stata a un gigante; et havea nel mezzo della fronte un solo occhio, il quale era così grande, et come specchio lucente, che nello rivolgermi che io feci dal capo a piedi tutta intiera mi vidi. Ma maravigliosa, et strana cosa mi parve poi da vedere, che non co' i panni in dosso, come veramente havevo, ma ignuda come io nacqui in quel grande occhio mi raffigurai; et così bianche per ogni loco haver le carni mi vidi (eccetto dalla manca parte, dove mi parve una macchia vedermi) che quasi alla neve assomigliarsi parevami. Veduto c'hebbi quello così strano homiciuolo, che esser un horribile mostro credevami, tutta come io dissi, di spavento ripiena, et non sol di spavento, ma per vedermi così ignuda, di tal di me stessa vergogna, che harrei voluto esser in quel punto sanza occhi, et perciò per uscir della camera forte tremando verso l'uscio mi volsi. Ma egli vie più forte tenendomi, sì che partirmi non potea di quel loco, così mi disse: "Fermati, et non fuggire, ne ti dubitare che in conto alcuno offender io ti voglia; anzi io ti dico, che per giovarti, et non per offenderti mi ti faccio vedere. Et quando tu saperai cui io sono, non dubito che così contrafatto come mi vedi, harrai più caro d'havermi veduto, et conoscermi, che se un gran tesoro havessi acquistato; et perciò fa buon cuore, et con molta attentione ascoltami."

Io, che non potevo con tutto ch'egli così ragionevolmente parlasse, scacciar quel gran timore, ch'io havevo nel cuore, pur udendolo cotanto humanamente parlare, fatta alquanto, benchè poco più animosa, così gli risposi. "Quale che tu sei, che io non lo so, non ti maravigliare se di te fuori di misura io temo, et se dalla tua presenza fuggirei volontieri, perciò che alcune parti così spaventose mi

Urania: The Story of a Young Woman's Love

provided, that the best way to leave a vivid memory of me after my death was to give you the very image of myself. But the light of reason was not entirely extinct in me, for I could still discern that sculpture, appropriate for great personages, was hardly appropriate for someone of my sex, my degree, and especially my humble accomplishments.[1] Therefore I decided to leave you my image in painting, and I had only to think of the way in which I should have myself depicted.

One day, while I was pacing up and down alone in my room, pondering the most fitting way for me to show my love and devotion for you in a painting, I felt a strong tug from behind on my dress. Great fear struck my heart, for I was certain there was no one else in the room with me. I turned around to determine who had done this, and saw that a very deformed homunculus, smaller than a pygmy is said to be, had been responsible. This homunculus was entirely nude, and his head was so large that it would almost have been adequate for a giant. There was but a single eye in the middle of the forehead, and this eye was so big, and shiny like a mirror, that in turning I saw myself reflected therein from head to foot. This was a strange and marvelous thing, for even though I was actually wearing clothes, I appeared in that great eye without them, as naked as the day I was born. I saw that my flesh was so white that it nearly resembled snow, everywhere but on the left side, where it seemed to me I bore a stain. Once I had seen this strange little man, whom I took to be a horrible monster, I was, as I have said, filled with fear; and not only with fear, but also with so much shame at seeing myself naked that I would have preferred in that instant to be deprived of my eyes. Therefore I turned toward the door to escape, trembling hard, but he, who was much stronger than I, held me tightly so that I could not leave the place. He spoke to me thus: "Stop, and do not flee; nor should you fear that I intend to harm you in any way. Indeed I say that I have revealed myself to you not to hurt you, but rather for your benefit. When you learn who I am, do not doubt that you will be more glad to have seen and known me, despite my grotesque shape, than you would have been had you acquired some great treasure. Therefore be of good cheer, and listen to me closely."

No matter how reasonably he spoke, I could not banish the great fear that I felt in my heart. Still, hearing him express himself in such human tones, I became just a bit braver, and answered him thus: "Whatever you are (and I do not know what that may be), do not marvel if I am extraordinarily afraid of you and if I would gladly flee from your presence. Some of your aspects seem quite frightening

---

[1] See Pliny, *Natural History* 35.9 and 35.12 for similar notions on the decorum of sculpture.

pare in te di vedere, massimamente quando in quel tuo grande occhio mi miro, che io ti giuro tra la vergogna che io ho perchè così ignuda mi veggio, et la paura, la quale essendo così brutto mi fai, che giamai starò bene sin che in parte non mi ritrovo, dove più non ti vegga. Nondimeno di' quello che voi dir, che io ti ascolto; ma ben ti prego, che nel tuo dir tu vogli esser più breve che possi."

A questo mio dire sorridendo il picciolin[2] così disse. "Beato il mondo tutto, et te particolarmente, se di continovo voi humani in questo mio occhio vi voleste mirare; imperciò che nè ingiustitia, nè temerità non si ritroverebbe tra voi. Io sono il Giudicio, che se non mi conosci hora te lo dico, il quale assai poco da voi altri mi trovo nel modo, che mi si conviene osservato. Et queste mie parti, le quali mirandole paiono a te mostruose, quando de' loro significati sarai a pieno informata, non più mostruose, ma maravigliose, anzi divine ti pareranno. Et primamente questa mia picciolezza tu dei sapere, che non sanza gran significato fu ella in me ordinata; imperciò che ella non significa altro, eccetto che tutti quei giudici, i quali nel mondo sono a giudicare ordinati, debbono esser non superbi et alteri, ma humili di natura et benigni di cuore. Et il mio esser ignudo dimostra che così medesimamente quelli doverebbono esser ignudi nel giudicare da ogni odio, et affetto. Questo mio capo poi, il quale io ho di grandezza all'altre mie membra cotanto sproportionato[3], altro non dinota, eccetto i giudici, i quali quantunque debbono esser, come io t'ho detto, humilissimi di natura, vogliono perciò grandemente esser dotti et di sommo sapere, acciò che per ignoranza non venghino la giustitia, et la ragione a rimaner soffocate, la dove esser ben ministrate dovrebbono. Et perchè io ho solo un occhio vuol dire che i giudici, che vogliono giudicar rettamente, non debbono mai occupar gli animi in verun'altra cura, eccetto che in quella, che a far loro giudici sono ordinati. Ancora molto grande è questo mio occhio, che viene a darvi ad intendere come non basta che i buoni giudici siano assai dotti, et che altre cure che gli disturbi dal giudicare non habbiano; ma è bisogno ancora, che siano molto aveduti, et accorti. Imperciò che assai volte poco a i giudicati gioverebbe che'l giudice fosse ben dotto, et molto bene sapesse intender le leggi, et poi in sè stesso d'avedimento mancando, non conoscesse dove, et in qual modo le leggi usare si debbono. Ma credilo a me che rari giudici hoggi

---

[2] This word, with the apocope of the final vowel after *n*, is typical of Veneto dialect usage.

[3] *Spooportionato* in T (Trivulziana 88) fol. 6v. Corrected to *sproportionato* in P (Patetta 358) fol. 8r.

to me, especially when I look upon myself in that great eye of yours. Because of the shame I feel to see myself naked, and the fear that you instill in me because you are so ugly, I swear to you I will never feel at ease until I have gone to a place where I can no longer see you. Nonetheless, say whatever you wish, for I will hear you; but I pray, let your speech be as brief as you can make it."

The little fellow smiled at my words, and answered thus: "The whole world would be fortunate, and you in particular, if you humans had the desire to look continually upon yourselves in my eye; for if you did neither injustice nor temerity would be found among you. I am Judgment, and if you do not know me now, I tell you, it is because I am so seldom observed by you in my most appropriate form. My appearance, which seems monstrous to you, will not appear to be monstrous at all, but rather marvelous, indeed divine, once I have fully informed you of its significance. First of all, you must know that my small size was not ordained for me without considerable significance, since it means that all judges who have been established in the world in order to pronounce judgments must not be haughty and proud, but rather humble in nature and benign. My nudity shows that they should be without hatred or partiality when judging others. This head of mine, which is so disproportionately large in comparison to my other members, reveals only that judges, in spite of the need for humility which I have described, must nonetheless be very learned, and of the highest wisdom. At those times when Justice and Reason are to be properly administered, let them not be suffocated by ignorance. The fact that I have only one eye means that judges who wish to judge correctly must never give their minds over to any other concern but that which their calling demands. Moreover, this eye of mine is very large, which serves to show you that it is not enough that judges be very learned, and that they not have other concerns which distract them from the task of judging. It is also necessary that they be very clever and shrewd, since quite often it appears that the judge who may be learned and adroit at understanding the laws, yet still lacks shrewdness, and therefore the knowledge of how the laws should best be applied is of little help to those who are to be judged. But believe me, these days it is

si trovano, i quali se sono dotti, non siano superbi; et se non sono superbi, che non siano poco aveduti; et se sono aveduti, che gli loro occhi non chiudano per non mirare nel mio.

"Ma io voglio il dir de' giudici lasciar da una parte, poi che o bene, o male che i loro giudici sian fatti, per essere il loro ufficio, il giudicare gli si conviene; et dirò di voi altri, i quali quantunque non si convenghi a voi il giudicare; pure in pregiudicio di questo, et di quello volete tutti esser giudici. Et di tali vi sono tra voi che a pena in capo il naso si veggono, et fanno nondimeno spesse volte in altrui mille temerari giudicij. Et peggio è assai, che ci sono di quelli (et non pochi) i quali essendo carichi di molti bruttissimi vitij, hor con risa, et hor con sdegno vogliono altri d'ogni lor picciolo error giudicare, che se que' tali si mirassero nel mio occhio, nel quale come entro ad un specchio tutto il suo corpo ignudo ciascuno si vede, et ha proprietà (come so che hai in te stessa veduto) di far vedere a ciascuno le carni sue di tante macchie coperto, come quante sono le sorti de' vitij, de' quali l'anima sua tien bruttata. Se nel mio occhio dico si mirassero quelli, forse forse, che non sarebbono così solleciti investigatori de gli falli altrui, come sono. Et forse ancora che più utilmente spenderebbono il tempo a nettare, o almeno a coprire le lor gran macchie, che vanamente non spendono in discoprire, et manifestar gli altrui piccioli errori. O quanti usurai, quanti ladri coperti, bestemmiatori, scandalosi, giuocatori; et d'altri molti pessimi vitij macchiati, si fanno beffe, et infamiano tale homiciuolo, over donna, ne i quali perchè sono humani, che non potendo esser la humanità sanza difetto, salvo se per gratia particolare alcuno non è preservato da Iddio. Hanno qualche mancamento in lor conosciuto; et tanto que' maligni gli infamano, quanto, et forse più di quello meriterebbono loro d'esser non pure infamati, ma de lor gravi mancamenti puniti. Et spesse volte

hard to find judges who, if learned, are not haughty; if not haughty, lack shrewdness; if shrewd, do not close their eyes so as not to look into mine.[4]

"However, I would like to set aside my discussion of judges, inasmuch as judgment is their professional office, whether they do it well or badly. Instead I will speak of the rest of you, who, on account of your various biases, persist in acting as judges even if such activity is inappropriate. There are those among you who can barely see the ends of their noses, and yet they very often pass myriad reckless judgments on others. And what is much worse, there are those (and they are not few) who wish to judge every minimal error of others, sometimes with laughter, and sometimes with disdain, even though they themselves are loaded down with many of the most noisome vices. If only they would look upon themselves in my eye, wherein each person sees his entire nude body as in a mirror! For this eye has the property of showing a person his flesh covered with as many stains as there are vices to render his soul loathsome, and I know you have seen this in yourself.[5] If these people would look upon themselves in my eye, they just might cease to be such tireless investigators of the faults of others; indeed they might find their time more profitably spent cleansing, or at least masking, their own great stains, rather than uselessly uncovering and revealing the small errors that other people commit.[6] O how many usurers, covert thieves, blasphemers, sowers of scandal, gamblers, and others soiled with all the worst vices, are given to mock or defame certain humble men and women because they have discovered some failing in them, even though no human being can be without defect, unless the grace of God allows it. These evildoers defame others every bit as much as they themselves deserve not only to be defamed, but even punished for their

---

[4] For similar descriptions of the significance of the individual parts of allegorical figures see Leone Ebreo's allegory of Cupid in *Dialogo I*, 53, as well as his description of Venus in *Dialogo II*, 133 (ed. S. Caramella [Bari: Laterza, 1929]). See also Pietro Bembo's treatment of Cupid in *Asolani* 1.18, in *Prose e rime*, ed. C. Dionisotti (Turin: Unione tipografico-editrice torinese, 1960), 347–48. The mirror of Judgment's eye bears considerable resemblance to the mirror borne by Christine de Pizan's allegory of Reason, which shows all who look in it the error of their ways, and how they truly are (*Book of the City of Ladies*, 1.3).

[5] The symbolic association between the revelation of nude bodies and sinfulness can be traced back to the Old Testament; see Genesis 3:7–10, Isaiah 3:17, and Ezekiel 16:37 and 16:39. The motif is also present in Dante's episode of the "femmina balba" (*Purgatorio* 19.31–33).

[6] See Matthew 7:3–5, and Luke 6:41–42.

mi rido di tali che non credeno che l'esser finti o bugiardi sia troppo gran vitio; che se ben considerassero quanto la bugia, et la fintione siano vitij, i quali ponno ogni bell'animo (quantunque d'ogni alta sorte di vitio nettissimo fosse) oscurare, macchiare, et bruttare, e mi dà il cuore che molti sono che impararebbono a dire più spesso il vero che non dicono, et meglio portarebbono la vera imagine de' lor cuori nella fronte scolpita, che quella della bugia nelle labra non portano. Et particolarmente d'alcuni dico, i quali assassinando quel valoroso nome di gentilhuomo, indegnamente quello non da tutti conosciuto tesoro si attribuiscono, et non considerano da qual parte nasce, et per qual cagione quel titolo di gentilhuomo fu ritrovato. Chè ben sono sciocchi se si credono che l'esser nobili procedi da veruna disuguaglianza, la quale tra il sangue del gentilhuomo et quello del plebeo si trovi, et non più tosto da quella, che di costumi, et virtù tra lor si conosce. Ma ben voglio dirti, che s'io fossi humano, et che del mondo io fossi rettore non vorrei, come tra voi si costuma di fare, che la nobilità per heredità si ottenesse. Anzi vorrei che col valore della propria virtude se l'acquistasse ciascuno, et solo fosse colui per nobile conosciuto il quale per virtuoso venisse approvato. Et più, et manco si conoscesse nobiltade in ciascuno quanto maggiore, et minor virtude in un più che in un'altro si vedesse risplendere. Chè se così si facesse io ti faccio sicura che'l vitio, et l'otio non sarebbono seguiti come sono da tanti.

"Ma con la lor mala ventura voglio lasciar questi tali, io dico de i rei, et non di quelli, che sono buoni; et dir di voi infelicissimo feminil sesso, che tanto sempre sète dalla malvagità di molti pessimi huomini calunniate. Chè io non so molte volte come la lunga vostra patienza in osservarli, et servirli a fatto non si consumi: nè hanno riguardo assai vi sono di loro, perchè come ho detto siano di molti brutti vitij macchiati, che pur continovamente con lor venenose lingue in molti modi l'honore vi lacerano. Et di che poi vi accusano quasi sempre di cosa tale, che pensandovi stupefatto rimango. Forse che la somma della infamia, che vi danno è perchè non li vogliate ubidire, o pure perchè troppo ritrose, et superbe con essi loro vi dimostrate; overamente perchè voi siate di quale uno di que' vitij macchiate, de' quai loro sono bruttati. Anzi se di quelli a migliaia n'haveste io mi credo che tutti gli si tacerebbono, per ben potere a piene labra dir di quello, che più de gli altri dovrebbono tacere; cioè che gli ingrati quasi mai d'altra cosa vi infamano, eccetto che del grande error che voi fate ciascuna volta che troppo

serious misdeeds. I am often amused by certain people who believe that falseness or lying are not such great vices. If they were to reflect on the true degree to which these things are indeed vices, inasmuch as falseness and lying are capable of darkening, staining, or rendering ugly any beautiful soul, even if it be free of other vice, I am certain that many of them would learn to speak the truth far more often than they actually do; moreover they would be quicker to bear the true image of their hearts engraved upon their foreheads than that of the lie upon their lips. I refer particularly to those men who assassinate the worthy name of gentleman by inappropriately bestowing it upon themselves, even though that name is a treasure known only to a few. They do not consider the origin of the title nor the reasons for which it came to exist, and they are quite foolish if they believe nobility derives from an inequality of blood between aristocrats and plebeians, rather than the inequality of manners and virtue which can be found between them. Let me make this clear: if I were human, and ruler of the world, I would not allow nobility to be acquired through heredity, as is the case among you. Instead, I would want each person to acquire it for himself through the worth of his own virtue; indeed, the only man considered noble would be the one who was generally seen as virtuous. One would recognize greater or lesser nobility in this man or that according to the degree to which greater or lesser virtue could be seen to shine in them. If this were done, I assure you that vice and idleness would not be indulged in as much as they are now.

"But I wish to leave these wicked ones (and I have not been referring to good people) to wallow in their wretchedness. Now let me speak of you, members of that most unhappy feminine sex, who are always denigrated by the wickedness of the very worst men. Indeed, as you serve and observe such men, I often wonder why your patience does not wear completely thin. A great many of them lack respect, since as I have said they are stained with considerable vices; thus they relentlessly destroy your honor in many ways, with their venomous tongues. And what they almost always accuse you of is so foolish that it astonishes me just to think of it. Perhaps there is no greater infamy than their accusation that you do not wish to obey them, or else that you are too haughty or unwilling to cooperate with them; in effect they are saying that you are stained with one of those very vices with which they themselves are sullied. Nonetheless, even if you had all of their vices by the thousands I believe they would mention none of them, in order to give their full voice to one in particular, the one they should say the least about: that is, those ingrates defame you for nothing so much as for the great error

amorevoli vi dimostrate con essi loro, la quale è per dire il vero, empia, crudele, et fera natura ne gli huomini.

"Ma poi dall'altro canto io non so che mi dire, imperciò che così parimente voi donne conosco l'una con l'altra maligne, che delle molte ingiurie che gli huomini vi fanno in gran parte gli escuso. O quante quante sono donne tra voi, le quali oltre che non pare a voi, che altra sorte di vitio possa bruttar una donna eccetto che l'esser innamorata; nè vi accorgete da qual picciolo vostro valore cotale salvezza, di non poter esser d'altro vitio infamate da gli huomini vi vien conceduta. Quante sono dico donne tra voi, le quali essendo così ben macchiate di cotal difetto quanto più esser possano, non si ritingono perciò di continovamente con mille obbrobriose parole molte altre additare, le quali forse meno di loro hanno fallato; nè pur si vogliono in questo mio occhio mirare, il quale potrebbe scoprirle quanto meglio dal silentio, che dal troppo dire accompagnate starebbono. Et molte altre poi, che hanno in loro molti altri difetti, et perchè non sono di tal tinta macchiate, piene di superbia sdegnano di pur mirare alcune le quali d'ogn'altra bruttura nette, di quel solo difetto, il quale è pur naturalissimo, o per loro destino, che a ciò far le induce, o per altra non conosciuta cagione sono in cotal solo difetto cadute.

"Ma io non venni già qui," soggiunse egli, "per voler di cotal materia con essa te ragionare, quantunque nel dirne in un pelago assai più a dentro che a mezzo io sia entrato, anzi venni solamente per volerti avisar d'un giudicio, il quale da te medesima consigliata, assai sciocamente hai fatto. Et ben ti dico, che per te sola non sarei a darti un tale aviso venuto; ma havendomi in ciò a fare quello, che sempre nel mio occhio specchiandosi, alcuna macchia in sè stesso non trova. Nè con tutto ciò mai si vede ch'egli giudichi alcuno; et beato il mondo se molti giovani si ritrovassero simili a lui. Di quello dico, che tu pur hora pensavi della dipinta tua imagine farli presente. Buono, anzi ottimo aviso per certo di fare un tal dono a colui, al quale gli simulacri, et le statoe si converrebbono, se non ch'egli è tanto benigno et humile di cuore, che tali honor fuggirebbe di certo; et non è da maravigliarsi s'egli d'ogni ottima parte è ricetto, poi che al suo nascimento Natura, et il Cielo l'uno a gara dell'altro gli diedero beltà, gratia, et valore. Per la qual cosa tutti quelli, che di lui han conoscenza sono sforzati[7] a gara l'un dell'altro amarlo, desiderarlo, et riverirlo in un punto. Et tu pur hora con poco giudicio facevi disegno che la dipinta tua imagine a lui donata fosse convenevol soggetto per far che dopo

---

[7] *Sfozati* in T (fol. 11r). Corrected to *sforzati* in P (fol. 13r).

that you commit when you show yourselves to be too amorous with them. To tell the truth, that vice is typical of the wicked, cruel, savage nature of men themselves.

"But on the other hand I am not sure what I should say, inasmuch as I know you women often treat each other just as maliciously, to the extent that I can forgive men many of the injuries they do to you. O how many women there are among you who do not imagine that any other sort of vice, aside from being in love, can sully a woman; moreover, you do not realize how little you gain from the 'saving grace' of not being defamed by men for other things. I say that there are so many among you who are as stained as they could possibly be with that defect of loving, yet nonetheless cannot refrain from continually pointing the finger at other women who have perhaps sinned far less, reproaching them with innumerable insults. They do not wish to look at themselves in my eye, which can reveal their essence in complete silence, far more effectively than through excessive speech. Then there are numerous women who have so many defects, yet because they lack that particular stain of being in love, disdain even to look at those who might be free from every other shameful behavior save that one which is most plainly a part of Nature. Perhaps it is destiny, or perhaps it is some unknown force which causes these women to fall prey to this single failing, that of being in love.

"But I have not come here to speak to you about this subject, even though I have ventured rather far into a sea of words concerning it," the little man added. "Instead I have come for the sole purpose of warning you that the decision you have recently arrived at is indeed a very foolish one. I tell you truly that I would not have come to give this warning solely on your behalf, but also on behalf of that young man who has never found any stain in himself despite constant reflection in my eye. Moreover, he has never shown himself as a judge of others, and the world would indeed be blessed if it held many others similar to him. I am speaking of that youth on whom you have recently decided to bestow your painted image. It would be a good, indeed excellent idea to give a gift like this to the kind of man for whom such images and statues would be fitting. In the case of this young man, however, who has a heart which is so gentle and humble, a like honor would surely send him fleeing. It is no marvel that he is the possessor of every most excellent quality, inasmuch as both Nature and Heaven competed at his birth to bestow upon him beauty, grace, and valor. Because of this all those who come to know him are compelled to compete with one another in loving him, desiring him, and revering him all at once. Just now you conceived the notion that your painted image would be a suitable vehicle for keeping yourself alive, after death, within his memory. In so doing you showed poor judgment,

morte tu restassi ancor viva nella memoria di lui, poco considerando quanto cotal soggetto dal canto di lui, che 'l riceve sia basso; et dal tuo, che lo dai, disconvenevolissimo et fuor d'ogni proposito si dimostri; et come fuor di proposito sia dirotelo.

"Tu debbi sapere che tutte le cose sensate, et non sensate, che operano, overo che danno materia ad altrui d'operare; di quelle solamente dico però, le quali non hanno in sè uso alcun di ragione, non ponno operare, nè dar da sè stesse materia, che in elle operi alcuno se non in quella sola attione, nella quale Natura le ha destinate. Eccetto che se l'huomo, il quale per lo valor, che ha in sè di ragione, con la quale alla natura spesse volte resiste, et fa forza, non gli fa violenza con gli accidenti, come nelle cose sensate per isperienza si ha veduto più volte, che l'ingegno dell'huomo ha usato cane, uccello, overo altro animale a far tali cose tanto alla lor natura contrarie, che non più nella loro, ma in spetie d'altra natura paiono trasformati. Et il medesimo delle insensate si può veder nelle piante che innestando gli huomini una spetie di pianta con l'altra, fa che le radici dell'una fuori di sua natura produce il frutto dell'altra, il che non sarebbe di certo se l'humana cura cotal violenza non gli facesse. Et così voglio dir della imagine tua, la quale per sè sola non sarebbe buon mezzo, per lo quale si potesse cagionar quello effetto che tu desideri che in quel virtuosissimo giovine si cagioni, che essendo la imagine cosa materiale non potrà da sè sola sanz'altro aiuto in cosa, la quale fosse a sua natura contraria operare, come sarebbe ch'ella da sè havesse valore di poter l'animo a passione alcuna movere, et alterare. Imperciò che essendo, come più volte ho detto, la imagine cosa materiale, et l'animo, over lo intelletto nel quale ella ha da operare, essendo essenza dello spirito, l'uno nell'altro non operarebbono mai, se un'altro mezzo, il quale dell'una, et dell'altra natura partecipasse, non vi si interponesse. Et

little considering how low such an object would appear to him, the receiver of it; nor did you recognize that you would show yourself to be acting most inappropriately in bestowing it. I will now tell you just how inappropriate this is.

"You must know that all things, sensitive or insensitive, which function, or which provide material for the functioning of others, cannot in fact do these things save in that one specific action for which Nature has destined them; I am speaking only of those things which lack the use of reason.[8] Man is the exception, for through his innate power of reason he can often resist Nature and exploit its accidents without violating its laws; and this we have often seen among sensitive things, when human intelligence causes a dog, a bird, or some other animal to act in ways so contrary to nature that these creatures appear to have been transformed into different species.[9] We see something similar among insensitive things, as when men graft one species of plant onto another, causing its roots to produce a fruit contrary to its nature. This could never happen if human effort did not intervene, to violate natural laws. The same thing goes for this image of yours, which in itself would not be a good means to bring about the effect you desire in that most virtuous youth. For an image is but a material thing, and thus cannot, on its own and without external aid, act upon another thing which is contrary to its nature, as would be the case if an image had the power to instill passion in the soul, or effect change within it. As I have said more than once, an image is material, whereas the soul or intellect upon which it would act is the very essence of spirit. Thus the one could not function with the other, unless some external means, participating in the nature of both, were to interpose itself; this means is the sense of

---

[8] See Aristotle, *De Anima*, 3. 9–10 (432 a15–433 b20), trans. R. D. Hicks (Amsterdam: Hakkert, 1965), 147–53.

[9] For this notion see M. Ficino, *Five Questions Concerning the Mind*, trans. J. L. Burroughs, in *The Renaissance Philosophy of Man*, ed. E. Cassirer et al. (Chicago: University of Chicago Press, 1948), 193–212, here 206.

questo mezzo il senso del vedere s'intende, il quale, rispetto all'essenza di sè medesimo, tende allo spirito, et rispetto all'operatione con la imagine, la quale è cosa materiale, s'accosta.

"Non potendo adunque, la imagine altro che cose materiali, col mezzo però del vedere, all'intelletto rappresentare; le quali come due sono le essenze del senso, così due sono le cose, ch'egli dalla imagine trahendole, allo intelletto le rappresenta: ciò è il bello, et il buono, il qual buono per esser più che'l bello appropriato alla natura dello intelletto, per diritta linea in quello trapassa. Ma il bello, che è molto più a sua natura disgiunto, viene primieramente dalla imaginativa raccolto, la quale più che altra potenza dell'anima, con tutti i sensi tien parte. Et tanto ivi il bello si ferma, che viene a farsi habile a potere nello intelletto trascendere, il quale intelletto poi l'ha in sè stesso considerato, nè fa o piacendogli, o non piacendogli quel concetto, che più gli pare. Perchè se la cosa considerata et conosciuta gli piace, in conserva della memoria la manda, et se non gli piace disprezzandola da sè la discaccia.

"Hor se dunque la imagine altra cosa che 'l bello, o il buono allo intelletto non rappresenta, io non so conoscere qual cosa bella, o buona, che in te sia vogli che

sight. In terms of its own essence, sight tends toward the spirit; in terms of its function, it tends toward the image, which is a material thing.[10]

"And so, the image reveals only material things to the intellect, and it does this only by means of sight. The sense of sight has two essences, and thus is able to draw two things out of the image and communicate them to the intellect: these are the beautiful, and the good. The good passes directly to the intellect, inasmuch as it is more appropriate to the nature of the intellect than the beautiful. The beautiful, on the other hand, stands at odds with the nature of the intellect and thus is taken in primarily by the imagination, that part of the soul which, more than any other, is the abode of the senses.[11] The beautiful remains there so long that in time it gains the ability to rise up into the intellect, where the intellect takes it into consideration and forms whatever concept of it that seems appropriate, either pleasing or displeasing. If the thing, now having been known and given consideration, pleases the intellect, it is sent to be preserved in the memory; if on the other hand the intellect does not find it pleasing, it disdains it and drives it back out.[12]

"Now, inasmuch as the image does not reveal anything other than the beautiful or the good to the intellect, I cannot fathom which beautiful or good aspects

---

[10] Bigolina's notions of psychology and cognition, with their sensitive and vegetative souls, and their meticulous separation of faculties and functions, follow the prevailing neo-Aristotelian teachings of her day: see K. Park, "The Organic Soul," in *The Cambridge History of Renaissance Philosophy*, ed. C. B. Schmitt (Cambridge: Cambridge University Press, 1988), 465–68. Bigolina's interest in the appreciation of the beautiful and the good reflects as well a neo-Platonic influence: see P. O. Kristeller, *The Philosophy of Marsilio Ficino*, trans. V. Conant (Gloucester, MA: P. Smith, 1964), 263–69, and also M. Ficino, *Commentary on Plato's Symposium on Love*, trans. S. Jayne (Dallas: Spring Publications, 1985), 2.2. Bigolina's assertion that the intellect is pure spirit seems to place her far outside the lively debate, largely centered in sixteenth-century Padua, on the material and immaterial aspects of the intellective soul; indeed Pomponazzi, who was active at the University of Padua, was inclined to regard the intellect as more material than immaterial: see P. Pomponazzi, *On the Immortality of the Soul*, trans. W. H. Hay II, in *The Renaissance Philosophy of Man*, 280–381, here 317.

[11] On the relationship between imagination and the senses in the neo-Platonist Ficino and the neo-Aristotelian Pomponazzi, see Kristeller, *Ficino*, 234–35 and A. H. Douglas, *The Philosophy and Psychology of Pietro Pomponazzi* (Hildesheim: Olms, 1962), 55.

[12] A similar process, describing how images received in the imagination are stored in the memory, can be found in Ficino's *Commentary on Plato's Symposium* 6.6 (trans. Jayne, 113–15).

questa tua imagine a quel giovine rappresenti, non havendo tu giamai cosa alcuna tanto degna operata, la quale habbia in sè tanto potere, che a commovere un nobile animo bastevole fosse. Chè del bello non ne voglio teco altrimente parlare, imperciò che per me io giudico, che se non per lo buono, et non mai per lo bello dovrebbe di sè lasciare imagine alcuno, per esser per lo vero cosa da sè troppo vana, et lasciva. Et perciò io ti consiglio che non la imagine della tua faccia a quel gentilissimo giovine mandi, poi ch'ella per farlo di te raccordevole non è buona, ma più tosto quella della grande osservatione et amore che gli porti gli manderai, la quale nella sua memoria viva ti terrà di continovo."

Io, che sino a quel punto colma di gran maraviglia ascoltandolo haveva sempre tacciuto, parendomi ch' egli al presente cosa tanto fuor di natura m'havesse detto, che io non la poteva in modo alcuno capire, perciò così gli risposi. "Sapientissimo Giudicio, s'io volessi col mio basso sapere prender a lodare l'alta et giustissima tua sapienza, non sarebbe minore la mia arroganza di quello sarebbe la ignoranza di tale che si presumesse con un picciolo vaso d'acqua far crescere il mare, overamente con un lumicciolo far più risplendenti i raggi del sole. Et perciò le infinite tue lodi per non saper dire a bastanza taceromi. Ma ben diroti almen questo: che di tante et tante ragioni c'hai dette, quantunque in me sia poco sapere, io pur le ho assai ben tutte comprese, eccetto questa ultima, che m'hai detta, la quale io ben ti confesso, che perchè io pensi et ripensi non posso, nè mai credo poter intendere. Cioè, che tu di' che io mandi a quel giovine virtuoso, il quale honestamente amo contanto, la imagine dell'osservanza et amor che io gli porto, imperciò che io giamai non saprei imaginarmi come amendue naturalmente si potessero pingere."

"Non mi maraviglio di questo tuo poco sapere," disse alhora il Giudicio, "per esser sempre stato costume di voi humani di rare volte intender molto tosto le cose, che vi si dicono. Massimamente di quelle dico che sono qualche poco difficili, se con similitudini a forza non vi si pongono nel capo. Et che ciò sia vero tu vederai, che per similitudini capacissima di quello divenirai, che hora impossibile ti par di poterlo sapere. Dimmi adunque, con qual cosa ami, et con quale osservi tu cotesto giovine così valoroso?"

"O," gli risposi, "io l'amo col cuore, et con lo intelletto l'osservo."

"Sta bene," diss'egli, "se adunque col cuore tu l'ami, et l'osservi con lo intelletto, mandagli una imagine del cuore et dell'intelletto; o, per far meglio, il tuo proprio cuore, et lo tuo proprio intelletto gli puoi mandare."

"Dio mi aiuti," gli risposi io alhora, "tu mi confondi con cotesto tuo vario parlare, et per dirti il vero, o che io non ti intendo, overamente che tu nelle tue sentenze in te medesimo sei discorde. Pur mo' biasimavi chiunque lascia di sè

of yourself you expect this image of yours to communicate to that young man. You have not done anything of great worth which might have sufficient power to move a noble soul. I do not wish to speak to you any further about the beautiful, since I judge that one should leave to the world only images of good, and never an image of one's beauty; such a thing is truly too vain and lascivious. Therefore I counsel you not to send the image of your face to that most gentle youth, for it is not a proper means to make him remember you. Instead, you must send your great reverence for him, and your love; things which will keep you continuously alive in his memory."

I had kept silent all this time, listening to the man with great wonder. However, since it seemed to me that this last statement of his was so out of the ordinary that I could not comprehend it, I answered him thus: "O most wise Judgment, if I wished with my low intellect to attempt to praise your high and just wisdom, my ignorance would be no less than that of someone who wished to make the sea mount higher by adding a little vase of water, or to render the rays of the sun more resplendent by means of a tiny lamp. Therefore, since I could never know how to say enough, I will refrain from singing your infinite praises. But I will say at least this much to you: despite my lack of wisdom, I have understood all of the many points you have made, save this last, which, let me confess, I do not believe I can grasp even after much reflection. You say that I am to send to that virtuous youth, whom I love so very chastely, an image of the reverence and love I feel for him; yet I cannot possibly imagine how the nature of either of these things might be painted."

"I do not marvel at your lack of knowledge," replied Judgment, "since it has rarely been the custom of you humans to grasp quickly the meaning of the things you are told. This is especially true of those things which are a bit difficult to understand, unless they are placed into your heads by means of similes. You will shortly see how true this is, when, through similes, you will have been rendered quite capable of understanding a notion which at the moment appears to be beyond you. So tell me, what things do you employ in loving and revering this most valorous youth?"

"Oh," I replied. "I love him with my heart, and revere him with my intellect."

"Well then," said he, "if you love him with your heart and revere him with your intellect, send an image of your heart and intellect; or, even better, you can send him your very heart and intellect."

"God help me!" I answered then. "You are confusing me with this varied discourse of yours. To tell you the truth, either I do not understand you, or else you are contradicting yourself in your pronouncements. Just now you were blaming

imagine, se per lo bello, et non per lo buono le lascia, dicendo che è cosa troppo lasciva, ella è pur anco cosa così fanciullesca da fare, che io non so che mi dire. Et dici che parimente una imagine del mio intelletto gli mandi, la quale operatione quanto sia possibil da fare, lo lascio giudicare a te stesso, che tanto t'hai affaticato per farmi conoscere quanto le materiali cose siano a le spirituali in estremo contrarie, et come non si unirebbono mai, se col mezzo di cosa, che dell'una, et dell'altra natura partecipasse, non si venissero a unire. Onde io voglio dire (con tutto che io sappia assai poco) che pur mi par di conoscere come tutto il mondo, nè tu, nè la istessa Natura non potreste alcun mezzo ritrovare, per lo quale si potesse effettualmente lo intelletto dipingere. Et poi soggiungi ancora (il che non meno mi par strana cosa da udire) che assai meglio io farei, quando lo istesso mio cuore, et intelletto mio gli mandasse; il quale effetto se ben lo consideri t'accorgerai da te stesso quanto non meno l'uno sia inhumano di quello, che l'altro impossibile si dimostri. Imperciochè, come ho già detto, non essendo in alcun modo possibile il poter dipingere lo intelletto, così medesimamente sarà impossibile in alcun modo mandarlo. Ben concederotti che'l mio cuore potrei mandarli. Ma quando io penso poi, che oltre che quel gentilissimo giovine non potrebbe in cosa veruna del mio cuore valersi, parmi che essendo come egli è benignissimo, che vedendo in me tanta inhumanità, come sarebbe se da me stessa il cuor mi cavassi, che con tale operatione non pur non farei l'effetto, che fare io desidero, cioè di perpetuarmi nella memoria di lui, ma più tosto per la horribilità d'un tale empio effetto in me stessa operato, in tanto horrore et malavolenza di lui caderei che più tosto che di me, vorrebbe tener della morte memoria. Et perciò a dirti il vero, questi tuoi consigli a me non piacciono punto, et meno io intendo di voler questi tuoi avisi seguire."

Di questo mio dire assai si rise il Giudicio, et dopo ch'egli hebbe riso a suo modo, così mi disse. "Tu hai una gran ragione, et in questo molto forte io ti lodo. Nondimeno dimmi ti prego, se tu havessi nel tuo giardino un molto grande et bellissimo pero, il quale di assai vaghi, grossi, et dolcissimi peri facesse, et che un tuo carissimo amico ti dicesse più volte, che quell'arbore grandemente gli piace, et che assai pagherebbe che fosse suo quel bel pero, dimmi dico ti prego, se tu molto desiderosa fosti di compiacer quel tuo amico, non taglieresti dal piede quel tuo sì bel pero, et a lui ne faresti presente?"

"Ahì," gli risposi io, "troppo gran peccato farebbe chi struggesse così bell'arbore, sanza giovamento d'alcuno; già che so ben io che al mio amico non piacerebbe il bel pero, eccetto perchè produce i bei frutti, et che levatogli il valore di producere que' bei frutti, non più quel bell'arbore prezzarebbe. Et perciò io ti dico, che essendo da me conosciuto il piacer dell'amico, sanza che il pero io struggessi farei di tal modo, ch'egli potrebbe dir che 'l bello arbore fosse suo. Et ciò

anyone who provides a personal image that shows the beautiful and the good, saying that it is too lascivious. Now you tell me to send him an image of my heart, an act which is not only completely wanton, but also quite childish; I do not know what to say. You say moreover that I should send an image of my intellect. I leave it for you to judge how impossible this is to do, since you have made so great an effort to inform me how material things are the extreme opposites of the spiritual, and how the two can never come together except through the agency of some thing which shares the natures of both. Therefore, despite my lack of knowledge, I say that it seems to me that neither you nor Nature, nor indeed anyone in the world, can find a way to paint the intellect effectively. You also assert (and this appears no less strange to me) that I would do much better to send my heart as well as my intellect to him: yet if you consider this well, you will realize on your own how the first act is no less inhuman than the second is impossible. I have already said it is impossible to find a way to paint the intellect, and it is just as impossible to send it to anyone. I grant you that I would be able to send him my heart; nonetheless, when I reflect upon it, I realize that my heart would be of no use to that most gentle youth. Since he is quite mild-mannered, I believe that the act of removing my heart would appear so inhuman to him that I would fail in my task, that is, to perpetuate myself in his memory. Indeed, I believe this terrible act, committed upon myself, would make me appear so horrific and malevolent to him that he would sooner remember death than remember me. Therefore I tell you that these counsels of yours do not please me in the least, and I do not intend to follow them."

Judgment laughed a great deal at these words of mine. After he had had his fill of laughter, he said to me, "You are well endowed with the ability to reason, and for this I give you great praise. Nonetheless I pray you tell me, if you had a very large and beautiful pear tree in your garden, which produced big, beautiful, very sweet pears, and a most dear friend of yours told you repeatedly that he greatly liked this tree, and that he would pay anything to have it, would you not cut down the tree, wishing to please this friend, and give it to him as a present?"

"Ah," I answered him. "It would be too great a shame to destroy so beautiful a tree, and it would serve no purpose to anyone. I am well aware that my friend would not like the tree unless it produced good fruit, and he would no longer appreciate it once it had lost that capacity. Therefore I say, since I would know my friend's desire, I would make every effort to arrange things so that he could say the tree was his, without having to destroy it. I would do this by frequently giving

sarebbe col sovente donarli de' frutti di quello; et così servando l'essere al pero harrei sodisfatto all'amico."

"Lodato sia Dio," disse egli, "che pur da te stessa t'hai aperta la mia da potermi intendere. O come alcune volte è dura cosa, et dispiacevole per noi altri, quando per dispositione de' cieli, et per fare avisati voi humani d'alcuni non da voi conosciuti secreti siamo forzati ad apparere et ragionare con tali ignoranti, come essere tu hora ti manifesti, che sono di tanto oscuro, pigro, et addormentato ingegno che se vogliamo esser intesi da loro, noi, che siamo divini, in loro, che sono vil cosa ci convien trasformarci. Già di tutti io non dico, imperciò che di tali si trovano humani tra voi, a i quali, se non fosse la corruttione della carne che è in loro, gli si potrebbe degnamente nome di divinità attribuire, et sono di così alto et chiaro ingegno che non noi si trasformiamo in loro per fargli capaci di noi, ma loro in noi per assotigliar noi si trasformano. De' quali tra il numero de' maggiori quel nobilissimo giovine che è cagion del parlar nostro si debbe intender che sia.

"Ma per ripigliar il già da me lasciato proposito, dico, che ben la tua grande ignoranza aperta dimostri, poi che non sai conoscere, come questo, che io t'ho detto del pero, è similitudine di quello, che dianzi di te medesima io ti dicevo. Et benchè in sè stesso l'habbi saputo distinguer benissimo, non hai però tanto ingegno che lo sapessi appropriare a quello per lo quale io l'ho detto. Ma io lo ti voglio del tutto chiarire, et dicoti che debbi intendere che 'l tuo intelletto, col quale hai detto che quel valoroso giovine osservi, si debbia appropriare al pero, ch'io dissi. Imperciò che tale medesima operatione può fare il tuo intelletto in quel giovine, quale sarebbe il pero nell'amico, che pur hora dicevi. Ma odi cosa maravigliosa da udire: che quantunque a te paia che lo intelletto non si possa dipingere, et visibilmente mandar lo potrai; et all'incontro il cuore, il quale so che a te pare che impossibile sarebbe che si potesse mandare, et non si vedesse, conoscerai medesimamente com'egli mandare invisibilmente si puote."

"Cotesto che tu di' ben mi parrebbe gran cosa, se tu lo mi facessi vedere esser vero," gli risposi io alhora. "Onde io ti dico che io mi dubito che a fatto mi debbi fare impazzire, così con questi tuoi dubbij et varij detti mi rendi confusa."

"O sciocca che sei," mi disse egli alhora. "Non sai tu che le compositioni, le inventioni, et in fine tutto quello che ingeniosamente[13] si opera, così sono i frutti che producono gli humani intelletti, come gli peri sono i frutti, che 'l pero produce? Et se come tu hai detto mandando de' peri all'amico intendi di farli in quel modo del pero presente, perchè non intendi ancora che qualunque dona de' frutti

---

[13] *Igeniosamente* in T (fol. 18r). Corrected to *ingeniosamente* in P (fol. 20v).

him fruit from it; and in this way I would have preserved the tree, while satisfying my friend."

"God be praised!" said he. "On your own you have opened the way to understanding me. Sometimes it is a hard thing for us, and unpleasant, when the disposition of the Heavens forces us to explain certain secrets unknown to you humans; we must appear and reason with ignorant people, such as you are showing yourself to be now. These people have such lazy, vague, and dormant intellects that we who are divine must transform ourselves into things as vile as they are, if we wish to be understood by them. I do not mean they are all like that, inasmuch as there are certain humans among you upon whom, were it not for the corruption of the flesh, one could properly bestow the name of divinity. They are of such high, shining intellect that we do not transform ourselves into them in order to make them capable of understanding us; instead, they take our forms, and in so doing sharpen our wits. You must understand that among the greatest of these stands that most noble youth, the one who has been the subject of our conversation.

"But now let me return to the subject which I was discussing before. You openly show your ignorance when you say you cannot see how the situation of the pear tree is an illustration of what I had been telling you earlier about yourself. Even though you have been able to grasp the idea as a separate thing, you do not have enough wit to see the connection between it and the things I was telling you before. But I wish to make all this plain to you. I insist that you understand that your intellect, the very thing which you said you employ when you observe that valorous youth, must be compared to the pear tree which I described, inasmuch as the same action that you said would serve to bring the pear tree to your friend would also make your intellect known to that youth. Now hear something marvelous: even though it seems to you that the intellect cannot be painted, you will be able to send it in visible form. On the other hand you will also see how the heart, which I know you think cannot be sent without being visibly revealed, can in fact be sent just as well, yet invisibly."

"This would indeed seem a great thing to me, if you could show it to be true," I told him at that point. "But I fear that in fact you will make me go mad, since you leave me so confused with your objections and various pronouncements."

"O what a foolish woman you are!" he said. "Do you not know that compositions, inventions, and ultimately everything which derives from genius, are the very fruits which the human intellect produces, just as the pears are the fruits produced by the tree? And if, as you have said, sending pears to your friend is your way of making him a present of the tree, why do you not grasp that any

del suo intelletto ad altrui, così medesimamente il suo intelletto gli venghi a donare? Et perciò se dal tuo intelletto qualche inventione trahendo comporrai una qualche operetta, et a quel raro giovine la manderai, potrai ancora tu dire alhora che una imagine del tuo intelletto gli harrai donata, et che quello, ch'era invisibile l'harrai fatto visibilmente apparere.

"Et perchè facendo questo, si sa che non lo potresti giamai fare se 'l consenso della tua volontade non vi concorre; la qual volontade nel cuore si ferma, ne aviene che facendo col formar qualche tua compositione lo intelletto visibile, il quale è da sè per natura invisibile. Così con la dispositione della volontade, la quale nel comporre et nel mandar la cosa composta harrai operata. La imagine del tuo cuore, il quale è di natura visibile, harrai mandata invisibile; intendendosi sempre la volontade esser la vera imagine de' cuori humani.

"Hor dunque hai potuto intendere come havendo deliberato di pur lasciar una imagine di te stessa a quel virtuoso giovine nel quale ti compiaci cotanto, lasciare una imagine gli potrai, et lasciargliela tale, che a te più di honore et a lui vie più grata gli fia assai che se gli lasciassi la imagine della tua faccia in oro scolpita."

"O verace, o giusto, o divino Giudicio," gli dissi io alhora. "Quanto era il mio debole sapere da ignoranza impedito, se con gli sapientissimi tuoi avisi non m'havesti fatta capace a conoscere et intendere tai cose, che in migliaia d'anni non le harrei giamai da me stessa conosciute, nè intese. Ma dimmi ti prego, essendo io di così picciolo saper com'io sono, come potrò mai far cosa la quale per suo valore meriti d'esser lungamente nella memoria d'altrui conservata?"

"O," mi disse egli, "già che tu non sei Socrate o Platone, che sì ti convenisse per gli difficili et oscuri passi della profonda filosofia passare. Nè ancora sei veruno di quei celebrati poeti come furono Oratio o Virgilio, ne i quali le dilettevoli, ingeniose, et dotte inventioni pullulavano, et fiorivano sempre. Ma si sa che sei donna, et solamente tanta virtude et sapere possedi quanto parvero a i cieli che all'humile tuo essere bastevole fosse; quantunque (et forse fu per tua grandissima penitenza) un desiderio infinito di sapere assai, ti donassero.

"Fa adunque quello che sai, et fa cosa che dilettevole sia. Imperciò che perchè tu sei donna, sarai in gran parte escusata dell'humile et basso tuo dire. Et perchè quello, a cui donarai la da te cosa composta è giovine et gentilissimo; rispetto all'esser giovine, del dilettevole da te preso soggetto compiacerassi; et rispetto ch'egli è gentile, il tuo buon volere assai più che lo istesso effetto harrà grato."

person who bestows the fruits of the intellect upon others is in fact making a gift of the intellect itself? By the same token, if by drawing some invention out of your intellect you compose a little work and send it to that remarkable youth, you will be able to say that you have given him an image of your mind. Moreover, you will be able to say that you have made visible that which had been invisible.

"Everyone knows that you would never be able to do this unless your will assented to it, and the will dwells in the heart. Just as you make your intellect visible, even though it is by nature invisible, when you create a literary work, by the same token you will be sending forth the invisible image of your heart, even though the heart is a normally visible thing. This is because you must employ the disposition of your will in composing and sending the created work, and we must always understand that the will is the true image of human hearts.

"You have decided to leave an image of yourself to this virtuous youth, who has made you so glad; and now you have been able to grasp just how to leave him such an image, one which will bring you more honor, and him more satisfaction, than an image of your face sculpted in gold ever could."

"O just, true, and divine Judgment!" I said to him then. "My weak wit was so impeded by ignorance that, on my own, I never would have understood these things in a thousand years, if your most wise counsels had not rendered me capable of appreciating them. But tell me this, I pray: seeing how I have so little wisdom, however will I be able to create a thing of such worth that it will deserve to be long enshrined in the memory of another?"

"Oh," said he. "Surely you are no Socrates and no Plato, who has had to travel along the obscure and difficult path of Philosophy. Nor indeed are you one of those celebrated poets, such as Horace or Virgil, in whom delightful, ingenious, and learned creations continually sprang forth and flourished. Instead you are Woman, possessing only as much virtue and wisdom as it seemed fit to the heavens to bestow upon your humble being. The heavens did, however, bestow upon you an infinite yearning for knowledge, and perhaps this has been a very great cross for you to bear.

"Therefore do that which you know how to do, as long as it brings delight. And since you are a woman, you will be excused to a great extent for your humble and low style. The person to whom you will give your composition is young, and of a very noble character; inasmuch as he is young, he will take pleasure in whatever is delightful in your subject, whereas his noble character will lead him to be much more satisfied by your good will than by the result itself."

Et poi ch'egli così m'hebbe detto sanza che io lo potesse, come era il debito mio ringratiare, da gli occhi miei in un baleno si fu dileguato. Alla quale partita, come cosa, che è fuori di sè stessa io rimasi. Pur dopo poco spatio d'hora in me ritornando, et ripensando sopra la prima deliberatione che di mandarvi la imagine della mia faccia havea fatta, acciò ch'ella in voi la memoria di me viva tenesse, parvemi che assai sciocco fosse stato quel mio primo proponimento. Et perciò abbandonando il primo del tutto, al secondo mi venni accostando. Et così da quello aiutata, del mio basso intelletto una imagine trassi, la quale dalla volontà del mio cuore pigliando la effiggie et il colore da amendue insieme questa operetta ne è uscita, che *Urania* si chiama, pigliando il nome da quella sopra la quale tutta la istoria è fondata.

Et così quale si sia questa mia operetta la vi mando et dono, acciochè alcuna volta in ella leggendo paiavi entro vedervi scolpita la imagine del mio cuore, con lo quale come ancora ho detto, dopo che io vi conobbi per lo valore de gli alti meriti vostri honestamente sempre vi ho amato. Et se 'l dono mio non vi paresse che a gli eccelsi vostri meriti convenevole fosse, considerate voi che giudiciosissimo sète, come chi fa quello che può non fa poco. Et chi tutto dona quello ch'egli ha, di niente riman debitore, benchè il dono di picciolissimo valore fosse. Pigliate adunque gentilissimo giovine, così gratiosamente questo mio humile presentuccio, come io volontariamente per farvene libero dono lo feci. Et se vi degnarete questa mia operetta legger tutta, vederete come ancora i savi et accorti giovani possono (quantunque non siano donne, le quali come voi altri huomini affermate, per loro malvagia sorte sempre al loro peggio s'accostano); possono, dico, etiandio loro alcuna volta non molto bene sapere il loro amore dispensare. Et vederete ancora, come alcuna volta la loro buona sorte porgendoli il buono, da sè volontariamente scacciandolo al loro peggio s'appigliano; nè mai di cotale lor peggio si aveggono sino a tanto che 'l peggio in pessimo non si converte, come al giovine dalla Urania amato contanto, Fabio detto per nome, intervenne.

Onde io prego Dio, che voi il quale d'assai valore, et costumatissimo giovine sète, guardi et difenda che mai in tale errore, in tutti i giorni vostri non possiate cadere; et me nella buona vostra gratia fin che harrò vita conservi; et dopo che io sarò morta, tanto in voi revivi di me la memoria, quanto in me hora, ch'io vivo, et che nelle rare anzi singolari vostre qualitadi io mi specchio, doppia vita mi porge.

Urania: The Story of a Young Woman's Love

Just as he had finished saying this he disappeared from my eyes with a flash, without my having the opportunity to thank him, as I should have.[14] When he was gone I was left stunned, but then regained my wits after a short space of time. I thought over my original plan to send you the image of my face, so that you would keep me alive in your memory; it now seemed to me to be very foolish. I therefore abandoned it entirely, and turned instead to the second proposal. Aided by this, I drew forth an image from my low intellect, an image which took its shapes and colors from the will of my heart. This little work, deriving thus from both my intellect and my heart, is called *Urania*, and it takes its name from that woman who is the whole subject of the story.

Thus I send you this little work of mine as a gift, such as it is, so that within it, while reading, sometimes you will see engraved the image of my heart. As I have said, with this heart I have chastely loved you ever since I came to know your great worth. And if by chance this gift of mine might not seem to be worthy of your very high qualities, I pray you, who are so discerning, consider this: those who do whatever they can are indeed doing much, and those who give everything they have owe nothing more, even if the gift be of very little value. Therefore graciously receive this humble little present of mine, O most gentle youth, since I have willingly created it in order to bestow it freely upon you. If you will deign to read this little work in its entirety, you will see how even wise and astute young men are capable (even though they are not women, who, as you men insist, are always drawn by their ill fortune to the worst of things); capable, I say, of not knowing how to love properly. You will also see how young men sometimes willingly reject the benefits their own good fortune gives them, attaching themselves instead to things which do them harm. These youths are never aware that these attachments are bad, until such a time as the bad things become even worse; and this is what occurred to Fabio, the young man beloved by Urania.

On this account I pray that God preserve and keep you, a most worthy and well-mannered youth, from falling into such error. Moreover I pray that God keep me in your good graces for as long as I shall live, and that He will revive my memory in you after my death; even as He gives me a double life now, while I am alive and still able to mirror myself in your rare, indeed unique qualities.

---

[14] Cf. the departure of the ghost of Scipio in Caviceo's *Libro del Peregrino*: "Dicte le parole, sparve la sancta umbra; et dolseme de non puoterla in parte alcuna ringratiare" ["having said the words, the blessed shade disappeared, and it grieved me to not be able to give it the slightest thanks" (ed. Vignali, 234)].

VRANIA.

NELLA QVALE SI CONTIENE L'AMORE D'VNA GIOVANE DI TAL NOME.

I

Nel tempo che Giufredi Prencipe, più che altro Signore che 'n que' tempi vivesse bello et piacevole, il bellissimo stato di Salerno pacificamente reggeva, si trovava in quella città una giovane d'assai nobil famiglia, per nome Urania chiamata; la quale oltre che nelle volgari lettere fosse assai convenevolmente dotta, et che le Muse sì nelle prose, qual nelle rime le fossero amiche, era ancora d'un così nobile animo ornata, che più tosto che un sol vitio da quel suo così bel animo s'havesse veduto uscire, harrebbe eletto di morir mille volte. Et perciò tanto la virtù le piaceva che udendola posta in altrui raccordare, non potea far, quantunque molto lontani que' tali virtuosi le fossero stati, che tutta d'honesto, et virtuoso amore accesa non se ne fosse. Era costei per cagion di cotali sue virtudi, più che per gran bellezza che 'n lei si ritrovasse, da molti nobili giovani di Salerno amata, et desiderata. Ma lei, che sol di virtù compiacevasi, non conoscendone alcuno de' molti li quali sì per goder delle virtù sue, qual perchè tale era il costume in Salerno, spesse volte a visitar l'andavano, che degno le paresse ch'ella del cor suo gli havesse a far

URANIA

THE STORY OF A
YOUNG WOMAN'S LOVE

I

In the days when Prince Giufredi, the most handsome and pleasant lord of his age, peacefully ruled the lovely state of Salerno,[15] there lived in that city a young woman of a very noble family named Urania. Aside from the fact that she was quite properly skilled in vernacular literature, so that the Muses were her companions as much in prose as in verse, she was also endowed with so noble a spirit that she would have chosen to die a thousand times rather than see her lovely soul give way to a single vice. She loved virtue so much that whenever she heard that it resided in others, she could not help but burn with chaste and virtuous love for them, even if they lived far away. This quality, more than any great beauty she may have had, caused her to be loved and desired by many noble youths of Salerno. As was the custom in Salerno, many of these young men would go to visit her, in order to appreciate her qualities; but she, who took pleasure only in virtue,

---

[15] No prince of Salerno bearing this name is attested in histories of the Sanseverino dynasty, such as those of Colapietra and Carucci. It does not seem that Bigolina intended to establish a firm historical time frame for her narrative, although it is possible that her portrait of the virtuous Giufredi was inspired by Ferrante Sanseverino (see Introduction, 19–20).

dono. Et quantunque a tutti assai grata et benigna si dimostrasse, et con accoglienze honorevoli ricevesse ciascuno, stavasi nondimeno in sè stessa assai lontana da ogni pensiero amoroso.

Ma Amore, che come di molte altre suol fare così havea deliberato di far di costei crudele scempio. Imperciò che contra la forza di così potente signore, forza, ricchezza, et virtù poco, o nulla vagliono, fece perciò che un nobile giovine di quella città Fabio detto per nome, havendo da molti udito le virtuti della Urania sommamente lodare, ch' egli di conoscerla, et d'haver seco qualche honorevole pratica fuor di misura s'accese. Et cotesto così gran desiderio, ch' egli havea di conoscerla, dalla somiglianza de' costumi, et virtù ch' egli teneva con essa lei procedeva. Imperciò che oltre ch' egli fosse nelle latine lettere assai dotto, era ancor di belle creanze sommamente adorno, et d'una gratia dal ciel concessagli, la quale ad ogni virtuoso cuore lo facea grato, di modo che egli rendea maraviglia a chiunque lo conosceva.

Costui adunque così desideroso ritrovandosi di conoscer la Urania, tanto con un parente di lei s'adoprò che da quello per compiacerli, una sera di verno a veghia vi fu condotto dove tanto dalla Urania gratiosamente venne raccolto, ch' egli di ritornarvi dell'altre volte prese ardir di chiederle in gratia. Perchè lei, che di bei modi et gentil maniere di lui stranamente compiacciuta s'era, con vie maggior affetto et con più pronto volere che giamai ad alcun' altro fatto havesse, risposegli, che cosa nel mondo non potrebbe haver che di maggior contento le fosse, come sarebbe ch' egli si degnasse spesse volte venirle a vedere. Della qual risposta parve che 'l giovine Fabio un sommo piacer ne sentisse, et ben di tal suo piacere dimostronne l'effetto. Imperciò che non lasciava da una volta all'altra molti giorni passare che con infinito contento sì dell'una, qual dell'altra parte a visitarla non andasse. Et que' giorni che andar non vi poteva, non mancava con amorevoli et dotte lettere di supplire; alle quali (sì come da colei, che bene il sapea fare) erano non men gratamente, che dottamente risposto. Et spesse volte alle lettere aggiongeva de' molti vaghi et dotti sonetti, con altre qualità di rime. Et di maniera tra 'l termine di pochi mesi crebbe tra questi due amanti l'amore, che un solo cuore, un sol volere, et una sola anima pareva che 'n trambi due tenessero.

Ma come la si fosse non so, che molti giorni hebbero a passare dopo che l'amor loro al sommo grado fu gionto, che quantunque Fabio infinitamente amator di virtù per lo innanzi si fosse dimostrato, nondimeno poco considerando alle molte virtuti che di giorno per cagion del suo amore, sempre maggiori nella Urania si dimostravano. Et scordatosi le tante et tante cortesie da lei ricevute, rivolse gl'occhi, et dopo il cuore nell'amor d'altra giovane, la quale per dire il vero, era assai della Urania più bella, ma di virtute poco al paragone presso le sarebbe durata.

did not know these men, and did not think it right that she give her heart to any of them. Even though she was kind and pleasant, and received each one with honor, she kept herself far from any thoughts of love.

But Love, as he often does with so many other women, had in his cruel way decided to make her look foolish. Steadfastness, wealth, and virtue can do little or nothing to counteract the strength of so powerful a lord as Love, who now saw to it that a noble young man of the city, named Fabio, fell madly in love with her. This Fabio had heard much praise of Urania's virtues from others, and thus resolved to meet her, and get to know her in an honorable fashion. On account of his virtuous habits, which so resembled hers, he was able successfully to satisfy his great desire to make her acquaintance. Aside from his great knowledge of Latin literature, he was also adorned by heaven with the best manners, and a grace which made him pleasing to every virtuous heart; in this way he made all who knew him marvel.

Therefore this man, who had so great a yearning to make the acquaintance of Urania, managed one winter evening to get a relative of hers to bring him to a party at her house. There he was so graciously welcomed by Urania that he made bold to ask her permission to see her on further occasions. Finding herself strangely attracted to his pleasing and genteel manners, she answered him with much more affection and good will than she ever had to any other suitor. She told him nothing in the world would make her happier than if he were to agree to visit her often. Fabio seemed to be quite pleased at this response, and showed his pleasure by not letting many days pass between his subsequent visits to her, to the infinite contentment of both. On those days when he could not come to see her, he did not fail to make up for this by sending her polished love letters; and she, who was highly skilled in this pursuit, answered them with letters of her own which were no less polished or pleasing. Often she added many beautiful and erudite sonnets to her letters, along with other types of poetry. In this fashion, within a few months they so grew to love each other that it seemed as if they held but a single heart, a single will, and a single soul between them.

How it happened I do not know, but many days after their love had reached its highest pinnacle, Fabio, despite having previously shown an infinite fondness for virtue, now began to show little consideration for the many virtues which Urania had been displaying every day, and to an ever greater degree, in the name of love. Forgetting the many, many courtesies he had received from her, Fabio turned first his eyes, then his heart to the love of another young woman. To tell the truth, she was much more beautiful than Urania; nonetheless, with regard to

Per la qual cosa mancando in Fabio il già tanto conceputo amor verso la Urania, incominciò seco a mancar parimente quell'ardente desiderio che di vederla o di lei novelle udire parea primieramente che tanto gli calesse. Et se pur alcuna volta vi andava, il che più per suo honore che per amor che a lei portasse faceva, erano assai scarsi e suoi ragionamenti et molto lontani da ogni suo primo usato modo. Perchè la Urania, che accortissima era, quantunque egli del tutto negasse d'haver fuor che 'n lei rivolto il suo cuore, nondimeno lei molto tosto se ne fu accorta. Et perciò essendosi a molti segni della inconstanza dell'amator suo a fatto chiarita, nè sapendo bene quale potesse esser colei per la quale abbandonata si conosceva, quantunque certissima fosse che di virtù non le si uguagliarebbe, quando ben l'avanzasse in bellezza, sentiva nondimeno di cotal novo accidente un così smisurato dolore, che per lo grande affanno si pensava di certo morire.

Et perciò per non incorrere in così gran scandalo, com'era di dover così vilmente lasciarsi condure a morte, et per non far del suo male allegra colei, per la quale d'ogni suo contento et d'ogni sua gioia era priva, deliberossi che che incontrar di ciò le ne potesse di volere sanza indugio vestita da huomo et sola fuor di Salerno partirsi, et andar pe' 'l mondo errando sin tanto che il lungo patire et molti disagi che per lo camino harrebbe sofferti, il soverchio amor che a Fabio portava, anzi più tosto la insania le levasser del cuore, et di sè stessa la facesser pietosa. Imperciò che di là dove amor scolpito nel cuor le lo haveva, per accidente che incontrar le potesse, non conosceva di poterlosi altrimenti levare.

Et perciò fatta una determinatione cotale, fece che un suo fedelissimo servo secretamente sì che la madre di lei non se n' accorse, alla qual sola si trovava di ubedire obligata, di honorevolissimi panni da huomo, et d'un buon cavallo, l'hebbe in pochi giorni fornita. Il qual servo perciò assai fece, et disse acciò ch'ella da tal reo proponimento si rimovesse; ma vedendo poscia come le parole sue alcun frutto, che buon fosse non facevano, si dispose di volerla in ogni modo sodisfare, et ubedirla.

Ma lei, che quantunque havesse del tutto deliberato il partire, perchè non le dava il cuor di poter sofferire di vedersi dinanzi gli occhi la cagion del suo male et non mille volte morire, nè volendo perciò che 'l tanto da lei amato Fabio le havesse questa sua partita ad alcun' altra vergognosa cagione imputata, et insieme desiderando di farlo conoscere, come lei sola più di quante altre donne l'amasse, o amarlo potessero mai, lo haveva amato, et amavalo ancora, et che altrettanto lei sopra ogn'altra meritava d'esser da lui amata, et tenuta cara. Perciò tolta carta, penna et inchiostro, di tal tenore una lettera gli scrisse:

URANIA: THE STORY OF A YOUNG WOMAN'S LOVE

virtue she could not match Urania at all. On account of this new state of affairs, Fabio's once firmly established love for Urania began to diminish; and with it went that ardent desire, once so important to him, to see her or to hear news of her. If occasionally he still paid her a visit, he did it more for her honor than for the love that he bore her, and in a departure from his established custom he now had little to say to her. Urania was very shrewd, and quite soon became aware that he had turned his heart away from her, despite his denials. Many signs made the inconstancy of her lover clear to her, and even though she did not know what woman had caused her to be abandoned, she was quite certain that this rival could not match her in virtue, however much prettier she may have been. Despite this certainty, Urania felt such boundless grief at this state of affairs that she thought she would surely die.

Yet she desired to avoid the great scandal that would arise if she allowed herself to die in such a vile fashion; moreover, she did not wish to give her rival, the one who had deprived her of all her joy and happiness, any cause to rejoice at her demise. Therefore she resolved, no matter what might come of this course of action, to flee Salerno without delay, dressed as a man, and wander the world until such a time as the great suffering and considerable discomfort that she would undergo along the way might free her heart from its excessive, indeed insane, love for Fabio; only thus could she prove merciful to herself. She could think of no other way to remove love from her heart, once it had become engraved therein, unless it be by some accident.

Therefore, having arrived at this decision, Urania had a most faithful servant secretly furnish her with very proper men's clothes and a fine horse; this he did within a few days, and in such a way that her mother knew nothing of what was going on (there was no one else to whom Urania owed obedience, save her mother). This servant did and said all he could to dissuade her from her misguided plan, but when he saw that his words were doing no good, he resolved to do everything she wanted, and obey her.

But even though Urania had determined to leave because she could not lay eyes upon the cause of her distress without yearning to die a thousand times, she still did not want her beloved Fabio to imagine that her departure was due to anything shameful on her part. She also wished to let him know that only she had ever loved him; and that she still loved him, more than any other woman ever had, or ever could. Moreover, she wanted him to know that she, and she alone, deserved to be loved and held dear by him, above all other women. Therefore she procured paper, pen and ink and wrote a letter to him, which reads as follows:

"Fabio mio, sopra ogn'altra cosa del mondo da me desiderato che mio con gran ragione ti posso chiamare, poi che havendomiti di tuo libero volere donato, non mi ti puoi, s'io non lo consento, con alcuna ragione ritogliere. Io non so s'io mi debba o più lodare o più dolermi de' cieli, perchè essi m'habbino più accorta, et di maggior conoscimento del comune uso dell'altre donne creata. Imperciò che quando l'utile et piacere co'l danno et dispiacere io misuro, li quali da questa mia accortezza, et conoscimento ho spesse volte tratti, così pari ad una bilancia gli trovo che differenza alcuna non vi so discernere.

"Ma lasciando da parte gli altri molti utili, et danni li quali in diversi modi dal mio troppo conoscere ho tratti, dirò di quei solamente i quali essendo da maggior soggetto, che altri mai fossero cagionati, ragionevolmente maggior utile, et piacere; et dopo più gran danno et dispiacere m'hanno arrecato. Grande, anzi grandissimo fu l'utile et piacere che io mi conobbi d'haver ricevuto alhora che io primieramente t'hebbi a conoscere; et che per cagion del mio grande conoscimento mi fu conceduto di potere per ciascuna tua interna virtute discorrere, et di quanto valore, et pregio fosse conoscerla. Et massimamente oltre l'altre tue ottime virtù, conoscendo quanto d'ogni fintione ignudo, di cuore mi amavi, per lo cui conoscere l'anima mia, et tutti e' miei spirti d'un'estremo piacere si colmarono; et fu poscia cagione che di altrettanto amore il cuor mio verso il tuo s'accendessi.

"Ma non minore trovo hora esser il danno et dispiacere il quale dall'istesso mio conoscimento io ricevo, essendomi egli stato parimente cagione che a molti da te celati segnali, assai tosto mi sia accorta del poco conto che tieni di me fuor di ragione, la quale cognitione oltre il danno che da lei infinito io ricevo, un fuor d'ogni humana credenza smisurato dispiacere nell'anima, et nel cuore mi cagiona. Et per dirti il vero Fabio mio, io non so imaginarmi perchè io pensi et ripensi, dove habbia havuto origine in te un così sinistro pensiero. Io dico in te imperciò che in ciascun'altro giovine men di te virtuoso, un tale accidente cosa nova non mi parrebbe. Ma in te, che d'ogni ottima virtù sei soggetto, non pur nova ma novissima, anzi quantunque apertamente io lo vegga, quasi incredibile parmi. Chè qualhora io considero non esser molti mesi passati, dapoi che tu da te stesso sanza esser da me ricercato; et meno non conoscendoti desiderato, venisti cotanto affettuosamente a visitarmi, et dopo a maggiormente amarmi incominciasti. Per la qual cosa si può affirmare che tu eleggesti me per amata, et non io te per amante, quantunque dopo che io mi conobbi da te d'esser amata m'ingegnassi d'amore, et di cortesia vincerti sempre.

URANIA: THE STORY OF A YOUNG WOMAN'S LOVE

"My Fabio, whom I have greater reason to call mine than any other thing in the world which I desire, since you gave yourself to me of your own free will; thus you cannot take yourself back again, for any reason, unless I consent to it. I do not know if I should have more cause to praise the heavens or complain about them, considering that they created me with more shrewdness and a greater ability to reason than is typical in women. Because of this, when I measure what is useful and pleasant in these qualities of mine against those aspects which are harmful and unpleasant, I find the balance is even, and I can discern no difference between them.

"But let me leave aside the majority of these useful and injurious aspects which coexist in various guises within my excessive reasoning powers, so I may speak only of the ones which are of greater importance. These, quite logically, have either been more useful and pleasant to me, or else they have caused me greater harm and displeasure, than the others. When I met you for the first time, I realized that the meeting brought me a very great deal of both the useful and the pleasant. At that moment my great reasoning powers allowed me to assess each of your inner virtues, and to know their worth and excellence. And beyond knowing your other great virtues, I also became aware that you loved me with all your heart, and that, stripped bare of all falseness, you knew my very soul. When this was clear to me, all of my spirits overflowed with extreme pleasure, causing my heart to burn with a love just as great as yours.

"But now I find that I am suffering no less from the harm and displeasure which my same reasoning powers have brought me. For these powers quite quickly allowed me to see through your many hidden signs, and thus become aware of how little you care for me, in defiance of all reason. Beyond the infinite harm which it has done me, this awareness has also brought tremendous sorrow, a sorrow beyond all human comprehension, to my heart and soul. To tell you the truth, my Fabio, even after constant reflection I cannot imagine how so sinister a notion ever came to reside in you. And I mean you in particular: for in any other young man, less virtuous than you, such an occurrence would not surprise me. You, on the other hand, are endowed with every most excellent virtue; therefore your action seems to me not only a very strange thing, but indeed incredible, even though I am able to see it plainly. I often consider how few months have passed since you came to visit me so affectionately, completely on your own with no signal from me, and with you not even knowing if I desired you; then afterwards you fell so deeply in love with me. From this, one can see that you chose me as your beloved, and I did not choose you, however much I subsequently endeavored to outdo you for all time in love and gentility, once I knew you loved me.

"Nondimeno io ti veggo assai fuor di proposito, in pochi giorni esser del tutto da quel tuo primo volere cangiato; nè saprei perciò imaginarmi giamai a qual mio mancamento io dovessi una tua cotanto subita mutatione imputare. Chè se due sono le bellezze nella donna dall'huomo amate et desiderate, cioè bellezza di corpo et bellezza d'animo, le quali quanto sia più l'una che l'altra da esser tenuta cara, et in pregio il fa manifesto lo incorrottibile, et immortal esser dell'una, et il corrottibile, et fuggace dell'altra. Hor se due sorti di bellezza nelle donne si amano io vorrei intender da te circa le parti mie corporali, o belle, o brutte ch'elle si fossero, quando primieramente ti piacquero quanto in così breve tempo ponno men belle, o men desiderabili esser divenute di quello alhora esser ti parvero. Ma lasciamo tutto da parte il dir di queste tali bellezze, poscia ch'elle presso gli virtuosi et elevati ingegni, quale è il tuo, debbono esser, anzi sono le meno prezzate, et solamente della bellezza dell'anima sia il dir nostro. Della quale dico che io non credo che men chiara, o di minor valore in me ti dovrebbe parere, di quello che ne' primi giorni esser in me la conoscesti, anzi più tosto maggior assai (come è pur per lo vero) la ti dovrebbe parere, poi che ritrovandosi la virtù mia sanza soggetto il quale la inalzasse; alla similitudine del ferro, che lontano dalla cote si trovi, quasi ruginosa si dimostrava. Et poi che alla cote dell'ottima tua gratia, la quale in tanto pregio io teneva, vicina si fece io posso dire (et tu ne dovresti esser buon testimonio) ch' ella già così chiara et lucida diveniva, che se punto amata m'havesti, in te gioia, et contento, et in altrui maraviglia harrebbe posta.

"Ma ben mi pare che per quello che sin'hora ho detto, et per molto più che in questa mia lettera son per dire, di troppo ardire, et arroganza mi dannerai, con dir che nè a huomo, et meno a donna che virtuosi siano è convenevole il tanto dar lode a sè stessi come par che me, di me stessa io faccia. Et io parimente teco circa alcuni termini lo confermo, ma ancora d'altra parte rispondoti, che molte operationi si trovano le quali da loro propria natura malvagie et vituperose sono, nondimeno ad alcun tempo et loco, et per tal cagione operate, vedesi come non tanto quel nome di malvagio et vituperoso perdeno, ma nel loco di quello, nome d'honore et di giustitia n'acquistano. Et chi vuol più vituperosa o più malvagia cosa vedere et udire, come è che l'huomo uccida l'altr'huomo, et ch' una man micidiale habbi tanto ardire di disunir quello che'l sommo Iddio et la gran madre Natura di concorde volere unirono insieme. Nondimeno pur vediamo spesse volte il mastro giustitieri hora a quello et hora a quell'altro in diversi modi levare la vita, nè perciò alcun si ritrova che per tale operatione il riprenda, nè che ella con nome di rea si possi chiamare; et ciò aviene perchè in cotal caso, la natura delle cose, dalla necessitade astretta, nell'accidente si converte, et similmente hora di me potrà

URANIA: THE STORY OF A YOUNG WOMAN'S LOVE

"Nonetheless, I see you are very much on a different course, since you have completely changed your mind in the space of a few days. I cannot imagine how I have failed, and to what I should attribute this sudden change of yours. If there are two beautiful aspects of a woman which a man loves and desires, that is, the beauty of the body and the beauty of the soul, the degree to which one is to be esteemed and held more dear than the other is shown by the incorruptible and immortal nature of the one, as well as the corruptible and ephemeral nature of the other. So, inasmuch as one loves two sorts of beauty in women, I would like to hear from you which parts of my body, either beautiful or ugly, could have become less beautiful or desirable to you in so short a time, even though at first they were pleasing to you? But let us leave aside the discussion of these beautiful parts, since they must be, and indeed are, the things least appreciated by high and virtuous minds such as yours. Let us talk only about the beauty of the soul. I do not believe the luster and worth of my soul should seem at all diminished to you now, in comparison to the way it appeared in the first days of our acquaintance. Indeed, my soul should appear all the more beautiful at present (as it truly is); whereas before, my virtue had not yet found an object which could elevate it, and it appeared to be almost rusty, like a sword kept far from its whetstone. Then, when the whetstone of your most excellent grace came near to me (and it was a thing which I held in the highest esteem), I can say that my soul became so bright and shining, that it would have imparted joy and contentment in you, and wonder in all others, if you had loved me at all.

"I am well aware that you will condemn me as too audacious and arrogant for what I have said thus far, and for what I will go on to say, in this letter. You will say that it is inappropriate for the virtuous, either men or women, to praise themselves as much as it seems I am doing; and I acknowledge that to some extent this is true. On the other hand, let me tell you that there exist many actions which by their nature are wicked and disgraceful; and yet, in certain times and places, and for certain reasons, it becomes plain that they can be called wicked and disgraceful no longer. Instead, they acquire new names in place of the others: honor and justice. What more wicked and disgraceful thing might we witness, or hear about, than the murder of one man by another? What is worse than a murderous hand that might dare to tear asunder that which God Almighty and great Mother Nature, in common agreement, have united? Nonetheless, we often see the High Executioner take the life of one man or another, in various ways: and no one reproaches him for such a deed, or calls it wicked. This is so because in such cases necessity forces the nature of things to convert itself into an accident; and now

avenire. Che quantunque non mi sia lecito il dar lode a me stessa, anzi più tosto devrei fuggir che d'altrui alla mia presenza mi fosser date. Nondimeno ritrovandomi in termine di dover da me stessa la propria ragion difendere et sostentare, et havendo deliberato di farti conoscere come non per cagione che io sia di te indegna, et che da te non meriti di ritrovarmi sopra ogn'altra sommamente amata, quasi mi spregi, et fuggi; ma perchè tale è la contraria mia sorte, mi è cotale amaro accidente incontrato.

"Dico perciò che per questa volta solamente, et non più ritrovandomi dalla necessitade astretta, voglio mi sia conceduto a sostentation delle mie ragioni quelle parti che 'n me buone io conosco sanza esserne da altrui ripresa poterle dire, offerendomi ancora tutto quello c'harro di me a lodare, a doverlo con buone ragioni farloti conoscer per vero. Dico adunque ragionando perciò teco, come con giovine virtuoso, et non del volgo, li quali più tosto a quello che e' sensi gli dettano che a quello che la ragion gli consiglia si accostano; chè sanza comparatione più dovresti nella bellezza dell'anima mia compiacerti, che di ogn'altra bellissima donna la quale fosse men di me virtuosa, et la ragione di questo mio vero dimostrativa, un sottile argomento la ti farà manifesta.

"Come tu poi sapere, due sono gli sensi nelli quali il virtuoso amante nell'amata sua si compiace, cioè nel vedere, et nell'udire; delle quali due parti mentre alla amata sua donna si trova l'amante presente, gli occhi et l'orecchi pasce et nodrisce. Et dopo che da colei che egli ama si è fatto assente, volendo pur ancora di quelle dolcezze gustare, le quali nel vederla et nell'udirla havea prima gustate, necessaria cosa è per esser il vedere, senso alle parti del corpo appertinente, ch'egli una imagine di quella bellezza nella Idea si formi, et col mezzo di quella la desiata bellezza miri et consideri; chè sanza un tale interposito mezzo, non potrebbe in assentia di quella bellezza gioire. Imperciò che le attioni materiali et quelle dello spirito sono due estremi che giamai da loro stessi si unirebbono, se per opera d'alcun mezzo non venissero a unirsi.

"Ma così dell'udir non aviene, chè essendo egli parte all'anima pertinente, subito che le parole escono di bocca a quel che le dice sanza ritrovare impedimento

URANIA: THE STORY OF A YOUNG WOMAN'S LOVE

something similar is occurring with me. Even though it is not right for me to sing my own praises (indeed I should rather flee them, if they are sung by others in my presence), nevertheless I find it necessary to defend and support my own reasoning, on my own. For I have decided to make you see how it is not because I am unworthy of you, or because I do not deserve to be loved by you above all other women, that you flee from me and nearly disdain me; instead, it is because of my own ill fortune that I have suffered so bitter a fate.

"Therefore, on this one occasion, while I am constrained by necessity, I wish that I may be granted the right to speak in defense of those aspects of my reasoning which I know to be good, without incurring the blame of others. I will put forward everything I have that is praiseworthy, and with effective reasons make you see the truth of it. I will speak to you in rational terms, as befits a young man of quality, rather than someone of the vulgar masses who listens more to the dictates of the senses than to the counsels of reason. Without a doubt you should take more pleasure in the beauty of my soul than in the great physical beauty of another woman, who might be less virtuous than I; and a subtle argument will demonstrate plainly to you the reason why this is so.

"As you know, the virtuous lover takes pleasure in his beloved through two senses, sight and hearing: thus he feeds and nourishes two parts of his body, the eyes and the ears, while the beloved is in his presence. When he is away from her, yet still wishes to partake of the sweet pleasures which he first tasted through the sight and sound of her, it is necessary for sight to form an image of her beauty within the Idea, inasmuch as sight is a sense which appreciates the physical body.[16] By means of that image the lover can gaze upon and contemplate the beauty he yearns for; and he could not enjoy that beauty in the beloved's absence, unless he has the image as an intermediary. The workings of matter and spirit are two extremes which, on their own, would never be able to come together unless some intermediary strove to unite them.

"But hearing cannot work in this same fashion, inasmuch as it is the sense appropriate to the soul. As soon as words exit the mouth of the person who pronounces them, they pass into the intellect of the hearer without encountering any

---

[16] The term Idea, referring to the goal of the natural appetite of the soul, derives from the neo-Platonic notions of Ficino (Kristeller, *Ficino*, 189–90). For the notions that an Idea exists within each individual see Ficino, *Commentary on Plato's Symposium*, 6.19 (trans. Jayne, 144–45).

che l'arrestino, passano all'intelletto dello ascoltante, il quale intelletto poscia che quella dilettatione che gli pare ne ha presa alla Memoria le raccomanda, et ivi si fermano. Onde ciascuna volta che lo intelletto vuol delle già udite parole compiacersi ancora, sanza adoprare alcun mezzo a sua natura disgiunto, dalla Memoria riducendosi quelle medesime, et non l'imagini di quelle vi trova, et in quelle considerando, quella dolcezza ne sente che prima udendole havea sentita. Hor se dunque non può lo amante in assenza, nella corporal bellezza della amata sua donna mirare se gl'interpositi mezzi non vi intervengono, et lo intelletto della sua che son le parole udite, le quali la bellezza dell'anima gli scuoprono, può molto ben sanz'altri mezzi da sè stesso mirarla, et intenderla. Manifesta cosa è adunque che assai più nobile la bellezza dell'anima sia da tenere, et tanto maggior la bellezza nell'una che nell'altra anima s'intende essere, quanto è più atta a riempir de' sue varie bellezze gl'intelletti, et le memorie di quei che la mirano, et delle bellezze sue varij ritratti può fare.

"O che io ti farò hora miracoli udire, et forse altre volte non uditi più mai; et pur mi dà il core di far sì che per verissimi gli conoscerai. Io so che altra donna, et più di me bella tu ami, chè se di me più bella non fosse, per così cieco non ti

Urania: The Story of a Young Woman's Love

impediment. The intellect, upon finding something delightful in these words, consigns them to the Memory, and there they remain. Whereupon each time that the intellect wishes to take pleasure yet again in what it has heard, it goes into the Memory without using any means foreign to its nature; there it finds not an image, but the very words themselves. Contemplating these, the intellect feels once more the sweetness it knew when it first heard them. Thus, even if the absent lover cannot gaze upon the corporeal beauty of his beloved lady without some means which functions as a go-between, the intellect can still regard and appreciate the words it has heard, which reveal the beauty of the woman's soul, without any intermediary at all. It is therefore quite obvious that the beauty of the soul must be regarded as the nobler of the two by far. One can see that a given soul may be so much more beautiful than another if it has a greater capacity to instill its varied beauty into the intellects and memories of those who look upon it, and if it can create diverse portraits of that beauty.[17]

"Oh, now I will tell you of miracles, miracles which perhaps have never been heard of before! I am inspired to strive to make you see the truth in them. I know that you love another woman, one more beautiful than I. She must be more

---

[17] For a similar distinction between sight, which appreciates the beauty of physical forms, and hearing, which takes note of the beauty of the soul, see Bembo, *Asolani* 3.6, in *Prose e rime*, ed. Dionisotti, 468. Renaissance theories on the perception of beauty do not all agree on this casuistry: in his third dialogue Leone Ebreo provides a more overtly neo-Aristotelian process, associating beauty perceived by the eyes with the "primo intelletto" (the first intellect) and that taken by the ears with the world soul, "l'anima del mondo," without implying that one is more effective than the other (*Dialoghi*, ed. Caramella, 326–28). Baldassarre Castiglione, for his part, is inclined to exalt the role of the sense of sight in the love process: *Il Cortegiano* 4.62, in *Opere*, ed. C. Cordié (Milan: Ricciardi, 1960). See also Tullia d'Aragona's *Della infinità di Amore*, in *Trattati d'amore*, ed. G. Zonta (Bari: Laterza, 1912), wherein sight is said to be the noblest and most perfect sense (230), and Giuseppe Betussi, who says the ears are closer to the intellect than the eyes, among those senses which are capable of appreciating beauty: *Il Raverta*, in *Trattati d'amore*, ed. Zonta, 3–149, here 18. However, Betussi mentions the same three senses, sight, hearing, and mind, in his dialogue *La Leonora*, without claiming one is closer to the intellect than the others (*La Leonora*, ed. Zonta, 307–49, here 336). No theorist, to my knowledge, describes a process like Bigolina's, with its lower esteem for the sense of sight. For a discussion of this problem in an art-historical context, see M. Rogers, "The Decorum of Women's Beauty: Trissino, Firenzuola, Luigini and the Representation of Women in Sixteenth-Century Painting," *Renaissance Studies* 2 (1988): 47–75, here 71.

tengo, che per altra men di me bella io credessi che abbandonata m'havesti; quando certissima sono, ch'ella più di me virtuosa non sia. Hor dunque se di questa tua bella donna per la quale hai lasciato di amarmi, dovendoti da lei dilungare, un ritratto volesti portar teco, il quale la sua bellezza a gli occhi tuoi rappresentasse, come faresti quando ancora Apelle o Zeusi et gli altri eccellentissimi pittori fossero vivi, che più d'un ritratto potessero fare, overo facendone molti, che più d'una sola somiglianza della tua donna tenessero. Ahì ingrato et sconoscente, che pur son forzata a doverti così dire, et ben nel cuore infinito affanno mi preme, non già di dirloti, ma che tu m'habbi dato cagione che io l'habbia a dire! Dimmi adunque, ti prego, quanti ritratti ti trovi haver teco i quali la bellezza mia ti rappresentano tutti? Et ecco il loro miracolo grande, che quello che dar non ti può la tua bella donna in eterno, nè tutti i più eccellenti pittori, nè ancora la gran maestra Natura lo ti potrebbe dare, io già te l'ho dato; che quante volte miri, et consideri le tante et varie sorti di rime et prose che da me composte tieni nelle tue mani, tanti ritratti vedrai esser quelle, quantunque diversi fossero, li quali ciascun da per sè et tutti insieme quanta sia in me bellezza ti manifestano. Hor vedi che già ti ho fatto conoscere come le bellezze, le quali ciascun giorno tu poi vedere, quando in me et in molti miei ritratti con lo intelletto tuo ti degnassi mirare, più meritano d'esser da te amate et tenute care, che qual'altra maggior corporale bellezza esser si voglia. Ma so che potresti rispondermi che assai delle virtù mie ti compiaci, nondimeno che essendo giovine la cui natura è di non molto in amare nè desiderar cosa alcuna stabilirsi, anzi sempre di vedere et udir nove cose son vaghi; et perciò come giovine di variare, et veder nove et belle cose ti diletti. Deh Fabio mio, come ti veggo traviato per strani sentieri! Et dove voi tu ritrovare, quantunque in molti

beautiful, for I know you are not blind, and you would not have abandoned me if she were less beautiful than I am. And yet I am absolutely certain she is not more virtuous than I. Therefore, if you were to have to go far away from this beautiful lady of yours, for whom you have ceased loving me, you would want to bring along a portrait that would still show her beauty to your eyes, just as you would have done in the days when Apelles, Zeuxis, and other most excellent painters were alive.[18] These artists might produce more than one portrait, or perhaps they would make many of them and provide you with a variety of images of your lady. Oh, you are a thankless ingrate, to force me to speak to you in this way! It is not the mere act of telling you this that causes my heart such grief, but rather the fact that you have done things to make it necessary that I do so. Tell me then, I pray you, how many portraits do you have with you that show my beauty? Here is their great miracle: I have already given you something which your pretty lady cannot give you for all eternity, nor all of the most excellent painters, nor indeed that great artist, Nature. Every time you look upon and contemplate in your hands the many and varied works which I composed, both poetry and prose, you will see they are all portraits, even if they are each different; and each of them by itself, as well as all of them taken together, show you how much beauty there is inside of me. Now you see what I have already made plain to you: that those beautiful things which you can see in me every day (that is, at such times as you might deign to use your intellect to regard me and my many portraits), deserve more to be loved and held dear by you than any other greater physical beauty one could want to have. I know well what your answer could be: that you do take great pleasure in my virtue, but nevertheless you are young, and it is ever the nature of young people not to yearn for stability in loving or desiring anything; indeed they are always drawn to seeing and hearing new things. Therefore, as a young man, you delight in variation, and in seeing things that are new and lovely. O my Fabio, I see you are drawn down very strange paths! No matter

---

[18] Apelles (fourth century B.C.) and Zeuxis (late fifth century B.C.) were Greek painters who were highly regarded in ancient times, and as a consequence in the Renaissance as well (see Pliny, *Natural History* 35.61–66 and 35.79–97). The inadequacies of artistic representation as a means of preserving the memory of one's beloved is also a theme of Niccolò Franco's prose romance *Philena*; here the author imagines at first that only Titian or Michelangelo could properly depict Philena's beauty, only to conclude despairingly that no representation could ever be adequate, save that of the memory (*La Philena di M. Nicolo Franco* [Mantua: Ruffinelli, 1547], fols. 14v–18v).

lochi cerchi, et ricerchi cose così varie, così nove et così dilettevoli et belle, come meco dimorando, hai ritrovato sempre. Deh dimmi ti prego, qual volta ti ritrovasti mai dove io fosse, che cose nove, et dilettevoli non vedesti? Et forse tali (et so che no'l negherai) che ti hanno fatto più volte maravigliare.

"Adunque se in me sola molte cose nove, varie, et belle, et dilettevoli sempre ritrovi, a che dunque duri fatica per ricercarne altrove? Et dove forse nè di tal natura, nè di cotal perfettione di gran lunga ritrovar potrai; et meno che così inchinevoli fossero, a sempre rinovarsi per compiacerti. Et se forse ti persuadesti che questa tua novella donna per la quale, sanza alcuna pietade havermi, tante pene mi fai sostenere, più di me ti amasse, nè per alcun tempo più di me amar ti potesse, credi certo che grandemente t'ingannaresti; et faroti il tuo errore con aperte ragioni conoscere. Credo che sappi come l'amore et benevolenza co'l quale questo et quello amiam noi, non più altre si estende di quello che a noi par di conoscere che sia il merito di quel tale, che amiamo. Et più et meno amiamo di quello ci pare che quel merito vaglia, overo quanto siamo capaci a ricever la conoscenza del valor di quel merito, et daroti uno essempio, et darotelo tale che opporre non gli potrai.

how many places you search, and how often, where do you expect to find things as varied, as new, as delightful, and as beautiful as what you have always found by remaining with me? Oh, tell me, I pray you, on what occasion did you ever find yourself with me without seeing new and delightful things? Perhaps these things were such (and I know you will not deny this) that they made you marvel at me, more than once.

"Therefore, if in me alone you always find many new, varied, beautiful and delightful things, for what reason do you go to the trouble of looking for them anywhere else? There you will not, by any means, find these things to be of the same nature and perfection as mine are; and even less will they have the inclination mine have ever to renew themselves, with the aim of pleasing you. And if perhaps you persuaded yourself that this new woman of yours, on account of whom you have pitilessly made me suffer so much, loved you more than I (not that she could possibly have loved you more than I, even for a moment), I am certain that you greatly deceived yourself; and I will show you your error with clear reasoning. I believe you know that the affection and benevolence that we feel whenever we love someone go only so far, as far as we have convinced ourselves that the person we love deserves. We love either more or less, depending on our perception of the degree to which the beloved deserves to be loved, or to put it another way, we love as much as we are capable of understanding the worth of the beloved. I will give you an example, one that you will not be able to refute.

"Tu sai che nove sono e' chori de gli angeli delli quali come dicono i teologi, quello de' Serafini è il più supremo et più de gli altri vicino al sommo Iddio; et che quegli angeli più che gli altri penetrano ne' grandi secreti suoi, et perciò dicono che essendo vie più quelli conoscitori della infinita sua sapienza et bontà, perciò sono più ardenti assai nell'amore di esso Dio che quegli altri, nelli quali tanta eccellenza di conoscenza non si ritrova. Hor se dunque chi più conosce la perfettione della cosa amata più ama, come mi negherai che io più d'ogn'altra, et più perfettamente non t'ami? Quando io son certissima che da alcun' altra non è, nè esser potrebbe l'ottime interne tue parti così perfettamente come da me conosciute giamai; et non potendosi perfettamente amare quello, che perfettamente non è conosciuto, seguita adunque che io, la quale sola perfettamente ti conosco, etiandio sola perfettamente ti amo; il chè più volte a molti espressi segni innanzi che hora hai potuto conoscere. Et Dio voglia che cotesto tuo novello amore a peggior termine non t'habbi a condure, di quello che sin hora il mio t'ha condotto; dal quale più tosto avanzar che perderne potevi. Nè creggiomi che a te minor gloria fosse che da me fosti amato, di quella che io mi tenevo quando da te mi conoscevo d'esser amata. Et ben parmi che d'avantaggio dovresti conoscere, come io conosco, quanto io meriterei più da te che da ciascun'altro d'esser amata et tenuta in pregio. Nondimeno non potendo, nè volendo più oltre di quanto a te piace compiacermi, voglio perciò questo tuo novello piacere lasciarti godere in pace.

"Ma non mi dando il cuore di poter la grande ingiuria che io da te ricevo con li propri occhi vedere et sopportarla, ho eletto per minor mio male la propria Patria abbandonare et lasciare; et così sarai tu cagione, ch'ella resterà priva di tale, che forse un'altra simile non ne ritenerà seco. Onde nome d'ingrato meco con la Patria, et che è peggio assai teco stesso t'havrai acquistato. Gliè vero che insopportabile doglia sarammi lo scacciare, anzi più tosto svellere quel radicato et perfetto amore che nel mio afflitto cuore pose radice alhora, che le notabili tue virtudi me ne dieder cagione. Nè saprei a qual'altra gravissima doglia et affanno questo mio smisurato dolore assomigliar potesse, eccetto a quello che nella privatione d'alcuna delle proprie membra si sente, che picciolo, presso questo mio, reputo ciascun altro grande affanno, et cordoglio.

"Chè quando io considero al duol che ci preme quando Fortuna le facultadi nostre ci leva, overo quando d'alcuno de' nostri amici morte ci priva, parmi che

Urania: The Story of a Young Woman's Love

You know that there are nine choruses of angels. Of these, as the theologians say, the Seraphim are the highest and the closest of all to God Almighty, for they are the angels who know His secrets most profoundly.[19] Because of this, the theologians also assert that the Seraphim are very much more aware of God's infinite wisdom and goodness, and therefore they are more ardent in their love of Him than the other angels, in whom such excellent awareness does not reside. If it follows that one who knows more fully the perfection of the beloved object must also love more, how can you deny that I love you more than any other, and more perfectly? For I am certain that no one else knows, or ever could know, your excellent inner substance more perfectly than I do; and one cannot perfectly love what is not perfectly known. Therefore it follows that I, the only one who knows you perfectly, am also the only one who loves you perfectly, and this you have been able to understand on many occasions, through the signals which I formerly communicated to you. May God grant that this new love of yours bring you to no worse end than that to which my love has so far brought you. Indeed, from my love you stood to gain rather than to lose. I do not believe that you exulted any less in the love I gave you than I did, when first I knew you loved me. It seems clear to me that you should be well aware, just as I am, that I deserve to be loved and esteemed by you more than by any other man. Nevertheless, unless you take similar pleasure in it, I can find no satisfaction in this love; nor do I wish to. Therefore it is my intention to let you enjoy your new love in peace.

"But, since I lack the strength either to withstand or to contemplate the great injury I have received from you, I have chosen to lessen my pain by leaving my homeland. You will have been the cause of this: my country will be deprived of someone of great worth, and perhaps it will never see the likes of me again. For this reason you have made yourself an ingrate not only in my eyes, but in the eyes of our homeland; and what is worse, you have become an ingrate to yourself. It is true that it will be unbearably painful for me to banish, indeed tear out, the deep-rooted and perfect love which grew in my afflicted heart as soon as your remarkable virtues gave it cause. I could not imagine what other great pain and suffering would compare to this enormous affliction of mine, save the pain one feels at the loss of a limb. I would call all other sufferings and grief small, in comparison to mine.

"When I consider the pain which oppresses us whenever Fortune takes away our powers, or whenever death deprives us of one of our friends, it seems to me

---

[19] For a similar view of the place of the Seraphim in the celestial hierarchy, derived from the Pseudo-Dionysius, see Dante, *Convivio* 2.5.9.

non doveressemo, se dalla ragione venissemo regolati, di tai perdite attristarsene molto; et la ragione è questa, che regolando in noi con ragione gli affetti et desiderij nostri, con il loro fine misurandoli sempre, non è dubbio che a cosa alcuna non porressemo affettione et amore, se non quanto fosse da noi conosciuto che quella cosa giovar ci potesse, overo che con essi noi ritener la potessimo. Onde sapendo noi come le facultadi et ricchezze che possediamo non son nostre, ma di Fortuna, et che nel voler suo sta lo ritoglierle et darle qual'hor più le piace, et perciò all'amor nostro havendo i termini posti harressimo intentione che tanto l'amor di quelle durasse in noi, quanto in essa Fortuna durasse il voler di lasciarcele. Per la qual cosa avenirebbe, che qualunque volta lei ce le ritogliesse, essendo col mancar di quelle finito l'amore, non ne sentiressimo doglia alcuna, et così a punto della perdita per morte d'uno amico sarebbe. Chè se quando incominciamo ad amarlo tanto discorso et ragione havessimo in noi che ci bastasse a considerare come egli sia mortale, et come era prima a lui ordinata la morte che tra noi fosse l'amicitia contratta, noi compartiressimo l'amor nostro con la sua vita, overamente con quella di noi medesimi. Onde se avenisse poi che morte ce lo togliesse sapendo come egli era innanzi a lei che a noi dedicato, et ch'ella perciò non ci fa ingiuria alcuna, et havendo col termine della sua vita l'amor nostro compartito, assai quietamente cotal doglia passaressimo.

"Ma non così aviene nella privatione delle membra, la qual sola parmi che a questa disgiuntione d'amore, la quale hora mi sforzi a far teco, come cosa a questa più di ogn'altra somigliante, et propria io possi uguagliarla. Chè havendoci Natura questi nostri corpi di tante belle et differenti membra ornati con intentione ch'elle con essi noi si stiano, et che noi le possediamo sin tanto che la vita ci dura, convenevolissima cosa è perciò, che dovendo compartir l'amor co'l durarci di quelle, che per tutto il tempo della vita nostra cotal nostro amore in elle s'estenda; rendendosi noi securi, che sino a morte accompagnar ci debbano. Et perciò se per cagion di pessima sorte ci avien mai che di mano, di braccio, o d'occhio siam privi, si può pensare che l'affanno et il dolore, il quale per cagione di cotal privatione si sente incomparabile sia. Chè essendosi tutte le membra con l'anima nostra d'uno indissolubile amore concatenate et unite, si dee credere che all'asprissimo dolore, il quale nel disunire, troncare, et frangere tale unito et radicato amore si gusta niun'altro dolore eccetto il mio uguagliare si possa.

"Tale adunque, et non d'altra sorte debbi pensar Fabio mio, ch'esser debba l'affanno, et il duolo, il quale nel irradicare dal mio cuore il tenacissimo amore,

that we should not be too saddened by such losses, as long as our lives are regulated by reason. And this is the reason: if we regulate our affections and desires according to reason, and measure them constantly against their aims, there is no doubt that we would never show affection or love for anything that we know cannot do us any good, or that we know we cannot have. Therefore we are aware that the powers and riches we possess are not actually ours, but rather belong to Fortune; for what we gain and lose is subject to her power and whim.[20] Thus if we would place limits on our love for these things, such love would last only as long as Fortune's will to grant them to us lasted. Because of this, any time she took them away from us we would not feel any pain at all, since our love for them would end as soon as they were gone; and so it would also be if one of our friends were to be claimed by death. This is because from the moment we began to love him, our rational powers would be sufficient to make us realize that he was mortal. Just as death was ordained for him long before our friendship was formed, we would make our love last only as long as his life, or indeed as our own lives. Then, if it were to happen that Death, fully realizing that our friend lay more in his domain than in ours, came to claim him, it would cause us no grief whatever. Inasmuch as we had made our love for him last only as long as his life, we would quite tranquilly avoid grief at his loss.

"But such a thing does not occur when one loses one's limbs; and it seems to me that the separation of your love, which you have just forced upon me, resembles the loss of a limb more than anything else, and is indeed the equal of it. Nature has endowed our bodies with so many lovely and differing members, with the intention that they remain attached to us for as long as our lives should last. It is therefore most proper that love last as long as our limbs do, and that love extend itself through them for the duration of our lives: this assures us that these things will accompany us until our deaths. Thus if it ever happens that ill fortune causes us to be deprived of a hand, an arm, or an eye, one can imagine that the suffering and pain caused by such a privation would be incomparable. All of our members are conjoined and united with our souls in an indissoluble bond of love; for this reason, we must believe that the bitter suffering that one feels in detaching, severing, or shattering so bonded and deep-rooted a love could not possibly be equaled by any other pain, save that which I am feeling now.

"And so, my Fabio, you must not imagine that the suffering and woe, which come from uprooting from my heart this most tenacious love for you, could be

---

[20] See Boethius, *The Consolation of Philosophy* 2.1 (trans. Watts, 54–56).

che io ti porto, che havendo nel mio concetto un fermo proponimento formato, il quale era di tanto tempo amarti quanto io conoscessi che 'n te le nobilissime tue virtudi havessero albergo; le quali sapevo io di certo, che mentre ti durasse la vita non t'harrebbono mai a lasciare. Per la qual cosa, a somiglianza del Tempio della Pace, presso di me perpetuo cotale amore dover esser tenevo. Ma accorgendomi hora come non svelto o troncato è da te quell'amor che già mi portavi cotanto, ma più tosto dalla radice seccatosi; et conoscendo impossibile esser che io troppo longamente potesse viver, non essendo da te reamata, et io così smisuratamente t'amasse, conviemmi per salvar mia vita necessariamente lo smisurato amor ch'io ti porto a men di mezzo il camino, et ancor troppo verde troncare, svellere, et irradicare; et quanta la doglia che io provo, et ch'io son per provar debba esser, credo che le già dette tante ragioni la ti possano far manifesta. Nè più altra cosa diroti eccetto pregarti che nelle tue grandi felicitadi alcuna volta di me ti sovenga, come per tua cagione d'ogni mia pace mi trovo priva; et sovengati ancora, come già non ti sdegnasti chiamarmi Maestra. Il Cielo ogni tuo fatto prosperi, et ogni tuo desiderio a felice fine conduca."

Urania: The Story of a Young Woman's Love

any different from the sort I have just described. In my mind I had formed a firm proposal to love you for as long as I knew that your most noble virtues continued to reside in you; and I was certain that they would never leave you while you lived. Because of this I imagined such a love would last perpetually in me, like the Temple of Peace.[21] Now, however, I realize that the love you once bore me was not cut off, nor pulled up from the ground, but rather dried up at the roots. I know it is impossible for me to live long if you do not resume loving me, since I loved you so deeply; therefore if I am to save my life it is necessary for me to cut off, uproot, and tear out this all too green love, which I have borne for you only less than half of its intended course. I believe the amount of pain which I bear now, and will continue to bear, should be evident to you from the many reasons which I have already explained. I will say nothing more to you, save to pray that you remember me sometimes in the midst of your great happiness; and think of how on your account I find myself deprived of all peace. Remember also that at one time you did not disdain to call me your teacher. May Heaven allow all your deeds to prosper, and lead your every desire to a happy end."

---

[21] The Temple of Peace, in Rome, is mentioned by Pliny (*Natural History* 34.19, 35.36).

II

Scritta et sigillata c'hebbe la sua lunga lettera, la diede al servo acciò che a Fabio, sanz'altro dirli la appresentasse. Et indi de' panni che da huomo s'havea fatti vestitasi, et sopra un'ottimo roncino salita, nascosamente n'uscì di Salerno et verso Napoli prese il camino dove qualche giorno havea deliberato fermarsi. Ma come vi fu giunta, il che fu co'l maggior affanno che alcun'altro cuore amoroso sentisse giamai, sì dal patir cagionato, che ne' viaggi non si può fuggire, massimamente essendo avezza ad haver tutti e' suoi commodi sempre, et sì ancora per cagion dell'amoroso strale il quale fuor di misura la pungeva, che vedendo come ogn'hora più s'andava dilongando da quello il quale mal grado di lei stessa, era suo cuore et sua vita, et sanza il quale parevale che sanza spirto s'andasse. Così poco riposo parvele di ritrovare in quel loco, che non fermandovisi più d'un sol giorno, il seguente matino salita a cavallo di Napoli si partì, facendo disegno di andar primieramente a Roma, et poscia di parte in parte tutta la Italia cercare et vedere; così pensandosi, et con tal pensiero ingannando sè stessa, che per molte et varie cose vedere et per lo assai patire dovesse venir a sciemarsi quella accerba passione della quale Amor con sue proprie mani il suo cuor le havea colmo, non sovenendole (quantunque molte isperienze havesse vedute) come egli ne' gentil cuori con maggior forza et valore, ne' più grandi affanni si facesse sentire.

Hora essendo costei di Napoli uscita, et così fuor di sè che non più accorgendosi che a cavallo fosse, havea abbandonata la briglia et lasciavalo gire di qual passo et in qual parte più gli piaceva. Et erasi mal grado suo, con l'animo tornata a rivedere lo ingrato suo amante, et indi aprendo le fonti de gli occhi alle lagrime, et alle parole sciogliendo la lingua, incominciò un così pietoso lamento, c'harrebbe ogni crudel cuore mosso a pietade, dolendosi del suo destino, et di Amore, me vie

II

When she had written and sealed her long letter she gave it to her servant so that he could present it to Fabio without saying anything else to him. Then she dressed in the men's clothes that she had prepared, mounted upon an excellent horse, and secretly departed from Salerno. She took the road to Naples, where she had planned to stay a few days. But she arrived there having suffered the greatest woe that any amorous heart had ever experienced; and this was partly due to the discomforts which one cannot avoid while traveling, especially in her case, since she had always been used to having her amenities. But it was also due to the arrow of Love, which pierced her very deeply even though she saw she was continually getting farther away from him who was the cause of it. In spite of herself, he was her heart and her very life: without him, it seemed to her that she was wandering about deprived of her spirit. And so she found little rest in Naples, and stopped there for only one day. The next morning she got on her horse and left Naples, planning to go first to Rome, and after that seek out and visit all the places in Italy. Thinking in these terms she deceived herself into believing that by seeing much, and suffering much, she could reduce the bitter passion that Love had poured into her heart with his own hands. Despite the many experiences she had witnessed, she did not remember that Love makes himself felt with greater force and valor, and greater suffering, in gentle hearts.

Now having left Naples she was so out of her mind that she no longer realized she was on horseback, so she released her hold on the reins and let the horse wander at whatever pace it wanted, and in whatever place. Her spirit had gone back to contemplating her ungrateful lover, in spite of herself; so she opened the fountains of her eyes to tears, loosened her tongue to form words, and began so piteous a lament that it would have moved any cruel heart to compassion. She

più assai di Fabio, che a cotal reo termine l'haveva condotta; et tra l'altre molte sue lamentevoli parole così diceva:

"Deh Fabio mio, come esser può che 'n così corto spatio di tempo il tuo cuore cotanto grande mutatione habbia fatto? Chè s'io voglio ad alcuna subita cosa rassomigliarla, così subita è ella stata che a null'altra cosa eccetto al baleno rassomigliar non la posso. Chè così come il baleno co'l suo tanto splendore in un punto gli occhi ci abbaglia, et in quello istesso punto da noi dipartendosi come ciechi ci lascia, così tu medesimamente in me meschina ha operato; chè havendo lo splendor dell'eccellentissime tue virtudi, et il valor della tua gratia lo mio cuore abbagliato, a pena d'esserti in gratia m'accorsi, che da quella esser abbandonata m'avidi. Deh perchè non mi è conceduto, Fabio mio, che tu hora potessi vedere come della tua luce ritrovandomi priva, io sia cieca nel tutto rimasa; onde a me tosto quello avenirà che ad ogni cieco, et sanza guida avenir suole, che non sapendo ove si vadi, o in fossa, o in fiume dove la vita vi lascia trabocca. So ben certo che tu sai come tu solo eri mia luce, et che già t'eri accorto come la luce tua in me rilucendo faceva la luce mia di doppia luce tralucere, et che se più nell'amarmi perseveravi, c'harrei cose per tuo amore maravigliose operate. Et dove pensi tu ritrovar donna più mai, che come io l'harrei fatto, così volontieri lo facesse? Overamente, che quanto io sono, fosse atta con mille modi le eccellenti tue virtudi in carte lodare, come tra le tue mani già buon'arra n'havevi. Ma e' mi convien questo amarissimo calice con patienza bere, poi che io conosco il mio destino esser tale. Nondimeno assai più te, che'l mio destino, ne incolpo, chè potendo il reo suo corso impedire, sopra di me l'hai lasciato ogni sua malvagia influenza sfocare. Chè come molti savi dicono, l'astri del cielo sono da sapienti predominati, et sforzati; et quale è più di te nella professione tua sapiente, nè più di me meritevole teco, et perciò alcuna iscusa non si potrebbe trovare la qual meco salvar ti potesse, che pur tu solo d'ogni mio mal sei cagione."

Queste et molte altre simili affettuose parole con grande spargimento di lagrime andava l'innamorata Urania dicendo; et tai focosi sospiri le usciano fuori che parea d'intorno a lei che l'aria accender si volesse, et havendo per più di sei hore sempre cavalcato sanza mai accorgersi quello si facesse, o in qual parte s'andasse, nè accorta se ne sarebbe ancora, se non che all'entrar di un piacevol boschetto dove

URANIA: THE STORY OF A YOUNG WOMAN'S LOVE

lamented her destiny, and Love; but mostly she lamented Fabio who had brought her to such a wretched pass. Among her many plaintive words, she said these:

"O my Fabio, how can it be that in so short a span of time your heart has changed so completely? For if I am to compare your heart to any swift thing, I can find nothing to match it save a thunderbolt: just as a thunderbolt dazzles our eyes in an instant with its brilliance, and in that same instant departs, leaving us blinded, so have you dealt with me, wretch that I am. For the brilliance of your most excellent virtues and the power of your grace dazzled my heart, and no sooner did I realize I was in your favor, than I saw I was out of it. O why, my Fabio, is it not granted to me that you should see how completely blind I remain, now that I find myself deprived of your light? A blind man who lacks a guide usually does not know where he is going, and thus falls into a ditch or a river,[22] wherein he loses his life; and the same will shortly happen to me. I am certain that you know that you alone were my light. I am likewise certain that you were aware how this light of yours was resplendent within me, and thereby made my own light shine forth at twice its power; moreover, I believe you knew that if you persevered in loving me, I would have done marvelous deeds in the name of your love. Where do you think you will ever find another woman who would willingly do what I would have done? Or who would be as ready as I am to praise your excellent virtues in a thousand different ways, in writing? You have already received fine guarantees that I would do this. But it is proper that I drink from this most bitter of chalices with patience, for I know it is my destiny. Nevertheless I blame you far more than I blame destiny: you were in a position to stop its evil course, and yet you allowed it to bring all its wicked effects down upon me. Many wise men say that the stars of heaven are dominated by the wise,[23] and can be controlled by them; and who is wiser in your profession than you are, and who is more worthy of you than I? Thus no excuse may be found which could exonerate you in my eyes, for you are the sole cause of all my ill fortune."

All the while the lovesick Urania went on saying these and many other similar lover's words she wept copious tears, and sent forth such hot sighs that it seemed the very air around her wished to ignite. She rode on for more than six hours ever unaware of what she was doing or where she was going; nor would she ever have known, if she had not entered a pretty little wood. A very lovely spring was

---

[22] Cfr. Matthew 15:14, and Luke 6:34.
[23] This is the well-known proverb "Sapiens dominabitur astris," often found as a heraldic device (see L. A. Smoller, *History, Prophecy, and the Stars: The Christian Astrology of Pierre d'Ailly, 1350–1420* [Princeton: Princeton University Press, 1994], 30).

era una bellissima fonte, la quale da verdi et diritti alberi che la circondavano era da meridionali raggi del sole difesa. Chè a punto in quell'hora, di poco il mezzo giorno passava, da due bellissime giovani donne di cinque che erano a quel bel fonte ridotte, venne da una per le redini del cavallo arrestata, et dall'altra per uno de' bracci presa, che tanto l'hebbono a scuotere, che pur in se stessa fu ritornata. Per la qual cosa fu da infinita maraviglia et vergogna assalita, come non sapendo in qual parte si ritrovasse, et che fosse stata in tale esser fuori di sè da quelle belle donne compresa. Et perciò tutta di vermiglio colore, per cagion della ricevuta vergogna la faccia tingendosi, con dolce riso, et con un rotto sospiro in cotal forma a quelle che arrestata l'havevano disse:

"Belle donne, se'l proprio giudicio non m'inganna, a quello che giovani et belle vi veggio, che possiate facilmente essere innamorate io giudico. Il che se è vero, spero che ne' cuori di ciascuna di voi (havendo provato in sè stessa quanto siano d'estremo potere le passioni amorose) più tosto pietà che scherno per havermi in cotal modo colto, potrò ritrovare."

Le belle donne, che tale et non altrimenti desideravano ch'egli si fosse, perciò quella che delle due era più ardita in cotal modo gli rispose, "Vago et amoroso giovine, gli è vero che la pietà primieramente, la quale punse e' cuori di tutte noi vedendoti in tai termini, ci mosse et spinse a doverti ritornare in te stesso. Ma un'altra cagione ci inviò ancora a dover fare un cotale effetto, la quale a te scopriremo quando per tua cortesia farci manifesto ti piaccia (non essendoti perciò disconcio) di qual paese sei, il tuo nome, di ove vieni et vai, et quale sia la tua professione."

"Gentilissime donne," rispose la Urania, "il manifestarvi l'esser mio a me poco disconcio può donare, et a voi lo intenderlo men utile creggiomi che porger vi debba. Chè ritrovandomi di così picciolo grido, come mi trovo, quando ben quale io mi sia v'habbia detto, non perciò più mi conoscerete di quello che nel semplice vedere dianzi mi conosceste, nondimeno per farvi conoscere quanto d'ubidir belle donne mi compiaccio, quello da me ricercato vi farò manifesto.

"Dovete dunque sapere il paese dove io nacqui esser molto da queste parti distante, et quasi ne' confini della Italia in un poco raccordato et assai humile castelletto chiamato per nome Geraci.[24] Fabio è il mio nome, et da quelle parti c'hora dissi, per cagione di contraria sorte amorosa mi parto. Dove vado non lo so, per non havere al partir mio altri che Fortuna et il destino tolti per guida, come alli segnali esservene già accorte potete; et la professione mia già tutta fu con

---

[24] This name is written in Roman square capitals in T (fol. 41v).

URANIA: THE STORY OF A YOUNG WOMAN'S LOVE

there, protected from the rays of the noonday sun by the straight green trees which surrounded it. At exactly that moment, a little past noon, Urania was stopped by two very beautiful young women, from a group of five women who had arrived at the spring earlier. One of these stopped her by seizing the reins of her horse, while another took hold of one of her arms; then they shook her so hard that she came to her senses. Urania was overcome with infinite wonder and shame, since she did not know where she was, nor how she came to be in such a situation; that is, out of her senses and apprehended by the lovely women. Because of the shame she felt, her face flushed a bright red color. With a sweet laugh and a broken sigh, she spoke thus to those who had stopped her:

"Lovely ladies, if my judgment does not deceive me, I believe that you could easily be in love, as young and pretty as you are. If this is true, and each one of you has felt the extreme power of the passions of love, then I hope that in your hearts I will find pity instead of disdain, for the state in which you have found me."

The lovely ladies desired only that Urania's hope be fulfilled. The bolder of the two answered, "Handsome and lovestruck youth, it truly was pity, piercing the hearts of us all when we saw you reduced to such extremes, that primarily motivated us to make you return to your senses. But another reason drove us to do this, and we will reveal it to you as soon as it may please you courteously to let us know (as long as you do not mind) your country of origin, your name, whence you have come and where you are going, and what your profession might be."

"Most gentle ladies," replied Urania. "It is hardly a problem for me to reveal my identity to you, and I believe that hearing it will not help you much, for I am of so little renown that when I tell you who I am you will not know me any better than you did before, when you simply saw me stand before you. Nevertheless, just to show you how much pleasure I take in obeying beautiful ladies, I will reveal to you the things you seek.

"You must know then that the land in which I was born is very far away from these parts, almost on the borders of Italy. I come from a scarcely known, very humble little castle called Geraci; Fabio is my name. I am leaving that land on account of my bad fortune in affairs of love. I do not know where I am going, since upon my departure I took no other guides but fortune and destiny; and you can see the signs of this in my appearance. My profession was formerly dedicated

sommo studio nelle volgari lettere posta, et di compor rime et prose dilettandomi assai; ma hora in ramarichi, in singulti, in lagrime, et in sospiri amorosi tutta tramutata si trova. Et se in cosa alcuna quale io mi sia vi pensate che per voi possa valere, con quella medesima libertà mi vi offero a valervene, con la quale voi tutte, una con l'altra fareste."

Le Gentildonne udendolo così cortesemente parlare un sommo contento ne presero, et perciò quella che ancora parlato gli havea così di novo gli disse: "Già non si può negare, gentilissimo giovine, che tutti que' cuori che da dovero amano, da dovero cortesi non siano, et d'ogni virtù soggetti in ciascun loco non cerchino dimostrarsi, come in te manifesto hora si vede, della quale cortesissima offerta quelle gratie te ne rendiamo, che maggiori da noi render si ponno, et il tuo cortese offerire accettiamo, et vogliamoti pregare che ti piaccia di darci in dono un consiglio sopra una determination nella quale tutt'hoggi affaticate tutte si siamo; ne perciò alcun frutto habbiam fatto. Del qual dono se ti è in piacere di sodisfarci, sarai contento da cavallo smontando con esse noi presso questo bel fonte sedere, del qual loco spero non partiremo che da te chiare et sodisfatte ritroveremosi, come da quello, il quale sì per scienza qual per isperienza sapendone assai, ottimamente ci potrà insegnare et ammaestrare."

Fabio, che di tal nome la chiameremo per hora, intendendo il desiderio di quelle donne, subitamente da cavallo discese, et essendo da tutte loro gratiosamente raccolto, poi che nel mezzo d'elle si fu assettato, così incominciò a dire. "Belle donne, quantunque i consigli miei non dovrebbono meritare di esser d'altrui come buoni seguiti, quando per cagione del reo consiglio, il quale ho dato a me stesso, ignudo d'ogni pace et d'ogni bene mi trovo. Nondimeno, perchè molti di cotal sorte di natura sono, li quali savi et ottimi consigli sanno dare ad altrui, et per loro stessi a' peggiori si pigliano sempre; et perciò persuadendomi d'esser io uno di quelli m'ingegnerò (quantunque il saper mio poco innanzi si estenda) di darvi consiglio; di qual sorte si sia quello, che da me ricercate, migliore assai di quello che per me stesso m'habbi mai preso. Hor dite adunque, che altro che conpiacervi non desidero."

Le gentildonne udendolo cotanto amorevolmente verso loro parlare, di buonissimo cuore lo ringratiorono tutte; et colei poscia, la quale parlato havea sempre

to the highest studies of vernacular literature, and I once took great delight in composing works in poetry and prose; now, however, it has completely converted itself into laments, sobs, tears, and amorous sighs. If you think knowing who I am can be of any value to you, I offer you my services with the same willingness that you would each employ on behalf of one another."

The gentle ladies became quite content, hearing the man speak in so courtly a fashion. So the same one who had spoken before spoke to him once again. "Most noble youth, one cannot deny that all those hearts that truly love are truly courtly, and that no matter where they may be, they seek to show that they are inclined to every virtue; these qualities can be clearly seen in you now. We accept your most polite offer, and give you the greatest thanks we can for it; we also pray that it please you to give us as a gift your advice regarding a question which we have been laboring over, without resolution, all day. If you are willing to satisfy us with this gift, please be content to dismount from your horse and sit with us beside the spring, from which I hope we will not depart until such a time as we may consider ourselves enlightened and satisfied by you. I hope you will be the man who will be able to teach and instruct us in a most excellent fashion, and who will know a great deal about our problem, either through learning, or through experience."

Fabio, by which name we will refer to her for the time being, understood the desire of those women, and descended from the horse.[25] After being graciously welcomed by them he sat down in their midst, and began to speak. "Lovely ladies, my advice should not deserve to be followed as if it were the best, inasmuch as I am presently deprived of all peace and happiness on account of the bad advice which I have given myself. Nevertheless there are many who are by nature wise and capable of giving excellent advice to others, yet incline toward poor judgment in their own affairs; and I have persuaded myself that I am one of these. Still, I will make every effort to give you advice, even though my knowledge does not go very far. Whatever counsel you might seek from me, it will be much better than any which I have ever given myself. Now speak, for my only desire is to please you."

When the gentle ladies had heard him speak so fondly to them, they thanked him with all their hearts. Then the one who had spoken to him earlier addressed

---

[25] After this sentence, all pronouns and adjectives in the text which refer to Urania become masculine, and remain so until the end of the episode of the five ladies. For a study of grammatical shifts of gender in narratives involving women disguised as men see Nissen, "The Motif of the Woman in Male Disguise from Boccaccio to Bigolina."

seguitò in tal guisa il suo dire. "Valoroso giovine, noi siam qui cinque donne raccolte d'assai nobili famiglie di Napoli, che non meno di carnal sorelle tutte cinque insieme si amiamo. Et perchè da noi non fu mai considerato come Amor tra humani cosa necessarijssima[26] fosse, et che se in molte cose nuoce, in molte più può giovare si siamo perciò sino a questa presente hora sempre conservate lontane da ogni pensiero amoroso, quantunque molti, et molti ci siano di quelli, che con ogni loro ingegno, et sapere s'affaticano per farci credere che di cuore ci amano, et noi nondimeno sempre ostinate et ritrose ad ogni loro richiesta et preghiera ce gli siam dimostrate.

"Ma considerando poscia tra noi come Amore è grandissimo incitamento alla virtù, et come chi non è innamorato, quasi alla similitudine di corpo sanza spirto si può tenere; et particolarmente noi donne, che levateci dalla diligenza di coteste nostre famigliari cure, io non so veder da quel, che noi siamo, poi che voi huomini acciò che la gloria tutta sia di voi soli ci impedite che nelle discipline delle lettere, et nelle belle et utili scienze si possiamo essercitare. Onde se Amor qualche poco in noi non desta lo ingegno, questa nostra, per lo vero, infelicissima vita passiamo ignude et prive d'ogni piacere, et sapere; et peggio è ancora, che le più volte la nostra troppa bontà, presso voi altri huomini nome di sciocche ci acquista.

"Ma lasciamo pur cotal dire, poi che al presente poco ci importa, et seguitiamo quello, che a noi è d'importanza grandissima. Dico adunque come dopo che tra noi tutte varij et diversi discorsi habbiam fatti, tutte in una sola determinatione si siamo risolte; la quale è di volere al tutto ciascuna di noi ritrovarsi uno amante. Ma tale vorressimo ch'egli fosse, che dopo che donate se gli fossemo, non havessimo poi cagione (come molte soglion far) di pentirsi. Gli è vero che come pur hora ti dicevo, che da molti di diverse qualità, et sorti ciascuna di noi vien guardata, et sollecitata, ma fuor di misura temendo d'errare, che non potendosi ne' cuori de gli huomini vedere, per lo quale certificar si potessimo se quelle loro amorose dimostrationi sono effettive, o pure apparenti, perciò siamo in dubbio a quali di tanti debbiamo per nostro meglio appigliarci.

"Onde per terminare una così grande questione, et chè da alcun' altro fatto non fossemo disturbate, hoggi in questo loco sole ci siamo ridotte, nè altro sino alla tua gionta habbiam fatto che hora una di noi dire, et hor l'altra soggiongere, et ragione a ragione aggiongendo, nè mai perciò si siam potute accordar, nè risolversi di qual sorte et conditione debbe la donna eleggersi amante. Perchè tale di

---

[26] This unconventional spelling, with doubling of the *i* to reflect the addition of the absolute superlative ending, occurs in both mss. (T fol. 43v; P fol. 46r).

him again, with these words: "Valorous youth, we are five women of very noble Neapolitan families all gathered together, and we are no less fond of each other than real sisters. We have never given consideration to the fact that love is a most necessary thing between people, and that even if it causes harm in some respects, in many more it does good; because of this, until now we have always kept ourselves far from any thought of love. A great many men strive to convince us that they love us with all their hearts, yet we are continually obstinate, and reluctant to accede to any of their pleas and requests.

"But then, we have also considered how love is so great an incitement to virtue, and how one who is not in love may be regarded as a body without spirit. This is particularly true of us women, for if you take away the responsibility of our duties to family, I do not know what would be left of us. You men keep us from working in the field of literature and in the sciences, both aesthetic and practical, so that all the glory they bestow is yours alone; therefore we spend our lives, which are truly unhappy, deprived of all pleasure and knowledge, unless love awakens our wits to some extent. And what is worse, we are mostly thought of as foolish by you men, on account of our inherent great kindness.

"But let us leave aside such things, which are of little importance at present, and return to that issue which matters so very much to us. After all of the varied and diverse arguments which we have been putting forth, we have all reached a single conclusion: and that is, each one of us wishes to find herself a lover. But we wish this lover to be the kind of man who will not afterwards give us cause to regret, as is true for so many women, that we have given our hearts to him. It is true, as I was telling you a moment ago, that each of us has been looked at and sought after by many men of diverse types and qualities. However, we are all very much afraid of making a mistake, since we cannot see into the hearts of these men in order to verify, if that be at all possible, whether their demonstrations of love are heartfelt or superficial; therefore we are in doubt as to which of these men is best for us to accept.

"We came to this place today alone, in order to resolve this great question without being disturbed by any other concern. We have done nothing else but this until your arrival: now one of us would speak, then another would have her say, with argument added to argument; yet we have not been able to come to an agreement or resolve the question of which sort of lover a woman should choose.

noi dice che la donna dovrebbe più tosto vecchio amante, che giovine eleggersi; imperciò che oltre che stabile et fedele le sarà sempre (la qual cosa rarissime volte in giovine si può vedere) le molte isperienze passate et vedute saranno cagione ancora ch'egli molto meglio saprà sè stesso, et l'amata sua donna ne gli occorrenti pericoli con prudenza et discorso salvare, et forse prevenirli ancora. Et tale dice poi che meglio è assai che l'amante sia giovine poi che, come più volte per isperienza si vede ne' casi amorosi, più tosto una buona sorte che molti savi avisi giova. Et perciò assai meglio è che l'amante sia giovine, il quale per virtù dell'ardir del suo cuore dalla giovanezza cagionato, sanza piangere il male assai prima che gionga, in gioco et festa l'amata sua terrà sempre; il che non farà il vecchio amante, il quale essendo di tema et dubbio soggetto, dalla gelata vecchiezza cagionato, già fatto presago che egli homai più non debbe haver bene, piange, et sospira i mesi, et gli anni innanzi che 'l male, ch'egli teme d'havere gl' incontri.

"Alcuna altra di noi dice poi che al parer suo nè molto giovine, nè ancor troppo vecchio dovrebbe esser l'amante dalla donna eletto, ma che dell'uno et dell'altro partecipasse. Imperciò che molto giovine essendo, è gran pericolo che 'l troppo ardir del suo cuore, in cosa men che buona traboccar non lo faci; et troppo vecchio ritrovandosi, nel molto timor non venghi a confondersi. Onde se dell'una parte et dell'altra sarà partecipe, avenirà che quanto la ragion porta, temerà gli pericoli et con ogni suo ingegno cercherà di schermirli, et pur quando verranno valerà con ardito cuore per affrontarli et ribatterli.

"Un' altra dice poscia che voglia di quale etade l'amante si sia somma avvertenza si debbe havere, ch'egli per due cagioni sia nobile, et ricco. Ch' egli sia nobile acciò che quando per alcun tempo il fallo di cotal donna (come spesse volte aviene) si venisse a scoprire, non venghi quella doppia vergogna a ricevere che soglion ricever quelle, le quali ad huomini ignobili, et vili hanno gli loro amori donati. Et poi che sia ricco, acciò che in mille sinistri casi, li quali ponno occorrere, con denari et tesori possi l'amata sua donna coprire, et difendere.

"Ma l'ultima poscia a questa di parere in estremo contraria, dice che ogni donna accorta, la quale desidera d'haver amante per sodisfattione et piacer di sè stessa et non d'altrui, debbe ogni suo studio porre, et con somma diligenza cercar di tutti que' disturbi fuggire, i quali questo vario Amore suole ne' cuori amorosi seminar spesso, cioè gelosia, dubbio, tema, et sospetto; et perciò debbe la donna eleggersi giovine amante, ma di minor conditione ch' ella non è, et che più tosto che ricco, sia povero. Imperciò che cotal giovine conoscendosi per cagione dell'humile sua conditione, di quella nobile donna indegno, et da lei vedendosi amato, tanto nel suo amor compiacerassi che sempre temendo di perderla, et che da

Urania: The Story of a Young Woman's Love

One of us says that a woman should select an older lover rather than a young one, and not only because he will be more reliable and faithful to her (which is only rarely the case with the young). The older lover's many experiences in life will also allow him to employ prudence and clever speech in order to save both himself and his beloved lady from eventual dangers, and perhaps even prevent them in the first place. Then another of us asserts that it is much better that the lover be young, since experience often shows that success in love affairs is more often due to good luck than to wise advice. A young lover is better because his youth imparts boldness to his heart, and thus he will refrain from weeping about ills long before they ever come about; moreover, he will always remain playful and festive in the presence of his beloved lady. This the old lover will not do, for he is subject to the fear and doubt brought on by frigid old age. Since he already has forebodings that nothing good will ever happen to him again, he weeps and sighs over the months and years that remain before he will encounter the fate that he fears.

"Then, another among us says that in her opinion the lover chosen by the woman should be neither too young nor too old, but rather should have qualities of both extremes. For if he is too young, there is a great danger that his heart will be too headstrong, leading him to excess, and to some improper deed. If he is too old he may well be confused by great fears. Yet if he shares the qualities of both youth and advanced age, he will fear dangers only as far as it is reasonable to do so, and he will use all his skill to fend them off; and even if he must meet them, his heart will be bold enough to allow him to confront them and defeat them.

"Yet another says, no matter how old the lover is, the most important thing is that he be noble and rich, and there are two reasons for this. He should be noble, so that if the lady were ever discovered to have committed some fault (as often happens), she will not feel the double shame that typically comes to those who have given their love to ignoble and lowborn men. He should also be rich, so that he can shield and defend his beloved lady with money and treasure in the event of one of those myriad grim situations that might arise.

"The last among us declares herself completely opposed to the last opinion. She says that every wise woman who wishes to have a lover for her own satisfaction and pleasure, and not that of others, should use all her wiles and keen diligence to flee from all the disruptions which fickle Love is accustomed to sow so frequently in loving hearts; namely, jealousy, doubt, fear, and suspicion. Therefore the woman must choose a young lover, but one of lower station than she, and poor instead of rich. Such a youth will know that he is unworthy of the noble woman on account of his humble state, so when he sees that she loves him he will do his utmost to please her when he returns her love. Since he will always be

qualche un'altro di lui più degno cotanto suo contento levato gli sia, più tosto che una sol picciola offesa farle, torrebbe mille volte a morire; et così quella donna di non perder il suo caro amante essendo secura, in pace, et longamente goderà lo suo amore.

"Hor dunque vedendo amoroso giovine, come per cagione di tante differenti openioni non potevamo accordarsi, et già disperate essendo di dover più ritrovare alcun mezzo, che questi nostri discordanti pareri accordar potesse, da questo loco, nel quale tutt'hoggi sanza alcun profitto fare siam state, ci volevamo partire. Ma havendoti assai dalla longa veduto, et a molti segnali ciascuna di noi giudicandoti innamorato facessimo perciò subita deliberatione, se qualche cortesia potevamo comprender in te, di chiederti in singolar dono, che ti fosse in piacere consigliarci, anzi liberamente quello insegnarci, del quale per la poca isperienza ignorantissime tutte ne siamo; ciò è, che havendo ciascuna di noi al tutto deliberato di non più star sanza amante, di quale etade, et conditione lo si debbiamo eleggere, et poscia qual modo debbiamo tenere, prima che di noi libero dono gli facciamo, acciò certificar se potessimo se da dovero siamo da loro amate o se pur fingono. Già sappiamo che essendo, come sei, innamorato, da alcun' altro non potressimo come da te ritrovar più sano et più verace consiglio; hor dunque dalla tua grande cortesia pigliando speranza aspettiamo la tanto da noi desiata risposta." Et qui la bella donna pose fine al suo dire.

Fabio, come vide la donna tacere, mandando primamente un grandissimo sospiro dal petto, in cotal modo poscia diede principio anch'egli al suo parlare. "Gratiose donne, di troppo grande importanza è il carico che dato m'havete, et da dover esser sostenuto da più forti homeri che i miei non sono. Gli è vero che innamorato mi trovo, et forse più assai di quello alcuna di voi si pensa, ma non veggio perciò che l'esser grandemente innamorato sia quello, che tale inteligenza mi presti, sì che per insegnarvi cose di così gran stima mi vaglia.

"Ma ben dirò questo, donne mie care, che a me parrebbe che essendo stato da voi veduto et compreso nel modo, che fuor di me stesso mi vedeste, et quasi somigliante ad un morto, dovrebbe esservi uno essempio, il quale più tosto vi inducesse a cercar di dispaniarvi quando nell'amorosa pania vi ritrovaste, che ritrovandovi fuori durar fatica per potervi entrare. Et pensatevi donne mie, se io che sono huomo, tanta amarissima pena per cagion d'Amore patisco; quanto maggiormente a voi, che donne sète, le quali io non dubito che assai più di me, di minor valore et forze havete gli animi vostri, in estremo amare vi si faranno sentire. Et Dio sa

URANIA: THE STORY OF A YOUNG WOMAN'S LOVE

afraid of losing her, of having someone else who is worthier than he take so much happiness away from him, he will prefer to die a thousand times rather than offend her in the slightest. Thus the lady, assured of never losing her dear lover, will long enjoy the love affair with peace of mind.

"So now you see, amorous youth, how it is we could not reach an agreement on account of these many differing judgments, and why, having become desperate, we had to find some means which could reconcile our discordant opinions. We wanted to leave this place, in which we have remained all day without profit. But when we saw you in the distance, we each judged you to be in love on account of the signals you displayed. So we immediately decided to ask you for a singular gift, provided that we could discern a measure of courtesy in you: we wanted to know if it would be your pleasure to advise us, indeed, freely teach us, about that which we are all most ignorant because of our lack of experience. As each of us has decided no longer to go without a lover, we wish you would teach us what his age and status should be, and then how we must act before freely bestowing ourselves upon these men, in order that we may be certain whether they really love us or are just feigning. You are in love, and thus we know we could never get truer and more beneficial advice from anyone else than from you. So now, drawing our hope from your great courtesy, we await the response for which we yearn." Here the lovely lady ended her speech.

When Fabio saw the lady fall silent, he heaved at first a great sigh, then began his own speech in return. "Gracious ladies, the weighty task which you lay upon me is of such great importance that it ought to be sustained by stronger shoulders than mine. It is true that I find myself in love, and perhaps more deeply than any of you imagine; nonetheless I do not see how being in love is sufficient in itself to lend me the wisdom that would allow me to teach you about such precious things.

"But I will say this, my dear ladies: since you saw me and understood from my appearance that I was out of my senses, and almost like a dead man, it seems to me that this ought to better serve as an example to inspire you to try to free yourselves from the birdlime of love, should you fall into it, and not make every effort to get stuck there while you are still free. And just think, my ladies, I am a man, and yet I suffer so much bitter grief for love: I do not doubt it will be much worse for you to fall into love's extreme throes, for you are women, endowed with souls less stout and strong. God knows how much it grieves me to have to

quanto mi duole di dovervi dir quello che volendo fedelmente consigliarvi, sono astretto a doverlovi dire; sì perchè contra al mio sesso dirò, come etiandio, perchè gli amorosi vostri cuori verrò a conturbare.

"Dico adunque donne belle che quantunque paia, come è per certo, che nelle leggi amorose, et tra l'uno et l'altro amante poca fede et men stabilità di usar si costuma, nondimeno (et pur forza è ch'io lo dica) minor fede, et maggiore instabilità ne gli huomini, che nelle donne si trovano sempre. Et quando altra isperienza non lo dovesse far manifesto, dovrebbe manifestarlovi le antiche istorie, le quali tante, et in tanti diversi lochi di cotali amorosi scempi[27] gridano; et pur in ciascun loco vederete le infelici donne della infedeltà de gli huomini sempre dolersi, dove rarissime volte si vede che gl'huomini habbino da dolersi delle donne cagione. Et questo aviene per la influenza de' più benigni pianeti, et per maggior partecipatione de gli elementi più molli nelle donne che ne gli huomini, li quali più benigne, et compassionevoli verso chi le ama le fanno, che all'incontro d'una donna infedele, mille infedelissimi huomini ritrovarete. Et all'incontro di mille donne fedeli, a gran fatica un solo fedel' huomo si potrà ritrovare; il quale poi per mala sua sorte, in quella sola infedele, tra mille fedel donne abbatterassi; come a me meschino è avenuto.

"Et perciò il miglior consiglio che dar vi potesse sarebbe, donne mie, che tanto da questo empio Amore vi dilongaste, quanto di farlovi vicino havete pensiero. Nondimeno poi che nell'aria vi conosco che pur di seguirlo sète al tutto disposte m'affaticherò a darvi quel consiglio, che a me parrà che men dannoso vi possa essere: persuadendomi che Amore in tutti i tempi non possa altro che danno recare.

"Dico adunque che quantunque (come ho già detto) Amore sia sempre reo, debbe nondimeno la persona, che a seguirlo si dispone, ogni suo ingegno porvi per farlo men reo che possibile sia. Et questo sarà quando una somma diligenza, sì l'huomo userà nello eleggersi donna, qual la donna nello eleggersi huomo amante. Assai bene ho intesi i discordanti vostri pareri; li quali, per non havere alcuna di voi quella parte toccata, la qual più dell'altre assai era mestieri che toccata fosse; voglio perciò tutti lasciarli da parte. Et dirò così, che a me non pare che tanto debbiate haver cura alla età, nobilitade, o ricchezza di quello che elegger per amante vi volete, quanto maggiormente dovete esser bene avertite che d'ottimi costumi sia ornato, et di qualche particolar virtù si diletti. Ma sopra tutto dovete

---

[27] *esempi* (the meaning here follows that of the Latin etymon *exempla*, rather than modern usage).

tell you this, for even though I wish to give you faithful advice, I am forced to speak against my own sex, and moreover what I will say will disturb your amorous hearts.

"Thus I say, lovely ladies, no matter how much it seems certain that between all lovers little faith and even less steadfastness are typically displayed with regard to the laws of love, nevertheless (and I am forced to say this) there is always less faith and greater untrustworthiness among men than among women. If no other experiences have made this plain to you, the ancient histories should suffice to do this, for so many of them shout out examples of such love stories, occurring in many different places. In each of these places you will always see unhappy women lamenting the unfaithfulness of their men, whereas only in very rare instances does one see the men having any cause to lament what the women do. This is due to the influence of the more benign planets, and the greater presence of the softer elements in women than in men, which makes women more benign and more compassionate towards those who love them. For each unfaithful woman you will find a thousand most unfaithful men; while for every thousand women you will find (and only with great difficulty) a single faithful man. And yet that man will have the ill fortune to run into that one unfaithful woman among the thousand faithful ones, as happened in my own wretched case.

"And so, my ladies, the best advice I could give you would be to get as far from this pitiless love as you were formerly willing to approach it. However, since from your attitudes I see that you are still completely disposed to follow this course, I will endeavor to give you a counsel which seems to me to be the least harmful, even if I am persuaded that love at all times can bring nothing but harm.

"Therefore I say, as I have already said, that even though love is always evil, the person who is committed to following it must use every expedient to make it the least evil it can be. This is possible when the man uses the most care in choosing his lady, and the lady does the same in choosing the man. I have understood your discordant opinions very well; but since not one of you has touched on the essential point that needed to be dealt with the most, I wish to set your opinions to one side. And I will say this, that it does not seem to me that you should worry about the age, nobility, or wealth of the man that you wish to choose as lover as much as you should be sure that he is adorned with excellent manners, and that he takes delight in some particular virtues. But above all you must keep in mind

havere a mente che tale amante non sia vano, cioè ch'egli come per arte non tenesse il fare a molte donne il vagheggio, che guai a voi donne mie, se in cotal sorte d'amanti vi inciampaste, li quali mille volte il giorno vi farebbono di gelosia morire. Chè così come i mercanti non si contentano d'una sol sorte di mercatantia, anzi s'affaticano che di molte et varie per le mani gli passino. Così quelli, essendo lo fare il vagheggio lor' arte, non contendandosi d'una o di due sino alla decina tutte ad un tratto arrivar vogliono; hor dovete pensarvi quanto alcuna ne possono amare, non potendosi il cuore, come non si può per certo, in più parti dividere. Et per me vi dico quando donna io fossi, più tosto che darmi in preda ad uno di questi tali, che dell'otio, et del tempo son creditori, io non so a quale altra cosa non mi esponesse.

"Buona cosa sarebbe, donne mie, se come sono i pareri d'alcune di voi, poteste amante ciascuna ritrovarvi il quale giovine, nobile, et ricco fosse; ma cotai ricchezze più tosto vorrei che in bei costumi in un nobile animo et in molte virtudi, che in assai accumulati tesori si estendessero. Perchè dovete sapere che più sa il giovine accorto che'l vecchio ignorante, nè può l'isperienza da sè fare esperto colui, lo ingegno del quale si trova nell'ignoranza sepolto. Et assai più gli savi avisi le più fiate giovano, che e' gran tesori non fanno; che quelli in istante, et quest'altri con intervallo di tempo operano. Ma ben vorrei che cotesto suo bell'animo a qualche lodevole opra havesse applicato, come sarebbe che d'armeggiare, o di agricultura, o di caccia, o di musica, overo d'altra sorte d'operatione tra lodevoli gentilhuomini usata si dilettasse, pur che in otio non vivesse, nè dietro il vitio non caminasse. Gliè vero che a me più d'ogn'altra cosa aggradirebbe, ch'egli assai dotto nelle greche, nelle latine, et etiandio nelle volgari lettere fosse, quando perciò non come morte in sè le tenesse, anzi honorevolmente in elle essercitandosi sempre. Perchè io vi faccio sapere esser peggiore assai più l'huomo letterato, il quale lasciando da parte i frutti che le scienze producono et al vitio s'accosta, che 'l semplice et ignorante, con quanto mal' animo può havere, non sarà mai. Et guardatevene, donne mie care, da questi tali, come dal foco fareste.

"Vorrei che avertiste ancora che l'amante da voi eletto fosse modestissimo et rispettoso, di poche parole, et non de' propri fatti vantatore; et che non molto curioso fosse. Imperciò che essendo per natura rispettoso et modesto, non potrà mancare che in ogni tempo et in ogni occasione gran rispetto et honor sempre non vi porti. Onde s'egli immoderato et prosuntuoso sarà, non mancherà mai hor con una sorte d'operationi, et hor con un'altra di spesse volte offendervi; et similmente vi avenirebbe s'egli troppo cianciatore per natura fosse, che per la troppa

that such a lover must not be vain, that is, that he not have the habit of pursuing many women. Woe to you, my ladies, if you mix yourselves up with such a lover, for he will make you die of jealousy a thousand times a day. Just as merchants are not satisfied with one type of merchandise, these men work hard in order to make many different pieces of goods pass through their hands. Since courting women is their profession, they do not content themselves with one or two, but want to take on ten at a time. Now imagine how much they are capable of loving a single one, since the heart certainly cannot be divided into many parts. And then as far as I am concerned, if I were a woman I would expose myself to just about any other risk, rather than have myself preyed upon by one of these men who thinks idleness and wasted time are his due.

"It would be a good thing, my ladies, if you could each find a lover who was young, noble, and rich, as some of you have said you preferred. But I would much rather such wealth included fine manners, a noble soul, and myriad virtues, than great quantities of amassed treasures. For you must know that the clever youth knows more than the old ignoramus, and experience in itself cannot make an expert of that man who finds his intelligence buried in ignorance. Very often wise counsels are far more useful than great wealth, since the former take effect in an instant, whereas the latter only after a delay. I would like to see the beautiful soul of this lover applied to some praiseworthy task, such as warfare, agriculture, hunting, music, or some other activity which typically brings pleasure to proper gentlemen, so that he not live in idleness, nor run after vice. Truly nothing would please me more than that he be very learned in Greek and Latin literature, and in vernacular letters as well, as long as he did not keep them as dead things, but rather continually practiced writing them in an honorable fashion. I want you to know that the literate man who abandons the fruits of his learning and turns to vice is far worse than the simple and ignorant man can ever be, no matter how weak his spirit. Beware, my dear ladies, of men like these, as you would beware of fire.

"I would like you to take care that the lover you choose be a man of few words, quite modest, respectful, and not inclined to boast of his own deeds. And he should not be too curious. For if he is by nature respectful and modest, he will not fail to show you great respect and do you honor at all times, and at every opportunity. If he is immoderate and presumptuous, you can expect he will often offend you, now with one sort of deed, now with another. The same thing will occur if he is by nature a prattler, since his too abundant words can easily overflow,

abondanza di parole facilmente traboccar potrebbe, et alcuna volta quello manifestare che si dovrebbe sotto a gran silentio custodire. Et parimente potrebbe incontrarvi, quando esser vantatore si ritrovasse, che quanti più et maggiori fossero e' favori che gli fareste, da tanto maggior volontà d'avantarsene sarebbe assalito. Et così similmente s'egli poi molte, et varie cose da lui vedute, et tentate, di voi satierebbesi tosto.

"Ma quando di tutte quelle ottime parti che io v'ho già detto ornato si ritrovasse, esser forse potrebbe che fortunate d'amante potreste tenervi; se perciò cosa alcuna che buona sia sperar si può che da Amore uscir potesse giamai. Gliè vero che io non saprei troppo secura regola darvi, per la quale certificar vi poteste, quanto et di qual sorte il da voi eletto amante vi amasse, et massimamente nel principio ch'egli incominciasse ad amarvi, nel qual tempo tutti gli amanti, sì gli finti, quale i veri ugualmente d'ardentissime fiamme amorose accesi vi si dimostrano, tutti costumati, tutti riverenti, et tutti rispettosi vi si fanno conoscere, et in somma non è osservatione, che 'n quel tempo non v'habbiano; non honore, et cortesia, che non vi facciano, et usino; nè operatione lasciano a dietro, o si scordano (quantunque faticosa o di danno lor fosse) pur che ella loro possa valere, per far che la gratia vostra a pieno s'acquistino. Per la qual cosa io conchiudo esser cosa non pur difficile, ma quasi impossibile il poter discernere et conoscere in que' principi' amorosi quali più o meno vi amano, et di qual dovete o non dovete fidarvi, poi che tutti ugualmente amanti, et osservatori dell'honor vostro, et della data fede vi si dimostrano.

"Ma ben tosto che di voi gli harrete fatti signori, quali siano accorger ve ne potrete; imperciò che essendo rei, subitamente tutto il reo che in loro si troverà vi si farà manifesto; et se anco saranno tali per natura, qual primieramente vi si forono dimostrati, in quel buon esser con esse voi conserverannosi sempre. Perchè io vi faccio sapere non ritrovarsi sorte o qualità di gente nel mondo che più patienti et sofferenti siano, di quello con le loro amate son sempre gli veri amanti; et all'incontro non è più gravosa o insopportabil soma come è la patienza et sofferenza presso quelli che fingono d'amare, et non amano.

"Et perciò io direi che per meglio chiarirvi quanto foste amate da loro, che qualche assai leggiera offesa gli faceste; ma guardatevi bene, che tale offesa non fosse di sorte che punto del loro honore a pericolo si ponesse, perchè quantunque vi amassero assai gli dareste nondimeno ragionevolmente cagione di non mai in tutti i loro giorni più amarvi. Et siate ancora avertite che per cosa del mondo, per cagion d'altro amore non gli offendeste; che qual' hora avenisse che la malvagia

and on occasion he will reveal something about which he ought to keep silent. Something similar may be your lot if he turns out to be a braggart, for the greater and more numerous favors you bestow upon him, the more he will be assailed by the desire to boast about them. You may well imagine that he will soon become just as tired of you, having seen and tried many different things.

"But if this man is endowed with all the best features, which I have described to you, it may well be that you will be able to consider yourselves fortunate in your choice of a lover. Therefore one may hope that some good thing can yet come out of love. Truly I am not certain how to give you the most sure rule, by which you can ascertain how much and in what way the lover you have chosen loves you. This is especially true with regard to that time when he first begins his courtship, for then all lovers, both false and true, show themselves to be equally enveloped in the most ardent flames of love. They all make themselves appear well-mannered, reverent, and respectful; and in short, there is no observance that they do not keep in that time, no honor or courtesy that they do not show you. They leave no deed undone or forgotten (however much it may be wearisome or risky for them), as long as it can serve to put them fully in your good graces. Because of this I conclude that in the case of these incipient lovers it is not only difficult, but nearly impossible to discern and come to know which ones love you more, or less, and which ones you may or may not trust; for they all equally make themselves appear to be true lovers and keepers of your honor, as well as the trust you have granted.

"But no sooner have you made them lords over you, than you will be able to tell what they are really like. For if they are bad, immediately all the evil in them will make itself plain. And if they really are by nature the way they first showed themselves to be, they will always treat you in that same benign fashion. Nor do I think it would make much difference if you were to do something to try their patience, for I tell you there is no kind of person in the world more patient and enduring than true lovers always are with their beloved ladies. On the other hand there is no burden more weighty and insufferable than patience and endurance in those who pretend to love but actually do not.

"Therefore I would suggest that you do some minor thing to offend your lovers, in order to confirm how much you are loved by them; take care, however, that this offense not be the sort that puts their honor at risk, for no matter how much they might love you, in such a case you would give them reasonable cause never to love you again as long as they live. In addition be warned that you must never offend them by means of love for anyone else, for any reason whatever. For

gelosia per cagion vostra gli entrasse nel capo, non mai più con quel sincero amor vi amarebbono, con lo quale primamente vi havessero amate. Ma se l'offesa, che gli farete di veruna di coteste due sorti non sarà, assai tosto quanto da loro sarete amate potrete chiarirvi. Imperciò che non amandovi da dovero alla prima, o alla seconda offesa, che gli facciate, gli vedrete da tanta furia di sdegno assaliti che nè per amanti, nè per amiche in alcun conto più vi vorranno conoscere. Ma non in cotal modo faranno già i veri amanti, li quali patientissimamente ciascuna offesa da voi fattagli sopporteranno, anzi temendo di esser abbandonati da voi, quantunque in alcun conto offese non vi havessero, ogni vostra colpa sopra loro assai volontieri si arrecherebbono. Per la qual cosa esser secure alhora potrete che cotali amanti più care che le lor proprie vite vi teniranno.

"Ma non vi pensaste[28] già che cotesto modo d'offenderli debba essere da voi posto in costume, et in uso; chè certe vi faccio, che la lor tanta sofferenza, et patienza dopo non molto tempo verrebbe del tutto a mancare, onde poscia (et con ragione) sareste da loro come superbe et ingrate, più che la morte odiate et fuggite. Anzi come alle due, overo alle tre offese che patientemente da voi harranno sofferte vi sarete chiarite quanto di cuore vi amino; dovrete alhora lasciando ogni modo d'offenderli a dietro, con tutt' il cuore disporvi a sempre compiacerli, et amarli; che così facendo verrete i cari amanti a longamente conservarvi in pace amorosa.

"Ma ben parmi hora, piacevoli donne, che sopra tal materia si sia detto a bastanza; et s'io non havesse così a pieno sodisfatto il desir vostro nel darvi consiglio, pregovi che non il voler mio, il quale verso voi è ottimo, ma il mio non più sapere ne vogliate incolpare. Et se d'altro per hora non vi piace valervi di me, sarete contente darmi licenza, che con buona gratia vostra al mio viaggio ritornerommi."

Le donne, che d'ogni suo dire sodisfattissime erano rimase, et havendo un gran desiderio ciascuna d'elle di poter gratificarlo in parte d'un tanto beneficio, che le parea da lui haver ricevuto, perciò poi che l'hebbero assai ringratiato, et sommamente lodati gli accorti avisi, li quali dati gli haveva, una cortese forza gli fecero; chè circondandolo tutte lo astrinsero a dovere il rimanente di quel giorno, et la notte appresso restarsi con loro. Fabio quantunque più assai la solitudine che la compagnia havesse grata, nondimeno per non parer discortese, dimostrando co'l farsi tanto pregare che le cotanto affettuose pregatrici sprezzasse, volse per ciò il cortese invito accettare. Et così dopo poco ivi dimorarono che i servi delle belle

---

[28] I have translated this unconventional use of the imperfect subjunctive as an imperative.

if it should ever happen that you cause evil jealousy to enter into their heads, they will never again show you the same sincere love that they felt at the beginning of the relationship. But if the offense that you do them is of neither of these two types, very soon you will be able to confirm how much you are loved by them. For if they do not really love you, at the first or second offense that you commit you will see them assailed by such a storm of disdain that they will want you neither as lovers nor friends. True lovers will not act this way, for they will put up patiently with any offense you do them; indeed, fearing to be abandoned by you, they will quite gladly accept every misdeed of yours, even if they themselves have done nothing wrong to you. On account of this, you will then be able to rest assured that such lovers will hold you more dear than their very lives.

"But do not imagine that such a pattern of offenses should become habitual. I assure you that their great endurance and patience would slip away before too long, whereupon they would have good cause to consider you haughty and ungrateful; thus you would be abandoned by them and hated more than death. After they have borne two, or possibly three offenses patiently, you will have come to realize how deeply they love you, and you should therefore stop committing any kind of offense whatever, and dedicate yourselves to pleasing them always, and loving them. In this way you will cause your lovers to stay with you a long time, in loving peace.

"But it really seems to me, pleasant ladies, that I have said enough about this subject. If I have not fully satisfied your desire with my advice, I pray you not blame my inclinations, which are most benevolent with regard to you, but rather my lack of knowledge. If you have no further need for me at the moment, may it please you to give me leave to go, and I will resume my travels with your good graces."

The women, who had been quite satisfied with everything he had said, each had a great desire to bestow on him some reward for the great service they thought he had rendered. Thus when they had thanked him, and praised very highly the wise advice he had given them, they pronounced a courtly decree: flocking around him, they all compelled him to stay with them for the rest of the day and throughout the night. Even though Fabio much preferred solitude to company, nevertheless he decided to accept their polite invitation, in order not to seem discourteous, nor scornful of his sweet petitioners for making them plead at great length. Therefore, after they had stayed there a bit longer, the servants of the

donne co' cavalli furono arrivati; et perchè già s'avicinava la sera, et havevano a far qualche miglio, subitamente perciò tutti su cavalli salirono, et verso il palagio d'una di loro, il quale più a quel loco vicino era, si aviarono. Al qual gionte et smontate che furono, nel mezzo loro il gentil Fabio si tolsero, et così tutto quel poco di giorno che avanzava, per bellissimi giardini diportandosi, et hor l'una, et hor l'altra per mano tenendolo, in piacevoli ragionamenti, con lor gran diletto passarono. Poi fattosi sera dopo una honorevolissima cena tutte n'andarono a letto.

Ma quanto fosse differente il riposo di quella notte della infelice Urania da quello, che tutte l'altre hebbero, non è chi potesse crederlo a pieno, poi che a quelle parendo d'haversi già ritrovato l'amante tale quale il giorno innanzi loro havea designato Fabio, che esser vorrebbono tutti, tanta gioia, et contento si sentivano ne' loro cuori, che non poterono mai per la soverchia allegrezza dormire. Dall'altra parte la troppo innamorata Urania conoscendosi esser sè sola colei la quale, per dire il vero, amava giovine che tutte quelle eccelse virtudi et costumi teneva, che ogni vero amator doverebbe tenere. Et parimente sè stessa conoscendosi tale, che ben degna dell'amor suo poteva tenersi, et nondimeno poco o nulla da lui vedendosi amata, nè sapendo fuor che'l suo destino incolpare, che così poco grata al suo Fabio l'havesse fatta, perciò da maggior passione assalita, che più altre volte sentisse mai, quasi fu quella notte su'l punto d'uccidersi. Pur da miglior consiglio aiutata, con speranza di trovar pace si dispose di voler viver ancora.

Perchè fattosi giorno con gran dispiacer di quelle donne tutte, le quali harrebbon voluto che sempre con esse per dar loro de' buoni consigli si fosse stato, si volse in ogni modo partire. Et forse che alcune d'elle, havendolo conosciuto di così bei costumi et gratiose maniere ornato, se ne erano si invaghite che sanza desiderar di ricercare altrove meglio di quello che poco loro havrebbe potuto giovare, volontieri accomodate se ne sarebbono.

lovely ladies arrived with their horses. As evening was coming on, and they had some miles to go, they promptly mounted the horses and set out for the closest lodging, a palace belonging to one of their number. Upon arriving there and dismounting, they placed the gentle Fabio in their midst and amused themselves in the gardens for what was left of the day. Now one lady took him by the hand, now another, as they passed the time in pleasant conversation and great delight. When night came they had a most proper dinner, then all went to bed.

But no one would ever believe how different the unhappy Urania's repose was from that of all the other ladies! Since it seemed to each of them they had found the lover they wanted in the form of the man who had been introduced to them as Fabio the day before, they felt such joy and contentment in their hearts that they could not sleep. On the other hand, Urania, too much in love, knew herself to be the only one who truly loved a young man who had all the high virtues and manners that a true lover should have. She likewise knew that she could consider herself completely worthy of that man's love, and yet she saw that he loved her but little, if at all. She did not know whom to blame save her destiny, which had made her so displeasing to Fabio; thus, assailed by greater sadness than she had ever felt before, she was nearly on the point of killing herself that night. She thought better of it, however, and decided to continue to live in the hope of finding peace.

The next day dawned, and Fabio resolved to depart, to the great displeasure of all the women who would have wished he stay on with them always and give them good advice. And perhaps some of them, having seen that he was endowed with such lovely habits and gracious manners, had fallen in love with him, and would willingly have settled for him without wishing to look any further for someone better. But of course he could not have served their purpose.

III

Hor dunque la Urania dalla fera passione amorosa cacciata, a men d'un miglio si fu dal palagio di ove s'era partita, dilungata, ch'entrò nel [...]²⁹ [co]me era solita di fare, nel suo interno amoroso pensiero; per lo quale, non più di quello che 'l giorno dinanzi havesse fatto, nè di sè stessa, nè del cavallo, nè di regger la briglia havea cura. Et così circa quatro miglia hor qua, hor la errando in una bellissima prateria fu arrivata, dove alcuni giovani gentilhuomini di Napoli un loro assai bel falcone approvar voleano, li quali vedendo quest'altro, che un giovine essere stimavano così fuori di sè, et simile ad un morto verso loro a cavallo venire furono da grandissimo stupore assaliti. Et perciò scordandosi di provare il falcone per voler la novità di questo caso vedere, ad un batter di ciglio hebbero la meschina Urania di tutti loro circondata; et incominciarono quale a scuoterle la sella, quale per le braccia a tirarla, et quale col pomo della spada hor per la schiena, hor per li fianchi spingendola. Onde la infelice quantunque fuor di misura internata nel suo amoroso pensiero si fosse, nondimeno da tante fiancate et punsate³⁰ offesa, assai tosto fu in sè ritornata; et vedendosi da que' giovani al parer suo come da nemici assalita, et oltraggiata, non havendo la vergogna tempo di prender in lei il suo loco nel cuore, per haverlo già tutto l'ira et lo sdegno per loro soli occupato. Perciò con la faccia

---

[29] Lacuna due to probable scribal omission in T (fol. 56r); reproduced in P (fol. 58v). The third line of the chapter ends "... ch'entrò nel ..." and the fourth begins "... me era solita ..." It would seem an entire line was skipped between the two.

[30] This noun is unattested in dictionaries, but it either derives from the past absolute of *pungere* (*punsi*), or else it is a variant form of *punzone* (in archaic usage, "blow of the fist").

III

Thus driven on by the savage passion of love, Urania had scarcely gone a mile from the palace when she entered [. . .] as she was accustomed to do, reflecting on the thoughts of love within her. Because of this, she paid no more heed to herself, to her horse, or to the reins than she had the day before. After going about four miles, wandering now here, now there, she arrived at a very beautiful meadow where some young gentlemen of Naples were training a marvelous falcon of theirs. When they saw this person whom they took to be a young man approaching them on a horse, so out of his mind and looking like he was dead, they were greatly astonished. They so wished to see this strange case that they forgot about training their falcon, and in the blink of an eye they had all surrounded the miserable Urania. They began to shake her saddle, and some pulled her by the arms, while others prodded her back and sides with the pommels of their swords. Despite being profoundly lost in her amorous thoughts, the unhappy woman was irritated by so many proddings and blows to her sides that she quickly returned to her senses. Seeing herself assaulted and offended by those young men as if they were her enemies, her heart was so filled with anger and scorn for them that shame could not take its accustomed place therein. With her face tinged by those

dal color di quelli depinta così gli disse: "Non potrebbe far la Natura, che se gentilhuomini sète, come il vestir vostro ne dimostra segno, che giamai i cuori vostri habbiano in loro alcuna favilla d'amor gentile sentita. Chè innamorato in gentil soggetto non si ritrovò mai ch'egli similmente gentile et cortese in ciascun suo affare non si dimostrasse sempre, nè crederò che la più discortese discortesia di questa, che a me fuor d'ogni proposito havete usata, per alcun tempo si usasse più mai. Non vogliam poi noi altri huomini confessare (et pur forza è che io 'l dica) che dalle donne in molte et molte buone parti siam vinti; ma particolarmente di cortesia sempre da loro superati siamo. Eccovi come hoggi da voi, che huomini sète, malissimo trattato mi trovo; dove ritrovandomi (per lo creder mio non guari lontano di qui) da cinque non men belle che virtuose donne, nel medesimo modo compreso, nel quale voi al presente con mio gran danno m'havete colto. Nondimeno elle come è pur d'ogni gentil cuore usitato costume, poscia che m'hebbero non men con cortesia che con destrezza in me ritornato, tra loro, et tra e' suoi dilettevoli et accorti ragionamenti cortesissimamente mi raccolsero, nè ch'io mi partissi tutto heri, et a gran fatica questo mattino, hanno voluto mai consentire: della quale somma cortesia, mentre ch'io vivo, son per tenirne memoria."

I giovani, che cinque erano, et l'un l'altro insieme carissimi compagni, et amici; et che per aventura dal loro canto, delle già dette donne erano amanti, nè per altra cagione s'havevano tutti insieme uniti in quel loco, cioè ad un palagio d'uno d'essi poco d'indi distante, eccetto che havendo inteso come le loro donne tutte cinque insieme s'erano, per diportarsi in quel loco dove si trovavano, ridotte; per poterle alcuna volta vedere, et la lor ventura tentare. Et perciò sentendosi ciascun di loro tutto in un punto dall'amoroso strale rinovar le loro piaghe, et in un mar di vergogna sommersi, udendosi la lor gran discortesia rinfacciare, ritirandosi a dietro vergognati, et muti rimasero.

Ma vie più assai Amore potendo in loro che vergogna non puote; chè considerando come gli havrebbe questo giovine più fresche novelle potuto delle lor donne donare; et massimamente ardendo d'infinito desiderio e' lor cuori di saper di qual sorte que' ragionamenti fossero stati, li quali egli havea detto, che dilettevoli et accorti furono. Perciò uno di loro, che assai più de gli altri era loquace, in cotal modo al giovane prese a dire. "Gentilissimo giovane, noi per lo vero confessiamo che scortesissimi i diportamenti nostri furono, ma con tutto ciò vogliamo ancor dire ch'essi non furono tali malitiosamente da noi usati, anzi più di mezzo morto ciascun di noi giudicandovi, sanza pensarci più oltre così facevamo, havendo solamente la intentione nostra a ritornarvi in vita. Et che ciò sia vero che

overwhelming emotions, she spoke to them: "Even if you are gentlemen, as your clothing indicates, Nature could not have provided that your hearts have ever felt any spark of noble love; for there has never been a lover who turned his affection to a noble purpose without revealing himself to be similarly noble and courtly in his every deed. Nor will I believe that such an uncalled-for discourteous discourtesy, which you have shown me, has ever been seen before at any time. We men do not like to confess that we are outdone by women in many of the proper things. Nevertheless, though I hate to say it, we are particularly outdone by them when it comes to courtesy; and here I stand today, very poorly treated by you who are men. I believe I was hardly far from here when I was surprised by five women who were no less beautiful than virtuous, in the same way you have just encountered me, causing me so much harm. However, when these women had tactfully and courteously returned me to my senses, in a fashion customary to those who have noble hearts, they welcomed me among them in a most courtly fashion and invited me to join their delightful and intelligent discussions. They would not allow me to leave them all day yesterday, and indeed this morning they only gave grudging consent; thus as long as I live I will remember their great courtesy."

There were five of these young men, all very dear comrades and friends, who by coincidence happened to be in love with the women Urania had met the day before. They had come together at one of their nearby palaces for no other reason than to amuse themselves in the area where they had heard that their five ladies had already gathered, in the hope of seeing them and trying their luck. Now, in an instant, each one felt himself wounded by the shaft of love yet again. When they heard themselves reproached for their great discourtesy, they were submerged in a sea of shame and drew back, disgraced and mute.

But love had much greater power over these men than shame. They considered how this youth could provide them with more recent news of their ladies, and they especially burned in their hearts with infinite desire to know more about these conversations, which the youth had said were delightful and intelligent. Therefore one of them, much more loquacious than the others, began to speak to the youth as follows: "Most noble youth, we truly confess that our behavior was most discourteous. Nonetheless we wish to add that we were not being malicious: we all imagined that you were more than half dead, so without giving it another thought we acted as we did, having no other plan but to revive you. We were quite innocent and free of all evil thoughts when we committed this outrage

da noi semplicemente, et ignudi d'ogni reo pensiero v'habbiamo oltraggiato, il buonissimo animo nostro, il quale hora a voi si farà manifesto, intiera fede ve ne potrà fare. Imperciò che oltre che dell'offesa, la quale fatta v'habbiamo confessiam d'esser mal contenti et pentiti, si esponiamo ancora ad ogni sorte di penitenza fare che a voi più parrà che meritevoli siamo."

La gentilissima Urania, nel cuore della quale non mai discortesia hebbe loco, udendo le assai humili parole de' giovani, et parendo a lei che in atti tutti rimessi fossero, non puote perciò mancare che etiandio lei ogni ricevuta ingiuria scordandosi, tutta humiliata non si commovesse nel cuore; et con accomodata, et benigna risposta, non gli facesse conoscere quanta in lei cortesia et gentilezza regnasse. Ma i giovani li quali sodisfatti non erano perch'ella perdonato gli havesse, anzi più oltre desiderando da lei cioè di sapere quali fossero stati e' suoi ragionamenti nel precedente giorno con le lor donne, perciò l'astrinsero et le fecero forza a dover quel mattino rimanere a desinare con essi loro, dicendo che mai non crederebbono che la grande sua cortesia perdonato gli havesse, quando una così picciola gli negasse.

Perchè la Urania non volendo alcun sospetto dare di sè a' giovani, quantunque mal volontieri, pur lasciossi al palagio condurre; dove gionti et smontati de' cavalli che furono, pareva che satiar ciascun di loro non si potesse di farle accoglienze et honore; et parimente a tavola più che altra volta si ritrovasse mai si ritrovò avantaggiata, et servita. Ma poscia che al fine dello abondante desinare furono gionti, quel giovine il quale più de gli altri era bel parlatore, assai dalla longa incominciò a tentarla, acciò che que' ragionamenti che lor desideravano di sapere manifesti gli facesse. Ma lei, che a maraviglia era accorta, subito come propriamente era fece giudicio, che que' cinque giovani erano delle cinque donne dal giorno dinanzi innamorati; et perciò con assai piacevole vista così gli rispose:

"Amorosi giovani, per quanto mi par di conoscere, a voi piacerebbe che io tutti e' secreti del mio cuore vi aprissi, et e' vostri molto ristretti et rinchiusi si stessero; et parmi che cotesta parte non sia de' buoni compagni. Onde io vi faccio sapere che se voi altrimenti non vi lasciate intender da me, nè voi altresì di quello che io so molto a dentro intenderete; che a me non poca discortesia parrebbe verso quelle cortesissime donne usare, quando fuor di proposito i loro secreti con tali che con esse loro interessati non fossero io manifestasse."

I giovani, accorgendosi come quest'altro giovine assai più di loro era accorto, et come la radice de' lor desideri havea già conosciuta; perciò sorridendo tutti et di concorde volere i loro amorosi pensieri et desiri non sanza mandar dalli loro

against you, and our very good intentions, which we will now reveal to you, can reassure you of the truth of this. Thus we will not only show you that we are very sorry for the offense which we committed, but also that we are prepared to do any act of penitence you deem appropriate."

When the most noble Urania, whose heart had never known discourtesy, heard the humble words of the young men, it seemed to her that they were acting quite meekly. Chagrined, she could not help feeling profoundly moved, and even forgot all the injuries she had received. In her benign and most proper response she let them know the extent to which courtesy and nobility reigned within her. But the young men were not satisfied that she had pardoned them, for indeed they desired more from her; that is, they wished to know what sort of conversations she had had with their ladies the day before. Therefore they put pressure on her and compelled her to stay and have lunch with them that morning, saying that they would never believe her great courtesy had pardoned them, if she were to deny them so small a favor.

Since Urania did not wish to appear suspicious in the eyes of the men, she allowed herself to be conducted to the palace, however unwillingly. When they had arrived there, and dismounted from their horses, it seemed that none of the men could tire of welcoming her and doing her honors. It was the same at the table, where she thought herself better served and treated than she had ever been before. But when they had reached the end of the abundant meal, the young man who spoke better than all the others began to entice her at great length, so that she would reveal to them the conversations that they all wished to hear about. However, Urania was marvelously clever, and she swiftly adjudged the five young men to be in love with the five women she had met the day before. With a pleasing expression, she answered them thus:

"Amorous youths, as far as I can tell, you would be pleased if I opened all the secrets of my heart to you, even while yours remained hidden and closed. Since I do not think this is fitting behavior among good companions, I will tell you that if you do not open yourselves to me, I will not reveal much of what I know to you. It seems to me that I would be showing no small discourtesy toward those very courteous women, if I were to reveal improperly their secrets to certain men who might not be interested in them."

At this, the young men became aware that this other fellow was much more clever than they were, since he had found out the root of their desire. Therefore they all smiled, and on one accord they opened all of their loving thoughts and desires to him, not without sending forth from their bosoms the most ardent sighs.

petti focosissimi sospiri, gli apersero tutti, soggiongendo che humilmente lo pregava ciascuno d'essi che non volesse cosa alcuna con loro tacere, la quale di quele donne havesse veduta, o sapesse; offerendosi tutti loro in maggior cosa operarsi per lui.

Grandissimo contento sentì la Urania d'essersi in que' giovani di quelle donne amanti abbattuta; et perciò in cotal modo gli disse: "Quantunque con verità io possa il più infelice et mal fortunato giovine che hoggi dì si trovi nel mondo chiamarmi. Nondimeno uno infinito cordoglio io sento, quando a giovani virtuosi io veggio in quello, che io patisco, patire; et all'incontro sommo piacere io gusto qualunque volta io mi accorgo che lor desideri a felice fine sortiscono. Et tanto più me ne compiaccio quando io conosco che qualche parte della lor felicitade da me, et per mia cagione gli deriva, come spero che hoggi in voi mi verrà fatto. Chè se tali sarete, et nel modo vi diporterete, quale debbe essere, et diportare ciascun virtuoso et leale amante con quella donna ch'egli si dispone d'amare, io vi do nova che tutti voi tosto et felicemente delle cinque già dette donne, adempirete gli amorosi vostri desiri."

Et indi dal principio al fine tutti i ragionamenti tra lei e le donne fatti sanza una sola parola lasciare a dietro lor' hebbe aperti et manifestati. Non si potrebbe mai raccontare con quanta attentione gl' innamorati giovani stavano, le a lor cotanto grate parole ascoltando; che ben mi creggio di queste più dilettevoli, nè più soavi altre alla lor vita non udissero mai. Et poi che ella hebbe fornito di dire, et essi ciascun per sè, et tutti insieme l'hebbero tante et tante gratie rendute; che soverchio sarebbe il volerle ad una ad una tutte narrare; quel giovine, ch'altre fiate havea detto seguitò nel dir così ancora:

"Cortesissimo giovine, io non so vedere qual cosa così grande o pretiosa potesse con essi noi ritrovarsi, nè di qual maggior valore la vita nostra esser potesse che l'una, et l'altra spendendo, et operando per voi, (quando bene il tutto misuro) alla minor parte del debito, che v'habbiamo havessimo poi sodisfatto. Et per farci vie più che non siamo (se più del tutto può esser) a voi obligati, vogliamo la somma vostra gentilezza pregare che quella cotanto grande cortesia, la quale di voi si estese a quelle gentildonne consigliando, et insegnando di qual conditione et sorte dovevano eleggersi amante, così etiandio vi piaccia d'estenderla in noi; et altretanto consigliarci et insegnarci di qual sorte et conditione debbe l'huomo eleggersi donna amata. Imperciò che da noi per lo innanzi non fu mai considerato che in altra cosa eccetto nel compiacimento de' sensi nello innamorarsi s'havesse ad essercitare, et credevamo che pur che gli occhi nella lor vista sodisfatti fossero, che ogn'altra parte di noi dovesse star queta, et contenta.

Urania: The Story of a Young Woman's Love

Each of them humbly begged him that he not fail to tell them any detail of what he had seen, or found out, from the ladies, and each one offered his complete services to him.

Urania was quite content to have come upon the very same young men who were in love with those ladies, and she answered them thus: "Even though I can call myself the most unhappy and unfortunate youth that exists in the world just now, I still feel an infinite sorrow when I see virtuous young men suffer from the same ill that I suffer. On the other hand I experience the greatest pleasure every time I see their desires happily fulfilled, and I am pleased even more when I have been the cause of some part of their happiness, as I hope will be the case today. For if you act and behave in the way each faithful and virtuous lover must act and behave with the woman he has decided to love, I can tell you that before long all of you will happily fulfill your loving desires with the five ladies in question."

At that point she told them all of the discussion that had gone on between her and the ladies, without leaving out a single word. No one could ever recount how attentively the amorous youths listened to her words, so pleasing to them; and I am quite certain they never heard any that were sweeter, nor more delightful, in their lives. When she had finished speaking, they all thanked her, both individually and in chorus, more than words could ever tell. Then the young man who had spoken before addressed her again.

"Most courteous youth, I cannot imagine what thing we might have that would be great or precious enough, nor of what greater value than our very lives; yet if we spent these things, or dedicated them to you, we would have satisfied only a minimal part of the debt we owe you, in my estimation. However, we would like to make ourselves much more obliged to you than we already are (if it were possible to exceed the infinite): we would like to impose upon your kindness, and ask you to extend to us that courtesy which you showed the gentle ladies, when you advised them and taught them the kind and quality of lover they should choose for themselves. We would like you to give us the same advice and instruction, regarding the kind and quality of woman that a man should choose for his beloved. For in our case, up to now we imagined that nothing but the pleasure of the senses mattered in affairs of love; and moreover we thought that as long as the eyes were content with what they beheld, every other part of us could remain tranquil and contented.

"Ma hora considerando come quantunque l'huomo di assai maggior perfettione sia che la donna non è, onde d'alcuni savi fu opinione che più vaglia il più vile et da poco huomo che si ritrovi nel mondo che la più nobile et valorosa donna che viva. Nondimeno voi con tante ragioni ammaestrate le donne havete che ogni loro studio pongano nello eleggersi amante, che di tali et tante virtù sia dotato quando io mi crederei rispetto alla dignità et al valore, che huomo così tristo non fosse che ogn'altra donna non se ne dovesse degnare. Et perciò dico che ciò considerando prendo argomento, et giudico dover esser cosa vie più necessaria assai che l'huomo usi maggior diligenza nel conoscere e leggersi tra le molte imperfette donne la meno imperfetta; che alle donne non è tra molti perfetti scegliere lo migliore. Imperciò che a quelle così gran disgratia è se errano mai, come a noi gran ventura sarebbe lo indovinarla pur una volta."

"Assai male sète informati, et assai peggio questa cosa intendete," rispose alhor la Urania, "per la qual cosa non poco mi maraviglio come così prudenti giovani quali sète, v' habbiate una così grande follia lasciata di bocca uscire, non havendo avertenza; come quelli, che prima la dissero non da ragione mossi, ma da passione sospinti in cotal modo falsamente parloromo; chè quantunque siam huomini non sopporta perciò la ragione che le donne siano da noi a torto calunniate, et oppresse. Non dirò già ch'elle di tutta quella perfettione siano che noi huomini siamo. Ma ben dirò almeno che loro poco men perfettione di noi tengono, intendendosi perciò sì dell'una qual dell'altra parte de' più perfetti, che gl'imperfetti et tristi huomini sanza alcun dubbio avanzano di gran lunga d'imperfettione, et tristitia le più triste, et imperfette donne che ritrovar si possino; la qual verità voglio con manifeste prove sostenerlavi.

"Ma veniamo alle perfettioni primieramente, nelle quali considerando noi vederemo come tra gli huomini rade volte alcuna nobil' arte, alta scienza, overo altra sorte di virtù si trovò mai, che parimente tra le donne, se non di tanta perfettione almen di poco minor, non se ne ritrovasse ancora; tanto perciò, quanto a loro è stato lecito di potere entromettersi. Onde se voi loderete gli huomini circa le cose divine, dicendo che molti santi spargendo il loro sangue in sacrificio al magno Iddio hanno la cristiana fede aggrandita; et io rispondervi non meno haverla fatta ampia tante virginelle, le quali nel santo martirio costantissime si son dimostrate. Et se voi direte che tra gli huomini vi fossero de' profeti assai, et io dirovvi che tra

Urania: The Story of a Young Woman's Love

"We have considered how man is so much more perfect than woman, which has led some wise men to the opinion that the lowest and least of men on earth is worth more than the most noble and most worthy woman alive. Nevertheless, you have employed much reasoning in order to teach these women that they should put all their efforts into choosing a lover who is endowed with so many of the best virtues; whereas I would say that with regard to dignity and worth, there is no man so wretched that any woman should not deign to accept him. Therefore, after giving it thought, I judge that it is far more necessary that a man employ great diligence in discovering and selecting the least imperfect among the many imperfect women, than it is for women to choose the best out of many perfect men: for it is such a huge disgrace for women if they ever err, just as it is so great a misfortune for us if we surmise that they have erred even once."

"You are very badly misinformed, and your understanding of this matter is even worse," answered Urania at this point. "Because of this, I marvel greatly that young men as prudent as you are have incautiously allowed such great foolishness to escape your lips. The people who first said those things were not moved by reason, but rather by passion, and thus spoke falsely. The fact that we are men does not justify our reasoning that women should be wrongly denigrated and oppressed by us. I will not say that they reach our level of perfection, but at least I will forthrightly affirm that they have only a little less perfection than we do. By this I mean they share in the various aspects of the most perfect men; and without a doubt the most imperfect and wicked men far exceed the imperfection and wickedness of the most wicked and imperfect women that one can find. I wish to provide you with clear proof to demonstrate this truth.

"First of all, let us consider perfections, for in these we will see how only rarely has some noble art, lofty science, or other kind of skill ever been found among men that has not also been the domain of women. If women have not done these things quite as perfectly as men, their degree of perfection has been only slightly less; that is, if it has been permitted to women to participate in these fields at all. So if you praise men for their involvement in divine things, by saying that many male saints have advanced the Christian faith through the shedding of their blood in sacrifice to the almighty God, I answer that so many young virgins have advanced it no less, and have shown themselves to be extremely steadfast in the face of holy martyrdom.[31] And if you say that there were a great many

---

[31] This is a common patristic topos in both Western and Eastern Christendom. See G. Clark, *Women in Late Antiquity: Pagan and Christian Life-Styles* (Oxford: Clarendon Press, 1993), 56–57.

le donne di molte savie sibille non vi sono mancate. Et se nelle mondane scienze direte esser stati molti huomini scientiati, delli quali tale poeta, tale oratore, tale filosofo, et tale d'altra qualità di virtù dotato si ritrovò; vi si potrebbe a questo rispondere che tra le donne vi son state una Safo, una Carmente, una Hortensia, et molt'altre poco men de gli allegati huomini dotte, et savie; et in Atene assai di quelle vi furono, che nelle accademie di filosofia nelle catedre a gli huomini scolari leggevano.

"Poi se della grandezza dell'animo et valor della persona vorrete assai valorosi huomini lodare; non vi si può rispondere che non men forse di quelli le quatro figlie di Antione, la Pantasilea, et Tamiri meritassero honore, et pregio? Et non credete voi, che hoggi dì tra noi non si trovino di molte donne ancora, le quali in

URANIA: THE STORY OF A YOUNG WOMAN'S LOVE

prophets among men, I will respond that among women there has been no lack of wise sibyls.[32] You might affirm that in the worldly sciences there have been many learned men, including this poet, or that orator, or so and so who was a philosopher, or someone who had some other sort of ability; yet one could reply that there have been among the women a Sappho, a Carmenta, an Hortensia, and many others hardly less wise or learned than the men who have been mentioned.[33] In Athens there were many such women, who lectured to scholarly men from the lecterns of the academies of philosophy.

"And then, if you wish to praise men who have shown great valor, acknowledging their greatness of soul and disregard for personal risk, could one not respond that the four daughters of Antione, Penthesilea, and Tamyris are no less worthy of honor and esteem?[34] And do you not believe that even today one may

---

[32] Christine de Pizan describes the sibyls in *The Book of the City of Ladies* 2.1–3 (trans. Brown-Grant, 91–95).

[33] Sappho (sixth century B.C.) was one of the best known of all Greek poets. Carmenta or Carmentis was a Roman goddess who was often regarded as a prophetess; indeed she appears thus in Boccaccio's euhemeristic *Famous Women (De Claris Mulieribus)*, ed. and trans. V. Brown (Cambridge, MA: Harvard University Press, 2001), 105–13. Boccaccio stresses Carmenta's keen intellect, for she was supposedly the creator of the Latin alphabet (*Famous Women*, 106–9). Carmenta receives even greater praise from Christine de Pizan, who makes her a founder of Western civilization; see *The Book of the City of Ladies* 1.33, 1.37–38, 2.5 (trans. Brown-Grant, 64–66, 70–72, 98). Hortensia (fifth century B.C.) was a Roman noblewoman who gained fame as an orator for a remarkable speech against the taxation of women. Both Sappho and Hortensia also appear in *Famous Women* (192–95; 348–49), as well as in Christine de Pizan (1.30; 2.36; trans. Brown-Grant, 60–61, 140).

[34] For Penthesilea, queen of the Amazons, and Tamyris (or Tomyris), warrior and Queen of Scythia, see Boccaccio, *Famous Women*, 128–31 and 198–203, as well as Ariosto, *Orlando furioso* 37.5 and Christine de Pizan, *Book of the City of Ladies*, 1.18–19 and 1.17 (trans. Brown-Grant, 41, 43–46, 38–39). The identity of the "four daughters of Antione" is more problematic; I am not certain which figure from classical mythology or history the author had in mind. I am indebted to Enrique Fernandez for the suggestion that Bigolina, or her copyist, might have misspelled the name Antiope, the name of the Amazon captured by Theseus. According to Paulus Orosius (*The Seven Books of History Against the Pagans*, trans. R. J. Deferrari [Washington: Catholic University of America Press, 1964], 1.15), Antiope was one of four daughters of Sinope, queen of the Scythians; the passage in Orosius is notoriously corrupt, however, and has often confused subsequent commentators. According to Prof. Fernandez, a bad reading of Orosius might have led Bigolina to conclude that Antiope (misspelled as "Antione") was actually the mother of the four warlike daughters. For Antiope, to whom no daughters are actually attributed, see Boccaccio, *Famous Women*, 82–85, 128–29 and Christine de Pizan, *Book of the City of Ladies*, 1.18 (trans. Brown-Grant, 41).

ciascuna di cotal professioni potrebbono a molti huomini, che d'assai si tengono, far vergogna? Onde io conchiudo non potersi con ragione alcuna dire che 'l più vile, et da poco huomo più vaglia, che la più valorosa donna non vale, giudicio per lo vero assai sciocco et insano. Ma per farvi conoscere ancora come le più triste donne di tanta imperfettione et tristitia non sono, come i più tristi huomini si trovano esser; dicovi che molto bene dovete considerare da quale de' due sessi vengono il più delle volte le tante sceleragini et tristitie di che il mondo n'è pieno; gl'inganni, le usure, i tradimenti, gli furti, le rapine, et gli homicidij da cui vengono se non da gli huomini sempre? Poco huopo sarebbono le leggi cotanto tra gli humani hoggidì necessarie, se gli huomini, l'uno con l'altro con fede, et pace, come le donne fanno, vivessero."

Havevano i giovani sino a quell'hora con somma attentione ascoltando, sempre tacciuto, ma parendogli poscia che queste ultime parole dal giovine dette in troppo gran biasimo del viril sesso fossero, et ch'egli assai più che non si conveniva delle donne partiale si dimostrasse. Perciò quel giovine il quale più de gli altri havea parlato, interrompendo alla Urania il suo dire, così le rispose: "Gran maraviglia, valoroso giovine, ci porgete vedendovi così fuor di misura a tutte le donne affettionato, massimamente non volendo consentire come per lo dir vostro vi lasciate intendere ch'elle alcuna parte o piccola o grande habbino, che tutta buona, tutta pura, et tutta fedele non sia; et dall'altro canto volete che tutte le più pessime sceleragini siano de gli huomini soli. Ben vogliamo confessarvi che tutte quelle lodi, che prima nel dir vostro date le havete sian vere, poi che con così aperte ragioni per le vere ce le havete fatte conoscere; ma non vogliamo già hora credervi c'elle di tanta perfettione siano, che con noi huomini insieme di molte tristitie non partecipino, quando noi certo sappiamo, anzi in fatti habbiamo di molte la lor prava natura conosciuta. Et sappiamo di certo ancora come di rado aviene, et massimamente ne gli homicidi, che da alcun'altra cagione eccetto che dalle donne pervengono; et ve ne sapressimo de' moderni tempi molti essempi dare, ma lasciamo stare i moderni de' quali i più sono occulti, et consideriamo gli antichi a tutto il mondo manifesti, et più d'ogn' altra la nobilissima Troia, parvi ch'ella per cagione d'una feminella così fosse disolata che pietra sopra pietra a pena non vi rimase? Non si armorono per cagion di lei sola tanti esserciti? Non vi guadagnorono per cagion sua cotanti valorosissimi huomini la morte? Delle quali uno solo più valeva assai, di quante donne fabricò mai la gran madre Natura. Non sappiamo di vera scienza ancora com'elle maravigliosamente sono vendicose, et crudeli? Nè mai s'acquetano

still find plenty of women among us who could put to shame, in each one of these professions, many men who are inclined to think highly of themselves? Because of this I conclude that no one could reasonably say that the most vile and insignificant man is worth more than the most worthy woman; I consider anyone who holds this opinion to be very foolish, and insane. To show you even further that the wickedest women are not as imperfect and wicked as the most wicked men, I ask you to consider well from which of the two sexes come most often the many evils and villanies which fill the world. Who but men bring about deceits, usuries, betrayals, thefts, plunderings, and murders? The many laws which are necessary to the human race would serve little purpose, if men would only live together in good faith and peace, as women do."

Up to this point the young men had listened very attentively, in silence. But now it seemed to them that the youth's last pronouncement put too much blame on the virile sex, and that he had showed himself to be far too partial to women. Therefore the one who had spoken more than the others interrupted Urania. "You offer us a great marvel, O valorous youth," he said, "when you reveal yourself to be so inordinately fond of all women, and especially when your words make it plain that you cannot imagine any female aspect, great or small, that is not all good, all pure, and all trustworthy. On the other hand you hold that all of the worst evils are confined wholly to men. We freely admit that all those first praises which you pronounced seem true to us, since you used such clear reasoning to make them understood. However, we cannot believe that women are of such perfection that they do not participate in many evils alongside us men, for we are aware of their depraved nature, and indeed we have often experienced it firsthand. Moreover, we certainly know that it is rarely the case that these evils, especially murder, are not caused by women. We could give many many modern examples of this, but let us leave these aside, for they are for the most part little known, and consider the ancient ones which are familiar to all the world. The most famous example is that of the noble Troy: are you aware that she was so ruined on account of a woman that hardly one stone was left upon another? Or that so many armies took up weapons because of this woman alone? Or that so many very brave men went to their deaths on her account? Just one of those men was worth so much more than all the women whom the great Mother Nature ever created. Do we not know, and know it truly, that women are remarkably vengeful and cruel? For they cannot rest until they find satisfaction in cruel vengeance for every

d'ogni picciola ingiuria che a lor vien fatta sin tanto che per crudel vendetta sodisfatte non restano. Chè lasciando il dir delle moderne da parte, ditemi, chi puote mai la maggior crudel vendetta imaginarsi di quella della crudelissima antica Medea? Et parimente di quella di Progne? Nè direi che men di queste crudelissima si dovesse Circe tenere, poi che in ricompensa de' ricevuti piaceri da tanti vaghi et amorosi giovani, in horribili et mostruose fere gli tramutava.

"Hor dunque non dite più di gratia che le donne cotanto buone siano, ch' elle non sapino se non sempre bene, et mai alcun tristo atto operare, poi che vi habbiam fatto conoscere come sanno fare, et fanno de' mali assai; et a molti, li quali per la lor debolezza non ponno porvi entro le mani s'ingegnano di dar materia a gli huomini che gli le ponghino. Per la qual cosa si può conchiudere ch' elle sempre danno di male, sanza esser una sol volta di bene cagione. Se forse da quelle per loro avocato salariato non foste; chè se così fosse gran ragione harreste a difender così valorosamente la ragion loro. Ma con tutto ciò non siamo noi obligati a così leggiermente credervi tutto quello che in favor loro a voi piace di dire."

"Certamente, et non poco di me v'ingannate, signori," rispose alhora la Urania, "havendo in cuore che mosso da passione io habbia alcuna cosa in favor delle donne detta; anzi dovete credere che la ragione sola, nè veruna altra cagione mi potrebbe mai movere a pigliar la difesa d'alcuno. Hovvi detto et dimostrato, et creggiovi haver detto et dimostrato il vero, sì come voi medesimi già confessato l'havete, esser le donne, se non di tanta, almen di poco men perfettione di quello che noi huomini siamo; intendendosi perciò delle buone, et non delle ree. Et dicevo poi, non per voler dir che di ree et di malvagie tra loro assai non se ne trovino ancora; anzi vi dico, che quando il raccontare i loro difetti in proposito mi venisse, sì come hora di difenderle mi è data cagione, di quei tutti, che io sapessi non ne tacerei uno.

URANIA: THE STORY OF A YOUNG WOMAN'S LOVE

little injury that is done to them. Leaving aside the moderns, tell me, who could imagine a crueler revenge than that of the ancient and most ferocious Medea? Or similarly, that of Procne?[35] Nor would I say that one should hold Circe any less vicious than these others, since in return for the pleasures received from many handsome and amorous young men, she would turn them into horrible monstrous beasts.[36]

"Therefore please refrain from saying that women are so good that they know how to do only good, and never evil. For we have shown you what they are capable of, and they do many wicked things to many people; and when their weakness prevents them from getting their own hands on people, they find ways to get men to place their victims within their power. Because of this one can conclude that they are always inflicting evil, and are not responsible for anything good. Perhaps you are a paid advocate of theirs; for if you were, you would have a fine reason to defend their point of view so valorously. Nonetheless, we are not obliged to believe so easily the things it pleases you to say on their behalf."

"You have certainly gotten quite the wrong impression about the kind of person I am, if you imagine that passion has moved me to say anything in defense of women," answered Urania at that point. "Indeed, you must believe that only reason, and nothing else, could ever move me to speak in anyone's defense. I have told you, and demonstrated to you (and I believe to have told and demonstrated the truth, since you yourselves have already admitted it), that women are only a little less perfect than we men. In this regard I was referring only to good women, and not evil ones; and I did not mean to say that no wicked or evil women exist. Rather, I say to you that as soon as it is proposed that I tell of women's defects, in the same way that I have just spoken in their defense, I will not omit a single relevant point.

---

[35] For Medea and Procne, see Ovid, *Metamorphoses* 6.426–674 and 7.1–424.

[36] See Ovid, *Metamorphoses* 14.8–74 and 14.242–415. Neither in the *Metamorphoses* nor in the tenth book of Homer's *Odyssey* (10.133–574; trans. Murray, 1:355–85) is Circe seen to seduce men before transforming them. However, such a process is indeed emphasized in Boccaccio's *Famous Women*, in the context of Boccaccio's usual euhemerism, which stresses symbolic over actual transformations: ". . . this woman . . . was forceful and eloquent but not overly concerned with keeping her chastity untarnished as long as she got something she wanted. With her wiles and charming words not only did she entice many who reached her shore to join in her wantonness: some she pushed into robbery and piracy . . ." (trans. Brown, 153).

"Io dicevo, dico, o pur volea dirvi che chi vole le sceleragini de' più tristi huomini con quelle delle più triste donne uguagliare quasi incomparabili sono; et voi dite che quei mali ch'elle non possono da loro fare, s'ingegnano di dar materia a gli huomini che gli facciano; et che elle di verun bene, ma solamente di male sono cagione; argomento per lo vero d'ogni fondamento privo. Nè saprei dir giamai qual ragione mover vi possa a dover creder quello che nè si sa, nè si vede; onde date più tosto indicio che l'uso del mal pensare, che alcuna pur verisimile ragione, a ciò dover dire vi spinga. Ma poscia che in dispregio loro adutti quegli essempi havete di crudeltà, di vendette, et di ruine per loro cagione, voglio con l'istesse vostr'armi difenderle, facendovi con quei medesimi da voi adutti essempi conoscere, come elle men de gli huomini sono crudeli, men vendicose, et meno d'alcuna ruina cagione. Et prima voi dite che per cagione di Elena la infelice Troia fu disolata, et tanti valorosissimi huomini furono a morte condotti; ma volgete l'ordine vi prego, et dite più tosto che il vano, et disordinato appetito di Paris primieramente, et dopo la sua tenace ostinatione fu cagion d'ogni male et ruina. Havete mai forse presso alcuno auttore veduto ch'ella per invitare il Troian nel suo amore a Troia n'andasse? O pure per tutti i lochi leggete sempre ch'egli per lei sviare in Grecia si conducesse; et s'egli con le amorose et dolci parole, con i lusinghevoli atti, et con le alte proferte a' suoi piaceri la indusse? Che volete voi dunque dire? Ma d'avantaggio il so che voi direste che come savia doveva alle dolci preghiere et lusinghe chiuder gli orecchi. O sciocca opinione di molti, le quali più a dentro che la scorza rade volte considerano! Chè se non hanno delle cose sensate inteligenza alcuna, dovrebbono pure almeno alle insensate assimigliandole qualche vero, et qualche proprio ritrarne. Non veggono questi tai tutto il giorno come la goccia dell'acqua della qual, cosa più molle et tenera non si trova; nondimeno ella ha forza, et potere di cavare, et forare il durissimo marmo, se spesse fiate sopra gli goccia. Quanto maggiormente dunque sarà arrendevole il cuore di donna gentile, la quale a sè vegga dinanzi colui che l'ama over finge d'amarla; et che con calde lagrime, con focosi sospiri, et con lamentevoli et dolci parole dirà che per lei arde, si consuma, et si strugge.

URANIA: THE STORY OF A YOUNG WOMAN'S LOVE

"I was saying, or was trying to say, that if one wishes to compare the evil deeds of the most wicked men with those of the most wicked women, one finds there is almost no comparison. You assert that women find ways to make men do those ills that they cannot do by themselves, and that they are never the cause of any good, but only evil; but this argument truly lacks any foundation, and I could never say what reason might cause you to believe this, for it is not apparent and could not occur to anyone. Therefore you should come to the conclusion that wrong thinking, instead of true reasoning, drives you to make these statements. But inasmuch as you have brought forth examples of cruelty, revenge, and ruin caused by women, in order to condemn them, I wish to use the same weapons to speak in their defense, showing you through the very examples you have mentioned how women are less cruel than men, less vengeful, and less likely to cause any ruin. First of all you say that Troy was brought down on account of Helen, and so many brave men were led to their deaths. But I pray you to reverse the order of things, and admit rather that the vain and immoderate desire of Paris in the first place, and subsequently his tenacious obstinacy, were the cause of every evil and the city's downfall. Have you perhaps read in the works of some author that Helen went to Troy for the purpose of seducing the Trojan? Or rather, do you not read in every source only this: that he went to Greece in order to lead her astray, and that he seduced her to his desires with sweet and loving words, with flattery and lavish gifts?[37] What would you say to that? But I know what you would say: that she, if she were wise, should have closed her ears to the sweet entreaties and the flattery. O foolish opinion of the multitude, who rarely look beyond the surface of things! For if they do not have any knowledge of sensible things, they should at least compare them to those which make no sense, so that they can draw some quality of truth from them. These people never see how a drop of water is the softest and weakest thing of all, yet it has the force and strength to wear away and perforate the hardest marble, if it drips thereon repeatedly. In view of this, how much more pliable must be the heart of a gentle lady, who sees before her the man who loves her, or who pretends to love her, and who expresses himself with warm tears, hot sighs, and sweet lamenting words, saying that he burns for her, melts for her, and is wasting away for love of her.

---

[37] Bigolina's vision of Helen as victim of a seducer is reflected in Ovid's *Heroides* 17. She would not have found so sympathetic a treatment of Helen in Boccaccio's *Famous Women* (trans. Brown, 146–47), nor in Christine de Pizan (*Book of the City of Ladies*, 2.61).

"Certamente chi bene il tutto considera, da pessima sorte per cagion di noi huomini è perseguitato questo infelicissimo feminil sesso; et lo voglio pur dire poi che alcuna donna qui presente non ci è, la quale mi possa udire. Elle miserelle sono da noi con tante vie et modi, con tanti ingegni, et molte fiate inganni sollecitate, che ogni alta et forte torre alla metà de combattimenti, ch'elle sopportano, dalla cima al basso ruinerebbe; et che peggio poi? Che s'elle s'arrendono sono donne di mala conditione, da quelli istessi, che grado lor ne dovrebbono havere, in ciascun loco divulgate. Et se dall'altra parte dure, et pertinaci a' lor preghiere si dimostrano sempre perfide, crudeli, discortesi, ingrate, et d'ogni virtù nemiche le chiamano. Onde io non saprei alle infelici in cotai casi qual altro men pericoloso consiglio donarle (quantunque questo assai spiacevole sia) eccetto che pregassero Dio, che di così poco grata vista, et men desiderati costumi le facesse, che alcun' huomo non se ne potesse invaghire. Chè altrimenti non è loro possibile di potersi dal mal dir delle nostre lingue schermire.

Ma per ripigliar dove la loro difesa lasciai, dico che havendovi dimostrato come non la greca donna, ma più tosto il frigio giovine fu cagion che l'antica Troia giacesse distrutta. Restami a dirvi come havendo le donne dato poca cagione di mali, hanno di molti bene et utili cagionati. Ditemi, non fu grande et memorabil utile quello che la hebrea Giudit con viril animo occidendo Holoferne al suo popolo diede? Nè forse minore fu quell'altro che la Reina Ester col suo savio ingegno et sapere al Re Assuero suo sposo persuadendo cagionò alli popoli suoi. Non furono ancora delle Sabine le operationi miracolose? Poi c'hebbero forza et sapere che que' due tanto nemici popoli cotanto amorevolmente in un sol popolo s'havessero a unire? Et che direm noi di quella savia Veturia Romana, madre di quel gran Coriolano? La quale quel che non poterono ottenere tanti grand'huomini legati et ambasciatori de' Romani, hebbe sola potere d'ottenere; et humiliò et intenerì il duro et depravato cuore del figliuolo. Chè s'ella non era, non potea Roma un grave eccidio, et forse estremo fuggire. Parvi forse che cotesti piccioli

URANIA: THE STORY OF A YOUNG WOMAN'S LOVE

"Certainly anyone who gives all of this due consideration will conclude that this most unhappy feminine sex is persecuted by ill fortune, and we men are the cause; and I wish to say this while there is no woman present here who might hear me. We chase after those poor wretches with so many ways, means, expedients, and at times even deceptions, that any tall fortified tower under siege would collapse from top to bottom if subjected to even half of what women bear. And what is worse, if they surrender they are considered women of ill repute, and those very men who should love them reveal far and wide what has occurred. If on the other hand they prove to be stubborn and resist all entreaties, men call them disloyal, cruel, discourteous, ungrateful, and enemies of every virtue. Because of this, in such cases the least risky advice I could give to women, even though it would be unpleasant, would be that they pray to God to make them so unattractive and ill-mannered that no man could possibly be attracted to them. Otherwise, it is not possible for them to defend themselves against our evil tongues.

"But I must return to where I left off in the defense of women. I have shown you how the Phrygian youth, and not the Greek woman, caused ancient Troy to lie in ruins. Inasmuch as women have been the cause of little evil, it remains for me to say how they have brought about many good and useful things. Tell me, did not the Hebrew Judith give something of great and memorable benefit to her people, by killing Holofernes in a spirit befitting a man?[38] Nor perhaps was the gift of Queen Esther to her own people any less useful, when she used her wisdom and skill to persuade King Ahasuerus?[39] Moreover, were not the deeds of the Sabine women miraculous, seeing that they had the power and the ability to unite lovingly, as one race, two peoples who were such great enemies?[40] And what are we to say about the wise Roman Veturia, the mother of the great Coriolanus? She alone was able to obtain what so many great men, who were legates and ambassadors of the Romans, could not; and she did this by humiliating and softening the hard, depraved heart of her son. If she had not been there, Rome could not have avoided a terrible massacre, one which might have brought disaster

---

[38] Judith 8–16. See also Christine de Pizan, *Book of the City of Ladies*, 2.31.

[39] Esther 5–9. See also Christine de Pizan, *Book of the City of Ladies*, 2.32.

[40] Livy, *Ab Urbe Condita* 1.13. See also Christine de Pizan, *Book of the City of Ladies*, 2.33.

benefici, et utili fossero, c'hanno dalle donne gli huomini ricevuti, sanza de gli altri molti, li quali per non tanto tedioso dimostrarmi lascio da parte?

"Voi dite poi ancora ch'elle più sono di noi huomini vendicose et crudeli; et io vi dico che noi vie più assai di loro crudeli siamo, et provar ve lo voglio. Ditemi, vi prego, di qual loco traggono le vendette la origine loro? So che dalle ricevute ingiurie mi risponderete, et è il vero: hor dunque se le donne vendicose sono, necessariamente seguita che da noi primieramente habbino ricevuta la offesa, poi che sempre la ingiuria alla vendetta precede. Et perciò noi siamo i crudeli, et non loro, ingiuriando noi prima, chi a noi ingiuria non fece; onde elle di noi vendicandosi, vengono quelli ad ingiuriare da i quali primieramente ingiuriate furono.

"Ma se mi diceste che Circe crudelissima fosse, la quale sanza alcuna ingiuria havere da que' giovani ricevuta, ignuda d'ogni pietade in diverse fere li tramutava. Ben dirò veramente con essi voi, ch'ella fosse crudele; nondimeno dall'altro canto possiamo quella tanta sua crudeltade in gran parte attribuire al troppo amore che a sè stessa portava. Imperciò che dubitandosi che andassero que' giovani la sua troppo lasciva vita manifestando, con incanti gl'impediva il potersi d'indi partire; et così del suo dubbio s'assicurava. Hor vedete come non era crudele, chè se crudel fosse stata, così come in fere li tramutava, et non gli uccideva, potendo medesimamente ucciderli, da intentione come non odio, che a quelli portasse, ma l'amore, c'haveva a sè stessa a ciò far la spingesse.

"Ma dite di gratia, con quai ragioni vogliamo noi tra gli huomini salvar Mario, Silla, Mezentio, Nerone, Falari, Ezzellino, et molti altri crudelissimi Tiranni? Li quali sanza ricever ingiuria da alcuno facevano de gli huomini crudelissimo

Urania: The Story of a Young Woman's Love

upon the city.[41] Do these things, which men have received from women, seem to you to be of minimal benefit and usefulness? I am leaving aside many others, so that my exposition not grow tedious.

"Then you say that women are more vengeful than men, and more cruel. I tell you that we are much more cruel than they are, and I wish to prove this to you. I pray you tell me, from what source do they draw their acts of vengeance? I know your answer: from the injuries they have received, and this is true; thus, if women are vengeful, by necessity it follows that first of all they have received offenses from us, since injury always precedes vengeance. Because of this we are the cruel ones, and not they, since we cause the first injury to those who have done us no wrong. Thus they come to do us harm, taking their revenge on us, after first having suffered at our hands.

"But perhaps you might say that Circe was most cruel, since she had received no ill treatment from those young men, and yet, deprived of all pity, she turned them into beasts. I tell you truly that she was indeed cruel; nonetheless from another perspective we can attribute that great cruelty of hers to a great extent to the excessive love which she felt for herself. Fearing that those young men would go off and make known her way of life, which was too lascivious, she impeded their departure from that place by means of incantations; by these means she dispelled her fears. Thus you see that she was not cruel, since she turned them into beasts and yet did not kill them. She could have killed them, as easily as she transformed them; but it was not hatred for them which moved her, but rather love for herself.

"But I pray you tell me, what reasoning would make us wish to excuse such men as Marius, Sulla, Mezentius, Nero, Phalaris, Ezzelino, and many other most cruel tyrants?[42] Without having received injury from anyone, they slaughtered

---

[41] Livy, *Ab Urbe Condita*, 2.39–40; Boccaccio, *Famous Women*, 222–31; Christine de Pizan, *Book of the City of Ladies*, 2.34. Bigolina follows the example of these three in providing the name Veturia for Coriolanus' mother. Plutarch (and Shakespeare) call her Volumnia (Plutarch, *Masters of Rome*, trans. I. Scott-Kilvert [Baltimore: Penguin, 1965], 46–49).

[42] For Marius and Sulla, see Plutarch, *Fall of the Roman Republic*, trans. R. Warner (Harmondsworth: Penguin, 1958), 11–98. For Mezentius, see Virgil, *Aeneid* 7.647–54 and 7.689–908. For Nero, see Suetonius, *The Twelve Caesars*, trans. R. Graves (Harmondsworth: Penguin, 1979), 213–46. Phalaris, the tyrant of Acragas who was famous for his brass bull in which he roasted his enemies, is mentioned in Orosius, *History*, 1.20 and Dante, *Inferno*, 27.7–15. For Ezzelino da Romano, Ghibelline ruler of Padua in the thirteenth century (whom Bigolina also mentions in "Giulia Camposanpiero"), see Cappelletti, *Storia di Padova*, 1:143–73, and Dante, *Inferno*, 12.109–10.

scempio; le quali lor crudeltà non si ponno con veruna ragione coprire, o escusare. Et perciò conchiudiamo vi prego, che se le donne non sono di noi huomini migliori, almeno non siano peggiori di quello siamo noi. Et conchiudiamo ancora potersi beato chiamar quell'huomo al quale da' cieli fu dato in sorte, che valorosa donna gli fosse compagna."

"Tante et così buone sono state le ragioni in favor delle donne da voi assignate," rispose alhora il giovine, "che homai possiamo confessar esser tutto vero quello, che detto ci havete; et per certo in grande errore eravamo, quando cotanto sinistro giudicio facevamo di loro. Nè vorrei vi giuro havere un gran tesoro guadagnato et non esser uscito di così folle credenza ch'io havevo, ch'elle altra cosa non potessero valere, eccetto che nell'accommodarcene ne' bisogni nostri, et alcuna volta seco trattenerci per fuggir l'otio, et non per altra cosa. Ma ben vi dico che da hora in dietro per cagion del dir vostro in quella somma veneratione le harrò tutte, nella quale debbono haversi, et tenere le cose quasi sacre, et divine."

"Troppo sète precipitoso," rispose al giovine la Urania; "et troppo vi lasciate da gli affetti vostri, ne gli estremi lontano dalla ragion trasportare. Poco fa non volevate che le donne alcuna cosa valessero, et mo' come divine tutte adorar le volete. Ben mi piace che di quel primo error siate fuori, ma non vorrei perciò che in un forse non minor foste entrato. Chè non minor fallo reputo il fare soverchio honore a cui di honor non è degno, di quello sarebbe il mancar di fare honore a cui meritevole ne fosse; et la ragione è da sè stessa chiara, et aperta.

"Dovete sapere signori, che assai rare sono le donne le quali meritino d'esser di vero et perfetto honore honorate; ma a migliaia ve ne son poi di quelle, le quali anco elle d'honor meritevoli sono, ma di quell'honore perciò dico, il quale tra nobili universalmente come hereditario distribuir si suole. Ma di quel particolare, et segnalato, il quale per heredità non viene, con gran tesori non si compera, nè per gran favori d'amici si può ottenere; anzi col proprio valore, con virtù, con l'ingegno, ma sopra ogn'altra cosa con un generoso, et bellissimo animo s'acquista, poche vi dico ritrovarsene al mondo. Et perchè pregato mi havete che io voglia consigliarvi et insegnarvi di qual conditioni dovete eleggervi donne amanti, cosa che a me par molto nova da udire; chè essendo gli accorti giovani, che dimostrate di essere non so come tale prosuntione potrà cadere in me sì che io debba credere d'esser io solo bastevole ad insegnare a tutti voi cinque. Nondimeno per farvi conoscere come assai mi compiaccio a tutti i virtuosi di compiacere, quel poco, ch'io saprò dirollo tutto.

"Dico adunque che l'huomo saggio, il quale ha già determinato a sua elettione d'innamorarsi, la qual cosa per lo creder mio a rari interviene che non vi siano

men very ferociously, and no reasoning can hide their cruelties, or excuse them. I pray you let us reach a conclusion: if women are not better than we men, at least they are not worse. And let us also conclude that any man may call himself blessed, if by chance the heavens have given him an excellent woman as a consort."

"The arguments in favor of women which you put forth are so many, and so worthy, that at this point we can admit that everything you have told us is true," responded the young man. "We were certainly quite wrong when we judged them so badly, and I swear I would not have wished to gain a great treasure, and yet not abandon a belief as absurd as the one I formerly held, that is, that women could not have any other value save to take care of our needs and amuse us from time to time, to alleviate our boredom. But I tell you truly: from this time on, because of what you have said, I will hold all women in the same lofty veneration that one should feel for things which are very nearly sacred and divine."

"You are too hasty," Urania answered him. "And too inclined to let your feelings run to extremes, far from reason. A little while ago you were not willing to believe that women were worth anything, and now you want to worship them all as if they were divine. I am well pleased that you have abandoned that first error, but I would not wish you to enter into a new one which might be no less grave than the other. For I believe doing high honor to those who are not worthy of it is just as grave a fault as failing to do honor to those who deserve it, and the reason for this is clear and apparent.

"You must know, gentlemen, that those women who deserve to have true and perfect honor bestowed upon them are quite rare. There are thousands of others who are deserving of honor; and in this case I am referring to the hereditary honor which is universally accorded to the noble class. But there also exists that particular, distinctive honor which cannot be inherited, which cannot be bought by great wealth, nor obtained through the great favors of friends. This honor is acquired through one's own personal worth, through virtue, through intelligence, and above all else through a generous and most lovely soul; and very few women who display this can be found in the world. You have requested that I advise and teach you as to which sort of women you should choose as lovers, and this seems a very strange thing to me, inasmuch as you have shown yourselves to be astute young men, and thus I might run the risk of appearing presumptuous if I thought myself capable, on my own, of teaching all five of you. Nonetheless, in order to show you how much I take joy in giving joy to those who are virtuous, I will tell you what little I know.

"I say therefore, that the wise man who has already chosen to fall in love (something which I believe happens to very few, since love catches most people

all'improviso colti; ma diciamo del saggio, che fa come il buon mercatante, il quale vole la mercatantia vedere, et conoscere prima che la comperi. Et così farà, al mio giudicio, il saggio huomo, chè innanzi ch'egli nell'amorosa pania ponga il piede, assai bene sopra e' casi suoi andarà avertito, poi che inveschiati che noi siamo non è in poter nostro lo a nostra voglia uscirne. Anzi a creppa core o vogliamo o non, siamo forzati entro starvi, quantunque molte volte ci è manifesto et aperto che colei, per la quale si struggemo non è soggetto tale, che meriti che debbiamo per lei tanto patire. O quante fiate una bella treccia et un vago ciglio assai perfidia, overo molta ignoranza ricuoprono! Chè quanto l'una et l'altra sia dannosa lo lascio a voi stessi giudicare. Ma perchè è necessario primieramente dire di qual grado ella dovrebbe essere, et poscia alle particolarità discendere, dico per quanto il mio giudicio mi detta che a me parrebbe che per molti sì honorevoli qual securi rispetti non dovrebbe l'huom saggio a niun modo in donna qual maritata fosse innamorarsi; ma che donzella o vidua fosse, quale delle due sorti li fosse più grata. Ma sopra ogn'altra cosa vorrei ch'egli havesse avertenza, che molto accorta et di un bell'animo ornata si ritrovasse; la qual cosa oltre che sommo diletto nello trattenersi seco riceverà, avenirgli ancora che da molti occorrenti pericoli egli, et sè stessa saprà salvare. Anzi più vi dico che ne' casi d'amore giudicherei che per la conservatione dell'uno, et dell'honore dell'altro, più necessaria cosa esser che la donna sia assai accorta che l'huomo, poi che l'honore dell'uno, et la vita dell'altro quasi sempre dall'accortezza, et buon reggimento della donna dipende, che quanti habbiamo veduti ne' loro amori pericolare, et a doloroso fine pervenire. Chè se ben consideraremo, tutto il male incontrato, dalla trascuragine, et poco accorgimento della donna lo deremo esser proceduto.

"Et perciò dovrebbe la donna amata maravigliosamente esser accorta, ma d'una accortezza, la quale da fintioni, da falsità, da inganni, et da molt'altre malvagie qualitadi non sia accompagnata; come ritrovarsi in molte, spesse volte si vede. Della quale accortezza un'altro non minor beneficio ne potrà l'huom saggio cavare, il quale sarà che essendo egli saggio, et ella accorta meglio le sarà il valor dell'amante suo manifesto; et assai più conoscerà quanto egli vaglia, che una ignorante, et sciocca non farebbe. Alla qual cosa seguirà che quanto più meritevole lo conoscerà, tanto l'harrà più in pregio, et ameralo, il quale effetto poi un'altro non minore nel saggio huomo cagionerà; cioè che conoscendosi tanto amato, di doppio amore accendendosi, un sommo contento goderà in sè stesso.

URANIA: THE STORY OF A YOUNG WOMAN'S LOVE

by surprise) acts like a good merchant who wishes to see and become familiar with his merchandise before he buys it. In my judgment a wise man should do the same thing, before putting his foot in the sticky snare of love: he should be warned in advance about love's nature, since once we are trapped it is beyond our power to escape, and we are forced to stay there whether we like it or not, even if it kills us. So often it becomes obvious and clear to us that the woman we are pining for is not the sort that is worth so much suffering — oh, how many times do beautiful tresses or a lovely set of eyelashes serve as a mask for much disloyalty, or ignorance! Which of these is the more dangerous I leave to you to decide. But inasmuch as it is my task first of all to tell you what the quality of the woman you choose should be, and then get down to the details, I say that, as far as my own judgment dictates, it would seem that for many sure reasons, and honorable ones, a wise man should by no means fall in love with a woman who is married. She should be a maid or a widow, whichever of the two he finds most pleasing; but above all else, I would like him to be sufficiently shrewd to select a woman who is wise and adorned with a beautiful soul. Aside from the great delight he will derive from her company, if she has these qualities, such a woman will know how to save him, and herself, from the many perils which might occur. What is more, in love situations I am convinced that it is more necessary that the woman be much more intelligent than the man, as far as her well-being and his honor are concerned, for the honor of the man and the very life of the woman depend almost always upon the cleverness and proper comportment of the woman. We have seen so many encounter dangers in their love affairs, and come to tragic ends, and if we consider carefully, we see that all of these evils derive from carelessness and the lack of cleverness on the part of the woman.

"Therefore the beloved woman must be marvelously clever, endowed with a cleverness that is not conjoined with lies, falseness, deceptions, and various other evil qualities, as is often seen in the case of many a woman. A wise man will be able to derive one other considerable benefit from this woman's cleverness, for if he is wise and she is intelligent her beloved's merits will be made plainer to her, and she will also have a far greater awareness of his value than would an ignorant or foolish woman. It follows that being aware of his merits she will esteem him and love him even more. This in turn will have an effect on the wise man which is no less important: that is, knowing that he is so loved by her, his own love will burn at double strength, and thus he will enjoy the greatest contentment.

"Vorrei che il saggio huomo havesse avertenza ancora che questa donna da lui eletta non fosse del tutto vana, cioè ch'ella havesse il suo cuore inchinevole; et disposto d'andar quà et là vagando sempre. Chè s'ella nell'altre sue attioni tenerà un cuor vario et instabile, nelle cose d'Amore vario, et instabilissimo terrallo; il chè è poi cagione di molti sospetti, et d'infiniti disturbi di mente.

"Harrei piacere ancora che la donna alquanto, anzi molto dotta nelle volgari lettere fosse, et di quelle assai se ne dilettasse; et di molte antiche istorie havesse vedute; la qual cosa due buonissimi effetti farebbe, cioè che stando sempre in honorevole essercitio di mente, non occuperebbe l'animo in tanti pensieri, et meno in dishonorevoli operationi. Chè in fine io non so conoscere il maggior spogliatore de buoni costumi, deviator d'ogni buona opera; et per conchiuderla struggitor di virtute come è il pessimo otio, il quale all'incontro è poi d'ogni mal vitio soppiantatore. Chè non potendo lo intelletto humano di sua propria natura mancare, la quale è di continuamente discorrere, et varie imaginationi in sè stesso formare, pur che occupato nelle varie alterationi de' sensi non si trovi, overo ne gli ordini et essercitij di tutto il corpo, perciò ritrovandosi la persona otiosa, et volendo lo intelletto al solito suo effetto dar opera, avien che di qual tinta egli è macchiato, di tal colore genera, et partorisce li suoi concetti. Imperciochè ogni seme produce il frutto a sua natura conforme; et vengo con cotesto mio dire a significarvi che quella persona, la quale a qualche virtuosa operatione non si ritrova l'animo haver aplicato da necessitade è astretta tutt' il tempo che da suoi ordinarij negotij le avanza, o vanamente o vitiosamente dispensare, come la isperienza in quelle donniciuole delle contrate vediamo; le quali i giorni delle feste facendo massa, et di loro stesse circolo, dicono una a gara dell'altra tutto quello che di questo et quell'altro fanno, et molte ve ne sono, le quali per dimostrar più di qualch'un'altra saperne dico, ancora aggiongendovi di quel, che non sanno, nè ponno sapere; onde aviene che assai volte tal cosa vengono a far manifesta, la quale con la tortura si dovrebbe negare.

"Hor vedete dunque come è dannosa et pericolosa cosa, sì all'huomo quale alla donna, lo starsi mai punto otiosi, et questo dico per quelli che virtuosi non sono. Imperciochè mai il virtuoso sta in otio, quantunque esteriormente non si essercitasse, anzi più è lontano dall'otio, et più opera mentre attualmente non si essercita, che quando porta per essercitio gran fatica; come il vitioso all'incontro per fatica, ch'egli faccia mai non ha operato, non intendendosi esser da tenere operatione quella, la quale seco alcuna lode non porta.

Urania: The Story of a Young Woman's Love

"I would like this wise man to have certain knowledge that the woman he chooses not be at all vain; which is to say she must not have a fickle heart, inclined ever to wander here and there. For if she has an inconstant and changeable heart in her other actions, it will be inconstant and most changeable in love, and this will cause much suspicion and endless mental distress.

"I would also like the woman to be somewhat, nay, extremely knowledgeable in vernacular literature, and to take great pleasure in it. She should be familiar with many ancient tales, for this would have two most excellent consequences: it would provide a proper activity for her mind, so that her soul would not be occupied with many dishonorable thoughts and deeds. Indeed, I know of nothing more inclined to deprive one of proper manners or distract one from good deeds, in sum, nothing more capable of destroying virtue, than that most wicked thing, idleness; and in fact such idleness is the root of every evil vice. For the human intellect cannot fail to act according to its nature, which means it must be continually engaged in discourse, and continually form images within itself, provided that it is not distracted by various shifting sensory perceptions, or else by the disciplined exercises of the entire body. Therefore when a person becomes idle, and yet the intellect wishes to go about its customary activities, it happens that such an intellect is colored by idleness, and thus conceives and gives birth to concepts of that same color. Every seed produces fruit according to its nature. By saying all this, I mean to show you that a person who does not apply his or her soul to deeds of virtue is compelled, by necessity, to spend all the time that remains after normal duties in useless or improper activities, as we see in the case of those small-minded neighborhood women who gather in crowds on feast days and compete with one another in telling what this or that person is up to. In order to show they know more than anyone else, many of these women add comments about things they do not know, and cannot know; and thus it occurs quite often they reveal certain things which must then be denied under torture.

"So you see what a hurtful and dangerous thing it is to remain the least bit idle, and this goes for men and women both. I intend this for those who are not virtuous, for the virtuous person is never idle, however much he or she may appear on the surface not to be doing anything. Indeed, it is not during a great physical effort that such a person is most active, and farthest from the state of idleness, but rather when he or she is not actually moving. On the other hand, a person given to vice is never truly active when engaged in physical effort, and does not understand that such effort does not constitute real activity, and is not in itself praiseworthy.

"Quanto debba esser poscia la donna dal saggio huomo eletta di modestia, di bei costumi, et d'humili, et belle maniere ornata, non m'affaticherò a estenderlovi altrimenti, poi che si sa che tale è donna a cui veruna di queste parti manca, quale arbor sanza fronde, prato sanza herba, et fonte sanza acqua sarebbe. Ma sopra ogn'altra cosa questo saggio huomo consigliar vorrei, chè se la buona sua sorte gratia gli concedesse (la quale a rari conceder suole) ch'egli in tal donna s'abbattesse, la quale tutte queste buone conditioni da me raccontatevi havesse seco; lo consiglierei dico, che oltre che per haver la gratia di colei fortunato dovrebbe tenersi, che anco si disponesse a non giammai farle un pur così picciolo torto, che punto il cuor di lei havesse a turbare; anzi con fedeltà, et sincero amore cara tenerlasi sempre."

Di poco mancò che mentr'ella quest'ultime parole diceva, le lagrime fuor de gli occhi non le uscissero; et a gran fatica le ritenne, con tanta efficaccia dal cuor le venivano. Imperciò che parendo a lei d'esser ella stessa tale, che sopra ogn'altra tutte le già dette ottime parti seco portasse; et per le quali parevale che più d'ogn'altra doveva dal suo Fabio esser tenuta in pregio, et amata. Nondimeno vedevasi per cagione del poco conto ch'egli di lei teneva esser condotta a dover andare pel mondo errando; et perciò da uno incomparabile affanno in quel punto assalita poco vi mancò che contra sua voglia non facesse a que' giovani l'error suo manifesto. Ma pure perché di grandissimo cuore era fece forza a sè stessa, et nel travagliato petto l'amoroso incendio tenne rinchiuso.

Ma essendo fuor di misura desiderosa di levarsi di quel loco per potere alle lagrime allargar la via, et etiandio con voce sfocare l'amarissima sua passione, perciò con bel modo chiese a' giovani di partirsi licenza, li quali quantunque fossero stati estremamente contenti che quel così savio non da loro conosciuto giovine per qualche giorno si fosse seco rimaso. Nondimeno vedendolo pur d'andar deliberato, poi che l'hebbero assai ringratiato, et molto più offertisegli, li dieder buona licenza; et vollero ancora per emmenda della usatagli discortesia forse tre miglia di camino contra la voglia di lei tenerle compagnia.

Urania: The Story of a Young Woman's Love

"I will not make any further effort to demonstrate to you the extent to which a woman chosen by a wise man must be modest, and must display the best manners, as well as habits which are both genteel and humble; for it is well known that any woman who lacks even one of these qualities is like a tree without branches, a meadow without grass, a spring without water. But above all else I would like to give this wise man the following advice: if his good luck should grant that he find such a woman (and rare is the man who is so lucky), that is, a woman who has all the qualities I have just described, I would advise him not only to think himself lucky to be in her good graces, but also to see to it that he never does her the slightest wrong, that he never brings distress to her heart. Instead, he should always hold her dear, with a true and faithful love."

As she was saying these last words, Urania could scarcely refrain from weeping. Her heart was all too ready to send forth tears, but with great difficulty she kept them in. For it seemed to her that she herself was that very woman, the one who displayed more of those aforementioned excellent qualities than all other women; moreover, those were the very qualities which she imagined should have caused Fabio to esteem her above all others, and to love her. Despite this, she saw that his low regard for her had caused her to wander through the world. Thus it was that at this point she was assailed by an incomparable sense of anguish, so that in spite of herself she nearly revealed her deception to the young men. However, her stout heart allowed her to take control of herself, and she managed to keep the amorous flame enclosed within her troubled breast.

Still, she greatly desired to leave that place in order to allow her pent-up tears to flow freely, and also to give vent to her most bitter passion; therefore with polite words she asked the young men's permission to depart. They would have been extremely content to have that youth, so wise and yet so mysterious, remain with them a few days; but since they saw that he was resolved to be on his way, they gave him leave, thanking him profusely, and offering him many favors. Moreover, in order to make up for their previous discourtesy, they insisted on accompanying Urania for three miles, despite her objections.

IV

Ma come i giovani da lei tolti si furono ritornò la infelice più che altra volta facesse, nel suo amaro pianto e lamento. Et così tra lagrime, sospiri, et lamenti molte città della Italia hebbe cercate; poco però in ciascuna fermandosi. Ma essendo già ne' i confini di Toscana arrivata, si ritrovò un giorno più de gli altri da tanto fera et crudel passione amorosa assalita, che diffidandosi di poter sanza il suo Fabio più vivere, lasciossi dalla disperatione vincere, et deliberossi al tutto di non voler più mangiare, et in tal modo lasciarsi morire. Et havendo quel giorno sino passato il mezzo per luoghi habitati cavalcato, et dopo essendo in una solitaria et gran campagna entrata, che sino alla sera sanza mai persona veder la condusse.

Et come di molti suole avenire, li quali chiamano et desiderano la morte ogn'hora, ma poi quando la si veggono vicina cercano con ogni lor saper et poter di fuggirla; così avenne della infelice Urania, che vedendo avicinarsi la notte, et che sola in quella solitudine si ritrovava, stanca dal cavalcare, et assai debole pel lungo digiuno, da così grande paura del proprio male sentì pungersi il cuore, che se havesse saputo dove la notte ricoverarsi per salvarse la vita assai volontieri l'havrebbe fatto, nè per cosa del mondo parevale di più voler così vilmente morire. Et perciò dati de' sproni al cavallo, il quale più di riposo et di mangiar che di trottar havea voglia, come la buona sua sorte volse nel tramontar del sole, quasi nel fine di quella grande campagna ritrovò una osteria, della quale accortasi parvele (tanta fu l'allegrezza che 'n quel punto sentì) che da morte a nuova vita ritornata fosse. Et essendo colà gionta, et chiamato l'ostieri chiedendoli di smontare et alloggiarsi, si sentì una molto contraria risposta al suo bisogno dare. Imperciò che le fu risposto, come una grande gentildonna fiorentina giovane et vidua, la quale per sodisfare a' suoi voti, con gran compagnia di servi, et serve a nostra Donna di Loretto n'andava,

IV

As soon as the young men had left her, the unhappy woman resumed her bitter weeping and laments, even more than before. With such tears, sighs, and complaints she passed through many cities of Italy, pausing only a little while in each. One day, however, when she had reached the border of Tuscany, she found herself more assailed than ever by a love passion so savage and cruel that she came to doubt that she could ever go on living without Fabio. Allowing herself to be overcome by desperation, she resolved to stop eating and thus bring about her death. It was past noon, and after she had ridden through inhabited areas, she came to a wide and deserted region, which she traversed until evening without seeing anyone.

It is often the case that those who desire death, and continually cry out for it, still employ all their power and wisdom in an attempt to flee when they see it approach. So it was with the unhappy Urania, when she saw she was alone in that solitude, with night approaching. Tired from her ride, and very weak from her long fast, she felt her heart pierced by so great a fear that she gladly would have sought shelter for the night, if she but knew where to find it, in order to save her life. It no longer seemed to her that anything in the world could have made her wish for so vile a death. So she put spurs to her horse, which had a keener desire for rest and food than trotting, and as fate wished it she found an inn almost at the end of the desolate region, just as the sun was setting. When she saw this she felt such great joy that it seemed to her that she had come back to life, after being dead for a time. She rode up and called to the innkeeper, asking if she could dismount there and find lodging; however, the answer she heard was completely contrary to her needs. She was told that a grand Florentine lady, a young widow who was on her way with a great entourage of serving men and women to fulfill

tutta l'osteria haveva occupata, et che havea comandato che alcun'altro non vi si dovesse alloggiare. La Urania udendosi dare così contraria risposta a sua aspettatione et bisogno, fu da così improviso, et fiero dolore assalita che sanza potersi ritenere, con gran voce, "Ahimè meschina, sventurata," gridando, et aperte le braccia lasciossi giù del cavallo cadere.

Non mancò chi tosto la novella di cotale accidente alla bella Emilia rapportasse, che tale fu il nome di quella giovane gentildonna, ch'ivi s'era alloggiata. Ond'ella, ch'era benigna assai, inteso il pietoso caso, molto tosto ella stessa colà si condusse, dove mossi da pietade e' suoi servi insieme con l'oste s'ingegnavano di ritornar nella tramortita Urania gli vaganti spiriti; nè cosa vi giovava, che le facessero. Ma essendovi giunta la bella donna, et vedendo a tai termini quel bel giovine condotto, et assai nobile all'ornato vestir giudicandolo, si sentì nel cuore da una insolita pietà et tenerezza tutta commovere.

Perchè fattolo da' suoi servi soavemente da terra levare, lo fece su quel proprio letto riporre, che per lei preparato s'era. Et indi con acqua fresca di sua mano il viso brufandole, molto tosto la fece in sè rivenire; et ritornata essendo, nè accorgendosi bene, tra il male et la passione che le lo vietavano, dove ella si fosse, incominciò con un grande lamento da molte lagrime accompagnato a maledir la dura sua sorte, che mal grado suo, et per dovere tanto stentare l'haveva ancora in vita serbata.

La gentildonna che quantonque non l'haveva se non quasi simile ad un morto veduto, et erale nondimeno tanto nell'aria piacciuto, che già si sentiva tutta del suo amore accendersi; et perciò volendolo, pur che possibil le fosse, consolare, più vicina al letto facendoglisi, et postagli la mano su la fronte, così amorevolmente gli disse: "Vago giovine, io non posso pensarmi da qual sinistra fortuna potete esser cotanto combattuto, che habbia havuto forza di così malamente offendervi che sprezzando la vita, debbiate la morte cercare. Chè se 'l giudicio non mi inganna alla gentil' aria vostra, et alle belle creanze parmi di dover credere che ancora di nobil sangue esser debbiate; per la qual cosa parrebbemi che etiandio di nobilissimo animo doveste essere. Il che sarebbe non lasciandovi tanto da gli aversi casi della Fortuna oprimere, che poi havesser potere nella vile disperatione condurvi. Ma comunque si sia, perchè sommamente di voi son divenuta pietosa, et non men

Urania: The Story of a Young Woman's Love

a vow to Our Lady of Loreto,[43] had occupied the whole inn, and had commanded that no one else be permitted to stay there. When Urania heard a response so contrary to her expectations and needs, she was suddenly overcome by terrible anguish. "Alas, what a wretched and miserable woman!" she cried out in a great voice. Then, opening her arms, she let herself fall from her horse.

It did not take long for the news of this incident to be reported to the lovely Emilia, the young noblewoman who was staying at the inn. She, who was very kindhearted, went straight to the place as soon as she heard the sad tale, whereupon she found that her servants and the innkeeper, all moved to pity, were trying to restore the unconscious Urania's vanished spirits. None of their efforts were successful, however. When the lovely lady arrived, and saw that fair youth reduced to such a state, she judged him to be of very noble rank on account of his dress, and felt herself moved within her heart by extraordinary pity and compassion.

She had her servants gently lift him from the ground, and place him on the very bed that had been prepared for her. With her own hand she bathed Urania's face with fresh water, and very soon made her come to her senses. When she was conscious, yet not fully aware of where she was on account of her weakness and emotional distress, she began a great lament, accompanied by much weeping, and fell to cursing the hard fate which, in spite of her sufferings, had kept her alive.

Even though the lady had thus far only seen him looking like a dead man, she had already found the youth so pleasing that she was beginning to burn with love for him.[44] Therefore, wishing to comfort him as much as might be possible, she moved closer to the bed. Placing her hand on his forehead, she spoke to him with loving words: "Fair youth, I cannot imagine what ill fortune could have been strong enough to strive against you, and cause you so much harm that you disdain life, and seek death. If my judgment does not deceive me, I take your genteel ways and good manners to indicate that you are of noble blood; and thus it seems to me that you must also possess a noble soul. Yet such a soul should not allow you to be so oppressed by contrary turns of fortune that you reach a point of extreme desperation. But whatever the case, I have so much pity on you that I now

---

[43] Loreto, near Ancona, is the site of the Holy House of the Blessed Virgin, reputedly transported there from Nazareth by angels in the thirteenth century (see H. Gillett, *New Catholic Encyclopedia*, 8:993–94). Bigolina is consistent in her use of the spelling "Loretto."

[44] On the motif of the cross-dressed woman who unintentionally attracts other women in the context of the medieval French romance, see V. R. Hotchkiss, *Clothes Make the Man: Female Cross-Dressing in Medieval Europe* (New York: Garland, 1996), 105–24.

desidero di porgervi aiuto di quello c'hora nel consolarvi mi vedete pronta; pregovi perciò che siate contento, come a carnal sorella fareste, tutti gli amari casi vostri scoprirmi, et insieme manifestarmi quale è 'l nome vostro, chi siete, et dove, et per qual cosa così errando andavate."

La Urania vedendosi quella bella giovane sopra, et che così dolcemente la confortava, pregandola che le volesse la sua disgratia raccontare; et parendole costei più che alcuna altra mai vedesse cortese, et gentile. Perciò assai humilmente, poscia che più focosi sospiri hebbe dal profondo del cuore cavati, così le rispose. "Nobilissima Signora, se mai per alcun tempo hebbi cagion di dovermi della malvagia mia sorte dolere, hora più che mai ne havesse me ne trovo haver cagione, poi ch'ella m'ha a tale condotto ch'io non vaglio in conto alcuno per render condegno guidardone alla troppa cortesia, che mi usate. Chè non havendomi più che hora veduto, con tanta amorevolezza et con le gentilissime mani vostre m'havete da quelle della morte levato, et non ancora di giovarmi satia, di darmi ancor maggior aiuto mi vi offerite. Onde non sapendo altro che mi fare, almen questo dirovvi, che quel tanto poco, o assai, ch'io vaglio tutto alla somma vostra cortesia et gentilezza lo dedico.

"Ma per dirvi chi et quale io mi sia, dicovi, Signora mia, che di così picciol grido è la fama del nome mio, che quantunque io lo vi dica, non è perciò che vi giovi per farmivi più conoscere di quello, che tacendolo mi conosceste. Nondimeno perchè la mia intentione è d'obedirvi dirolovi adunque. Io sono, Signora, uno sventurato giovine d'assai humile sangue nato in Salerno, Fabio è il mio nome. Et essendo (come ne gli huomini suole incontrare) da strana fortuna perseguitato, la sorte della qual pregovi che non vi vogliate curar di altramente intenderla, sonmi deliberato perciò da quella arrabbiata fortuna cercando di fuggire, di mai non restarmi sin tanto che o gentilhuomo, o gentildonna io ritrovi, che virtuosi siano, al servigio de' quali io possa quel resto di tempo, che m'avanza almeno in pace, se non contento, passare."

Poi che la Urania hebbe fornito di dire, la piacevole Emilia crollando il capo così le rispose. "Deh Fabio, ch'io non voglio già che vi pensate di farmi credere che, come dite, d'humile sangue siate nato; imperciò che i nobilissimi costumi vostri, et l'accorto parlare mi danno ad intendere che non pur nobile, ma nobilissimo siate. Nè piaccia a Dio che questi vostri rari et bei costumi, li quali non perchè voi serviste ad altrui, ma perchè vi facessero d'altrui esser servito, et amato, vi furono da' Cieli conceduti; che io voglia, pur che da voi non manchi, ch'essi servino ad alcuno mai. Io son gentildonna di Firenze, et da molti nobili parenti

URANIA: THE STORY OF A YOUNG WOMAN'S LOVE

desire to offer you not just consolation, as I have so readily demonstrated, but also help. I pray therefore that you agree to reveal to me all of the terrible things which have befallen you, as if I were a sister of your flesh and blood; and moreover I would like you to tell me your name, who you are, and what you were seeking when you were wandering about."

As Urania beheld this beautiful young woman above her, who so sweetly comforted her and requested her to tell of her hard fate, it seemed to her that she had never seen a woman who was more courteous or kind. Therefore, drawing hot sighs from the depths of her heart, she answered. "Most noble lady, if ever I have had cause to grieve over my ill fortune, now is a more fitting time than ever, inasmuch as this fortune has led me to such a state that I lack all means to bestow upon you a suitable reward, in return for the too great courtesy which you show me. Even though you had never seen me before this moment, with much kindliness and with your own gentle hands you have saved me from the clutches of the hands of death; and now, not yet tired of acting as my benefactor, you are offering me even greater help. Not knowing what else to do, at least I will tell you this: whatever I am worth, be it little or much, I dedicate it all to your very great courtesy and kindness.

"But with regard to letting you know who and what I am, I tell you, my lady, that the renown of my name resounds so little that you will know me no better if I reveal it than you would if I kept silent. Nonetheless, since my intention is to obey you, I will tell you about myself. I am, my lady, a wretched young man of very low degree who was born in Salerno. My name is Fabio. As often occurs to men, I am afflicted by bizarre turns of fortune, the nature of which I pray you not to seek to know. In an effort to flee my wrathful fortune I have decided not to rest until I find a virtuous gentleman, or a gentle lady, in whose service I can pass what time remains to me; in peace at least, if not in contentment."

Urania had finished speaking, so the lovely Emilia, shaking her head, answered her thus: "Ah, Fabio, I do not accept your efforts to make me believe that you are lowborn, inasmuch as your very noble manners and your refined speech give me to understand that you are not only noble, but most noble. Moreover, let it not be God's will that these remarkable and pleasing manners of yours, which were granted to you by the Heavens not so that you should be a servant, but rather that you should be served, and beloved, by others, ever be employed in service to anyone; or so I would wish it, provided there be no failing in you. I am a noblewoman of Florence, descended from many noble ancestors, and it has been little

discesa, et di poco è passato l'anno che d'uno gran cavalier che mi era marito io restai vidua; il quale d'ogni sua ricchezza, che abondantissimo n'era mi ha lasciata herede, et hora ne vado per sodisfare ad un voto, ch'io feci per cagione d'una grande infirmità che io hebbi già alcuni mesi, a Nostradonna di Loretto. Et se volete venir meco, sodisfatto che io harrò al voto si ritornaremo in Firenze, dove ben servito, et honorato da tutti sarete, et come carnal fratello terrovi; nè voglio che men habbiate libertà di poter delle facultadi mie a vostra voglia disporre, di quello, che io stessa mi habbia. Nè altra cosa a farvi così larga offerta m'induce, eccetto il gentil aere vostro, et i vaghi et rari costumi, delli quali ornato vi veggio; et che mi danno ad intendere che tale sarete, quale il mio cuore vi desidera."

Infinite furono le gratie, che la Urania alla cortese gentildonna hebbe rendute, et parendole che la Fortuna le havesse miglior ventura preparata, ch'ella stessa non havrebbe saputo imaginarsi. Imperciò che con costei poteva salvandosi da vergogna, commodamente vivere, fin tanto che l'amorosa pazzia le si fosse levata del cuore; che essendo homai di tanto vagar stanca, era fatta di riposarsi volontarosa. Et perciò dopo mille et mille gratie con gratissimi modi rendutele, la cortesissima offerta hebbe accettata; offerendosele altretanto d'esserle, per quanto s'estendevano le sue forze, amorevol fratello, et fedel servitore.

Et indi poco stando, di letto levandosi, allegramente cenarono insieme; et la matina per tempo la vaga Emilia, per ritrovarsi quel giovine, che tanto le piaceva sempre a canto, ritornò più allegra che altra volta mai fosse, nel suo viaggio. Et la Urania, che ad altro in quel tempo non attendeva, che di farsi grata alla gentildonna, tenendo l'amoroso tormento nel mezzo del cuore appiatato, sempre cavalcandole appresso, con la faccia più allegra, che far potesse, hora con dolci motti, et hora dotte rime cantando, et alcuna volta assai dilettevoli successi amorosi raccontandole s'ingegnava in piacere et gioco tenerla. Le quai cose erano cagione che di doppie amorose fiamme il cuor della Emilia verso lei s'accendesse.

Ma poi che tra tali piaceri hebbero col debito tempo il loro viaggio, sì dell'andar, qual del ritorno fornito, et che in Firenze furono ritornati, dove in amorosa pace la gentil Emilia godevasi la dolce vista del caro amante, non passorono molti giorni che alcuni suoi parenti le furono a casa, li quali per nome d'un nobilissimo Conte assai giovine et valoroso, acciò li fosse moglie la richiesero. Il quale già più mesi essendosi di lei acceso, haveva con sommo desiderio aspettato che l'anno del pianto, per lo morto marito passasse, et poscia a' suoi parenti chiederla; non si

Urania: The Story of a Young Woman's Love

more than a year since I became a widow at the passing of my husband, a great cavalier. He left me the heir to all of his wealth, which was considerable. Now I am on my way to Our Lady of Loreto in fulfillment of a vow which I made a few months ago on account of a severe illness which afflicted me. If you wish to accompany me, as soon as I have satisfied my vow we will return to Florence, where you will be well served and honored by all, and I will keep you with me as if you were a brother of my own flesh and blood. Moreover, I would not wish you to have any less freedom of access to my goods and resources than I myself have. Nothing else but your genteel air, and those rare and lovely manners which I see adorning you, induce me to make so generous an offer to you, and these are the very traits which give me to understand that you will acquiesce to my heart's desire."

Infinite were the thanks which Urania bestowed upon the courteous gentlewoman, and it seemed to her that fortune had provided her a better outcome than she could ever have imagined. For with this gentlewoman she would be able to live comfortably, and without shame, until such a time as her love madness would be lifted from her heart. By now she was tired of wandering, and desired to take some rest. Thus after thanking the lady thousands and thousands of times, in a very polite fashion, she accepted the very kind offer, offering to act both as a loving brother and faithful retainer to the lady, inasmuch as it was in her power to do so.

A little while later Urania got out of bed and the two had a merry meal together. In the morning the lovely Emilia resumed her journey in a happier state than she had ever been before, because she so enjoyed having that young man by her side. For her part Urania wanted nothing else at this point than to be pleasing to the gentlewoman, and so, concealing her love torment within her heart, she rode ever by her side with the most joyful expression she could muster. She also contrived to entertain and give pleasure to the lady, at times employing sweet witticisms, or else singing intricate rhymes; and sometimes she even recounted very delightful love stories. These things caused Emilia's heart to burn two times over with flames of love for her.

With pleasures such as these they finished the journey, both going and coming back, in a suitable space of time, and returned to Florence, where the gentle Emilia rejoiced in the sweet sight of her dear lover, and basked in amorous peace. Not many days had passed when some of her relatives came to her house, acting on behalf of a very noble count who was both youthful and valorous. They asked her if she would become his wife, since he had been burning for love of her some months, and had been waiting with great anticipation for the requisite year of mourning for her deceased husband to pass, so he could ask her relatives for her

pensando mai non ottenerla, massimamente essendo nobile, et ricco assai. Ma passato di subito l'anno essendosi posta la donna in viaggio per sodisfare al suo voto, gli fu perciò necessario l'aspettare il ritorno; il quale inteso, erasi a dimandarla a' suoi parenti condotto; li quali, come io dissi, da lei ridottisi, con grande instanza per nome del conte la chiesero, et assai a dovere a sì buon partito appigliarsi la confortarono.

Ma lei, che tutto il suo cuore haveva al suo caro Fabio rivolto, et considerando ch'ella era ricca a bastanza, per la qual cosa parevale che non dovesse, come d'avaritia spinta, per posseder maggior ricchezza, pigliar marito, che grato non le fosse; et restar di sodisfare al piacer di sè stessa, alla quale più desiderava, et parevale d'esser tenuta di compiacere, che a tutto il resto del mondo insieme. Et perciò fatto buon viso gli suoi parenti ad un tratto fece chiari, come per alhora non faceva conto di rimaritarsi, però ringratiandoli assai della loro amorevolezza verso lei dimostrata; soggiongendo ancora, che sommamente il partito di quel nobile Conte le piaceva tanto, che quando havesse havuto animo di voler marito non l'harrebbe cambiato con altro huomo del mondo.

Assai sopra tal materia le fu da suoi parenti detto, et ridetto; ma nulla lor valse, ch'ella pur sempre salda sopra il primo suo proposito si tenne. Perchè vedendo loro di non poter, come era il lor desiderio, sodisfare al Conte, mal contenti da lei si partirono; et ella, che all'incontro era doppiamente allegra, vedendosi da quel gran stimolo liberata, per far maggior la sua allegrezza, et a dieci doppie il suo piacer raddoppiare, non potendo più sopportar l'amoroso ardore, che dentro per lo suo Fabio il cuor le coceva, et parendole che di tutto il mal, ch'ella pativa, lei istessa ne fosse sola cagione, poi che potendo, tanto tardava a rimediarvi, rendendosi secura che della medesima sorte d'amore, co'l quale amava lei Fabio, esser riamata da lui; chè ben sapeva che essendo, come egli era, accorto, già aveduto si sarebbe quanto, et qual sorte focosamente l'amasse. Nè per altro pensavasi ch'egli di discoprirle il suo amor rimanesse, eccetto che per la gran modestia, che in lui conosceva, quasi che si credesse col suo dire, di doverla offendere.

Et perciò sì per levarli questa tema, et dubbio del cuore, come ancora credendo di dar rimedio a tante sue pene amorose, quel giorno istesso seco solo nella sua camera il trasse; et fattolo presso di sè sedere in cotal modo incominciò a dirli. "Fabio mio carissimo, perchè assai accorto ti conosco non mi affaticherò

hand. He never expected he would not receive it, especially since he was extremely rich and highborn; but since at the end of the year the lady had gone off on her journey, in order to fulfill her vow, he was forced to wait until she returned. As soon as he heard she was back, he betook himself to her relatives in order to ask for her; and they, as I have said, went to her and earnestly presented his petition, encouraging her to accept so fine an offer.

But the lady had turned her whole heart to Fabio, and since she considered herself to be quite rich enough already, it did not seem right to her to accept a husband whom she did not love, as if driven by avarice to possess even more wealth. Nor did she think it right to abandon all thought of her own pleasures, for she desired to satisfy herself above all else; indeed, she felt more obligated to follow her own interests than those of all the rest of the world taken together. Therefore, when she received her relatives, she thanked them warmly for the kindness they had shown her, but told them straight out that for the moment she had no plans to remarry. She added that the noble count's offer was quite pleasing to her, and whenever she would be in a mind to marry, she would not exchange him for any man in the world.

Her relatives belabored the issue over and over again, but to no avail, since she remained firm in her original decision. Seeing they were getting nowhere in satisfying the count, as they had desired, the unhappy relatives went on their way. For her part, the lady was twice as happy as before, seeing that she had managed to free herself from that great annoyance. Now she began to think of ways to make her joy even greater, and increase her pleasure tenfold; for she could no longer withstand the flames of her love for Fabio, which were cooking her heart from within. It seemed to her that she herself was the cause of all her suffering, for she was taking so long to resolve a problem that she was well capable of resolving. She made up her mind that Fabio loved her with the same sort of love that she bore for him; and inasmuch as she knew well that he was wise, she decided he must already have realized how much she was in love, and what sort of burning desire she felt for him. Moreover, she imagined that he had only refrained from revealing his feelings for her on account of his great modesty, a trait of his that she knew well; she convinced herself that he was probably thinking any revelation would offend her.

Therefore she brought him to her room alone, on that very same day, with the aim of not only removing this fear and hesitation from his heart, but also alleviating her own myriad sufferings of love. She had him sit down beside her, then began to speak: "My dearest Fabio, since I know you are very wise, I will

altrimente per farti conoscere quanto sia smisurato l'amor, che io ti porto. Imperciò ch'io son più che certa che prima che hora aveduto te ne sei, ma ben ho deliberato di farti hora manifesto, come l'intentione mia è stabilita di volerti, mentre che io vivo amare, et tenerti caro.

"Sappi Fabio mio, che que' miei parenti che hoggi vennero qui, non per altra cagione vi vennero, eccetto che per volermi con un molto nobile et ricchissimo Conte maritare, il quale già più mesi sono che di me fuor di misura innamorato si dimostra. Ma io, che in altra parte ho riposto il mio cuore per ritrovarmi havere in te solo fermato ogni mio desiderio, et pensiero, gli ho perciò, benchè con gran fatica licentiati, sopra questo saldo proposto solo fermandomi, ch'io per hora rimaritar non mi voglio. Hor Fabio dolcissimo, se a te par d'accettare una grata offerta, che colei che assai più che sè stessa t'ama ti appresenta, a te sta; benchè io so che essendo di nobilissimo core come sei, non ti mancherebbe l'animo d'accettare ogn'altro maggior dono di questo; come quello, che d'ogni gran bene sei degno.

"Il dono, che io t'offrisco è che ti degni d'accettarmi per moglie, anzi per serva, con quanto io possedo in dote; chè altro maggior desiderio in me non sento che di poterti tutti e' giorni di mia vita con fede servire. Hor dunque Fabio levami d'affanno ti prego, et tosto rispondi quello che ti detta il cuore di dover fare."

Quanto paresse acra, et amara alla Urania questa, che ad ogni huomo sarebbe parsa gratissima offerta, non è chi a pieno lo potesse raccontare; chè vedendosi tra tai termini ristretta si sentì in quel punto da un smisurato affanno stringere il cuore. Dubitavasi massimamente che se ella per donna si scopriva, vergognarebbesi la Emilia di molte parole et atti amorosi che fatto le haveva; et parendole d'esser stata da lei schernita, che in odio poi la togliesse. Nondimeno, perciò che fuor di misura era accorta, sanza molto pensarvi, assai tosto come risponder le dovea si risolse, et così le disse. "Signora Emilia, et padrona mia honoratissima, io non so se tra gli molti et feri assalti che m'ha fatti alli miei giorni la mia nemica Fortuna, io debba tener questo, che hora mi s'ha scoperto, per lo più memorabile di tutti gli altri quantunque tra gli altri uno così estremo me ne facesse, c'hebbe poter di levarmi fuor della propria patria et casa, et farmi andar per lo mondo errando; et forse ancora errante farei, se la mercede vostra con la tanta sua cortesia, et amorevolezza a miglior vita non mi recava. Io non so dico, se 'l duol ch'io sento hora,

not weary myself any further to make plain the great love I bear you. Though I am more than certain that you are already aware of this, I have decided to make it plain to you now that it is my firm intention to love you and hold you dear for as long as I shall live.

"I want you to know, my Fabio, that those relatives of mine who were here today came for no other reason than to marry me off to a very rich and noble count, a man who has shown himself to be madly in love with me for some months now. However, seeing that I have placed my heart elsewhere, and have fixed my desires solely in you, I sent my relatives away, which was no easy task, and insisted that it was my firm resolution not to remarry at the present time. Now, sweetest Fabio, it is your task to consider a pleasing offer, presented to you by the one who loves your more than she loves herself. I say this even though I know that a heart as noble as yours would never deny you the greatness of spirit to accept a gift even more lavish than this one; and this is fitting for a man such as you are, worthy of every good thing.

"Here is the gift which I offer: that you deign to accept me as your wife, indeed as your servant, with all that I possess for my dowry; for I can find no greater desire within me than to be able to serve you faithfully all the days of my life. Therefore Fabio, I pray you, banish my woes and give me a swift response, according to the dictates of your heart."

No one could fully describe how acrid and bitter this offer, which any man would have found extremely agreeable, seemed to Urania. Seeing the situation in which she was trapped, in that instant she felt her heart afflicted by limitless woe. She feared mightily that if she revealed her identity as a woman, Emilia would feel shame on account of the many words and deeds of love she had made plain; moreover, if Emilia were to feel herself scorned by Urania, her love would turn to hatred. Despite these fears, without a great deal of reflection Urania quickly came to a decision regarding her response, for she was so exceedingly intelligent. "Lady Emilia, most honored mistress," she said. "I wonder whether of all the ferocious assaults which fortune, my foe, has launched against me in my time, I ought to regard the one which you have just revealed to me as the most memorable, even though these assaults include one so extreme that it drove me from my home and country, and forced me to wander through the world. And perhaps I would still be wandering, if the great kindness and affection which your grace bestows had not led me to a better life. So let me repeat, I do not know if the pain

di non essermi conceduto di poter la tanto gratiosa, et liberalissima vostra offerta accettare, possa esser uguagliato da quello, che disperato da casa mi tolse. Anzi più tosto, se bene io considero, questo d'avantaggio vince et trapassa quello, poi che per quello io solo restavo offeso, et del mio mal solo sentiva il dolore; onde di questo del mio, et del vostro, che assai più mi grava sento pena, et cordoglio.

"Et per farvi, Signora, tutti i casi miei manifesti, et dirvi quello che io prima che hora non ho voluto dirvi; il giudicio, che di me primieramente faceste giudicandomi nobile, è vero, et punto non vi ingannaste. Imperciò che di Salerno assai nobile io sono; ma il più sventurato di me non credo che nel mondo la Natura altr'huomo creasse; che essendomi, come de' giovani è usanza, d'una nobile giovane innamorato; la quale per quanto il mio giudicio mi detta, et so che io non m'inganno; oltre che è assai bella, ella è poi la più gentile, et la più costumata, et di ciascuna sorte di bellezza d'animo la meglio qualificata, ch'altra donna si possa desiderare, et vedere. Et la mia buona sorte fu tale che per un tempo da costei, che Urania si chiama, tanto fui riamato che d'altro non parea che si pascesse, et nodrisce, che della vista, et della gratia mia. Della qual cosa a tanta gloria me l'arrecavo, che il più felice amante che nel mondo si ritrovasse mi reputava di esser; nè harrei la mia sorte con qual altra beata si ritrovasse, cangiata. Costei, che d'ogni honesto favore, che far mi potesse non mi mancava, a tale per compiacermi si condusse che d'essermi moglie con semplici parole mi promise.

"Ma non so, ahimè, da qual cagion procedesse che non passarono dapoi molti giorni, che mostrandosi fuor del suo costume di me schiva, venne a tanto poscia che non mi si lasciava nè poco, nè assai più vedere, del quale strano caso così dolente mi ritrovai, chè io fui quasi per lo gran dolore per impazzirne, et per morirmi d'affanno. Ma vedendo pur con mia grandissima doglia, che mai cotal sua rea opinion per cosa, ch'io mi facesse mutava, per mio men male, et per sodisfare a lei elessi di partirmi fuor della patria sperando ch'l tempo et li disagi ch'io patirei dovessero l'amorosa passione levarmi del cuore. Ma niente, vi giuro Signora mia, cotal pensier m'ha giovato, anzi quanto più dall'amato mio bene allontanando mi andavo, tanto di maggior fiamma et più forte desiderio di rivederla il cuore mi ardeva, et struggevamisi.

"Gliè vero che dapoi che la vostra mercede seco mi trasse (alla quale io sarò in eterno obligato) in gran parte ho sciemata la pena; che il continuo specchiarmi ne' vostri rari, et soavi costumi, il godermi incessantemente della grande bontà, et

Urania: The Story of a Young Woman's Love

which I feel now, on account of my inability to allow myself to accept your extremely gracious and magnanimous offer, can equal that which once sent me from my home, in a desperate state. Indeed, if I give it due consideration, my present grief overcomes and exceeds that other: for then I alone was hurt, and felt misery only for my own state, whereas now I feel pain and grief on both your account and mine, so that the condition weighs more heavily upon me.

"Now, lady, let me make known to you my entire situation, and tell you those things which at first I was unwilling to reveal. Your first judgment of me, that as I was a nobleman, is true, and you did not deceive yourself; for indeed I am a nobleman of very high degree, from Salerno. Yet I do not believe that Nature ever created another man more unlucky than I have been. In the fashion of young people, I fell in love; and the object of my affections was a young noblewoman who, as my own judgment tells me (and I know I am right in this), is not only extremely lovely, but also more endowed with gentility, good manners, and every sort of beauty of the soul than any other woman one could wish for, or ever hope to see. For a time my good fortune permitted that this woman, called Urania, loved me in return, and to such an extent that it seemed that she derived sustenance and nourishment from nothing so much as the sight of me, and from my good graces. So much did I glory in this that I thought myself to be the happiest lover in the world, and I would not have exchanged my good fortune for any other blessed state. She did not fail to bestow upon me every favor that propriety permits, and to please me she went so far as to promise, with mere words, that she would become my wife.

"But alas, for what reason I do not know, only a few days later she came to disdain me, in violation of her established custom; she would no longer let me see her, not even occasionally. This strange state of affairs left me so miserable that I nearly went insane, and nearly died, for grief. But, in spite of my tremendous pain, it was clear to me that nothing I did could change her cruel opinions, or work to my advantage; thus, in order to give her satisfaction, I decided to leave my homeland. I hoped that time, and the sufferings that I would undergo, would eventually remove all love passion from my heart. But I swear to you, my lady, this notion was of no benefit to me whatsoever: indeed, the farther I went from my beloved, the hotter my heart burned, consuming itself with desire to see her again.

"It is true that my pain has been greatly diminished ever since your compassion raised me up, and I will be forever grateful to you for this. I have been continually inspired by your sweet and incomparable manners, and have ceaselessly

cortesia vostra sono stati cagione, che per quanto io posso sono più vostro che mio divenuto, quantunque poco di libero mi sia rimaso, che quella ingrata della maggior parte di me fece acquisto, a benchè assai poco da lei tale acquisto prezzato sia. Hor dunque, Signora mia, potete conoscere quanto io sia libero per accettar la cortesissima vostra offerta; ma ben tutte quelle gratie di tanta vostra amorevolezza vi rendo, che per me maggiori render si possano."

O come trista, o come pessima parve questa insperata risposta alla bella Emilia, la quale con le lagrime su gli occhi così gli rispose: "Deh Fabio mio dolcissimo, ben sapevo io che gli meriti tuoi erano tali che altra maggior donna di quel che io sono non sarebbe ben degna di possederti. Nondimeno havendo dall'altra parte riguardo quanto sia la benignità tua mi confidavo in quella, rendendomi sicura che tu dovesti, non alla bassezza mia, ma alla grandezza del sincero amor, ch'io ti porto haver riguardo; et che il valor di quello presso il tuo gentil animo dovesse haver forza d'agguagliarmi con qual altra si voglia di me maggior donna. Chè già non son si sciocca Fabio mio, che io non conosca che non altro amor che ti occupi il cuore, ma il conoscermi di te indegna è cagione che con mia grandissima doglia così rifiutata m'habbi. Nè ancora crederei (di così nobile animo ti conosco) che mai dietro a donna che 'l tuo amor sprezzasse, per nobile et bella ch'ella si fosse, così vilmente ti volesti perdere. Ma sia che si voglia, io non voglio senon quel tanto che ti piace volere. Ma ben ti assicuro che da hora in dietro non sarà più alcuno, che giamai consolata, nè allegra mi vegga." Et qui spargendo un mar di lagrime fece fine.

La Urania, che si vedeva tra così stretti termini condotta, che essendo di simil conforto più ch'altra donna del mondo bisognosa, vedevasi hora quest'altra dinanzi languire, nè sapeva, che partito pigliare. Imperciò che 'l confortarla, poco, anzi nulla vedeva doverle giovare, et per darle aiuto non era buona; et perciò tutta conturbata nell'animo, et dal suo proprio duolo quel di lei misurando, et non men per la pietà che a sè stessa portava, che per quella, che alla Emilia haveva, piangendo anch'ella così le rispose. "Signora, quanta doglia io sento di non potere a gli comuni nostri desideri sodisfare, Iddio lo sa. Ma vie più di questo mi doglio assai, che in tale pessimo conto m'habbiate, come è, che non essendomi in maritaggio con altra donna legato, io di così altero, et superbo animo fosse, che negasse di pigliar voi per moglie; chè non che di me, ma d'ogni alto prencipe sareste degna. Oltre che l'obbligo che con essa voi tengo, dalla quale mi conosco haver la vita, è tale, che non che d'accettarvi per carissima moglie, come mi havete offerta, mi stringe, ma a dover farmi perpetuo servo de' vostri servi havrebbe forza di stringermi. Hor dunque Signora Emilia, io vi supplico et prego che se mai fede ad huomo

Urania: The Story of a Young Woman's Love

rejoiced in your great kindness and courtesy, to the extent that I have become more yours than mine; that is, inasmuch as it is in my power to do so, for there is so little of me left to give. That ungrateful woman took away the greater part of me, even if she barely appreciated what she had acquired. Therefore, my lady, you can see how free I am to accept your most courteous offer, even though I am as grateful as I can possibly be for the great love you have shown me."

O how sad, how terrible did this unexpected response seem to the lovely Emilia, who answered him thus with tears in her eyes: "Oh, my sweetest Fabio, I knew well that your great worth was such that a better woman than I am would not deserve to have you. Nonetheless I took your kindliness into account, and thus was confident that you would not consider my low state so much as the depth of the sincere love which I bear you. I hoped this love would work upon your kindly soul and cause it to regard me as the equal of any woman who might be better than I am. I am not so foolish, my Fabio: I am not unaware that your refusal of me, which has caused me much sorrow, is not due so much to another love which has taken over your heart, as it is to the fact that you regard me as unworthy of you. Nor could I believe that you would throw yourself away in such a vile fashion in the pursuit of a woman who disdained your love, however noble and beautiful she might be; for I know your greatness of soul would not permit this. Whatever the situation, I want nothing more than whatever it is your pleasure to desire. But I assure you, from this time forth, no one will ever see me joyful, or at peace." And with these words she fell silent, shedding a sea of tears.

Urania realized that she was in a very difficult situation. She, who was more in need of such comfort than any other woman on earth, watched this woman suffering before her, yet did not know what course of action to follow. She could see that any effort on her part to comfort Emilia would do no good, and nothing she could do would help. With her own soul in turmoil, Urania measured her pain against Emilia's, and felt no less pity for herself than she did for the other woman. Weeping, Urania answered her thus: "Lady, God knows the agony I feel at being incapable of satisfying our common yearnings. But what makes me suffer even more is your low way of regarding me; that is, that you think I am so haughty and arrogant that I would refuse to take you as my wife, even though I am not bound in marriage to any other woman, and even though you are more worthy to wed a lofty prince than one such as I. Indeed, since I know I owe you my very life, the obligation I feel to you is such that I should rather be bound to make myself a perpetual servant of your servants, than to imagine myself worthy to accept you as my beloved wife. Therefore, Lady Emilia, if ever you have put your trust in any loyal man, I beseech and pray that you trust me, one who is

leale per alcun tempo prestaste, che a me, che lealissimo sono la debbiate hora prestare, et credermi che io non posso con donna alcuna in maritaggio legarmi. Et s'io potesse farlo, che assai più volontieri di quello che voi richiesto m'havete il farei, nè lascierei voi, per prendermi qual si voglia altra maggior donna del mondo. Ma se vi piace darmi licenza che io torni a Salerno, et che forse maritata la ritrovasse, voi vedereste che alhora, parendomi dal canto mio d'esser assolto, et libero, potreste poi far quello di me, che più vi piacesse; che con doppia mia sodisfattione al tutto allegramente consentirei."

La Emilia, che assai era accorta, giudicando, come era per certo, che queste ultime parole le havesse non ad altra intentione dette, che per poter con suo conzo[45] levarsele dinanzi, et non mai più lasciarsi vedere; et benchè già fosse certa d'esser assai poco da lui amata. Nondimeno perchè Amor sua natura non perde; chè quando egli piglia alcuno al suo vischio, quantunque il misero impaniato espressamente conosca d'esser poco grato a chi egli ama, non però questo malvagio Amore consente ch'egli sciogler se ne possa; anzi l'infelice per naturale forza d'Amore, quanto più l'error suo vede, et conosce, tanto più da sè stesso, senza punto schifarsi, tutto dentro vi si immerge. Hor così dunque facendo l'innamorata Emilia, la quale con tutto che s'accorgesse come era poco dell'amor che ella cercava da Fabio desiderata, nè amata; nondimeno da più forte desiderio accesa di farselo suo in ogni modo, così gli disse. "Io non potrei mancar, Fabio mio, di crederti tutto quello che mi dicesti, chè considerando alle rare tue virtudi, non crederei giamai, che d'ingannar una semplice donna, come son'io, ti compiacesti. Credoti adunque il tutto, et piacemi assai la elettione che hai fatta di ritornare a Salerno per veder se forse la tua Urania maritata si fosse. Ma perchè io temo (come il proprio de' veri amanti fu sempre) quantunque maritata la ritrovasti, che dalla dolcezza della Patria, et de' parenti lusingato, potresti facilmente dilettandoti più di star ivi, a me non più ritornare. Et perciò sì per fuggir questo pericolo, come ancora perchè più che altra cosa desidero di veder colei la quale tien sola tutto quel pregio, che potrebbe molt'altre donne far degne, poi che sola nel mondo ella si trova del tuo amor meritevole, voglio, et ho deliberato che sanza me a patto alcuno non debbi andare; et per levare ogni vergogna, et sospetto, che ne' cuori di molti potrebbe nascere, io verrò teco vestita da huomo; nè altra compagnia con essi noi, fuor che un fedelissimo mio servo voglio che habbiamo."

Assai s'affaticò la Urania per levarle questo pensiero d'andar seco del cuore, dimostrandole con buone ragioni tutta la vergogna, et il danno, che così andando

---

[45] Veneto dialect form for *concio* (G. Boerio, *Dizionario del dialetto veneto* [Venice: Cecchini, 1856; repr. Milan: Martello, 1971]), s. v.

most loyal to you; and that you believe me when I say that I cannot join myself in marriage with any woman. If I could do it, I would, and with far more willingness than you have even shown in making your request to me; nor would I ever leave you for any grander woman on earth. But if it please you to grant me leave to go, I will return to Salerno. If I find that she is married, you will see that you will be able to do with me whatever you please, since I will consider myself at that point a free man; and I will be completely satisfied to consent, with joy, to your wishes."

Emilia, who was very shrewd, was quite certain that Urania's concluding proposal served no other purpose than to provide an opportunity for her beloved to escape, and never return. She was likewise certain that this man scarcely loved her at all. Nevertheless, the nature of Love never changes: for whenever he traps someone in his lime, this wicked one never lets the victim get free, no matter how clearly the victim knows that the person he loves does not want him. Indeed, by nature the power of Love is such that the more the unhappy victim sees his error, and is aware of it, the more inclined he is to get himself completely trapped, without feeling the slightest repulsion. So it was with the lovestruck Emilia; for even though she knew that Fabio hardly loved her, or desired her in the way which she sought, still she burned with an ever stronger desire to make him hers by any means possible. "I could not fail, my Fabio, to believe everything you have told me," she said. "Considering your rare virtues, I would never imagine that you could take pleasure in deceiving a mere woman, such as I am. Therefore I believe you completely, and I am well pleased with the choice you have made to return to Salerno to see if perhaps your Urania has married. However, as is typical of those who are truly in love, I am fearful, imagining that you might be so lulled by your relatives and your sweet homeland that you will find it more pleasant to remain there even if Urania actually is married, and not come back to me. Therefore, in order to avoid this danger, and moreover because I wish more than anything else to see this woman who alone holds as much excellence as would suffice to make many more women worthy of love (seeing that she is the only woman on earth whom your love esteems), it is my desire and decision that you will not leave without me, under any circumstances. I will come with you dressed as a man, in order to banish the shameful thoughts and suspicions which might arise in the hearts of many; furthermore, I do not wish us to be accompanied by anyone else, save by one of my very faithful servants."

Urania strove hard to drive this determination from Emilia's heart, employing clever arguments to convince her of all the dishonor and injury that could arise

le ne potrebbe seguire. Ma in fine nulla vi valse, anzi più sempre nel suo proposito ostinatasi diceva, che quando ben mille morti credesse non poter fuggire, che pur al tutto con esso lui volea andare; et che hormai più non s'affaticasse in cosa nella quale ogni fatica era perduta. Vedendo la Urania non poter altro fare, mostrò di contentarsi di quanto a lei fosse in piacere, con animo poi di scoprirsi come era ancor' ella donna, quando in Salerno fossero gionte.

 Et così la Emilia assai racconfortata fece tra il termine di pochi giorni, di molto ricchi et nobili panni da huomo, per sè et per lo suo Fabio preparare. Et indi fingendo d'andar in contado per starsi alquanti mesi a piacere, et dato ordine c'hebbe a' fatti suoi, con le accorte sue cameriere, lei, il suo Fabio, et il servo una mattina per tempo saliti su buoni cavalli, per Salerno si partirono.

 Ma lasciamoli andare, che per hora habbiamo di loro detto assai, et ritorniamo al vero Fabio in Salerno, il quale poi c'hebbe la lettera della Urania dal servo di lei ricevuta, quantunque assai strano gli paresse di restar d'una privo, dalla quale si conosceva ardentissimamente amato, et che molto maggior doglia sentisse, ch'una donna de gli meriti, ch'era lei, la qual meritava d'esser sommamente da ciascuno desiderata, et amata; per sua cagione dovesse andar così miseramente errando. Nondimeno conoscendo non potervi rimediare, che havendo inteso come già s'era partita, nè sapeva in qual parte fosse andata, si diede però al meglio che puote pace. Et perchè già per innanzi erasi alquanto d'una nobile et assai vaga donzella invaghito, il quale novello amore era stato cagione che egli si fosse men del solito verso la Urania dimostrato amorevole; ond'ella, che 'l maggior mal pressagava, per non le dare il cuore di poterlo sofferire, prima che maggior si facesse haveva eletto per men male partirsi. Hor dunque vedendo Fabio che la Urania s'era partita, con maggior cura, et sollecitudine, che prima non faceva incominciò l'amor della bella giovane, che Clorina havea nome, a seguitare. Et lei, che assai gentile et accorta era, ma non già che di gran lunga al valor della Urania si potesse uguagliare; essendosene accorta, et piacendole assai gli bei modi, et accorte maniere di Fabio, d'altretanto amore verso lui s'accese; et tutti i favori ch'ella honestamente potea darli tutti gli dava. Chè non essendo in quel tempo (come ho detto altre volte) vergogna alcuna in Salerno che le giovani donne fossero da' giovini di ogni sorte nelle lor case visitate, et con essi loro publicamente ragionare. Vi andava perciò assai volte Fabio a visitarla, et conoscendosi a molti segni grandemente amato da lei, tanto contento ne prese che in pochi giorni s'hebbe del tutto la infelice Urania, come se mai non veduta l'havesse, a scordare.

from such a journey. But in the end it was to no avail; indeed, Emilia stuck ever more obstinately to her plan, saying that even if she were certain she would suffer a thousand deaths, she would still wish to accompany her Fabio. Eventually Urania gave up, seeing that all her efforts were wasted. Inasmuch as there was nothing more to be done, she made a show of being content to do whatever pleased Emilia, and planned to reveal her own identity as a woman as soon as they arrived in Salerno.

Thus it was that Emilia, greatly pleased, had some very lavish and noble men's clothing prepared both for herself and for her Fabio, in the space of only a few days. Pretending she was going off to amuse herself in the countryside for a few months, and having set her affairs in order with the help of her astute maidservants, she then set out for Salerno early one morning in the company of her Fabio and the servant, all mounted on fine horses.

But now let us leave them on their journey, for we have said a great deal about them, and return to the real Fabio back in Salerno. After he had received Urania's letter from her servant, he found it strange to be bereft now of a woman who he knew was so fervently in love with him; moreover, he was quite saddened to learn that a woman of so much worth, who deserved to be greatly loved and cherished by all, was forced to wander about in such a miserable fashion. Nonetheless he consoled himself as best he could, since there was nothing he could do about the situation: he had heard the circumstances surrounding Urania's departure, and he had no idea where she had gone. He had for some time been considerably attracted to a noble and quite beautiful maiden, and this new love had been the reason why he had lately shown less affection than usual for Urania, causing her to choose to leave the city rather than suffer the even greater grief which she imagined would be her lot. When Fabio saw that Urania had left, he put greater effort into wooing this other young woman, whose name was Clorina, than he previously had done. She, who was very genteel and clever, but nowhere near the equal of Urania in excellence, soon became aware of Fabio's attentions, and since she liked his suave manners and dashing ways, she fell as much in love with him as he with her, bestowing upon him all those favors which chasteness allowed. As I have said, at that time in Salerno young women could be visited at their homes by young men, and converse with them in public, without suffering any shame whatsoever; therefore Fabio went often to visit Clorina. Realizing through many signs that he was greatly loved by her, he was so happy that in the space of a few days he completely forgot about the wretched Urania, as if he had never even seen her.

Venne tra questo tempo per fermarsi nella corte di Giufredi Prencipe di Salerno un giovine gentilhuomo Siciliano, che bellissimo era di corpo, et molto prode et valoroso della persona, ma nel resto poche altre buone parti erano in lui. Et tra l'altre ch'egli havea molte di ree, era un gran vantatore; et andando costui, come del più de' giovani è costume, per la città quà et là uccellando, vennegli per sorte la Clorina veduta, la quale assai più di quant'altre n'havesse ivi vedute gli piacque. Onde per starsi in essercitio amoroso si deliberò farle il vagheggio; non perciò ch'egli fosse di sorte, che molto nelle panie amorose si lasciasse inveschiare, et così fece, che mo' in un loco et mo' in un'altro vedendola, et sempre grande honore facendole, non restò mai fino che tra il termine di pochi giorni con buon mezzo hebbe il modo come Fabio, et de gli altri facevano, di andarla ad ogni suo piacere a visitare, et ragionar seco.

Perchè la Clorina, la quale non tanto adentro con l'ingegno penetrava, anzi le più soglion fare, che più tosto alla forma dell'huomo, che alla cagione per la quale è huomo tenuto considerano. Parendole Menandro (che tale del Siciliano era il nome) un bellissimo giovine, et ben della persona disposto; et più d'ogn'altra cosa parendole che fosse un bel ciarlatore, et che ciascuna ragione, quantunque più con fintioni che co'l vero, a suo commodo sapesse tirare, tanto que' suoi finti modi le piacquero, che sanza punto schermirsi, non parendole più in Fabio cosa bella nè buona vedere, tutto il suo cuore a voler solo costui amare rivolse. Non già però che gran conto non mostrasse tener di Fabio; ma lui, che accortissimo era, ben tosto s'accorse come era costei del suo amore assai raffreddata, et che più di lui amava Menandro.

Nondimeno perchè, come ho detto altre volte, Amor non permette che gli miseri innamorati, quando in error sono, et che si conoscono non esser amati, che si possano a lor voglia sciorre; perciò lo sventurato Fabio, per non noiar colei che noiar lui non temeva, tutta la sua gran disgratia portava in pace; et tanto era il rispetto che le haveva, che per non le dar noia quello dissimulava, che vedea in lei pur troppo chiaro, et troppo aperto. Et perchè non gli negava lo andar qualunque volta gli piaceva la dove ella era, egli perciò sperando che una volta dell'error suo s'accorgerebbe, et quanto più lui, che Menandro meritasse d'esser amato verrebbe a conoscere; con quei primi tenuti modi perciò, et spesse volte, come prima faceva la visitava; et in cotal modo l'innamorato Fabio tra dubbio, et tema la sua vita assai mal contento passava.

URANIA: THE STORY OF A YOUNG WOMAN'S LOVE

During this time a young Sicilian gentleman stopped at the court of Giufredi, the Prince of Salerno. In body he was very handsome, and in spirit very brave and valorous, but otherwise he was quite lacking in any good qualities. In fact, he had many wicked ones, and was a great boaster to boot. As is the custom with most young men, he went here and there about the city engaged in falconry, and in so doing, as fate would have it, he caught sight of Clorina, whom he found more pleasing than all the other women he had seen there. Thereupon he decided to pursue her, in order to stay in form as a lover (not that he was the sort to allow himself to be truly caught in the snares of love). Seeing her now in one place, now in another, and always showing her the greatest respect, he did not relent until, after a few days, he managed through his cleverness to get himself invited to see her, and to converse with her at her house whenever he liked, just as Fabio and others had done.

Clorina, who was not a very deep thinker, tended to give more consideration to a man's external form than to those things which made him appear to be a true man in the eyes of others. Thus it was that Menandro (for such was the Sicilian's name) seemed to her to be a man who was most handsome, and properly put together. His pretentious ways were pleasing to her no matter what line he spun out for her amusement; and even though he might be as full of lies as truth, she thought he was quite clever with words, and she made no effort to fend him off. Soon she no longer felt that Fabio held anything attractive or worthwhile for her, and she now dedicated all her heart to loving Menandro. Of course she did not make a great show of holding Fabio in low esteem; nonetheless, since he was exceedingly shrewd, he soon became aware that her love for him had cooled considerably, and that she now loved Menandro more.

As I have said before, Love does not permit those wretched people who love by mistake to be free of their desires, even if they know they are not loved in return. The unhappy Fabio bore his misfortune in peace, in order not to hurt her, a woman who had no scruples about hurting him. So respectful was he of her, and so unwilling to create a disturbance, that he pretended not to be aware of the new situation even though he could see it so clearly and openly in her demeanor. Since she did not deny him entry into her house whenever it pleased him, and since he hoped she would become aware of her error and recognize that he deserved her love far more than Menandro, he continued to visit her quite often in the same way he had before. In this way the lovestruck Fabio, consumed by doubt and fear, passed his days in a very unhappy state.

V

Ma perchè gliè necessaria cosa che alquanto da questi io mi diparta s'io voglio tutto a pieno il successo de' loro amori narrare, dico perciò che si ritrovava in que' tempi nella Calabria d'uno assai grande stato Duchessa una nobilissima signora, la quale per quanto affermavano tutti quelli, che veduta l'havevano, donna più di lei bella non si poteva in tutt' il mondo vedere, nè passava la bellissima signora d'età gli venti anni, et era di poco più d'un'anno (sanza alcun figliolo) rimasa vidua, et dello stato herede, con poco pensiero di più rimaritarsi, quantunque da molti nobili signori, et alti prencipi ne fosse continovamente sollecitata; et da' suoi popoli soventemente persuasa ne venisse. Ma lei, che con un vecchio et gelosissimo marito, con suo smisurato affanno et accerbissima pena era vissa due anni; et dubitando fortemente, che forse la seconda volta potrebbe inciamparsi ancora, haveva perciò tra sè stessa determinato di non mai più alcun marito volere, ma in perpetua viduità, et con honore viversi sempre.

Haveva costei (che assai catolica, et ornata d'ogni buon costume era, ma sopra tutto di tutte le sorti d'amor vano espressa nemica) quatro sapienti vecchi per suoi conseglieri eletti, alli quali tutto il governo dello stato, et di ciascun'altra cosa appertinente a chi regge la cura lasciava; et ciò faceva per poter più quietamente, et da ogni travaglio lontana la sua vita passare. Et de gli quatro eravene uno più grave d'etade, et di più maturo consiglio de gli altri; il quale lei proprio come se padre le fosse stato l'honorava, et amava; et in lui solo vie più che ne gli altri i suoi maggiori secreti tutti fidava.

V

However, it is necessary that I leave these people behind for a time, if I am to narrate fully the story of their love affairs. To this end, I will tell of a very great lady who was duchess of a large state in Calabria.[46] All those who saw her affirmed that there was no more beautiful woman in all the world. This lady was not yet twenty, and she had been a widow, with no children, for little more than a year. She had inherited the state, yet had little thought of remarrying, even though she was courted by many noble lords and princes, and often urged to remarry by her people. Since she had spent two years with an old and very jealous husband, who had caused her no end of pain and misery, and since she was quite afraid the same thing could befall her a second time, she had secretly determined never to marry again, and to maintain honorably a state of perpetual widowhood.

This lady, who was an avowed enemy of any sort of improper love, being very dedicated to the Catholic religion and endowed with the finest manners, had chosen four wise old men to act as her counselors, and to these she left the governance of her lands, and all the responsability for maintaining them. She did this in order to permit herself to live a more quiet life, far from any toil and trouble. Of these four there was one who was older than the others, and who could give wiser counsel. The Duchess loved and honored this man as if he were her father, and in him alone she confided all of her greatest secrets.

---

[46] In the fifteenth century the Aragonese kings of Naples also bore the title of Duke of Calabria. Masuccio Salernitano's *Novellino* (published 1476) is dedicated "a la illustrissima Ippolita d'Aragona e de' Visconti, Duchessa di Calabria," for instance (ed. S. Nigro [Bari: Laterza, 1979], 1), and his Novella II is addressed to "... Alfonso d'Aragona dignissimo Duca di Calabria" (19). Although Bigolina appears to avoid any precise identification of her character, she likely had this dynasty in mind.

Haveva questa gentil signora una sua certa particolar dilettatione, la quale era di haver presso di sè tutti i ritratti di quanti nobili signori, prencipi, et prencipesse nel mondo si ritrovassero. Et per ciò fare, teneva nella sua corte salariato il più famoso pittore che 'n que' tempi vivesse; il quale mo' in quella corte et mo' in quell'altra de' nobili prencipi ritrovandosi d'ivi non si toglieva, che de' signori et signore seco ne portava i ritratti. Et come alla Duchessa sua signora era giunto, et che gli haveva dell'opera sua a perfettione condotti, a lei li consegnava; la quale con quasi miracoloso artificio, tale in tavole d'avorio, tale di hebano, et tale in altre varie sorti li faceva riporre; et poscia che di molt'oro, perle, et pretiose gioie gli havea fatti (come il loro grado) maestrevolmente ornare, entro una bellissima stanza, che a lei era la più cara di tutte l'altre, ad ordine gli riponeva; nella quale ad assai pochi, et di rado, per gratia particolare era conceduto d'entrarvi. Ma lei havea per costume d'andarvi almeno una volta il giorno; et hor questo, et quello di que' ritratti mirando per buona pezza con sua grande sodisfattione vi si interveneva.

Hor avenne in que' giorni come volle sua sorte, o più tosto come piacque ad Amore, il quale di rado consentir volle che alcuno si presumesse di poter col proprio valore dalle sue forze schermirsi, et che con suo gran danno tosto non gli facesse conoscere, come ogni estrema possanza da noi humani usata presso la sua, che è infinita val nulla; volle perciò dico, così ancora questa gentil signora, che felicissima sino quell'hora era vissa, con suo smisurato danno, per essempio dell'altre vincere, et castigare. Avenne dico, che havendo il pittore molte parti dell'Italia et fuori di Italia scorse, per raccogliere a compiacenza di sua signora di varij signori et signore i ritratti più tosto a caso che con pensiero alcuno per Salerno fece passaggio, nel quale entrato, come la pessima sorte di sua signora permesse, si venne ad incontrare nel più bello, più cortese, et più gentil prencipe che tutto 'l mondo alhora tenesse; cioè Giufredi honoratissimo Prencipe di Salerno; il quale tanto estremamente piacque al pittore, che gli parve sino a quell'hora non haver veduta cosa nel mondo, in fuori la Duchessa sua signora, che di tanta sodisfattione gli fosse stata; et perciò per più giorni in Salerno fermandosi con somma diligenza, sanza che egli se ne accorgesse lo ritrasse.

URANIA: THE STORY OF A YOUNG WOMAN'S LOVE

The lady had a certain peculiar fondness for collecting and surrounding herself with portraits of all the noble lords, princes, and princesses that could be found in the world. In order to do this, she kept the most famous painter of those times at her court as a salaried worker. This painter, upon arriving at the court of a certain noble personage, would not leave until he could take with him the portrait of the lord or lady of the place. Once he had returned to his lady the Duchess, with his works brought to a pitch of perfection, he gave them to her. Some of these he executed on panels of ivory, some on ebony, and some on various other materials; and when he had masterfully decorated them with much gold, pearls, or precious jewels (according to the subject's rank), he would place them in a very beautiful room, which was the dearest room of all to the Duchess, and one which very few people were ever allowed to enter, and this occurred only rarely, and with special permission. The Duchess, on the other hand, had the habit of going in there at least once a day, where she would gaze for long periods, and with great satisfaction, on this portrait or that.[47]

Something occurred at this time that might have been a whim of fate; or perhaps it was the will of Love, who has rarely allowed anyone to presume to withstand his power by means of personal strength. Any person who tries to resist soon comes to know this power, and suffers great harm, since any extreme effort which we humans might employ is worth nothing in a contest with Love's infinite strength. Therefore it was Love's desire to overwhelm and punish this gentle lady, who had been leading a happy life up to this point, and inflict great harm upon her, as an example to others. In any case, as I was saying, something occurred: after this painter had visited many places both within Italy and abroad in order to acquire portraits of lords and ladies according to his mistress's pleasure, he happened, more by chance than by design, to pass through Salerno. After entering the city, as the Duchess's great bad luck would have it, the painter chanced to meet the most handsome, courteous, and genteel prince in all the world at that time: Giufredi, the exalted Prince of Salerno. The painter liked him so much that it seemed to him that he had seen nothing so pleasing in all the world thus far, apart from his mistress the Duchess, that is. Thus he stayed in Salerno for several days, and managed through great effort to paint the Prince's portrait without his being aware of it.

---

[47] In her description of the Duchess's personal portrait gallery, Bigolina may have been inspired by the humanist Paolo Giovio, who collected portraits of celebrities in a "museo" at his villa in Como in the 1530s: see L. Freedman, *Titian's Portraits Through Aretino's Lens* (University Park, PA: Pennsylvania State University Press, 1995), 15.

Et dovendo condursi più oltre, per dover di commissione di sua signora ritrarre un'altro gran prencipe, parvegli d'haver fatto così grande acquisto, havendo di questo il ritratto, che sanza andar più innanzi, più che mai fosse allegro, et contento dalla Duchessa ritornò in Calabria, dove giunto, et a sua presenza condottosi così le disse: "Signora, se mai cosa vi portai che fosse di qualche valore, al presente una d'estremo valore, et pretiosissimo tesoro vi porto. Eccovi, Signora mia, del più che ogn' altro bello, cortese, gratioso, et gentil signore il ritratto. Questa è la naturalissima effiggie di Giufredi Prencipe di Salerno, del quale non credo che Natura, nè i Cieli il più bello, o meglio di lui qualificato producessero mai; et ben da hora in dietro potrete gloriarvi d'haver il ritratto di tutte le bellezze del mondo nelle man vostre. Et se così io havessi potuto in questa tela ritrarre le gratie, gli ornati costumi, et le cortesissime maniere, come io con questi propri occhi gli vidi, io vi giuro Signora, che stupida et maravigliata mirandoli ne rimarreste."

Et indi in tante particolari lode (tra udite dire, et vedute) di quel gentil signor si diffuse, che quella meschina signora, la quale era incauta d'ogni fattione et pensiero amoroso, et forse con più attentione che non si conveniva, quantunque le parole affettuosissime del pittore ascoltava, si sentì da un non so che inusitato, et non più altre volte da lei sentito, pungersi il cuore. Ma come si fermò a riguardare il ritratto, parvele alhora che un mare di foco et un monte di giaccio tutto in un medesimo punto adosso le se riversassero. Imperciò che Amore, il quale sino a quell'hora havea tardato a farle il suo grande valor manifesto, et non volendo più differire s'havea ne' begli occhi di quel ritratto nascoso.

Chè quantunque fossero sanza obiecto et inanimati, essendovisi Amore entro riposto, fecero nondimeno quel medesimo, anzi maggiore effetto in lei, che gli vivi et animati del prencipe non harrebbono fatto; ch'ella in quelli mirando parvele, che da due folgori, anzi da due accutissime saette il suo cuore trapassato le fosse. Perchè la gentil signora sentendosi fuor del suo costume estremamente alterata, fece, con poche parole da lei dette, il bel ritratto di sua molta ruina cagione, nel più bel loco della sua camera riporre. Et dopo che'l pittor fu partito, il quale

URANIA: THE STORY OF A YOUNG WOMAN'S LOVE

The painter was supposed to continue on his journey, having been charged by his lady to paint another great prince. Nonetheless, it now seemed to him that he had already made a very great acquisition with the portrait he had just done, so without traveling further he returned to Calabria quite joyful and content. When he arrived there, he presented himself to the Duchess. "My Lady," he said, "if I have ever proffered anything that was of any worth, then the thing I am bringing you now is a most precious and extremely valuable treasure. Here, my Lady, is a portrait of the handsomest, most courteous and most gracious gentleman of all: Giufredi, Prince of Salerno, whom I have represented here in quite true-to-life fashion. I do not believe that Nature or the heavens have ever produced a more handsome or better qualified man than he, and thus from now on you can bask in the glory of holding in your own hands the very image of all the beauty in the world. Yet if I had been able to portray on this canvas all of the grace, the decorousness and courteous manners which I saw in him with my own eyes, then, my Lady, I swear to you that you would remain awestruck and stupefied to see them."

The painter went on, pouring out so much specific praise of what he had heard of the Prince, or seen for himself, that the poor duchess felt some sort of strange aching in her heart, something that was beyond her experience. Since she was incautious with regard to deeds and thoughts of love, she listened to the gushing words of the painter with more attention than perhaps was wise. Then, when she stood before the painting and looked at it, it seemed to her that both a sea of fire and a mountain of ice poured down upon her in the same instant. For Love, who had until then delayed in revealing to her the extent of his power, was now no longer willing to put things off, and had hidden himself in the beautiful eyes of the portrait.[48]

These eyes were formless and inanimate; yet once Love had come to rest in them they had the same effect on the Duchess as the living, animate eyes of the Prince would have had, or perhaps their effect was even greater. Looking at them, it seemed to her that her heart was pierced through by two lightning bolts, indeed by two very sharp arrows. Feeling herself much changed from her customary demeanor, and speaking very little, she ordered that the beautiful painting, the cause of her very ruin, be placed in the loveliest spot in the room. After the artist, who was all too aware of the great change that had been wrought in her, had taken his

---

[48] For the prevalence of the motif of falling in love with painted images in Renaissance culture, see C. E. Gilbert, *Italian Art 1400–1500: Sources and Documents* (Englewood Cliffs, NJ: Prentice-Hall, 1980), 121–22.

troppo ben della grande mutatione di lei s'era accorto, ritornolo ella con più attentione, et con maggiore affetto a mirare, et quanto più lo mirava sempre più bello, più gratioso, et amoroso parevale; per la qual cosa così fuor di misura s'accese, che tutta d'amore et di desiderio si sentia venir meno, nè molti giorni passarono, che a tale venne la troppo innamorata signora, che vedendosi continovamente dinanzi da gli occhi la cagion del suo male, nè da quello alcuno aiuto sperar potendone, s'era quasi vicina alla morte condotta.

Et ben spessissime volte dell'aventuroso Pimaleone si ricordava, et per ottenere un simil dono com'egli fece infinite preci alla dea dell'amore, da infinite lagrime accompagnate porgeva. Ma vedendo poi come nulla il suo pregar le giovava, et rincrescendole pure il morire, si dispose di voler in ogni modo vedere se qualche rimedio si potesse trovare, con lo quale, non rovinando l'honore, il quale lei sopra tutti i tesori del mondo pregiava, la sua vita salvarsi potesse. Ma conoscendo che da sè sola, et sanza gran consiglio non si sarebbe un così gran negotio potuto honorevolmente ispedire, deliberò perciò con quello suo più saggio, et antico, et da lei più de gli altri amato consigliero haverne di ciò parlamento, anzi tutto il carico di cotal cosa sopra le sue spalle riporre.

Perchè fatta una tal determinatione fecesi subito quel buon vecchio nella sua camera chiamare, et fattolo presso di sè sedere così gli disse. "Honoratissimo padre, so ben che vi sarete (et non poco) maravigliato della grande mutatione, che di me da pochi giorni in qua harrete veduta, et perchè, come si dice, non dovemo tenere il male nascoso a que' tali che qualche consiglio, o rimedio ci sanno, ci possono, et ci vogliono fedelmente donare; io adunque conoscendo il male, che io hora patisco esser acerbo, et pericolosissimo, per la qual cosa di sommo consiglio, et rimedio son bisognosa. Ho perciò, padre mio, voi eletto acciò che di consiglio, di rimedio, et etiandio d'aiuto bisognando mi soccorriate; ho voi solo eletto tra tutti gl'altri, acciò che come più antico d'anni, più isperimentato, et sapiente, meglio de gli altri mi sappiate consigliare. Et che come essendo più di ciascun'altro, che nella mia corte si ritrovi d'auttorità, et potente, più d'ogn'altro possiate sanza da veruno esserne ricercato, o ripreso essercitarvi nel ritrovar rimedio al mio male. Et finalmente perchè essendomi (come per lo vero sempre vi ho conosciuto) più d'ogn'altro amorevole, et fedele; più fedelmente, et amorevolmente con tutto il potere, et saper vostro a darmi aiuto vi habbiate a disporre."

Et così detto con calde lagrime, et affocati sospiri gli scoperse l'amoroso tormento ch'ella per amor di Giufredi Prencipe di Salerno pativa, narrandoli come il suo bellissimo ritratto era stato di ciò cagione; et soggiunse dicendo: "Padre mio

URANIA: THE STORY OF A YOUNG WOMAN'S LOVE

leave, she returned to look at the picture even more attentively, and with greater affection than before. The more she looked at it, the more lovely, graceful, and amorous it seemed; and thus she fell completely in love with it, and her feelings of love and desire made her feel faint. Before many days had passed the Lady, far too lovesick, was nearly on the point of death; for she had been staring at this harmful object continuously, even though she could never hope it would give her any relief.

Very often she recalled the fortunate Pygmalion; and so she offered countless prayers, accompanied by countless tears, to the goddess of love, in the hope of receiving the same gift he had.[49] But she did not wish to die. Realizing that her prayers availed her nothing, she decided to see if she could find any remedy that would save her life, as long as it would not compromise her honor, for that was the thing she prized above all worldly treasures. She knew that on her own, and without good advice, she would never be able to handle this situation in an honorable fashion, so she decided to discuss it with her wisest, oldest, and most beloved counselor, and place the responsibility for the entire affair in his hands.

Once she had reached this decision, she called the fine old man to her room. She bade him sit beside her, then spoke: "Most honored father, I know that you must be amazed at the great change which you have seen in me these last few days. As it is commonly said, we should not keep our misfortunes hidden from those people who are willing and able, in good faith, to offer us advice or a remedy; and inasmuch as I am aware that the misfortune I am currently suffering is most bitter and dangerous, I am in need of the best possible advice and remedy. Out of all the others, I have chosen only you as the one who would best know how to counsel me, since you are the most advanced in years, the most experienced, and the wisest. Moreover, as you have more power and authority in my court than anyone else, no one more suitable than you could be engaged for the purpose of seeking a remedy for my condition. And finally, I have always known you to be more loving and faithful to me than any other, and thus more capable of placing your power and wisdom at my disposal in a loving and trustworthy fashion."

Having said this, with hot tears and sighs she revealed to him all of the amorous torment she was suffering for the love of Giufredi, Prince of Salerno, and how his beautiful portrait had been the cause. "Sweet father of mine," she continued,

---

[49] For the story of Pygmalion, see Ovid, *Metamorphoses* 10.243–97.

dolcissimo, voi dovete pensare che grandissima forza ho fatta a me stessa innanzi che a manifestarvi uno tale mio amoroso pensiero mi sia condotta; che come a i diportamenti i quali sin'hora di me havete potuto vedere, non dubito che non siate sicuro che in me verun'altro amoroso pensiero non cadesse più mai. Onde potete pensarvi che ritrovandomi a cotali passioni novella, con vie maggior affanno che un'altra, la quale assuefatta le fosse non farebbe, io le sento, et sopporto; et che con maggior vergogna lo vi manifesti. Nondimeno, perchè come padre vi amo, et (come io so) perchè da voi parimente, come figlia son amata, più tosto che morire (che morir certamente converrami, se soccorso non mi darete) mi son condotta a scoprirvi il mio male. Et quello che io da voi desidero è, che io vorrei che tanto con lo ingegno vostro vi affaticaste, che con bel modo induceste quel Prencipe a richiedermi di suo istesso volere per moglie, et ch'egli non si accorgesse d'esser da me punto desiderato, anzi vorrei che essendo da lui richiesta, et io dimostrandomi schiva a preghiere vostre poscia io facesse mostra di consentirli; che per cosa del mondo non voglio ch'egli intenda ch io l'amo; et meno che si pensi d'esser da me ricercato.

"Hor dunque, padre mio honoratissimo, havete il bisogno et il desiderio mio tutto inteso, per la qual cosa potete conoscere come di me la vita et la morte nelle mani vostre si trova; per che son sicura, che voi volendo saperete, et insieme poterete aiutarmi; et voi similmente sicurissimo rendo, che non porgendomi tosto aiuto sarete dopo forzato a tosto piangermi morta."

Troppo gran cosa da udire parve questa nuova al buon vecchio, et massimamente essendo per lo innanzi così buon conoscitore stato della quieta et modestissima natura di lei; et perciò per buona pezza stette sopra di sè stesso, in questa cosa pensando, sanza alcuna cosa risponderle, nel qual tempo la bella signora pianse amaramente sempre. Perchè accorgendosi il vecchio quanto cotal fatto importasse, et conoscendo come ammonitioni, nè riprensioni non harrebbono havuto in quel tempo in lei loco, et havendole come a sua signora rispetto, et come a figliuola, portandole amore si dispose ad un tratto con ogni sua possa di darle aiuto, et perciò rompendo il lungo silentio così le rispose. "Già non mi maraviglio, signora et figliuola mia, quando all'età et bellezza vostra considero, et maggiormente quando alla smisurata vostra gentilezza ho riguardo, che Amor si sia impadronito del vostro cuore. Imperciò che, oltre che giovanezza et bellezza siano due soggetti per lor propria natura all'amore inclinati; la gentilezza poi non pure inclinato, ma appropriatissimo soggetto d'Amore parmi, che si debba da chi più intenda tenere; et di più dirovi, che io non credo che perfettione alcuna in quel cuore si possa trovare,

URANIA: THE STORY OF A YOUNG WOMAN'S LOVE

"you must imagine that it took a supreme effort on my part to bring myself to the point where I could tell you of such thoughts of love, for I am sure you do not doubt from the behavior you have observed in me thus far that no other amorous preoccupation has ever afflicted me. These passions are all new to me; therefore it should be plain to you that I feel them, and suffer from them, to a worse degree than someone else who might be more used to such things. In addition, I suffer greater shame than most people in revealing these passions to you. Nevertheless, since I love you as a father, and since (as I know) I am equally loved by you as a daughter, I have decided I must tell you of my condition in order to avoid the death which I will certainly suffer, if you do not help me. This is what I desire of you: I want you to employ all your skills to make that Prince ask me, of his own volition, to be his wife. Moreover, I do not wish him to have any idea that he is desired by me; on the contrary, once he has made his request of marriage, I intend to make a show of reluctance at your entreaties, before finally consenting to accept him. Under no circumstances do I want him to know that I love him, and I especially do not want him to think I am pursuing him.

"Now, my most honored father, you have heard all of my need, and my desire; and you are fully aware how you hold my very life and death in your hands. For this reason I am certain that if you desire it you will know what to do, and at the same time be able to help me. I have also made it very plain to you that if you do not help me right away, soon you will be forced to weep over my dead body."

To the old man these words seemed a very disturbing revelation, the more so because he had always known of her quiet and very modest nature. Thus for a long time he remained lost in thought over it, and gave her no answer, while the lovely lady continued to weep bitter tears. The old man knew how grave the situation was, and how little effect his warnings and reproaches might have on her at this moment. He also bore her great respect as his mistress, and great love as a daughter, and so he abruptly decided to do all he could to help her. Breaking his long silence, he answered her thus: "O my Lady and daughter, when I consider your age, your beauty, and most especially your very great gentility, I am not surprised that Love has taken over your heart. Both youth and beauty tend toward love by their very nature; but it also seems to me that gentility not only tends toward love, but is indeed a most appropriate subject of it, to be valued by all those who have the keenest insight. Let me also tell you that I do not believe that

nel quale Amore non vi ha per sè loco; nè d'altro mi maraviglio eccetto come tanto a innamorarvi sète tardata, essendo massimamente, come voi pur siete, più d'ogn'altra bella, virtuosa, et gentile.

"Ma quando poi bene dall'altra parte al tutto io considero, ogni maraviglia in me cessa. Chè se gliè (come è) vero, che ogni simile per natura brama, et cerca d'accostarsi al suo simile, non dovevate prima che a questo tempo innamorarvi, che non essendovisi se non hora parato soggetto innanzi, il quale in bellezza et virtute a voi fosse simile, non dovevate perciò per lo adietro innamorarvi in alcuno, et hor che lo a voi simile soggetto dinanzi vi s'è parato d'accendervi del suo amore non potevate fuggire. Hor dunque, signora mia, dovete sapere come non mi maraviglio, nè vi biasmo perchè innamorata io vi vegga; et più dicovi, che di buon cuore, et prontissimo in tutto quello affaticar mi vederete, che io saprò imaginarmi d'operare acciò possiate al vostro tanto desiato fine intieramente pervenire. Gli è vero che il modo che volete ch'io tenga assai mi par duro et difficile; nondimeno se sète contenta che sia meco il pittore consapevole et operatore di quanto intendo di voler fare, e' mi dà il cuore che la cosa propriamente passerà nel modo che voi stessa desiderate."

Non si potrebbe raccontar a pieno l'allegrezza, et la gioia, che sentì alhora quella signora udendo il suo buon consigliero così amorevolmente confortarla, et cotanto buono aiuto prometterle; et poscia che assai l'hebbe ringratiato dissegli ch'era contentissima che'l pittore d'ogni suo secreto consapevole fosse, perciò che se lo haveva conosciuto fedelissimo sempre. Perchè il buon vecchio, che sanza fine era desideroso di compiacerle, tolta c'hebbe da lei licenza molto tosto si ritrovò co'l pittore, et havendo la fede sua tolta in pegno, brevemente raccontolli il grande amore, che la lor signora al Prencipe di Salerno portava, et insieme quello, che egli havea deliberato di fare, per condure il suo desiderio a buon fine; il che fu ch'egli volle che lo accorto pittore con quella maggior diligenza ch'egli sapeva usare sopra uno nobilissimo quadro il giudicio di Paris pingesse; cioè le tre Dee, et seco Paris col pomo d'oro in mano, che fu di tanta ruina cagione. Et non sanza molta consideratione haverrvi volle che la Duchessa di Borbone, la quale era donna assai bella, ma di grandissima venustà ripiena; di maniera che a chiunque la mirava faceva nascer un gran desiderio di riverirla, anzi adorarla; ch'ella di Giunone il loco tenesse, et fosse co'l scettro in mano et la corona in capo, come Reina del Cielo. Et la figliuola del Re di Polonia, la quale in que' tempi era bellissima di persona,

any perfection can be found in a heart which Love has not come to occupy. Nothing has astonished me more than your long delay in falling in love, inasmuch as you are more beautiful, virtuous, and mannerly than any other woman.

"But, on the other hand, when I consider the whole situation, my astonishment fades away. For if it is true (as I know it is) that each type by nature yearns for and seeks its equal, then you could not have fallen in love before now, given that only at the present time has an object appeared which resembles you in degree of beauty and virtue. Now that a love object of your rank has appeared before you, you could scarcely avoid falling in love with him. Thus, my lady, you must know that I am not surprised to see you in love, nor do I blame you for it. Let me also tell you that you will ever find me ready to strive, with all my heart, to do anything I can conceive of which might bring you to the goal which you desire so completely. It is true that the method which you asked me to employ seems arduous and difficult. Nonetheless, if you will allow me to bring the painter along with me as an accomplice who has been fully informed of all my plans, I am certain that this thing will be brought to fruition in just the way you desire."

No one could adequately describe the exultation and joy that the Lady felt when she heard her counselor comfort her in such a loving fashion, and promise her so much succor. After thanking him profusely, she told him she was quite content that the painter be informed of all her secrets, since she had always known him to be most faithful to her. Thus the fine old man, who desired so much to please her, took his leave of her and went to see the painter. Once the old man had sworn him to secrecy, he swiftly told him of the great love which their mistress bore for the Prince of Salerno, and also of what he planned to do in order to bring about the thing she yearned for. This was his plan: the artist would use all of his skills to paint a very lofty image of the the Judgment of Paris, showing the three goddesses together with Paris holding the golden apple, the cause of so much ruin. Without pondering long the old man decided that the Duchess of Bourbon, who was a beautiful woman filled with such charms that anyone who saw her felt a great desire to revere and even worship her, should stand in for Juno, holding her scepter and wearing the crown of the Queen of Heaven. And then he wished the daughter of the King of Poland should be depicted as Pallas,

et di faccia, ma del tutto d'ogni amor vano rubella, per haver la virginità sua al grande Iddio consacrata, nè d'altra cosa che d'haver assai scienze pareva curarsi; volle egli che come Pallade tutta armata, et con la lancia in mano fosse dipinta. Et perchè havea più volte udito dire al Duca morto suo signore che non si poteva più bella cosa nel mondo vedere, come era l'ignudo corpo della Duchessa sua moglie; volle perciò, che la bella Signora nel loco di Venere con parte delle bellissime sue membra scoperte si pingesse. Chè facendole porre uno manto, overo bernia di carmesina seta, sopra l'ignude carni, la quale la manca spalla coprivale, et giù descendendo alla destra ascella tutta la destra spalla, il braccio, et la mammella scoperti restavano; et dalla parte sinistra il bel fianco, parte del ventre, la coscia con ambedue le gambe, et gli picciolini piedi tutta ignuda si dimostrava; et tanta era la vaghezza, et bianchezza, che da quelle bellissime, et ben proporzionate membra ne uscivano, che abbagliato da quelle, era stato più fiate il pittore in grandissimo pericolo di traboccare. Nè il canuto vecchione, d'anni forse settanta, l'havea passata

Urania: The Story of a Young Woman's Love

in armor and bearing a lance in her hand.[50] She was at that time a very beautiful woman in face and body, yet opposed to any form of earthly love because she had sworn her virginity to God Almighty; indeed she seemed to care for nothing else but acquiring great knowledge. Finally, since the old man had often heard his lord, the late Duke, say that there was no sight more lovely on earth than the nude body of his wife the Duchess, he wished that his comely Lady be painted in the place of Venus, with a part of her gorgeous body uncovered. He would have her place a mantle or cloak of crimson silk over her naked skin, covering her left shoulder, and descending down to her right armpit so that all of her right shoulder, arm and breast would be exposed. On the left side she would reveal in their nakedness her lovely flank, a part of her abdomen, her thigh and both legs, along with her tiny little feet. Those comely and well-proportioned limbs radiated so much loveliness, and were so white, that the artist was often dazzled by them, and he came close to committing some rash act.[51] Nor could the white-haired old

---

[50] As in other instances, it is difficult to say if Bigolina had actual historical personages in mind for these characters. However, her Polish princess might well have been inspired by Katarzyna Jagiełłonka, the daughter of Sigismund I, King of Poland, and his Italian queen Bona Sforza, granddaughter of Alfonso II, King of Naples (and, perhaps not coincidentally for Bigolina, Duke of Calabria; see note 46 above). At the time Bigolina was writing (ca. 1552) Katarzyna was still unmarried and known for her fervent Catholicism; she would marry the King of Sweden in 1561 (N. Davies, *God's Playground: A History of Poland*, 2 vols. [New York: Columbia University Press, 1982], 1: 147, 434). A Polish princess also appears in *favola* 3.4 of Straparola's *Le piacevoli notti* (see note 13 to "Giulia Camposanpiero"). The Bourbon situation in the mid-sixteenth century was rather more complicated, for the house had many branches; however, it is possible that Bigolina's Duchess was based on Louise de Montpensier, sister of the famous Duke Charles of Bourbon (who was killed in 1527 at the Sack of Rome). Louise died in 1561.

[51] From Bigolina's two descriptions of this painting, and the choice of personages whose likenesses the artist appropriates for the figures, it can be concluded that the goddesses Juno and Pallas (Minerva) are shown clothed, which serves to underscore Bigolina's ethical point. However, this flies in the face of established Renaissance iconography, which had long dictated that all three goddesses must be nude in a depiction of the Judgment of Paris; this could be traced back to no less an authority than Ovid ("tres tibi se nudas exhibuere deae" ["three goddesses will show themselves nude to you"], *Heroides* 17.118). Every painting I have seen of the subject shows the three goddesses in this way, including even that of Lambert Sustris, who painted the frescoes in the Bigolin family villa at Selvazzano in the 1540s, and thus could have known Bigolina directly (Mancini, *La Villa Bigolin*, 53–84). For Sustris's *Judgment of Paris*, which he painted on a wedding chest (*cassone*), see F. L. Richardson, *Andrea Schiavone* (Oxford: Clarendon Press, 1980), 201, and plate 235.

sanza sentir più volte pungersi l'anima e 'l cuore; nondimeno havendosi ambidue fatto scudo della ragione, la si havevano passata al meglio che potero.

Volle ancora il buon vecchio che presso la bella Venere fosse il Prencipe Giufredi in loco di Paris, et in habito di Pastore depinto; il quale fu dall'eccellente pittore pinto con tal maestranza che nella faccia della bellissima Venere tenea gli occhi fisi, et porgevale il pomo; che chiunque ambidue gli mirava, non potea tenersi che d'amor non sentisse tutto commoversi.

Ma poscia che 'l nobilissimo quadro fu con somma diligenza a perfettione condotto; et che hebbe il pittore tutto l'ordine havuto dal vecchio consigliero circa il modo che si dovea in tal fatto tenere, per più tosto ispedirsi salito un legno che verso Roma n'andava, in pochi giorni in Salerno si ritrovò; dove smontato, et con bel modo appresentatosi al Prencipe, dopo la convenevol riverenza fattagli in cotal modo gli disse. "Nobilissimo Signore, la fama della grande vostra bellezza già non molti mesi per haverne il ritratto, et dapoi fornirne un mio oggetto della Corte di Spagna mi trasse; et n'hebbi per gratia de' Cieli il mio intento; quantunque Vostra Eccellenza alcuna intentione non ne havesse. Et al presente il gran nome della smisurata sua virtù et gentilezza mi vi riconduce. Io, Signore, nell'arte mia sempre mi son dilettato se non di avanzare, almen d'uguagliarmi alli più eccellenti del mio tempo; et più d'ogn'altra cosa sempre dilettato mi sono, di tener meco i ritratti di tutti i più eccellenti et nobili prencipi; et delle più belle et valorose Signore del mondo. Et essendo, poco fa, passato un'anno, per buona sorte da un nobilissimo signor d'Italia richiesto a dover ritrarre una sua sopra ogni stima bellissima moglie, la quale egli volle (quantunque con infinito dispiacer di lei) che dal capo a' piedi io l'havesse a ritrarre; ben perciò con una bernia di carmesino zendato sopra la ignuda carne, la quale parte di quelle bellissime membra copriva, et parte ancora, con stupor di cui le mirava, lasciava scoperte. Et ben vi giuro Signore, che in tutti i miei giorni, membra più belle, o meglio di quelle qualificate gli miei occhi non videro mai, nè credo che Apelle o Zeusi di simile a quelle in una sola riposte,

Urania: The Story of a Young Woman's Love

man, who was about seventy years old, look upon these limbs without feeling shaken in his heart and soul on more than one occasion. Nonetheless each man made a shield of reason, and withstood the experience as best he could.

The old counselor also wished that Prince Giufredi be added to the painting next to Venus, in the place of Paris, and in shepherd's clothing. The fine painter executed this in such a way that the Prince was shown with his eyes fixed on Venus's beautiful face, handing her the apple. In fact, the artist's skill was so great that anyone who looked upon these two figures could not fail to be moved by the power of love.

No sooner had he brought this most noble painting to perfection through his great diligence, and no sooner had he consulted with the old counselor concerning the plan of action, than the painter boarded a ship bound for Rome, this being the fastest way to get there. In a few days he alighted in Salerno, and presented himself to the Prince in a civil fashion. After showing the Prince all due reverence, he spoke to him thus: "Most noble lord, it has not been many months since the fame of your marvelous good looks drew me here in order to paint your portrait, while I was on my way to finish a project at the court of Spain; and by the grace of heaven I accomplished my intent, even though Your Excellency had no intention that I do so. At the present time the great reputation of your infinite virtue and gentility has brought me back here. My lord, I have always taken pleasure in at least equaling the efforts of the most excellent artists of my time, even if I could not outdo them; and nothing has given me better pleasure than possessing the portraits of all the finest and most noble princes in the world, as well as the most beautiful and worthy ladies. A year ago I had the good fortune to be asked by a very noble Italian lord to paint his inestimably beautiful wife, whom he wanted painted from head to toe, in spite of the infinite displeasure which this caused her, on account of the fact that he wanted her shown with a only a mantle of crimson sendal covering her naked flesh. This mantle covered part of her very beautiful limbs, yet left part of them exposed, to the dumbfounded admiration of any who looked upon them. I swear to you, my lord, that in all my days my eyes have never seen a body more beautiful or more perfect. Nor do I believe that either Apelles or Zeuxis ever saw a single woman endowed with a body like this;

meno vedessero loro; chè se una simile veduta n'havessero, non sarebbe stato necessario a Zeusi far di tante belle raccolta, per formarne una sola perfetta; poi che questa ch'io dico in sè sola tutte le porta.

"Hor ritratta che io l'hebbi vollemi quel cortese Signore di mercede convenevolissima premiare; ma io giamai alcuna cosa non volli accettare, anzi di somma gratia gli supplicai ch'egli fosse contento di concedermi licenza che un'altro ritratto simile a quello, per me io facesse, chè s'egli cotal dono mi concedeva mi sarei reputato d'haver la maggior mercede da lui ricevuta, ch'altra io potesse ricevere. Non voleva per cosa del mondo cotal gratia quel Signore concedermi, nondimeno havendoli io la mia fede data, che giamai si saperebbe, et che io mai non manifestarei di cui fosse il ritratto. Pur s'acquetò, et fu contento che un'altro per me io ne facesse, ma nascosamente però sì che la bella et gentil Signora non se ne accorgesse, la quale son certissimo che giamai consentito l'harrebbe.

"Hor vedendomi ricco d'uno così pretioso tesoro, nacque in me un novo pensiero di voler dipingere sopra un quadro il giudicio di Paris nelle tre Dee; che ritrovandomi quella bellissima imagine, parvemi ch'ella sarebbe una Venere divinissima. Et così diedi principio all'effetto di questo mio novo pensiero; et posi la molto valorosa Duchessa di Borbone, nel loco della Dea Giunone: che essendo quella honorata Duchessa d'infinito honor degna convenevolmente gli attribui' un cotal degno loco. Posi poi nel loco di Pallade la casta et virtuosissima figliuola del Re di Polonia; et quest'altra ch'io dissi, la quale è non men gentile et virtuosa di quel che sia bella, la posi nel medesimo habito che io la ritrassi nel loco di Venere.

"Ma volendo poi ritrovare un'huomo, il quale dandoli il loco di Paris, ragionevolmente lo potessi a proportione con quella bellissima Venere accompagnare, mi ritrovai ben del tutto impacciato; che tutti sozzopra i miei ritratti rivolgendo, giamai uno non ne potei ritrovare il qual mi paresse per bellezza meritar d'esser presso una così bella Venere posto. Per la qual cosa come disperato di poterne più un degno ritrovare, quasi che dalla incominciata impresa mi distolsi; ma ritrovandomi

for if they had, it would not have been necessary for Zeuxis to have gathered the attributes of so many different beauties, in order to create a single perfect one.[52] As I say, this woman bears every attribute of beauty within herself.

"When I had painted her, this courteous lord wished to reward me with an extremely generous compensation. But I did not wish to accept any payment, and instead I begged him to allow me, if it pleased him, to make another portrait just like it for myself; and if he granted me such a gift I would consider it the greatest payment that I ever could have received from him. This the gentleman would not permit me, for anything on earth; but then once I had given him my word that no one would ever know of it, and that I would never reveal whose portrait it was, he relented. Now he was content to let me paint another portrait for myself, as long as I did it secretly so that the beautiful and gentle lady would not know of it, for I am certain that she would never have agreed to allow it.

"Now seeing that I was a rich man, for I possessed such a treasure, there arose in me a new plan, to paint the Judgment of Paris with the three goddesses standing before him. I had that very beautiful painting of the Duchess, and it seemed to me that she would make a most divine Venus. So I set about putting my new plan into effect. I inserted the most outstanding Duchess of Bourbon in the place of the goddess Juno, inasmuch as I considered such a role fitting for that honorable lady who merits infinite respect. I then added the chaste and most virtuous daughter of the King of Poland in the guise of Pallas. Next came this other, no less genteel and virtuous than beautiful, whom I have already described: I put her in the place of Venus, in the same costume which she was wearing in the portrait I had made.

"Now I needed to find a man, equal in stature to this beautiful Venus, to put in the place of Paris, but here I found myself at a loss. I went through all my portraits, tossing them into disorder, but could not find one that seemed to me attractive enough to deserve to be put beside so lovely a Venus. On account of this, I despaired of ever finding a portrait so worthy, and was on the point of giving up

---

[52] Zeuxis, unable to find a suitable model for his painting of Helen of Troy, compiled the attributes of five different women of Croton; see L. B. Alberti, *On Painting and Sculpture*, ed. and trans. C. Grayson (London: Phaidon, 1972), 99; and Boccaccio, *Famous Women* (trans. Brown, 143). On the prevalence of this story in Renaissance discussions of aesthetics, see Rogers, "The Decorum of Women's Beauty," 50, and P. Bettella, "Corpo di parti: Ambiguità e frammentarietà nella rappresentazione della bellezza femminile nei trattati di Trissino e Firenzuola," *Forum Italicum* 33 (1999): 319–35, here 327.

pochi mesi fanno in Spagna con un mio carissimo amico di questo mio fatto a parlamento, mi fu domandato da lui, se io mai havesse Vostra Eccellenza veduto; et gli risposi che no. Onde egli risposemi: 'Se non l'hai veduto lamentati adunque della tua negligenza, che non ha saputo ricercar la cosa desiderata dove ella si trova.' Et dopo in tante convenevolmente date lodi a Vostra Eccellenza sì della cortesia et gentilezza, qual della bellezza si diffuse, che un tanto desiderio di veder il vero mi pose nel cuore, che 'l giorno seguente, per ritrovarmi qui, m'imbarcai; dove giunto trovai, che l'effetto sopr'avanzava il suono delle lodi d'assai. Et tanto mi furono i Cieli cortesi che mi fu agio conceduto, sanza alcuna cosa farne intender a Vostra Eccellenza commodamente di potervi ritrarre; onde di voi medesimo Signor mio, componendo il mio Paris, condussi a perfettione il bel quadro; del quale la gran bellezza, et nobilità considerando, parvemi che non lo poteva in migliore et più degno loco collocare, come è facendo d'egli a Vostra Eccellenza presente. Et così Signor mio, lo vi ho portato acciò dall'humile vostro servo, con quel fedel cuore che egli lo vi porge, il picciolo dono vi degnate accettare."

Et poi c'hebbe così detto fece cenno a due servi, che discosti da quel loco stavano, che 'l bellissimo quadro gli recassero innanzi. Tra il qual tempo il cortese Prencipe assai gratiosamente ringratiò il pittore delle tante lode dategli, et del buon volere ch'egli verso di lui dimostrava d'havere. Ma giunto ivi il bellissimo quadro dal quale levando il pittore un panno di seta con lo quale stava coperto tutto ad un tempo così al Prencipe disse: "Cotesto è, Signore, il bello et nobilissimo quadro, non già cotanto nobile et bello per l'opera mia, quantunque ogni mia industria io vi habbia posta; ma maggiormente per cagione della grandissima nobiltà, che ne' soggetti ch' entro vi sono, si trova. Et prima mirate Signor mio vi prego, la gran maestà, la quale nella faccia di questa venerabile Giunone, et sapientissima Pallade si scorge; che non può far chiunque le mira, che sommamente maravigliato non resti. Ma per dire il vero poi, chi considera le sopra humane bellezze di questa Venere, gliè forza che vinto, abbagliato, et confuso rimanga.

"Deh per cortesia mirate un poco Signore, come queste aurate crespe chiome paiono reti da allacciar mille indurati cuori. [. . .][53] che la spatiosa, et lucida fronte; gli occhi, che a due stelle si assimigliano; quantunque la loro natural vivacità non vi si possa scorgere a pieno; le inarcate, et d'hebano ciglia; il ben proportionato naso, le gote di rose, la picciola bocca, le labra della quale vincono di

---

[53] Lacuna due to probable scribal omission in T (fol. 108r); reproduced in P (fol. 109r). As in the case of the first lacuna in this text (132, note 29), it occurs in the break between two lines.

the undertaking which I had already begun. Then, a few months ago while in Spain I found myself conversing about this situation of mine with a very dear friend. He asked me if I had ever seen Your Excellency, and I told him no, whereupon he answered me thus: 'If you have not seen him, you have cause to lament, for your negligence has not allowed you to seek out the thing you desire where it may be found.' He then poured forth such great praise of Your Excellency, speaking as much of your courtesy and gentility as your good looks, that he instilled in my heart a desire to see the actual item. Thus it was that the following day I embarked on the voyage which has brought me here, and upon arriving, I found that the reality greatly exceeded the sound of the praises I had heard. And so kind were the Heavens to me, that without Your Excellency's knowledge I was easily able to paint your portrait, then use the image to create my Paris, thus completing to perfection the beautiful painting. Considering the beauty and nobility of this work, it seemed I could find no better or more worthy purpose for it than to make a present of it to Your Excellency. And so, my lord, please accept this little gift which I have brought to you as your humble and faithful servant."

When he had finished saying this, he made a sign to two servants, who were standing nearby, indicating that they bring forward the beautiful painting. While they were doing this, the courteous prince very graciously thanked the painter for the great praise he had pronounced, and for the good will he had shown him. When the lovely painting had been brought to them, the painter lifted the sheet of silk which had covered it completely, and spoke to the prince. "This, my lord, is the beautiful and most noble painting. It is not so beautiful and noble merely through my efforts, even if I have worked very hard on it, but principally on account of the very great nobility which is to be found in the subjects it contains. First, my lord, look upon the great majesty which can be discerned in the faces of this venerable Juno and this most wise Pallas; indeed, no one who sees them could refrain from marvelling. But to tell the truth, whoever considers the superhuman beauty of this Venus is left overwhelmed, dazzled, and dazed.

"Please see, my lord, how these golden curls resemble nets which could entrap a thousand hard hearts. [...] than the shining expanse of forehead, and these eyes which resemble two stars, even though one cannot fully appreciate their natural intensity here. Notice her curved eyebrows, which are the color of ebony, and her well-proportioned nose, as well as her rosy cheeks and tiny mouth, whose lips

bellezza i coralli; nè d'altra cosa tanto mi doglio, quanto è del non haver potuto quelle orientali perle, ch'elle rinchiudono, come io le vidi in lei, così pingerle ancora. Il mento di giustissima misura, et che in parte alcuna non manca, o eccede, par che ciascuno dica da per sè, 'Qui, et non altrove tiene il suo regno Amore.'

"Ma che diremo poi noi di cotesta gola, et petto, che vincono di bianchezza le nevi? Et di quel poco rilevato pomo, che non vi è chi mirandolo tutto d'amoroso desio struggere il cuor non si senta. O Dio, che rotondo et ben formato braccio è questo! Della mano non dico, perchè troppo ben si assomiglia a quella che spesse volte l'arco, la faretra, et gli strali del fanciullo Cupido modera et regge. Al bel ventre et rilevato fianco non credo già che la Invidia alcun difetto vi ritrovasse. Ma mirate, Signore, più che ogn' altra cosa, con somma attentione vi prego, la bellissima coscia della quale altra più bella non credo che Fidia, o Policletto ne scolpissero mai. Et in fine chi da capo a' piedi ben la mira, et considera, dirà che la gran Maestra Natura giamai altro corpo più di questo d'ogni bellezza perfetto, nè creasse, nè potesse creare."

Mentre s'ingegnava il pittore di inalzar con somme lodi la eccellenza di quelle bellissime membra, il Prencipe, che fissamente il bel ritratto mirava, più di mille ardentissimi sospiri havea mandati dal cuore; della qual cosa essendosi accorto il pittore, et di certo credendo ch' egli di quelle singolari bellezze innamorato si fosse, et di ciò sentendone un'infinito contento, s'affaticava perciò più fortemente a lodargliele ogn'hora. Ma per dire il vero, il fatto in altro modo passava di quello ch' egli già divisato s'haveva; imperciò che essendo il buon Prencipe già più di due anni acceso nell'amor d'una assai bella donzella, la quale era figliuola d'un nobile conte suo vassallo; et che la savia damigella per compiacere al Prencipe veniva da tutti chiamata; mirando quelle estreme bellezze nelle membra di quella vaga Signora venne in consideratione, anzi in ferma credenza che tali, o forse anco più belle esser dovessero quelle della donzella, ch' egli amava contanto. Per la qual cosa d' un così novo, et intenso desiderio di vederle, et gustarle s'accese, che non

in their beauty put corals to shame. Regrettably I was not able to paint the oriental pearls which I saw enclosed within those lips; and nothing saddens me more. As far as her chin, which is of most perfect proportion, is concerned, it has no shortcomings or grossness whatever, and indeed it seems that each one who views it says to himself, 'Here, and nowhere else, Love has established his realm.'[54]

"But then, what are we to say about this throat, and this bosom, both of which are so much whiter than snow? And what of this slightly raised apple, which no man can look upon without feeling his heart melt with amorous desire? My God, how round and well-formed is this arm! And I have said nothing about the hand, which looks all too much like the one which so often is seen to handle the bow, quiver, and arrows of the youthful Cupid. I do not believe Envy has found any defect in her lovely abdomen, nor in her exposed side. But above all, my lord, pay the greatest attention to her most lovely thigh, for I do not believe Phidias or Policlitus ever sculpted one more lovely.[55] To sum up, whoever looks her over from head to toe, and regards her closely, will conclude that great Mother Nature never created, nor ever could create, a body more perfect than this one in every beautiful detail."

While the artist strove to exalt with the highest praise the excellence of those gorgeous limbs, the Prince fixed his gaze upon the portrait and sent forth from his heart a thousand most ardent sighs. When the artist became aware of this, he was certain that the Prince had fallen in love with her singular beauty; and, feeling infinitely content, he made an effort to praise her even more. But to tell the truth, the situation was proceeding in another direction from that which he had planned. For the good Prince had, for the past two years, been in love with a very beautiful maiden who was the daughter of one of his vassals, a noble count, and this wise maiden had been urged by everyone to stay in the Prince's good graces. As he looked upon the extreme loveliness of the fair lady's body, the Prince came to imagine, and indeed he was convinced that the body of the maiden whom he loved so much must be equal of the one in the painting; or perhaps it was even more lovely. For this reason he was seized by so strange and intense a desire to see

---

[54] This phrase echoes Petrarch's *canzone* 126.52 "... qui regna Amore" ["here Love reigns"].

[55] Phidias (Pheidias) and Policlitus (Polycleitus) were Greek sculptors of the fifth century B.C., regarded as paragons of their art during the Renaissance. See Pliny, *Natural History*, 34.19.

solamente li cagionò quei focosi sospiri, ma fu etiandio cagione ch' egli ponendo in quel punto tutti que' rispetti da canto; i quali infiniti haveva. Fece deliberatione subito ch' ella da Napoli fosse tornata dove da alcuni suoi assai nobili parenti era stata chiamata per nozze, di torlasi per moglie.

O maladetto sei tu Amore per sempre, poi che coteste sono delle belle operationi, che tu sai fare! Che giovò (inhumano) a quella infelice Signora il far palese la bellezza delle sue occulte et nobilissime membra, poscia che per tua malvagia operatione quello, che a lei dovea giovare con suo danno et scorno in utile d'altra rivolgesti? Ma non mi maraviglio di ciò perchè noi altri pingendoti cieco, ci fai in vendetta di te stesso conoscere come noi siamo gli ciechi, et non tu. Ma guai a quelli, delli quali ti piace di prenderti gioco, et del lor mal ti compiaci, come di questa infelice Signora di cui ragiono, facesti.

URANIA: THE STORY OF A YOUNG WOMAN'S LOVE

the maiden's body, and have a taste of it, that it made him heave hot sighs, and even caused him to set aside all of those scruples which he had once had in abundance. He immediately decided the maiden should return from Naples, where she had been called by certain of her noble relatives who wished to find her a husband, for now he would marry her himself.

O cursed be you forever, Love, for such are the intrigues of which you are capable! You inhuman thing! Of what use was it for that unhappy lady to expose the beauty of her hidden and most noble parts, if your evil machinations served only to bring shame and injury upon her, and to make her efforts on her own behalf work to the advantage of another woman?[56] But I do not marvel at this, because when we describe you in paintings as blind, you take your revenge on us by showing how we, and not you, are the blind ones. Woe to those whom you toy with for your amusement! For you take pleasure in their pain, just as you did in the case of this unhappy lady whom I have described.

---

[56] On the indecorousness of high-born, well-known persons allowing themselves to be depicted nude in Renaissance paintings, see R. Goffen, "Titian's *Sacred and Profane Love* and Marriage," in *The Expanding Discourse, Feminism and Art History*, ed. N. Broude and M. D. Garrard (New York: IconEditions, 1992), 110–25, here 113–14, and Rogers, "The Decorum of Women's Beauty," 50–52. For a discussion of the erotic potential of Cinquecento mythological paintings, as well as the link between such paintings and the portraiture of courtesans, see Carlo Ginzburg, "Titian, Ovid and Sixteenth-century Codes for Erotic Illustration," in *Titian's Venus of Urbino*, ed. R. Goffen (Cambridge: Cambridge University Press, 1997), 23–36. On the iconography of nudity see R. Goffen, "The Problematic Patronage of Titian's *Venus of Urbino*," *Journal of Medieval and Renaissance Studies* 14 (1993): 301–29, here 302–3; here Goffen notes that nudity was not always seen as the antithesis of chastity at this time, especially in the context of the depiction of a bride; however, Bigolina's case is clearly quite different. See A. C. Junkerman, "The Lady and the Laurel: Gender and Meaning in Giorgione's Laura," *Oxford Art Journal* 16 (1993): 49–58, for a study associating female nudity in portraits with the risks run by Renaissance women who sought a career in the public eye (especially as writers). For the Renaissance notion that portraiture could not adequately convey the beauty of character, a context in which *Urania* must clearly be viewed, see E. Cropper, "The Beauty of Woman: Problems in the Rhetoric of Renaissance Portraiture," in *Rewriting the Renaissance*, ed. M. W. Ferguson et al. (Chicago: University of Chicago Press, 1986), 175–90, here 181–83. For a study stressing Matteo Bandello's acceptance of pictorial methods of portraiture in the context of his *Novelle*, see M. Cottino-Jones, "The Pen and the Brush: Woman Portraiture in the Renaissance," in *Da una riva all'altra. Studi in onore di Antonio d'Andrea*, ed. D. della Terza (Florence: Cadmo, 1995), 229–32. As Cottino-Jones notes, Bandello had no problem praising a woman (Cecilia Gallerani, the mistress of Ludovico Sforza) both for her physical beauty as well as for her literary talent.

Ma poi che dopo lungo dire hebbe pur dato fine il pittore alle molte lodi di sua Signora, et che 'l Prencipe dopo molto guardare si fu satiato, vennegli quel desiderio il quale è quasi commune a ciascuno, cioè di voler tutte quelle cose sapere, le quali maggiormente negate gli sono. Vennegli desiderio dico di volere intender chi fosse quella sì bella Signora nel quadro dipinta; onde il pittore, che assai più voglia di dirlo havea, ch' egli non havea di saperlo, poscia che s'hebbe alquanto lasciato pregare facendosi dar la fede di mai ad altra persona ridirlo, gli manifestò cui, et quale ella fosse, fingendo che 'l Duca di lei marito quindeci giorni dinanci la sua morte, con infinito dispiacer di lei l'havea fatta così ritrare. Molto piacere hebbe il Prencipe di saper chi ella fosse, et infinitamente hebbe grato il bel quadro; il qual fatto riporre nella più cara stanza che egli havesse tutto si diede ad honorar il pittore et farli grate accoglienze, et honorevolissimi doni astringendolo forte a doversi restar seco per qualche giorno; il che con intentione faceva acciò ch' egli dopo fatte le nozze, gli havesse la sua savia damigella a ritrare, non facendogli perciò di tal cosa alcun motto.

Ma non passarono più di due giorni dopo la giunta del pittore in Salerno che 'l vecchio della Duchessa consigliero vi giunse simigliantemente ancor egli; il quale seco una bellissima ghirlanda di rose portava, della qual sorte ve ne erano forse poche altrove per lo mondo vedute; et di tali da molto lontani paesi venutale una sol pianta ne tennea la Duchessa. Havevano cotali rose una maravigliosa proprietade, la quale era che oltre che bellissime più dell'altre, et di smisurato odore fossero, havevano ancora una tal virtude, che un'anno intiero cotal bellezza et odore in somma perfettione le duravano.

Giunto adunque, che fu il vecchione con la ghirlanda in Salerno, et appresentatosi al Prencipe, dopo la convenevole riverenza fattagli in cotal modo gli disse. "Eccellentissimo Signore, so che Vostra Eccellenza non mi debbe conoscere, per esser molti anni che in queste parti non mi son ritrovato. Imperciò che dopo che io son fatto vecchio, mai di Calabria dalla corte del Duca Federico mio Signore mi son partito; et alla morte sua, la quale avvene di poco è un'anno passato, con le viscere del cuore mi raccomandò la sua bellissima, ma molto più virtuosissima sposa, dal servigio della quale nè mi son partito, nè sin ch'io sarò vivo giamai partire m'intendo.

Urania: The Story of a Young Woman's Love

The artist brought to a close his long speech of praise for his lady. When the Prince had sated himself with looking at the painting, he was seized by a desire (common to nearly everyone) to know those secrets which are most firmly denied to him. By this I mean that he now desired to know who the beautiful lady depicted in the painting was; whereupon the painter (who had far more desire to reveal the name than the Prince had to know it) allowed the Prince to plead for a bit, then made him swear never to repeat the name to anyone, before at last telling him her identity. In doing so he pretended that the Duke, her husband, had commanded that the lady be painted in this way, despite her infinite displeasure, only fifteen days before he died. The Prince was very pleased to know who she was, and thus he was infinitely glad to have the painting, which he had brought into his favorite room. He bestowed every honor upon the artist, and made him feel very welcome, giving him very honorable gifts and urging him to stay in his court for a few days. The Prince did all this with the intention of having the artist do a portrait of his wise maiden after the wedding, so he did not say a word about this to him.

However, no more than two days after the painter had come to Salerno, the old counselor of the Duchess arrived there as well. This man was bearing a most lovely garland of roses, of the sort which perhaps had hardly ever been seen anywhere else in the world. Of these roses, which had come to the Duchess from very distant lands, she maintained only one bush. These roses had a marvelous property: not only were they more beautiful than any others, and endowed with an extremely strong scent, but they also would keep their beauty and scent perfectly intact for an entire year.

When the grand old man had arrived in Salerno with the garland, and had presented himself to the Prince with suitable reverence, he began to speak: "Most excellent lord, I know that Your Excellency must not know me, since I have not been in these parts for many years. After I became old I never left Calabria, and remained in the court of my lord, the Duke Frederick.[57] Just before his death, which occurred a little more than a year ago, he charged me in all earnestness to look after his most beautiful (yet even more virtuous) wife, whose service I have never left, nor ever will leave as long as I live.

---

[57] This is not a clearly identifiable figure, although the brother of Alfonso II, King of Naples and Duke of Calabria, was indeed called Frederick (1451–1504). He too served as King of Naples for a time. See Masuccio, *Il Novellino*, ed. Nigro, 103–4, and notes 46 and 50 above.

Giulia Bigolina

"Ma per dir a Vostra Eccellenza brevemente la cagione, la quale al presente dinanzi a sua presenza mi conduce, dico, che ritrovandomi haver alcuni negotij da ispedire a Roma, et havendo ottenuta dalla Signora buona licenza d'andarvi, già pochi giorni sono passati mi posi in viaggio per terra, per non mi comportar molto il mare, et mi levava assai per tempo ogni giorno per far buon camino innanzi che 'l sole co' suoi raggi fortemente l'aria, et la terra scaldasse. Hor avennemi già due giorni, che essendomi (sì com'io dissi) assai a buon' hora levato, et postomi dinanzi di tutti i miei servi in viaggio per meglio poter dir le mie devotioni, et non esser da alcun disturbato, non fui a pena ito innanzi due miglia che su la riva d' un fiumicello, lungo il quale io cavalcava ritrovai una assai bella donzella (per quello, che io ne potei comprendere) la quale essendo ferita, et tutta nel proprio sangue allagata, quasi vicina alla morte in terra giaceva. Ond'io a così strano spettacolo fermandomi, et tutto per compassione sentendo commovermi il cuore giù del cavallo discesi, et tolta che io l'hebbi pietosamente tra le mie braccia le dimandai qual pessima sorte l'haveva a cotal doloroso fine condotta; et ella, che dimostrava homai più poter poco, così con gran fatica risposemi. 'Cortesissimo gentilhuomo, perchè io so certo che tanto la vita non mi durerebbe, che io potessi tutta narrarvi la crudel cagione, la qual trasse un pessimo cavaliero a condurmi a questo estremo fin così amaro; et perciò basteravi per hora il sapere che ingiustissimamente questa pena io patisco. Ma ben vi supplico, et prego per quanta cortesia et pietade si ritrova in voi, che siate contento hor hora sanza punto tardare così con le vostre braccia in questo fiumicello gettarmi, nè vi dubitate perchè io sia ancor viva di gettarmi nel fiume, imperciò che non così tosto sarò da quelle acque tocca; che miracoloso effetto di me vederete.'

"Ond'io, che quantunque una assai inhumana operatione da dover far mi paresse questa, nondimeno pur di tal fermo volere vedendola, et conoscendo come poco più di vita perder poteva, per sodisfarla, et per pietà lagrimando la vi gettai. O cosa maravigliosa, et quasi incredibile da udire, nondimeno io pure il vidi, et dirollo. Io vi giuro Signore, che non così tosto l'hebbi nel fiumicello gettata, come sino al fondo di quello passando subitamente sana, allegra, et bellissima se ne ritornò di sopra, et havendo questa così bella cassetta in mano, che a me vedete havere, in cotal modo con faccia ridente mi disse. 'Cortesissimo gentilhuomo, le gratie che io vi rendo del grandissimo beneficio che io ho da voi ricevuto, come è che co'l mezzo vostro io m'habbia ricuperata la vita elle sono infinite, ma perchè manca del debito suo quello, il quale con qualche effetto potendo, vuol con semplici parole sodisfar colui, dal quale un gran beneficio si conosce haver ricevuto,

Urania: The Story of a Young Woman's Love

"In order to tell Your Excellency briefly the reason I have come, I will say that I had some business to conduct in Rome, for which I obtained leave from my lady to go to that city. A few days ago I set out on a land voyage, so as not to suffer rigors at sea; each day I got up early in order to cover the maximum distance before the sun would heat the air and the earth with its rays. Now it happened just two days ago, when I had arisen so early (as I have just said), I set out ahead of all of my servants in order to say my prayers without being disturbed by anyone. I had not gone more than two miles when I discovered a lovely maid on the banks of the stream beside which I was riding. She was a real maid, at least as far as I could tell; she had been wounded, and was lying on the ground near death, covered with blood. At this bizarre spectacle I stopped and descended from my horse, feeling my heart greatly moved by compassion. I took her piteously in my arms, and asked her what evil fate could have brought her to so sad a condition. She, who by now appeared on the brink of death, made a great effort and answered me thus: 'Most courteous gentleman, I am quite certain that my life will not last long enough for me to tell you the whole cruel circumstance whereby an evil knight brought me to so bitter an end. Therefore, at present it will be sufficient for you to know that I suffer this fate most unjustly. But I beseech you, by whatever courtesy and pity may reside in you, that you be willing to throw me into this stream with your own arms, and without delay. Do not fear to throw me into the water while I am still alive, for as soon as I am touched by the water you will see it will have a miraculous effect on me.'

"Even though this seemed a most inhuman thing to do, I could see that she was firm in her desire; and since it was clear there was so little left of her life to lose, I threw her in just to satisfy her, all the while weeping for pity. O what a marvel then occurred, almost incredible to hear; and yet I saw it, and will recount it to you. I swear to you, my lord, that no sooner had I thrown her into the stream, so that she sank to the bottom of it, than she immediately returned to the surface unscathed, joyful, and so very beautiful. She was bearing a most lovely box in her hand, the very one you see me holding here. 'O courteous gentleman,' she said, her face all a smile. 'The thanks which I give you for your great kindness, whereby I have regained my life, are infinite. But a person fails to show due gratitude if he wishes to give thanks with mere words even when he is capable of more, and is fully aware he has received a great favor; such a person makes himself

ond' egli ingrato si faccia tenere. Et perciò non volendo io da voi esser giudicata tale, voglio un dono farvi, il quale pensomi che forse al presente parravi assai picciolo, per non esser cosa, la quale a voi si convenghi, nondimeno quando da qui a pochi giorni vederete il frutto, che questo mio dono producerà, più caro l'harrete che se un gran stato donato vi havesse. Questo dono, che io dar vi voglio è una ghirlanda di rose di maravigliosa bellezza, ma d'una infinita virtù, et la virtù sua è tale che quale huomo si voglia, che questa ghirlanda doni a chiunque donna egli ama et desidera, non così tosto farà da quella donna toccata, come cotanto nell'amor di colui che le l'haverà donata accenderassi, che cosa ch'egli le chiederà nè sapra, nè potrà negarli, et cotale amore sanza mai punto mancare sino alla morte di quella donna, nel cor suo conserverà sempre.

"'Et perchè io so che voi potreste dirmi: et che voglio far io d'un così fatto dono, essendo come io son, vecchio, per la qual cosa mi si disdice il cercar che alcuna donna più di cotal amore mi ami? Ma io vi dico, che essendo da me la cortese natura vostra conosciuta, et come assai più di giovare ad altrui, che a voi stesso vi compiacete, perciò questo dono particolarmente vi faccio, acciò che con questo habbiate a porger aiuto al più bello, al più gentile, et cortese Signore, che hoggidì viva; et questo è il virtuosissimo Giufredi Prencipe di Salerno, il quale al giunger vostro (che a lui drittamente vi consiglio che andate) per lo più meritevole soggetto, che si trovi nel mondo, acceso di tante amorose fiamme ritroverete, che a pena tante ne ardeno Mongibello, et ne ha ben giusta cagione, imperciò che tanto è degno il soggetto per lo quale egli arde, che ogni cuore aggiacciato tutto in fuoco convertirebbe.'

"Et poi che cotali parole m'hebbe dette, questa bella cassetta su la riva del fiumicello mi trasse, et tutto ad un tempo si tuffò giù nell'acqua, nè più la rividi; della qual cosa io rimasi così maravigliato, che io non potrei a pieno narrarlo. Ma dopo sopra le sue parole considerando m'avidi, che come havea detto ella cotesto dono più grato che se m'havesse ogni gran stato conceduto io doveva haverlo, essendomi co'l mezzo di questo dono dato il modo di poter far allegro, et contento uno così raro Signore come è Vostra Eccellenza. Et perciò i miei passi che in altra parte havea volti, subitamente più che mai fosse, allegro qui in Salerno rivolsi. Et così, Signor mio, di questa bella et amorosa ghirlanda vi faccio un dono, acciò che col valor suo da quella donna, che voi più amate tutto quello, che 'l vostro cuor desidera possiate ottenere." Et ciò dicendo il buon vecchio, et havendo già tratta la vaga ghirlanda fuori della ricca cassetta, l'una et l'altra con riverenza pose nelle mani del Prencipe.

URANIA: THE STORY OF A YOUNG WOMAN'S LOVE

appear ungrateful. Since I do not wish to judged so by you, I wish to give you a gift. I believe this gift might appear very small to you right now, for it might seem an inappropriate thing. Nonetheless, when you see the benefits this gift of mine will produce a few days from now, you will hold it dearer than any great kingdom I might have given you. The gift I wish to give you is a rose garland of marvelous beauty, but also of infinite power: its power is such that if any man gives this garland to the woman he loves and desires, that woman will burn with love for the man who has bestowed it on her as soon as it touches her. She will not be able to deny the man anything he asks of her, and she will preserve this love for him in her heart until her death, without fail.

" 'I know what you might ask me: why would I want such a gift, since I am an old man, and people say that it is inappropriate for me to seek anything more than the most innocent sort of love from any woman? But I tell you, your courteous nature is plain to me, and I know you take much greater pleasure in helping others than in helping yourself. Therefore I bestow this particular gift on you in order that you might give aid to the most handsome, kind, and courteous lord who is alive today; and that is the very virtuous Giufredi, Prince of Salerno. I advise you to go to him immediately, for when you arrive you will find him burning with more flames than those which consume Mount Etna; and the object of this amorous fire will be the most worthy that can be found in the world. And he has every right to burn thus, for the object of his desire could turn any frozen heart to fire.'

"When she had spoken these words, she tossed this beautiful box onto the shore of the stream, then suddenly dived down into the water, and I did not see her any more. I was more astonished to see this than I could ever describe. But afterwards I thought over her words, and realized that what she had said was true: I should regard this gift as more welcome than any great kingdom she could have given me, since I now had the means, through this gift, to make joyful and content a lord as rare as Your Excellency. Therefore I was glad, and even though I had been formerly headed in a different direction, I changed my course quite quickly in order to come here, to Salerno. And so I bestow upon you, my lord, this lovely and loving garland as a gift, so that by means of its power you may obtain everything your heart desires from the woman you love most." The good old man had already taken the fair garland from its lavish box, and now as he finished speaking he reverently placed both in the hands of the Prince.

Non si potrebbe a pieno narrare con quanta allegrezza et contento l'innamorato Prencipe il bel dono della vaga ghirlanda accettasse; chè havendo assai bene il dir dell'accorto vecchione inteso giudicava di certo che quella donzella, la quale glie l'haveva donata fosse una maga, la quale conoscesse come a lui pareva, che infiniti i meriti della sua savia damigella fossero; et che insiememente sapesse quanto fosse sviscerato l'amore, con lo quale egli l'amava; et perciò che così havesse con quel vecchio operato, acciò che quella virtuosa ghirlanda nelle mani sue pervenisse. Onde parendoli che i fati del Cielo di questo suo amore havessero cura, di doppie fiamme sentivasi l'infiammato cuor rinfiammare, et più sempre stabilivasi di volere in ogni modo pigliarla per moglie.

Per la qual cosa tanti ringratiamenti et tante grate accoglienze fece al buon vecchio, che ad uno Imperatore, che un regno donato gli havesse assai meno di quelle sarebbono state a bastanza; et poi gli soggiunse: "Padre mio honoratissimo, dinanzi che di qui vi partiate e' mi dà il cuore che io vi darò cagione che voi direte che quella accorta donzella saviamente, et il vero vi disse, lodandovi quel nobilissimo soggetto che io amo, et a quale io intendo di donar la bella ghirlanda." Et così dicendo, vi sopragiunse il pittore, il quale fingendo di non lo haver già più mesi veduto, molte honorate accoglienze gli fece, dimandandogli come la Duchessa sua Signora faceva; et poscia in molti, et honorevolissimi ragionamenti di lei entrambi due si diffusero, alli quali il Prencipe si ritrovò sempre presente. Ma poi ch'egli per dar ordine ad alcuni suoi fatti d'ivi si fu partito, et che gli due messaggieri della Duchessa rimasero soli, raccontò il pittore al buon vecchio tutto quello che egli haveva co'l Prencipe, mostrandoli il quadro, operato; soggiongendo nel raccontarli quanti focosi sospiri havea il Prencipe mandati dal cuore, mentre le bellissime membra della Duchessa mirava; et ch' egli le andava lodando. Per la qual cosa era come sicuro che la ghirlanda non ad altra che a lei manderebbe. Sommo contento ne senti di ciò lo buon vecchio; nè meno credea lui che la cosa dovesse nell'istesso modo passare nel quale egli con l'ingegno suo designato s'haveva di quello, che 'l pittor lo credesse.

Ma il Prencipe c'havea inteso di certo come tra il termine di tre giorni la sua savia damigella ritornava in Salerno; et perciò con quella maggiore allegrezza che mai più altra volta sentisse, haveva ordinato che di nobilissima tapezzeria fosse per ogni parte ornato il suo bel palagio. Il che fu tosto adempiuto; et acciò che da tutti fosser vedute, et l'odore gustato di quelle odorifere rose, fece la bellissima ghirlanda con una catenella d'oro al solaio della gran sala sospendere. Hor mentre che queste cose si facevano, et che già per tutto Salerno la bellezza et virtù della ghirlanda era divulgata, insieme con la comune opinione che 'l Prencipe altro non aspettasse eccetto della savia sua damigella il ritorno, per farne a lei di quella presente.

Urania: The Story of a Young Woman's Love

One could never fully describe with what joy and contentment the amorous Prince accepted the gift of the fair garland. For he had understood the wise old man perfectly, and was quite certain that the maid who had given the old man the garland must have been an enchantress who knew, just as he did, of the infinite merits of his lady. Moreover, he imagined this enchantress knew how fervently he loved his lady, and thus she had made good use of the old man, as a means whereby the magic garland would come into his hands. Concluding that the heavenly fates had taken an interest in his love, he now felt his already enflamed heart flare up twice over, and was all the more certain he wished to marry the maiden.

Therefore he thanked the man profusely, and gave him such honors as would have been sufficient for an emperor who had bestowed a kingdom upon him. "My honored father," he said, "before you depart from here, I will make bold to tell you that the clever maid spoke wisely, and told the truth when she praised the noble object of my affection, the woman whom I love and to whom I intend to give the lovely garland." As he spoke, the painter came up. He pretended he had not seen the old man for many months, and gave him a very honorable welcome, asking after the health of his lady the Duchess. Then both men began to gush the most flattering comments about her, while the Prince was still present. However, when the Prince left the room in order to see to his other affairs, and the Duchess's two messengers were alone, the painter told the old man everything he had accomplished by showing the painting to the Prince. He also mentioned the heated sighs that the Prince had sent forth from his heart, while viewing the beautiful body of the Duchess, and how he had exalted her. Hearing all this, the painter was quite certain that the Prince would send the garland to no one else but the Duchess. The good old man was mightily content to hear these things, and was no less convinced than the painter that the affair would progress exactly as his clever wit had planned.

But the Prince had learned with certainty that his wise maiden would return to Salerno within three days. For this reason, feeling greater joy than he had ever known, he ordered that every part of his beautiful palace be decorated with the noblest tapestries; and this was soon done. Then, so that everyone would have a chance to see and smell the scent of the roses, he had the lovely garland hung from the ceiling of the great hall on a golden chain. While these things were occurring, news of the beauty and magical powers of the garland was spreading through Salerno, along with the common opinion that the Prince was waiting for nothing less than the return of the wise maiden, so that he could present it to her.

Avenne che 'l secondo giorno dopo che la ghirlanda fu giunta, Fabio et Menandro si abbatterono ambi in un tempo, come la lor sorte permesse di andar a visitar la loro amata Clorina, come spesse volte erano usati di fare. Et poscia che vicendevolmente hebbero di quella et quell'altra cosa ragionato assai, nel ragionamento della ghirlanda entrarono, affermando ciascuno di loro che come la savia damigella fosse ritornata, che'l Prencipe a lei la ghirlanda darebbe, et che insieme la si torrebbe per moglie; imperciò che 'l così fuor dell'ordinario havere ornato il palagio, d'altro che di nozze non dava inditio. Ma la Clorina, che grande invidia et odio alla savia damigella portava, pensando come così aventurata fosse; chè non essendo al parer suo più di lei nobile o bella, et meritasse tanto dal Prencipe esser amata, che nè havesse a divenir Prencipessa. Perciò tutta sdegnosa, et con un sospiro che le venne dal cuore, verso que' giovani così disse. "O infelice Salerno, che io non credo che chi cercasse la Italia tutta, un'altra città simile a te vota de veri amanti si ritrovasse. Io mi maraveglio come voi altri giovani, i quali fate professione d'innamorati, per la vergogna non andate a nascondervi tutti, nè dovreste più havere ardire di mirar in faccia quella donzella, dalla qual ciascuno di voi desidera d'esser amato, poi che havendo sì commodo un tal tesoro come è quella ghirlanda, la quale potrebbe far beato quello, il quale alla sua amata donna la donasse; nè pur un solo si ha ritrovato di tanti che fanno professione amorosa, il quale habbia pur tentato d'haverla; chè se de veri amanti in questa nostra città vi si ritrovassero, come de' finti vi si trovano assai, questo sarebbe un soggetto (massimamente ritrovandosi la ghirlanda nel commodo loco per poterla rubare come ella si trova) da por sozzopra tutto Salerno, perciochè ciascun per donarla alla donna ch' egli ama dovrebbe sforzarsi d'haverla.

"Ma ahimè, che al presente veruno amante non si ritrova, il quale d'altro che di parole sia gagliardo, et cortese, et che quando a far di sè qualche dimostratione d'effetto tosto zoppo, et avaro non si dimostri; et così di uno, in uno al parer mio si dimostrano tutti. Et perciò non si debbe sperare che i giovani dal tempo d'hoggi voglino per amor delle loro amate donne, nè per conseguir loro amori alcuno incommodo patire; anzi a lor pare che facino assai, et che infinito merito presso le lor donne s'acquistino, perchè quando le veggono le fan riverenza, et parole di buona creanza le dicono, il che tutto in honor loro, et non d'elle riesce.

"Guardati che hoggi troppo in giostre, in torneamenti, overo in altra sorte di valorosa impresa (come già far si soleva) per amor non si pongano; già solevano gl' innamorati giovani, come si sa, con fatiche, et grandi pericoli nella vita, la vittoria de' loro amori acquistarsi; et al presente tutti in agi, et in piaceri s'acquistano. Ma

Urania: The Story of a Young Woman's Love

Two days after the arrival of the garland, it happened that fate permitted Fabio and Menandro to pay their customary visits at the very same time to their beloved Clorina, so that they ran into each other there. After they had discussed a little of this or that, their conversation turned to the garland, which they all believed the Prince would give to the wise maiden as soon as she returned, with the aim of marrying her at once. Indeed, the Prince's inordinate decorations in the palace suggested nothing less than a wedding. Clorina, however, felt great envy and hatred for the wise maiden and considered her entirely too lucky. In Clorina's opinion the maiden was neither nobler nor fairer than she, and thus did not merit to be so loved by the Prince, nor indeed to become Princess; therefore, all disdainful, she heaved a sigh from her heart. "O unhappy Salerno," she said in the presence of the two young men, "I do not believe that anyone searching through all of Italy could ever find a city as devoid of true lovers as you are. I marvel that all you young men, who have become professional suitors, do not hide yourselves for shame. You should no longer dare to look the maid whose love you wish to win in the face, seeing that you have a treasure like that garland near at hand, a treasure which could confer bliss on any man who gives it to his beloved lady. Of all those who follow the amorous profession, there is not a single one who has attempted to get hold of it. If true lovers were to be found in this city of ours, instead of the false ones who are everywhere, this garland would become an object to turn all of Salerno on its ear; the more so since it has been hung in a place from which it might easily be stolen. Each man should be making a supreme effort to acquire it, in order to give it to his lady.

"But alas, at the present time no lover can be found here who is brave or courteous in anything but words, or who fails to appear weak and stingy when the time comes to do anything effective. As it is for one, so it is for all of them, in my opinion. Therefore we cannot hope that the young men of our time wish to suffer any discomfort whatsoever, either for love of their ladies, or in order to bring their desires to fruition. Instead they think they are doing much, and gaining infinite prestige in the eyes of their ladies, if all they do is bow or say the proper words when they see them; but these things bring honor only to the men themselves, and not to the ladies.

"Notice how these men do not engage very often in jousts, tournaments, or in any other sort of deed of valor in the name of love, as they used to do. As we know, once upon a time young lovers triumphed in love by means of striving and great risk to their lives, but nowadays they acquire love through ease and pleasures.

per dire il vero, la maggior cagione di ciò le medesime donne ne sono; perciò che troppo amanti, et liberali d'ogni favore gli si dimostrano. Et ben vi giuro che se come esser mi trovo la minor di tutte l'altre in bellezza, così io fosse una di quelle, che sono, o d'esser belle si tengono, et che qualche giovine si ritrovasse in Salerno, il quale facesse professione di farmi il vagheggio, lasciandosi una cotanto sicurissima occasione uscir di mano, come è di tentar d'acquistarsi con la valorosa ghirlanda il mio amore, et insieme farmi conoscer quanto di cuore mi amasse, io vi dico che da mo' in dietro non vorrei ch'egli più mai havesse ardire di veniremi dinanzi da gli occhi."

A queste così altere, anzi superbe parole ambidue i giovani s'ammutirono, et per buona pezza stettero sopra di loro che alcuna cosa non dissero, et più Fabio, che l'altro fu quello, il quale quelle parole a cuore si prese, come quello che essendo accortissimo troppo ben comprendeva che per lui solo le haveva dette, et acciò ch'egli per tal cagione di più andar dov'ella si fosse, si distogliesse. Et perciò d'infinita amaritudine ritrovandosi pieno, sanza altrimente escusarsi da indi a poco pigliando da lei con riverenza commiato, di quel loco si tolse. Ma poi che si fu partito, et che la sua gran disgratia incominciò a considerare come così tosto l'havea levato dal cuor di colei, la quale egli più che altra cosa del mondo amava, et desiderava d'esser amato, tanto affanno lo sopragionse, che disperandosi di più poter viver, non considerando ch'ella come di lui nemica quelle arroganti parole havea dette fece ferma deliberatione in quel punto, quando ben fosse sicuro di lasciarvi la vita, di voler provar sua ventura, et rubar s'ei poteva, la bella ghirlanda, et a lei di tanto amore ingrata donarla, parendoli che non harrebbe fatto picciolo acquisto quando in quel fatto morisse. Imperciò che altro non haveva egli in cuore eccetto che di farla vera conoscitora com'egli più di Menandro svisceratamente l'amava; nè di vita o di morte si curava egli più molto.

Havendo tra sè, dunque, una tale deliberatione fermata, fecesi alcuni straci, et un capellaccio a un forfantone[58] prestare, dandoli di quelli buon nolo; et poi che i suoi nobili et ornati vestimenti s'hebbe spogliati, di que' vili, et indegni straci le delicatissime sue membra riccoperse,[59] et indi quel vago capo d'un cotanto nobilissimo intelletto degno ricetto sotto quel vil capellaccio nascose. Et tolta c'hebbe una picciola et oscura lanternuzza, et entro accesovi un lumiciuolo, et nascosasi tra que straci la spada sanza far motto ad alcuno in palagio se n'andò, et per quello

---

[58] *furfante*, with augmentative suffix.
[59] Corrected to *ricoperse* in P (fol. 121r).

URANIA: THE STORY OF A YOUNG WOMAN'S LOVE

But to tell the truth, the women themselves are mostly responsible for this, for they are too disposed to love and too liberal in their favors. Even though I find myself to be the least beautiful of all women, I swear to you, if I were one of those who is beautiful, or who thinks she is, and if some young man of Salerno professed to court me, yet gave up so sure a chance to gain my love by means of that powerful garland, and thus prove the depth of his love for me, I swear from that time on I would not let him dare appear before my eyes."

At these haughty, indeed arrogant words, both men fell silent, and said nothing for a long time. It was Fabio, more than the other, who took these words to heart, for he was quite intelligent, and understood too well that she had been speaking to him alone, with the aim of getting him to give up the idea of coming to visit her. Full of great bitterness, he made no further excuse for himself; instead he reverently asked for her leave, and made a swift departure from that place. But once he had left, he began to think about his wretched state, and how quickly the woman whom he loved more than anything else in the world, and who he desired should love him, had banished him from her heart. He was so overwhelmed by distress that he lost hope that he could go on living. Failing to realize that she had acted as an enemy when she said those arrogant words to him, he made a firm decision, as soon as he was certain that he must die, to try his luck and steal the lovely garland if he could, so he could give it to this woman who was so ungrateful for the great love he felt for her. It seemed to him he would gain a great deal if he died as a result of this endeavor, since his heart held no other desire than to make her realize how much more fervently he loved her than did Menandro. He no longer cared whether he lived or died.

Once he had reached this decision, he paid a good price and got a man of the common rabble to lend him some rags and a wretched hat. Removing his noble and lavish clothing, he covered his most delicate limbs with those vile and unworthy rags, then hid his handsome head, that worthy home of his most noble intellect, under the terrible hat. Afterwards he took up a small, feeble lantern and lit within it a small flame. Hiding his sword amongst the rags, he set out for the palace without saying a word to anyone. He wandered here and there through the

qua, et là caminando, nè mai essendo conosciuto d'alcuno gli vennero alcune tavole vedute, le quali a gran mucchi erano state ivi portate, per farne poi per le grandi solennità delle nozze, un teatro; et parendogli che quelle tavole assai al suo proposito fossero, perciò come incominciò a farsi sera dietro a quelle che d'alcuno non fu veduto si nascose.

Menandro dall'altra parte, che havea veduto Fabio così tosto et confuso dalla Clorina partirsi subito imaginandosi quello, che era, anch'egli da lei pigliando licenza, da quel loco si tolse. Et sentendosi d'amarissimo sdegno arder di dentro, per lo grande odio che a Fabio portava, tutto si diede a pensare il modo ch' egli havesse potuto tenere a chiarirsi di questo fatto, et insieme di poterli ogni suo disegno sturbare; et così pensando vennegli in mente come egli haveva assai stretta dimestichezza con uno de camerieri del Prencipe, la camera del quale per bel punto su la gran sala venia a riferire. Perchè ritrovato assai tosto lo cameriere, tanto seppe fare, et dire, parte molti denari donandoli, et parte con belle parole assai più promettendoli, ch'egli pur fu contento di far quanto gli era in piacere; et così in palagio condottolo, nella sua camera lo nascose, dove fin oscura notte si stette.

Ma quando fu notte oscura, et che ciascuno nel palagio parve acquetato, Fabio, che dietro quelle tavole si stava nascoso, uscì fuori pian piano, et aperta c'hebbe la sua lanternuzza n'andò là, dove alcune longhissime scale appoggiate si stavano, le quali per acconciar la tapezzeria furono ivi portate, et pigliandone una con la maggior fatica del mondo per la sua longhezza, la dove era apesa la ghirlanda la condusse; et indi non sanza gran pericolo di cadere, et fiaccarsi il collo, fino alla cima salito distaccò la bella ghirlanda; et per non guastarla, sopra quel vil capellaccio la si pose.

Gli restavano forse da dieci scaglioni ancora a descendere quando Menandro, che verso Fabio tutto fellone con la spada in mano, essendo già entrato nella gran sala, s'avide ch'egli della scala scendea. Onde avisandosi ch' ei fosse quello che gl' era, nè pensando di dover niente a sè stesso, ma solamente nocere a Fabio perciò con alta voce così gli disse. "Ahì traditore, io pur t'harrò colto, et non ti sarà gratia conceduta di poter com'era l'animo tuo, la bella ghirlanda alla Clorina donare; anzi in tuo dispregio sarò io pur quello, che quella, et insieme la tua indegna vita levandoti, l'amore della Clorina a fatto m'acquisterò con la bella ghirlanda."

Udendo Fabio cotali altere parole, et havendo alla voce riconosciuto che egli era, tosto saltò giù de que' pochi scaglioni che gli restavano a scendere, et tolta la sua spada di terra dove posta l'haveva, incontra gli si fece con suo disavantaggio grandissimo, imperciò che altro non havendo che gli riparassero i colpi che que'

URANIA: THE STORY OF A YOUNG WOMAN'S LOVE

palace without being recognized by anyone, then noticed some planks which had been brought there and left in great piles, so that a theater could be constructed for the great wedding celebration. It seemed to him that those planks perfectly suited his needs, so he hid himself behind them without being detected, as soon as evening came on.

For his part, Menandro also asked Clorina's leave to depart, once he had seen Fabio exit so quickly, and in such a troubled state; for he immediately guessed the true reason for Fabio's departure. Burning inside with scorn, for he bore such hatred for Fabio, Menandro began to cast about for a way to find out for sure what Fabio was doing, and at the same time frustrate his plans. Then it occurred to him that he knew one of the Prince's servants, a man whose room above the grand hall gave easy access to it. He went at once to this servant, and was clever enough to persuade him to let him do whatever he wanted, partly by giving the man a large sum of money, and partly with sweet promises of more money to come. It was thus that the servant let Menandro into the palace and hid him in his chamber, where he stayed until night fell and the darkness was complete.

But at this very moment of darkness, when it seemed everyone in the palace had quieted down for the night, Fabio quietly emerged from behind the planks where he had been hiding. Opening his tiny lantern, he went to where several very long ladders had been left, brought in for the purpose of installing the tapestries. One of these he lifted and carried over to where the garland was hanging, although he had to strain mightily because of the ladder's extreme length. There, despite the great danger of falling and breaking his neck, he climbed up to the top and unhooked the lovely garland, which he then placed around his ragged hat so as not to damage it.

He had perhaps only ten rungs left to go in his descent when Menandro, sword in hand and looking ferocious, came into the hall and saw him coming down the ladder. Once he realized that it was indeed Fabio, he forgot about his own safety and turned all his thoughts to harming his rival. "Ah, traitor!" he shouted. "I've caught you, and you've lost the chance to accomplish your plan and give the garland to Clorina. Indeed, I will be the one who will scornfully deprive you of both the garland and your life; and after that, I will use the garland to gain Clorina's love for myself."

When Fabio heard those haughty words he recognized Menandro by his voice. He swiftly jumped down the last few rungs and seized his sword from the place where he had left it. He then took Menandro on, despite the very great disadvantage of having only rags to fend off his rival's blows, whereas Menandro was quite

miseri straci ch'egli havea in dosso, gli harrebbe Menandro, che benissimo era armato di certo in poc'hora levata la vita. Ma come a Dio piacque che tanto male in un così nobile giovine consentir non volle, fu da alcuni del palagio i quali non erano ancora iti a letto, et a carte giocavano, la prima voce di Menandro udita et intesa. Perchè prese subitamente le loro armi forse sei, che erano, là dove haveano udita la voce corsero in un baleno; et prima gli hebbero ambidue presi che d'esser veduti si fossero accorti; et molto tosto dinanzi al Prencipe gli condussero; il quale a quel romore per intenderne la cagione anch'egli s'era levato. Et tosto riconobbe Menandro, ma non così fece di Fabio, mercè de gli straci et del capellaccio, che glielo impedivano. Et perciò dimandando a lui stesso chi egli era, nè volendo darli alcuna risposta per non esser da tanti, che ivi erano riconosciuto però tacevasi. Ma Menandro, che pur a nocerli tenea fisso il pensiero che gl'era Fabio, et tutto il fatto intieramente come stava scoperse, et disse ancora come ambidue erano nell'amor della Clorina rivali, et questo di più vi aggiunse cioè che havendo ad alcuni segnali compreso come Fabio havea intentione di rubar la ghirlanda, et alla Clorina donarla, ch' egli acciò che Sua Eccellenza non ricevesse un tal torto s'havea perciò nel palagio nascosto per levargliela a forza, et poscia a Sua Eccellenza restituirla.

Ma quelli che gli presero, et che havevano udito quanto havea detto Menandro, perchè più di lui amavano Fabio, perciò tutto quello che da lui sentito havevano narraron al Prencipe; il quale con un male viso così gli disse. "Ahì rinegato che sei, ben m'aveggio che tu sei un traditore, et che molto maggior castigo meriti tu che costui, poi ch'egli da semplice amor spinto, a far tale atto si mosse, onde tu di lui ti movesti. Nondimeno ambidue n'andarete in pregione, nè uscirete di là, che n'harrete debito, et convenevol castigo." Et così detto gli fece in diverse pregioni rinchiudere; havendo prima levata di capo a Fabio la vaga ghirlanda, della qual dopo miglior cura n'hebbe che dianzi non havea havuta.

Ma poscia che in camera fu ritornato, et che sopra questo caso si pose a pensare infinitamente di Fabio gli dolle, chè per cagion delle sue grandi virtudi amandolo sommamente, et sapendo come da tutta la città medesimamente era amato, più che volontieri s'egli l'havesse con suo honor potuto liberare, et quell'altro punire, l'harria liberato. Imperciò che un sommo odio per suoi mali vezzi et costumi portava a Menandro, et già più giorni una tale occasione di poterlo castigare a suo senno, harrebbe comperata a cotanti. Ma hora che con quel di lui, il danno di Fabio vi concorreva, mal contento a morte si ritrovava; et così tutta notte pensando

URANIA: THE STORY OF A YOUNG WOMAN'S LOVE

well armored and certainly could have soon taken Fabio's life. But as it pleased God, who did not wish to allow such an evil fate to befall so noble a youth, Menandro's first shouts had been heard by some men of the palace who were playing cards and had not yet gone to bed. Around six of them seized their weapons and ran in a flash to where they heard the voice; there they captured the two men before they were even aware they had been seen. They were swiftly brought before the Prince, who had also arisen in order to find out what all the noise was about. He immediately recognized Menandro, but could not do the same in Fabio's case, on account of the ragged clothes and the hat, which concealed his identity. Therefore the Prince asked him who he was, but Fabio was silent, not wishing to be recognized by the many people who were present. However Menandro, who still had his thoughts fixed on bringing harm to Fabio, revealed the entire affair, adding that both men were rivals for the love of Clorina. Moreover, he told the Prince that he had gathered from certain indications that Fabio intended to steal the garland in order to give it to Clorina; therefore, to prevent such a crime from being committed against His Excellency, he had hidden himself in the palace with the aim of taking the garland from Fabio by force, and returning it to the Prince.

But the men who had captured them were aware of what Menandro had said earlier, and since they were fonder of Fabio than Menandro, they told the Prince everything they had heard Menandro say. "Ah, renegade scoundrel!" said the Prince with a scowl. "I know full well you are a traitor, and deserve much greater punishment than this man, who was driven only by love to do what he did, while you acted instead out of malice towards him. Nonetheless both of you will go to prison, and you will not leave until you have suffered suitable and proper punishments." When he finished speaking, he had the two men locked into different dungeons; but first he removed the lovely garland, which he now looked after more carefully than he had previously, from Fabio's head.

Once the Prince was back in his room, and began to think about this situation, he felt profound sadness for Fabio, whom he loved greatly on account of his virtues. Since he also knew the rest of the city was equally fond of the young man, he would have been more than willing to set him free, and punish only Menandro, if his honor were to have permitted it. He greatly hated Menandro for his evil vices and bad habits, and there had been many days in the past when he would have gladly paid for an opportunity to punish this man as he knew he should. But now that Menandro's punishment was all mixed up with Fabio's, the Prince found himself mortified with unhappiness. After he had passed the whole

et ripensando come potesse Fabio liberare, et Menandro punire, et che l'honor suo macchiato non fosse, parvegli pure al fine d'haver ritrovato un'ottimo modo, il quale usando sarebbe da tutti pietosissimo giudicato, et non severo nè ingiusto.

Non fu a pena schiarito il giorno lo seguente mattino, che per tutto Salerno si seppe la novella come Fabio et Menandro erano impregionati per haver voluto la notte rubar la ghirlanda del Prencipe, et alla Clorina donarla; della qual cosa il padre di lei tanta doglia ne prese che se ne sentiva morire; massimamente intendendo come da tutti veniva la figliuola incolpata ch'ella di tanto scandalo era stata cagione; et le usò perciò di molte sconcie parole. Ma gli parenti, et insieme molti altri gentilhuomini, che amici gli erano come hebbero intesa la sua cattura dinanzi al Prencipe concorsero tutti; et ivi con le ginocchia chine gli supplicavano che volesse haver pietade alla giovanezza di Fabio, et all'Amor, che mal guidato l'haveva, offerendosi ciascun di loro a pagar gran quantità di denari per riscatto della sua vita. Ma il Prencipe, il quale quantunque ancora in favor di Menandro alcuno non comparesse, non volendo nondimeno per suo honor partial dimostrarsi, a quelli, che lo supplicavano in tal modo rispose. "Padri, et fratelli miei, voi sapete ben tutti come non si conviene a giusto Signore il lasciarsi da convenevol giustitia rimovere; et sapete ancora come in ciascun Signore, et in ciascun giudice manco che ogn'altra cosa la partialità convenirseli, per esser cosa da sè non manco degna di vituperio, di quello ch'ella sia molte volte de' gran danni cagione, sì come spesse fiate molti essempi in altrui si possono haver veduti; et perciò io vi prego che non vogliate cercare che'l Signor vostro, il quale sino a quest'hora sempre giusto si ha fatto conoscere, per opera vostra partiale, et ingiusto novellamente divenghi.

"Se ben volete considerare, voi vederete che l'error d'uno et dell'altro è gravissimo, onde s'io volesse con quella severità punirli, che merita il loro commesso delito gli farei ambidue sanza alcuno indugio morire. Nè la ragione sopporterebbe che perchè Fabio sia de' miei cittadini, et da voi tutti assai pregato io ne sia, che perciò più rispetto che a Menandro io gli havesse. Nondimeno acciò che voi conosciate come non manco io mi compiaccio d'esser misericordioso che giusto; et che tanto più d'usar misericordia mi piace, quanto più conosco che la ingiuria, et l'offesa si riverscia in me solo; che quando sopra d'altrui tale ingiuria cadesse, io vi accerto che in vano vi affaticareste a pregarmi.

"Ma conoscendo come del loro commesso errore io solo son quello, et non altri che la ingiuria, et il danno riceve; voglio per tanto, per amor di voi tutti, et

Urania: The Story of a Young Woman's Love

night thinking over and over again how he might free Fabio and punish Menandro, yet in such a way that would not besmirch his honor, he finally came up with a perfect plan that would be judged most merciful by everyone, neither severe nor unjust.

The light had scarcely come the following morning when throughout Salerno everyone heard the news that Fabio and Menandro were imprisoned for having stolen the Prince's garland, in order to give it to Clorina. When the news reached Clorina's father he was so grief-stricken that he felt he was about to die, especially when he heard that his daughter was blamed by everyone as the cause of so much scandal; therefore he reproached her with many harsh words. But Fabio's relatives, along with many other gentlemen who were friends of his, went before the Prince when the heard of his capture, and there on bended knees they begged him to have pity on Fabio's youth, and on the power of love which had led him astray. Each one of them offered to pay a great deal of money to save the young man's life. However, the Prince, though he scarcely seemed to lean in Menandro's favor, did not wish to appear partial, in order to protect his honor. To those who pleaded with him, he gave this answer: "My fathers and brothers, you well know that it is not fitting for a just lord to allow himself to be distracted from the application of proper justice. You also know that in any lord or in any judge nothing is less suitable than partiality, inasmuch as it is something quite worthy of blame, and often the cause of great harm; and we have seen many examples of this in others. For this reason, I pray that you not desire to see your lord, who has up to now always had the reputation of being just, become strangely partial and unjust as a result of your efforts.

"If you consider well, you will see that each man's crime is very serious, so serious that if I wished to punish them with the severity such crimes deserve I would put them both to death without delay. The interests of fairness would not allow that Fabio be treated any better than Menandro simply because he is one of my citizens, and because all of you are pleading on his behalf. Nonetheless, I want you to know that I take no less pleasure in being merciful than in being just, and I am especially more inclined to show mercy when I am aware that the offense was committed against me alone, and that I alone have suffered harm; for if such a wrongdoing were to have been committed against anyone else, you may be certain that your supplications would have been in vain.

"However, I am aware that I am the only one who has received injury and harm from the crimes that they have committed. Therefore, for the love of all of

della Clorina, la quale io so esser giovane bella, accostumata, et discreta, poi che io ho inteso che ambidue sono di lei amanti, voglio dico ambidue liberarli facendo perciò avantaggio a quello (sia quale si voglia) il quale si conoscerà, ch'ella più che l'altro ama et tien caro. Dicovi adunque, che quale di questi due giovani mi sarà dalla Clorina per marito dimandato, per amor di lei ogni ingiuria fattami gli son per rimettere, et a lei libero lo voglio donare. Et l'altro poi, acciò che per amar una così bella et valorosa giovane habbi meritato qualche cosa, voglio che ancora a lui la morte, et ogn'altra sorte di castigo, per amor di lei gli sia perdonato, quando perciò un'altra donzella egli trovi, la quale per amor suo tanto s'affatichi che con ingegno possi levare un bascio dalla mia Femina Salvatica. Et se tra il termine di tre giorni non potrà costui alcuna donzella trovare, la qual per suo amore voglia porsi a tal rischio, sentenzio, et determino che come indegno dell'amor d'ogni donzella, cada nella pena ch'egli essendosi per rubarmi nel mio palagio nascoso s'havea meritata. Nè altra maggior gratia possa egli da me ottenere eccetto che havendo egli meritato di morir su la croce gli sia il capo mozzato; con questa novella conditione, che se alcun' huomo si movesse a dimandar gratia per lui, cada subitamente nella istessa pena d'esserli mozzato il capo; et se fosse donna o donzella che tal gratia mi adimandasse, sanza alcuno intervallo sia per tre volte intorno il mio palagio con correggie frustrata."

Non hebbe ad altro effetto l'accorto Prencipe la sentenza fatta in tal modo, eccetto che essendo come sicuro che la Clorina gli harrebbe Fabio per marito richiesto; et pensandosi ancora che non si ritroverebbe veruna donzella, la quale a pericolo di basciar la Femina Salvatica si ponesse, perciò così verrebbe Menandro ad esser solo punito; nè di tal parere era il Prencipe solo. Ma tutti que' gentilhuomini, anzi la città tutta insieme, in tal parer con esso lui concorrevano; et di ciò infinitamente se ne rallegrarono tutti, et di tal sentenza innumerabili gratie ne renderono al Prencipe. Ma più de gli altri, che sommamente si rallegrasse, il padre della Clorina, il quale tra quegli altri si stava, era quello che somma allegrezza dimostrava d'havere. Chè rendendosi anch'egli più che sicuro, ch'ella Fabio dimandarebbe, tanto contento sentiva per la figliuola, che sarebbe in parte della infamia disgravata, et insieme d'haversi un così gentile, et virtuoso genero ritrovato, ch'egli non poteva quasi capir nella pelle.

Et perciò tolta c'hebbero dal Prencipe tutti licenza insieme col padre di lei dalla Clorina se ne girono; et le fecero intender come nel suo piacere la vita di Fabio si ritrovava, molto pregandola tutti che tosto ella a liberarlo n'andasse, poi che così benigno il loro Signore gli si dimostrava. Alle cui parole il padre di lei tante altre,

you, and also for my fondness for Clorina, whom I know to be a beautiful, well-mannered, and discreet young woman, beloved (as I have heard) by both of these men, I wish to set them free, and give at the same time a certain advantage to whichever one of them that Clorina may love most, and hold most dear. Thus I ordain that for the love of Clorina I will forgive all offenses committed against me, and moreover I will release and give to her whichever of the two young men she might ask to have as a husband. As for the other, inasmuch as he deserves something in return for having loved so fair and worthy a maid, I command that for the love of her he be spared death or any other sort of punishment; that is, as long as he can find another maid who loves him so much that she is able, through force or ingenuity, to receive a kiss from my Wild Woman. If within three days he cannot find any maid who is willing to run such a risk out of love for him, then I decree and establish that he, as one unworthy of the love of any maid, shall suffer the fate that he deserves for having hidden himself in my palace for the purpose of robbing me. He will get no better favor from me save that he will have his head cut off, instead of dying on a cross, as he deserves; and I likewise impose this novel rule: any man who attempts to plead that he be spared will immediately suffer the same sentence of decapitation. If any woman or maid ask that he be spared, she will immediately be flogged three times around my palace with leather whips."

The wise Prince had pronounced his sentence in this way for only one reason: he was certain that Clorina would choose Fabio for her husband. Moreover, since he imagined that no maid would risk the danger of kissing the Wild Woman, Menandro would be the only one to be punished. This thought occurred not only to the Prince, but also to all of the gentlemen present; and indeed all the city agreed with him. Everyone rejoiced greatly at this, and gave infinite thanks to the Prince for this sentence. No one was happier than Clorina's father, who was standing with all the others, for he was more than certain that his daughter would request Fabio. He was so happy for his daughter that he was nearly beside himself, for she would be freed of at least part of her shame, and he would moreover gain so genteel and virtuous a son-in-law.

Once they had taken their leave of the Prince, they all went to see Clorina, accompanied by her father. They told her how Fabio's life now depended on her whim, and pleaded with her to go out and set him free, since their lord had shown himself to be so merciful. To these words Clorina's father added many

et così lodevoli, in favor di Fabio esortando la figliuola a liberarlo vi aggiunse che ben fece manifesto a tutti, quanto egli vie più assai Fabio che Menandro desiderava che genero li divenisse.

La Clorina, che sino a quella hora per così strano accidente s'havea afflitta in pianto amarissimo; hora udendo così buona novella, come era che'n lei sola fosse tutta riposta la elettione di poter qual più le piacea liberare, alzando le mani al Cielo, et quelle lagrime che prima da fera passione tratta spargeva, hor da somma gioia mandando fuori sanza mai ad alcuno rispondere, poi che così qual si trovava hebbe presi suoi veli, insieme con la madre, et altre matrone ch'ivi erano concorse, et da tutti que' gentilhuomini seguita dinanzi dal Prencipe si condusse; al quale poscia che debita riverenza hebbe fatta, così disse. "Illustre, et eccellente Signore, quanto habbia a tutti noi vostri vassalli sempre giovato il ritrovarsi da così giusto, et benigno Prencipe governati, il quietissimo viver nostro da ogni tirannia lontano apertissimo lo dimostra. Ma quanto poi anco può particolarmente giovare a molti, che oltre che giustitia et misericordia abondantissimamente in voi si conosce albergare, che ancora siate vero conoscitore quanto in giovenil petto pungano le saette d'Amore, i giovani per lo commesso error della ghirlanda impregionati, e io insieme ne potremo render vera testimonianza; chè havendo i due giovani gran castigo meritato per haver havuto poco riguardo nell'usar tal violenza nello istesso palagio del loro così benigno Signore, et io insieme per havergliene forse dato cagione. Nondimeno voi benignissimo, perchè come ho detto sapete quanto in giovenil petto possa un desire amoroso, ci havete pietosamente a tutti dato il rimedio con lo quale salvar si potemo; del qual pietosissimo dono mi doglio nel cuore di non valere, et men saper ringratiarvene tanto, quanto all'alta bontà di voi, et al debito mio si converrebbe.

"Per la qual cosa poi io piglio ardire di dover sperare, che questo di voi sapere quanta forza habbia il foco d'Amore, sarà cagione che io sarò non solamente presso Vostra Eccellenza escusata quando io non facesse quella elettione di sposo quale so che quanti son qui presenti stanno in espettatione che io debba fare; ma ancora ch'egli presso quanti mi volessero di ciò accusare sarammi escusa. Io non dubito, Signore, che'l padre mio, et quanti altri qui si trovano, et forse Vostra Eccellenza con loro insieme, come cosa certa tenete, che io debba Fabio per sposo dimandarvi, la qual cosa io ragionevolmente devrei fare, quando da voi Signor mio non havesse imparato ad esser giusta et benigna. Già che non mi è nascoso come la nobilità di Fabio, le sue rare virtudi, et costumi, la singular sua bellezza, et più d'ogn'altra cosa l'esser ambi noi d'una medesima Patria cittadini vi danno materia

others, praising Fabio and exhorting his daughter to liberate him. He also made it plain to everyone that he would be much happier having Fabio as a son-in-law than Menandro.

Until now, this strange affair had been causing Clorina to weep bitter tears. Upon hearing the good news that she, and she alone, had been given the choice of freeing whichever of the two men she liked the most, she raised her hands to heaven; and the tears which she had previously shed on account of her great sadness now changed to tears of the greatest joy. Giving no answer to anyone, she took up her veils, and set off to see the Prince, accompanied by her mother and the other ladies who had gathered there. All of the gentlemen followed behind. When she had shown the Prince his due reverence, she spoke: "Illustrious and excellent lord, the fact that we, your vassals, have lived most tranquilly, free from all tyranny, plainly shows the great benefit we have received from the rule of so just and benign a Prince. But this benefit does not lie solely in the justice and mercy which we know reside in you, for those youths who have been imprisoned on account of the affair of the garland, and I as well, can all bear witness that many find it particularly helpful that you know full well how deeply the arrows of Love pierce young hearts. Those young men deserve harsh punishment for having thought so little of using violence in the very palace of so benign a lord as you are, and perhaps I deserve it too, for having given them reason to do this. Nonetheless you are infinitely kind, and you do know, as I have said, what amorous desires are capable of in young hearts; therefore, you have mercifully given all of us the means whereby we may save ourselves. It grieves my heart that I have neither the ability nor the wisdom to thank you as much as your kindness and my debt require, for this most merciful gift.

"Because of this, I am bold enough to hope that this capacity of yours to understand the power of Love's flame will suffice to allow me to be forgiven not only by Your Excellency, but also by all those who might wish to condemn me, should I not choose the husband whom I know everyone here expects me to choose. My lord, I do not doubt that my father, and all those who are present, including perhaps Your Excellency, are convinced that I must ask that Fabio be my husband. Indeed, it would be reasonable that I should do so, were it not that I have learned how to be just and kind from you, my lord. I am fully aware that Fabio's nobility, his rare virtues, his manners and singular beauty, and especially the fact that we are both citizens of the same land, must cause you to believe that

da dover credere, che io debba lui, et non Menandro volere. Le quali cagioni per lo vero sono quelle, che la materia a me danno di far altrimenti di quello, che ciascuno si pensa. Et la ragione è che ritrovandomi, come si sa, da ambidue questi giovani grandemente amata, li quali ambi nobili, vaghi, et virtuosissimi sono; per la qual cosa io son forzata indifferentemente amarli ambi due; et conoscendo come per li grandi meriti di Fabio, egli da tutto Salerno vien amato. Il che per esser forastiero non così avien di Menandro; parmi perciò cosa convenevole et giusta, sì perchè io l'amo molto, come ancora perche io so ch'egli non così ritroverebbe qui donna che a pericolo di basciar la Femina Salvatica si ponesse; parmi dico più tosto lui che Fabio, addimandandolo per sposo, di voler liberare. Chè ben sono io sicura, che di molte nobilissime donzelle non mancheranno in Salerno, le quali a gara una dell'altra per liberar Fabio si moveranno, che per liberar Menandro so certo non se ne moverebbe alcuna, et così per cagion mia l'uno et l'altro sarà liberato.

"Et perciò Signor mio, poi che alla somma benignità vostra parve di farmi un cotanto favore, come è che uno di due divenendomi sposo sia per mezzo mio liberato; et che a mia elettione sta il liberare quello, che più mi piace; pregovi perciò Signor mio, che vi piaccia concedermi per sposo Menandro; et insieme esser contento di escusarmi con tutti questi nobilissimi gentilhuomini, et rapacificarmi co'l padre mio, il quale so certissimo che fieramente sarà meco adirato, perchè io harrò più tosto Menandro addimandato, che Fabio, et così so che da ciascun'altro ancora non sarò meno odiata, che tenuta sciocca. Nondimeno io mi confido che quando harranno tutti d'avantagio il fine di questo effetto considerato, più tosto lode che biasmo me ne daranno; quand'io so che liberando io Menandro non ne mancheranno di molte, et forse di me più degne, le quali di liberar Fabio si offeriranno."

Quanto questa inaspettata dimanda della Clorina al Prencipe, et a gli altri paresse nova, et strana da udire non si potrebbe con lingua narrare; per la qual cosa spinti da doglia infinita tutti que' gentilhuomini gridavano ch'ella era una donzella insensata; et maggiormente che gli altri il vecchio suo padre era quello che tutto affannato la villaneggiava, et minacciavale di farla malamente pentire s'ella non rivocava la sua stolta dimanda. Ma il Prencipe, il quale quantunque nella più intima parte del cuor gli dolesse di veder passar la cosa in tal modo, pur non volendo farsi conoscer da alcuno per partiale, et ingiusto; poi che con amorevoli parole l'hebbe consigliata più d'una volta, come assai più honore, et utile le sarebbe stato il pigliar

URANIA: THE STORY OF A YOUNG WOMAN'S LOVE

I should want him and not Menandro. Instead those are the very reasons that have led me to do the opposite of what everyone imagines I will do. Here is why: as everyone knows, I have found myself greatly loved by these two young men, both of whom are noble, handsome, and most virtuous; and on account of these qualities I am forced to love them both equally in return. I am aware that Fabio's qualities have made all of Salerno fond of him, whereas the same has not occurred in Menandro's case, since he is a foreigner. Therefore, as much because I love him as for the fact that I know that no woman here would put herself in danger for him by kissing the Wild Woman, it seems to me proper and just that I should want to free him by requesting him in marriage, and not Fabio. I am quite certain that there will be no lack of most valiant maidens in Salerno who will compete with one another in order to free Fabio, whereas I know for a fact that none will make any effort to free Menandro; in this way both of them will be liberated through my actions.

"Therefore, my lord, since in your kindness you have decided to do me so great a favor, that is, you have allowed one of these men to be released so that he may become my husband, and you have allowed me to choose whichever of them pleases me most, I pray you, my lord, that it please you to grant me Menandro as a husband. In addition, I beg that you will deign to ask these noble gentlemen to forgive me, and also make peace between me and my father. I know for certain that he will be fiercely angry with me because I am asking for Menandro instead of Fabio, and on this account I am aware that I will be no less hated than thought a fool by everyone else. Nevertheless I am confident that they will give me praise rather than blame, as soon as they have given further consideration to the outcome of this plan, for I know that while I am freeing Menandro there will be no lack of others, perhaps more worthy than I, who will offer to free Fabio."

No tongue could tell how strange and bizarre Clorina's unexpected request appeared to the Prince and the others. Driven by infinite grief, all of the gentlemen shouted that the maid was insane; and her old father was the one who, sorely distressed, vilified her more than any other, and threatened to make her suffer terribly if she did not take back her idiotic demand. But the Prince still did not wish to appear partial and unjust to anyone, however much he felt sadness in the deepest recesses of his heart when he heard the direction this affair was taking. More than once he advised her with gentle words, saying it was more honorable and

Fabio, che colui per marito, et vedendola sempre con più forte animo nel constante della sua opinione fermarsi, volle perciò che'l padre di lei, et gli altri al piacer della stolta Clorina s'acquetassero tutti. Et facendo in quell'hora medesima trar di pregione Menandro, volle ancora che in quel punto istesso, egli la Clorina a sua presenza sposasse.

Et fattiglisi (con grande ramarico del padre della Clorina, et de' parenti et amici di Fabio) di subito levar dinanzi, non forse con minor suo dolore, fece fare una grida in tal modo, cioè, che qualunque donzella nobile, o non nobile si ritrovasse, la quale con ingegno, o con arte tanto s'affaticasse, che tra il termine de giorni tre potesse dalla sua Salvatica Femina levare un bascio, le fosse il gentil Fabio conceduto per marito con dote di diecimila ducati di quelli del Prencipe. Udita la grida molte povere giovani si mossero per voler la loro ventura provare, se havessero potuto un cotanto valoroso giovine per marito acquistarsi; ma come alla Femina Salvatica si avicinavano alquanto, tanto spaventate restavano, che se fossero state sicure d'acquistar tutto il mondo, si sarebbono da quello horribil mostro fuggite.

Et per farvi la cagion manifesta per la quale quella Salvatica Femina così spaventevole era, dico che essendo già due anni innanzi stati donati al Prencipe quella femina, et con lei un'huomo salvatico, il quale era tanto sdegnoso et spiacevole, che harrebbe spesse volte per poco, et per niente ucciso un'huomo; et veniva perciò co' gravissimi ceppi a' piedi tenuto sempre. Ma non così era la Femina, la quale essendo quasi come dimestica divenuta qua, et là per tutto il palagio con le donne della madre del Prencipe n'andava dimesticamente. Ma tanto era smisurato l'amore che'ella al suo Salvatico Huomo portava, che non lasciava mai un'hora passare che non lo ritornasse a vedere; et con grandissima affettione mille et più volte non lo basciasse.

Hor avenne come ne' fanciulli sogliono spesse volte delle strane voglie venire, che un paggio del Prencipe havendo una grandissima voglia di potere a suo senno fare sdegnar quell'Huomo Salvatico, per prendersene gioco et piacere; et havendo più, et più fiate fatta la guardia per poter coglierlo solo, acciò non venisse da veruno impedito, pure un giorno come la sorte volle, a punto come egli desiderava lo ritrovò, che nè la Femina Salvatica, nè alcun'altro vi era, ma tutto solo, et al solito suo sdegnoso in quella stanza si stava. Perchè il paggio più che altra volta mai fosse ritrovandosi alhora allegro, et contento, presa una sua certa lunga bachetta, la quale già più giorni per tale effetto preparata s'haveva, incominciò stando egli

URANIA: THE STORY OF A YOUNG WOMAN'S LOVE

practical for her to choose Fabio over Menandro as a husband; but when he saw her firmly resolved, with unshakable will, to stick to her choice, he ordered her father and all the others to be silent, as it pleased the foolish Clorina. Having Menandro brought forth from prison in that very same hour, he caused him to be married to Clorina at once in his presence.

He then sent everyone away, to the great regret of Clorina's father, her relatives, and Fabio's friends; and perhaps his own grief was no less than theirs. He issued a proclamation: any maiden, be she noble or common, who might succeed either through guile or stratagem to get a kiss from his Wild Woman, would receive the noble Fabio as a husband, together with a dowry of ten thousand ducats from the Prince. When they heard the proclamation, many poor young women set out to try their luck, to see if they could gain so valorous a man for a husband. But when they got at all near to the Wild Woman they were so afraid that they would have fled from that horrible monster no matter what, even if they had been certain they would have received the whole world as a reward.

Now I will make plain to you the reason why that Wild Woman was so fearsome. Two years before, the Woman had been given to the Prince as a gift, along with a Wild Man who was so irascible and repugnant that he would have killed a man for little or no reason. Because of this, his feet were always restrained by the heaviest shackles. But the female was not restrained thus, for she was almost like one of the household, wandering here and there about the palace in the company of the ladies who attended the Prince's mother. But so great was the love she bore her Wild Man that she never let an hour pass without going back to see him and kiss him more than a thousand times, with the greatest affection.

Strange desires often come over little boys, and so it was that one of the Prince's pages was seized with a great yearning to see if he could goad the Wild Man into a rage, for his own amusement and pleasure.[60] He kept an eye out on numerous occasions to see if he could catch the Wild Man alone, so that no one could stop him from doing it. One day, as fate would have it, he found the Wild Man just as he wanted, all alone and sulking in his usual fashion in the room, and neither the Wild Woman nor anyone else was there. The page, happier and more pleased than he had ever been, took up a long stick which he had prepared days earlier just for this purpose, and began to poke the Wild Man with it from a safe

---

[60] For a similar scene, in which a curious boy approaches a Wild Man kept in shackles by a king, see Straparola's *favola* 5.1 (ed. Pirovano, 1: 326).

lontano, a stucicare l'Huomo Salvatico, et così bene, et leggiermente lo sapea fare, che quantunque hora per gli occhi, hor per gl'orecchi, et hor per altra parte rincrescievole stucicando l'andasse, non però puote mai (sì dal ferocissimo sdegno era lo Salvatico huomo acciecato) dallo insolente paggio sbrigarsi; perchè vedendosi così fortemente instigato, nè sapendo schermirsi, in tanta rabbia divenne, che non potendo contra cui l'offendea vendicarsi, in sè stesso la ferocissima rabbia rivolse, et con spaventevoli urli le proprie mani si pose a mangiare.

Avenne in quell'hora, che a caso una delle donne del palagio di ivi passando et sentendo il gran rumor, che là entro si faceva, per veder quello che gli era, entrò nella stanza; et vedendo quello così spaventoso spettacolo, et come l'Huomo Salvatico s'havea quasi tutte mangiate le mani, et ch'era tutto dal proprio sangue bruttato, poi che con grandissime villanie hebbe di quel loco scacciato il paggio, prese un grosso bastone in mano, con lo quale il governatore dell'Huomo Salvatico spesse volte a segno lo facea stare, et incominciò quanto più forte poteva a percuoterlo, acciò che di mangiare sè stesso si distogliesse: ma come alla pessima sorte parve di permettere, la Femina Salvatica che già buona pezza non haveva il suo huomo veduto, et più che mai desiderosissima ritornandolo a rivedere, udì assai lontano gli horribili stridi ch'egli faceva. Perchè affrettando i passi, et entrata nella stanza ove egli era, vide quella donna meschina, che col grosso bastone lo tappellava, et sanza mani, et tutto sangue vedendolo s'avisò che quella donna in cotal modo l'havesse contio, però con un ferino furore addosso le si aventò per volerla uccidere; et l'harrebbe fatto assai tosto, se non che il governatore, et molti altri famigliari della corte havendo que' grandissimi gridi, che tutti tre facevano uditi, tostamente là corsero; il che quasi fu in un punto con l'assalir che fece la Femina Salvatica quella misera donna, et viva, ma tutta la faccia squarciata, le la tollero dalle mani; ma non mancò perciò che da ivi a poche hore la infelicissima non morisse; et così medesimamente dell'Huomo Salvatico avenne, il quale tra il dolor, ch'egli delle mangiate mani sentiva, et lo rabbiosissimo sdegno, c'havea in sè conceputo, in brevissima hora finì la sua vita. La qual cosa la sua Femina vedendo, et havendo fisso nel suo pensiero, che quella donna, et non altri fosse stata cagione ch'ella del carissimo suo huomo rimanea priva; perciò tanto odiosa, et nemica a tutte le donne divenne, che quante le si fossino parate innanzi, tutte le harrebbe malamente uccise, se non che subitamente nel medesimo modo la posero che primieramente il suo huomo tenevano, cioè co' ceppi a' piedi ancor lei.

URANIA: THE STORY OF A YOUNG WOMAN'S LOVE

distance. The insolent page did this so well and so deftly, poking him now in the eyes, now in the ears, now in some other part in an annoying fashion, that the Wild Man was blinded by his ferocious rage and could not get away from him. Seeing himself so harshly tormented, and not knowing how to defend himself, the Wild Man flew into such a state that he turned his fierce wrath upon himself. With terrifying shrieks, he began to eat his own hands, unable as he was to take any vengeance on the one who was abusing him.[61]

It happened by chance that one of the women of the palace was passing by at that time and heard the great noise. She entered the room to find out what was going on and saw the terrifying spectacle, with the Wild Man covered in his own blood because he had eaten his hands almost entirely. She drove the page out with the harshest words of reproach, then took up a great stick that the Wild Man's keeper often used to control him; with that she began to beat the Wild Man quite hard in an effort to get him to stop eating himself. But by the very worst stroke of fate the Wild Woman was on her way back to see her man, since she had not seen him for some time and was keen to be with him. Hearing his horrible cries from far off, she picked up her pace and entered the room. When she saw that poor woman beating the Wild Man, who had no hands and was covered with blood, with her big stick, she imagined the woman had done all this to him. With a savage fury she flung herself on the woman and tried to kill her; and she would have succeeded, had not the keeper and many other court servants run to the place quite swiftly in response to the cries that all three of them were making. They arrived almost at the same moment that the Wild Woman was assaulting the wretched woman, whom they pulled alive, but with her face all torn, from the Wild Woman's hands. The unhappy woman died of her injuries not many hours later, and so too did the Wild Man in a very short time, on account of the pain that he felt from his eaten hands, as well as the great wrath which he had aroused in himself. When the Wild Woman saw that he was dead, she was convinced that the woman, and no one else, had been the reason that she was now deprived of her dearest man. Therefore she became so hateful an enemy of all women that she would have killed any that appeared before her, had she not been immediately placed in the same circumstances that her man had been in, that is, with shackles on her feet.

---

[61] For a similar motif, in which a woman reduces herself to beggary because she has gnawed her hands out of grief and frustration, see the early Christian romance *The Recognitions of Clement* (*Clementine Recognitiones*) 7.13–18 (trans. T. Smith, 159–60).

Et questa era la cagione per la quale dianzi si ha detto, che tutte le donzelle, le quali per liberar Fabio basciarla volevano così da lei spaventate fuggivano; imperciò che qual volta alcuna le si avicinava, così mostruosamente digrignava i denti che molte ve ne furono che per la grande paura in terra tramortite cadevano. Et una vi fu vestita da huomo; imperciò ch'ella smisuratamente dietro gli huomini si struggeva; ma come le si fu avicinata, perchè perfettissimo havea l'odorato, perciò che quella era donna subitamente conobbe; et havendola così vicina che più a dietro non si potea ritirare, tra con mani, et co' denti tutta lacerata l'hebbe; nè mai fu possibile, nè con forze, nè con preghiere, se non morta dalle sue mani ritrarla. Per la qual cosa tutte le giovani così ricche, qual povere cotanto erano homai spaventate che più alcuna non si trovava, che così ardita fosse che pur in faccia la osasse mirare.

Onde il Prencipe, gli parenti di Fabio, et in fine tutto Salerno vedendo come al suo scampo più alcun rimedio non vi era, essendo homai passati due giorni et con dispiacere infinito aspettando il terzo, et la crudele Clorina bestemmiando piangevano tutti. Hor il giovine Fabio, al quale in pregione fu data la nova come il benigno Prencipe, sol per amor di lui havea così grande autorità alla Clorina conceduta di poter liberar de' due giovani quello, che più a lei piacea di pigliar per marito con ferma intentione ch'ella non Menandro, ma lui addimandar gli dovesse; et che poi anco la pessima nova havea intesa, come la mal consigliata giovane, havea non lui, ma Menandro per marito richiesto, anzi ottenuto, si era perciò in tanta amaritudine posto, che s'egli v'havesse il commodo havuto da sè stesso (per uscir del grande affanno, che sentiva) s'harrebbe data la morte.

Et tra questo suo estremo tormento ritornandoli a mente lo sviscerato et fedelissimo amor che la Urania soleva già così caldamente portarli, et come egli ingrato di tanto suo amore, quantunque alcuna grande nè picciola cagione ella mai dato gli havesse, per la quale egli, per altra (benchè più bella fosse) lei lasciar dovesse giamai; nondimeno così cieco era stato, che ella di lui amantissima, per una sua crudelissima nemica haveva non pur lasciata d'amare, ma ancora sofferto, anzi datole occasione che per lo Mondo errando, et forse dispersa n'andasse.

Et perciò con fiocca voce da un nembo di sospiri, et di lagrime accompagnata in cotal modo diceva. "Deh Urania, a me già fedelissima tanto, perchè non è stato in piacere del mio destino, che mentre mi ti ritrovavi vicina, et che io da te cotanto ero amato, così il valore, et fedele amor tuo havesse alhor conosciuto, come al presente che lontana mi sei, et che con grandissima ragione forse odio mi porti

URANIA: THE STORY OF A YOUNG WOMAN'S LOVE

This was the reason why, as I have said, all of the maids who wished to free Fabio by kissing her instead ran off in terror: for every time one of them got close, the Wild Woman gnashed her teeth in such a way that there were many of these maids who, for fear, fell to the ground in a swoon. One of these women was even dressed as a man, since the Wild Woman was inordinately fond of men; but as soon as she approached, the Wild Woman immediately knew she was a female because she had a very refined sense of smell. Since this maid was so close that she could not pull back, the Wild Woman tore her up with her hands and teeth; and it was not possible, neither through force nor cajoling, to get the maid out of her hands until she was dead. Because of this all the young women, rich and poor alike, were so terrified that not one could be found who was so bold that she dared look the Wild Woman in the face.

At this the Prince, Fabio's relatives, and finally all of Salerno wept and cursed the cruel Clorina, when they saw that there was no longer any way to save Fabio. Two days had passed and everyone awaited the third with infinite anxiety. In prison the young Fabio had received the news that the merciful Prince, moved solely by his great love for Fabio, and fully expecting that she would ask for Fabio instead of Menandro, had granted to Clorina the authority to be able to free whichever of the two youths she liked best. Subsequently he had also heard the terrible news that the imprudent young lady had not picked him as a husband, but had instead chosen, and indeed had already obtained, Menandro. Thus he fell into such bitterness that if he had had the means he would have taken his own life, in order to escape from the great distress that he felt.

In the midst of this extreme torment he recalled to mind the complete and most faithful love that Urania had so warmly borne for him at one time. He also remembered how he had failed to appreciate this great love, even though she had given him no reason, either great or small, to cause him to leave her for another woman (however more beautiful). Despite Urania's faithful love, he had been so blind that he had not only given up loving her in order to turn his attentions to a woman who was a most cruel enemy, but he had also allowed, or indeed even caused, Urania to wander off through the world; and perhaps she was even lost forever.

Thus he spoke, with his hoarse voice emerging from a fog of sighs and tears: "O Urania, once so faithful to me, why did it not please my destiny to allow me to be aware of your worth and your loyal love when I had you near me, and when you bore me such great affection? And why should it be granted to me to know this only now, when you are far away, and perhaps consumed with hatred

mi è conceduto perfettamente conoscerlo? Ahimè, che se ciò mi fosse avenuto, non mi ritroverei (et lo so certo) nello miserissimo stato che al presente mi trovo; che ben si sa, che così sei discreta, et gentile (se pur vivi ancora, et che l'ingiusto martir, che io t'ho dato, non ti sia stato di morte cagione) che in un tale obbrobrioso errore non sarei mai per tua cagione caduto; come io posso con la verità affermare, che mentre io ti amai un sol picciolo disconcio per tua cagione non hebbi mai a patire; anzi di più voglio dire, che così benigna, amorevole, et pietosa mi par di conoscerti, che se qui in Salerno al presente ti ritrovassi, overamente in parte così vicina che la mia grande miseria a tempo di potermi giovare intendesti, io non dubito punto che per venire dove io sono tu porresti le ali, et ogni possibile mezzo per potermi liberar tentaresti, quantunque manifesto ti fosse che per compiacere altra ingrata donzella a cotal miserabil fine io fosse condotto.

"Ma ahimè, misero, che dico io? Et come sono fuori di me stesso uscito? Che io non consideri come una di due cose necessariamente esser conviene cioè, o ch'ella è già morta; imperciò che allo esterminato dolore, il quale nella dolorosa lettera, ch'ella al partir suo mi mandò dimostrava d'havere, non è possibile che in una così amarissima vita habbia potuto longamente durare. Overamente, s'ella in vita pur anco si serba, impossibile è ancora che poco, o niente più mi ami; che il patir de' molti disagi, come nel far de' lunghi viaggi non si può fuggire, et lo sovente seco stessa rememorar la crudel cagione, la quale da null'altra convenevol cagione, fuor che da sè medesima derivando, g'ha[62] dato cagione di dover tanti disagi et affanni patire, penso che così l'harra fatta compassionevole di sè stessa, che in me, come in cagion del suo male, sommo odio harrà posto. Et d'altra parte debbo credere ancora che forse si sarà ritrovato qualch'uno, il quale più di me savio, miglior conoscitor de gli meriti, et virtù sue di quello fui io dimostrandosi; tanto la haverà riverita et osservata, ch'ella, la quale è tutta amorevole, et all'honeste cortesi richieste arrendevole, considerando quanto sia meglio l'amar dove lo amore è reciproco, che dove ingratitudine, et spregio, nè mai di meglio si spera (come da me si conosce haver ricevuto) tutta ad amarlo sarassi rivolta.

"Et io quale mi merito convenevol castigo della ingratitudine mia porteromi; la qual mala ventura, non credo che per altro mio maggior peccato mi sia incontrata, eccetto che per la gran crudeltade, che verso lei, che cotanto mi amava ho sanza alcuna ragione usata; che dovendo io amare chi più di sè stessa mi amava, et

---

[62] Veneto dialect form for *ha*, which typically includes the proclitic adverb *ghe*: G. Rohlfs, *Grammatica storica della lingua italiana e dei suoi dialetti*, 3 vols. (Turin: Einaudi, 1968), 2: 274.

URANIA: THE STORY OF A YOUNG WOMAN'S LOVE

for me, as you have every right to be? Alas, if I had known it, I would not find myself now in my present wretched state; of this I am sure. As everyone knows, you are so genteel and discreet (that is, if you are still alive, and if the unjust suffering which I caused you has not brought about your death) that I would never have fallen into such a shameful error through any action of yours. I can say truthfully that as long as I loved you I never suffered the slightest unease on your account; on the contrary, you appear to me to be so kind, loving, and compassionate that if I were to encounter you here in Salerno, or somewhere close enough to allow you to hear of my wretched state in time to come to my aid, I do not doubt that you would put on wings and employ every possible means to attempt to come to me and set me free. And you would do this even though it were plain to you that I got myself into this miserable state through my efforts to please another maid, an ingrate.

"But alas, woe is me, what am I saying? How could I be so out of my mind? For I am forgetting that only two things can have happened, that is, either she is dead, since it is not possible that she could have lasted long in the wretched state of endless grief that she indicated she was suffering in the letter she sent at her departure; or else, if she is still alive, it is impossible that she continues to bear any love for me at all. Since on long journeys one cannot avoid suffering grave discomforts, I believe that as she thinks over the cruel treatment which, more than any other possible reason, has caused her to undergo such suffering and hardship, she must have come to feel sorry for herself; whereas at the same time she must bear the greatest hatred for me, who am the cause of all her difficulties. Moreover, I am compelled to believe that perhaps she has found someone who has shown himself to be wiser than I, and better able to appreciate her fine points and virtues than I have been. Such a man will have revered and honored her to the extent that she, so inclined to affection and so easily swayed by one who woos in an honest and courteous fashion, will have come to love him. She will see that it is better to love when one is loved in return, instead of turning one's affections to someone who shows only ingratitude and disdain, and the promise of nothing better; and one can see that is all she has gotten from me.

"For my part, I will bear the fitting punishment I deserve for my ingratitude. I do not believe that my misfortune has come to me for any worse sin than the great cruelty that I have shown, for no reason at all, to the one who loved me so much. Even though I should have loved a woman who loved me more than

a ragion meritevole n'era, volli lasciando lei chi dell'amor mio era indegna, et che punto non mi prezzava, volli dico più che me stesso amare, et seguire. Hor togli dunque infelicissimo Fabio lo amarissimo et convenevole frutto, al seme dello irregolato amor, che alla Clorina hai portato." Queste, et altre simili molte dolorose parole d'ogni speranza homai privo lo affannato Fabio diceva.

Et perchè dopo ch'egli fu posto nella pregione non havea mai per dormir chiusi gli occhi; et essendo estremamente lasso, fu in quel punto da un molto profondo sonno assalito, et parveli in sogno di vedere, che egli entro uno assai dilettevole giardino si ritrovasse, nel quale non da altri che da una piacevolissima cagnolla era accompagnato, la quale co' più dolci vezzi, et carezze del mondo lusingando l'andava; et a lui parea che sommo piacer de cotali sue piacevoli lusinghe sentisse. Ma mentre ch'egli con maggior diletto, che più havesse sentito gustavale, vide dall'altra parte del giardino una assai bella donzella comparere; che a gran passo verso lui ne veniva. Della quale accortosi, poco più la cagnolla prezzando, similmente anch'egli tutto ridente verso quella i suoi passi rivolse: ma parendo alla cagnolla che gran torto così sprezzandola le facesse, perciò hor co' piedi, et hor co' denti nella veste tirandolo, quanto più potea d'arrestarlo s'ingegnava; ma niente giovavale, anzi essendo già egli sommamente divenuto desideroso d'avicinarsi a quella bella donzella, et parendogli che col suo frequente tirare, la amorevole cagnolla i suoi volontarosi passi alquanto gli ritardasse. Perciò gli tanti piaceri da lei ricevuti tutti ad un punto scordandosi, et tutto di sdegno carico, d'un piè nel petto alla cagnolla con tal furor diede, che assai da sè lontano la spinse; ma lei, che amorevolissima gli era, non per quello rimase di novellamente ritornarlo a tirar per la veste; nè meno egli mancò di pur sempre poco cortesemente da sè scacciarla, ma accorgendosi poi la infelice cagnolla, come che fatto ch'egli alla bella giovane si fu vicino, la quale con molte blanditie lo raccolse, più niente di lei curavasi, tanto gran doglia ne prese, che in suo idioma piangendo, et languendo subito dalla sua presenza si tolse, et molto a dentro nel giardin si nascose.

Ma dopo ch'ella d'indi si fu partita, parendo a Fabio che con la compagnia di quella bella donzella felicissimo fosse rimaso. Et ella per mano pigliandolo parvegli[63] che così gli dicesse. "Odi Fabio, io so che del mio amore sei acceso, et che

---

[63] *Pavegli* in T (fol. 138r). *Parveli* in P (fol. 139r). The P copyist (probably Borromeo) corrected the misspelled verb, but also changed the indirect object pronoun to reflect the archaic usage which predominates elsewhere in the text. I have corrected the misspelling and retained the original pronoun as it appears in T.

Urania: The Story of a Young Woman's Love

herself, and who rightly deserved to be loved, I abandoned her and chose instead one who was unworthy of my love, and who did not esteem me at all; in fact, I chose to love this woman more than myself, and to dedicate myself to her. O unhappy Fabio, now you must harvest your most bitter fruit; a fruit that you fully deserve, grown from the seed of the unbridled love you bore for Clorina." By now deprived of all hope, the miserable Fabio pronounced these words of woe, and many other similar ones.

At this point Fabio was overcome by a very deep slumber, not having closed his eyes since he had been placed in prison. In a dream he seemed to see that he was in a most delightful garden, with nothing more than a very sweet little female dog for company. He dreamed he was gently caressing the dog, and it seemed to him she took the greatest pleasure in his fond attentions. However, while he was enjoying this pursuit with more delight than he had ever felt before, he saw a beautiful maiden appear on the other side of the garden, coming swiftly toward him. Breaking into a smile, he likewise approached her as soon as he saw her, and forgot all about the little dog. Thinking a great wrong had been done her to be so scorned, the dog tried by every means possible to stop him, either by using her paws or by pulling at his clothes with her teeth. But it was no use. Indeed, seeing that he now felt the greatest desire to approach the maiden, and realizing that the lovestruck dog was slowing his advance somewhat, the dreamer forgot at once the many pleasures he had received from the dog. Filled with disdain, he kicked the dog in the chest with such anger that she was flung far away from him. But the dog was still so deeply in love with him that the blow did not suffice to keep her from returning to tug at his clothes again; nonetheless, the dreamer continued to drive her rudely away. When the unhappy dog saw that he had reached the beautiful young lady, and had been welcomed by her with many flattering words, she realized that he cared nothing for her. Weeping in her own language, the dispirited dog was so overcome by her great pain that she left the dreamer's presence and hid herself far off in the garden.

After the dog had gone, it seemed to Fabio that he was extremely happy in the company of the lovely maiden. She took him by the hand. "Listen, Fabio," she seemed to say, "I know that you are burning with love for me, and that you

che altra cosa maggiormente non brami come è di potere di questa mia vita goderti; la quale ad ogni tuo piacere paratissima ritroverai; quando perciò ti disponi all'incontro di fare ancor tu a me un gran servigio; il che è, che ritrovandomi per alcuni mie affari haver bisogno d'alcuni uccelletti, li quali in un nido su la cima di quel lunghissimo, et sottile albero sono; che qui a noi dirimpetto nel mezzo del giardino tu poi vedere; et che ti dia il cuore d'andar su quella cima a pigliarli, et che io dalle tue mani gli prenda; io ti giuro che subitamente, che io gli harrò da te ricevuti così potrai di questa mia vita disporre, come di cosa tua propria faresti: hor dunque risolviti tosto di quanto ti piace di fare."

Pareva a Fabio che quelle parole della donzella gli arrecassero un sommo contento, et perciò così le rispose. "Bellissima giovane, voi l'havete indovinato, che d'ardentissime fiamme acceso nel vostro amore io mi trovo; et che altra cosa non più tanto desidero, come è di poter tanto valere, che mi giovi per acquistarmi a fatto la gratia vostra; per la qual cosa io dico, che non su la cima di quello albero a prender gli da voi desiati uccelletti per amor vostro mi sarà facile il salire, ma ancor su nel Cielo per pigliar cosa che vi fosse in piacere vorrei tentar di andare; et perciò colà andiamo tosto, che d'altro che di compiacervi, et ubidirvi non tengo cura."

Et così detto, verso la lunga, et sottil pianta n'andarono, et ivi giunti parevali, che assai leggiermente su quella salisse; ma come egli fu quasi alla cima, et al nido vicino parvegli che sentisse quella pianta dal piede molto crollare, perchè mandando giù la vista lungo il tronco di quella, vide cosa la quale infinito spavento gli porse; imperciò che gli parve vedere, che quella donzella, la quale poco dinanzi così bella gli era paruta, da cintura in giù tutte le membra di bruttissima serpe tenesse, et parevali che con uno di quegli stromenti, co' quali si lavora il terreno, che homai quasi tutta la terra dalle radici dell'albero havesse cavata; per la qual cosa essendo l'albero quasi diradicato, perciò così fortemente crollava; et parevali ancor di vedere un bruttissimo fauno; il quale stando vicino al piè della pianta ad un suo gran bastone appoggiato, mirava la mostruosa donzella, che così ben s'affaticava a discalciar la pianta, acciò che cadesse.

La quale come le parve che tanta le ne havesse levata, che ogni picciolo crollo a terra l'havrebbe potuta mandare, riponendo lo stromento con lo qual lavorava, et rivoltatasi al fauno così gli disse. "Parti amor mio, ch'io t'habbia hoggi mai rassicurato del grande amor ch'io porto a costui, del quale in tanto sospetto vivevi? Hor vedi come per compiacerti io l'ho in parte condotto, dove egli non potrà (con tutto il suo ingegno) la morte fuggire. Andiamo dunque a goderci i dolcissimi frutti dell'amor nostro, et lui là suso col mal'anno lasciamo." Et così detto parveli

Urania: The Story of a Young Woman's Love

desire nothing so much as to be able to take pleasure in being part of my life. And you will find me most ready to provide you with every pleasure, just as soon as you are willing to do me a great service. I find I need some little birds for certain purposes of mine, and these birds are in a nest at the top of that tall slender tree, the one that you can see just opposite where we are, in the middle of the garden. I want you to find the courage to climb up there and get them, so that I can take them from your hands. I swear to you that as soon as I receive the birds my life is yours to be used however you wish, as you would do with your own. Therefore decide quickly what it pleases you to do."

Fabio imagined he felt great contentment at the maiden's words. "Most beautiful young lady," he answered her, "you have guessed rightly that I am burning with the hottest flames of love for you, and that I desire nothing more than to be worthy enough to be able to acquire your good graces. For this reason I say to you that it will be easy for me to climb to the top of that tree in order to get the birds you want; indeed, I would even be willing to attempt to climb on to heaven for anything there that you might desire. For I care for nothing so much as pleasing you, and obeying you."

Having said this, he accompanied her to the tall and slender tree. When they got there, it seemed to him as though he climbed the tree quite effortlessly. But as he approached the top, and also the nest, he seemed to feel the tree start to totter from its base. Looking down the trunk, he saw something that filled him with infinite terror: in his dream the maiden, so lovely to him just moments earlier, had now taken on the appearance of a hideous reptile from the waist up. He also had the impression that she had dug up almost all the earth from around the roots of the tree, using one of those tools that are used to work the fields; and because of this the tree had nearly become uprooted, and was about to fall. Now he seemed to see a very ugly faun, who was standing near the base of the tree, leaning on a big stick and watching the monstrous maiden work herself into a sweat to uproot the tree and bring it down.

When the maiden was convinced that she had removed so much earth that the slightest movement would make the tree fall, she put down her tool and turned to the faun. "Does it not seem to you, my love," she said, "that I have shown you today just how much love I bear that man, of whom you were so suspicious? See how I have gotten him into a place from which he will not be able to escape death, despite all his cleverness; and I have done this to please you. Therefore let us go enjoy the sweetest fruits of our love, and leave him up there in his misfortune." When she had said this, it seemed to Fabio that the two of them embraced, then

che ambidue insieme abbracciati, in un baleno da gli occhi suoi dileguassero; della qual cosa il parve, che tanto confuso, et spaventato rimanesse, che non sapea egli stesso quello, che far si dovesse; imperciò che gli pareva ogni poco che mosso si fosse, che la crollante pianta sarebbe con suo estremo precipitio a terra caduta, et lo ratenersi la su gli era sicura morte; et perciò parevali, non potendo altro fare, che fieramente la sua sventura piangesse.

Ma mentre così si struggeva, vide la amorevolissima cagnolla da quella parte uscire, dove prima s'era nascosa et al dritto venir verso la pianta; alla qual giunta, et con gemiti, quali alla sua natura si confacevano, parea che grandemente del mal di lui si dolesse; et dopo che dogliendosi, et guatando in su, alquanto fu stata; spinta da quella somma amorevolezza, con la quale ella ardentissimamente il giovine amava, si pose tra con le branche, et col muso, con tanto affetto a rincalciare la terra al piè della pianta, che in breve hora così ferma, et salda parve a Fabio di sentirla esser venuta, ch'egli sicuro, et facilissimamente giù ne discese. Et quando fu a terra, conoscendo come s'haveva per opera di quella cagnolla salvata la vita, per opera di quella, ch'egli per seguitar quella frodolente donzella havea tante volte con poca amorevolezza da sè discacciata; con amorevole affetto tra le sue braccia la prese; et mentre al suo petto la si stringeva, tanto fu il piacer, che nello accarezzarla sentiva, che vinto da soverchia dolcezza il sonno si ruppe.

Ma quando fu risvegliato, et che molto ben hebbe considerato quel sogno giudicò che non sogno, ma visione la poteva tenere. Et ben s'accorse, che la mostruosa donzella, altro che la falsa Clorina non poteva significare; la quale con arroganti persuasioni, nel pericolo, ch'egli si ritrovava l'haveva condotto, et che il fauno, lo da lei amato, et liberato Menandro significava; ma la fedelissima cagnolla, la da sè a torto scacciata Urania parevali che intender dovesse. Onde considerando come la cagnolla da quel grande pericolo di morte l'havea liberato, entrò in ferma speranza che la sua Urania, la quale egli già era ritornato ad amare, dalla mala ventura, nella quale egli era posto, medesimamente a liberarlo dovesse venire. Et perciò quantunque mancasse un sol giorno, et non più delli tre dopo i quali a morte era sentientiato; nondimeno tanto per questa visione prese conforto che parevali di certo non poter più di quella morte morire; della quale ei poco dianzi così stranamente haveva temuto. Ma lasciamolo alquanto da questa novella speranza racconfortato, chè buono sarà il ritornare a dir dela sconsolata Urania, la quale con la innamorata Emilia verso Salerno cavalcavano a gran giornate.

URANIA: THE STORY OF A YOUNG WOMAN'S LOVE

disappeared from sight in a flash, leaving him so confused and afraid that he had no idea what he should do next. Every little move he made appeared to cause the tottering tree to begin its final plunge, and yet staying where he was meant certain death. Seeing there was nothing he could do, he began to weep bitterly over his misfortune.

But while he languished thus, he saw the very loving little dog come out of the place where she had been hiding and head straight for the tree. When she reached it, she whined as dogs naturally do, and showed thereby that his miserable state had caused her to suffer as well. After commiserating for a while, and looking up at him, she stayed there for a time. Then, driven by they great love she felt for the young man, she set about affectionately kicking the dirt back against the base of the tree, employing her paws and her muzzle. In a short time it seemed to Fabio that the tree had become so firm and stable that he descended from it safely and with great ease. Once he was on the ground he picked the dog up lovingly in his arms, knowing now that she had saved his life through her efforts, despite the fact that he had shown her no great affection, and had driven her off in order to chase after that false maiden. While he was holding her to his breast, he felt such pleasure in caressing her that he was overcome by the sweetness and woke up abruptly from his sleep.

But when he was awake, and had thought about the dream at some length, he decided that he should consider it not a mere dream, but a vision.[64] He was well aware that the monstrous maiden could signify no one other than the false Clorina, who had led him into his present danger with her arrogant persuasiveness. The faun, whom she loved, stood for the freed Menandro, while the most faithful little dog had to be seen, he imagined, as Urania, wrongly driven away. Considering how the dog had saved him from mortal danger, he firmly began to hope that his Urania, whom he had begun to love again, would come to rescue him from the misfortune in which he had fallen, just as the dog had. Therefore, even though only one day, and no more, remained of the three that he had been given before the death sentence would be carried out, he still took so much comfort from this vision that it appeared certain to him that he was no longer bound to suffer that death which he had so greatly feared just a little while before. But now let us leave him for a bit, comforted as he is by this new hope; for it is right that we return to our account of the disconsolate Urania, riding toward Salerno for all she was worth, in the company of the lovestruck Emilia.

---

[64] For a similar typological distinction between dream (*somnium*) and vision (*visio*) see Macrobius, *Commentary on the Dream of Scipio*, 1.3 (trans. Stahl, 87–92).

VI

La Urania dunque essendo con la bella Emilia, ambe vestite da huomo, postasi in camino per gire isconosciuta in Salerno, con intentione di non lasciarsi a parente, nè ad amico veruno conoscere; ma come una sol volta havesse havuto gratia di poter vedere il suo Fabio, manifestar alla bella Emilia, come ancor ella era donna, et insieme tutta la sua sventura scoprirle; et se poi fosse contenta di volere ancor seco in compagnia ritenerla, havea deliberato in tutti i suoi giorni non più abbandonarla giamai.

Et perciò come fu giunta in Salerno volle, per non esser da alcuno riconosciuta, all'hosteria alloggiare. Ma non fu così tosto da cavallo smontata, come la mala nova di Fabio a gli orecchi le venne; imperciò che per tutto Salerno d'altra cosa che dell'empio caso non si ragionava; che essendo di quel giorno, il quale era il terzo, quasi hora di vespro, nè vedendo sino a quel punto alcuna per la quale si potesse sperar del suo scampo, teneva per cosa certa ciascuno ch'egli havesse il seguente giorno a morire: et perciò da tutti (perchè era amato da tutti) estremamente venia lamentato.

Come la Urania hebbe intesa la pessima nova, et che certificata si fu che quello da così fera ventura assalito era il suo amantissimo Fabio, ch'egli era quello, il quale pur fu suo spirto, sua anima, suo core, et sua vita; et quello per lo quale havea lei meschina tanti affanni, et tanti disagi sofferti, et sanza il quale malagevolmente di poter viver fidavasi, hora intendendo dico com'egli per lo amor della ingrata Clorina era a quell'estremo fine condotto, tanto fu amara et potente la doglia che al misero cuore le prese, che da i vitali spiriti abbandonata, sanza pur dire una parola giù in terra strangosciata lasciossi cadere. La qual cosa vedendo la di lei tanto amantissima Emilia, et parendole fuor di misura strana cosa da vedere, che questo suo Fabio, tanto s'havesse della rea sorte d'un'altro Fabio a dolere (quando ancora

VI

When Urania had set out for Salerno with the lovely Emilia, both of them disguised as men, her intention was to visit the city incognito, without revealing her identity to a single relative or friend. But once she had had the blessed opportunity to see her Fabio, she intended to tell Emilia how she too was a woman, and at the same time recount to her her whole sad story. Then, if Emilia were still content to remain in her company, Urania had decided that she would never leave her for the rest of her days.

When she reached Salerno she wanted to stay in an inn, so that no one would recognize her. But no sooner had she gotten off her horse than the bad news concerning Fabio reached her ears, for in all of Salerno no one spoke of anything but the terrible affair. Since it was nearly the hour of vespers on the third day, and no woman had yet appeared who could be hoped to bring about Fabio's rescue, all the people were convinced that he would have to die on the morrow. This was greatly lamented, because he was so much loved by everyone.

Once Urania had heard the terrible news, it was soon confirmed to her that this man who had been afflicted by such misfortune was indeed her beloved Fabio, still her spirit, her soul, her heart and her life, the man for whom she had miserably suffered so many trials and hardships, and without whom she could only expect to lead a wretched life. When she had also heard how he had been brought to this final state by his love for the ungrateful Clorina, her heart was assailed by such a deep and bitter pain that her vital spirits left her, and she fell in a swoon to the ground without a word. It seemed a very strange thing to Emilia, who loved her Fabio so much, to see him so grief-stricken at the hard fate of another Fabio

fratello gli fosse) che dovesse a tai termini lasciarsi condurre. Perciò poi che col maggior affanno, ch'ella altra volta sentisse più mai, gli hebbe con buoni rimedij, (et non sanza gran fatica) gli smarriti spiriti ritornati, da compassione, et da Amor spinta forte piangendo così le disse:

"Deh Fabio, unica speranza dell'anima mia, che mala sorte è questa, dalla quale al presente così afflitto ti veggio? Et chi puote esser costui giamai, per lo quale cotanto affanno della non ancora sua giunta morte ti prendi, che prima di lui par che tu voglia morire? Chè se del medesimo tuo nome udito nomar non l'havesse, crederei certo ch'egli ti fosse fratello. Ma sia che si voglia, per quanto teco io posso, et vaglio ti prego, caro mio amantissimo Fabio, che ti piaccia tutta scoprirmi la cagione, per la quale tanto acerbamente per lo danno di costui ti tormenti, acciò che essendoti quella amorevole et fedel compagna, che io ti sono mi sia conceduto, sì della cagione, quale del duol cagionato potermi teco insieme dolere; che ben sai amandoti, come svisceratamente io ti amo, in te non poter esser dolore, che in me dolore, et affanno non sia; come ogni tua allegrezza sarebbe medesimamente a me di sommo contento cagione."

Vinta la Urania dalle dolci parole della amorevole Emilia, poi che per buona pezza fu stata a poter rihaver la favella, come più tosto puote dire, così le rispose. "Signora Emilia mia honorata padrona, già non mi è cosa nova il saper quanto (sol vostra mercede) sanza punto io da voi meritarlo, pur troppo mi amate; della qual cosa presso i molti altri miei discontenti, non meno forse mi strugge il conoscermi poco atto a potere in tutti i miei giorni di cotanta vostra amorevolezza in parte alcuna meritarvi giamai; et il maggior affanno che di questo io sento è il vedere come questa mia misera vita (quantunque ella sia di picciol valore) non esser così mia, chè per quel poco, ch'ella vale facendovene dono io potesse almeno a qualche parte del debito mio sodisfare; chè se già mi fu impedito, perchè era d'Amore, al presente perchè è di morte soggetto, del tutto mi vien negato il poterlavi in conto alcuno offerire. Et acciò vi sia manifesta la cagione, per la quale insieme co'l dolore ho deliberato di finir questa mia infelicissima vita, poi che d'intenderla n'havete talento, dicovi, che dovete sapere come questo Fabio, il quale al presente in così strano pericolo di morte si trova, è tanto a me non di sangue, ma di amore congiunto, che quanto egli mi sia, difficilmente lo vi potreste imaginare. Questo Fabio Signora mia, è della da me tanto amata Urania fratello, nè cosa si trova nel mondo, la quale ella più, nè tanto come costui habbia caro, ami, et apprezzi. Nè

URANIA: THE STORY OF A YOUNG WOMAN'S LOVE

(even had he been a brother), and to let himself get into such a state. More distressed than she had ever been before, she employed good remedies and considerable effort to restore Urania's scattered spirits to her. Weeping greatly, and moved by Love, Emilia spoke to Urania thus:

"O Fabio, only hope of my soul, by what ill fate do I see you afflicted now? And who ever can this man be, whose death (which he has yet to suffer) has brought you so much grief that you seem willing to die yourself, even before he does? If I had not heard him called by the same name that you bear, I would certainly believe that he is your brother. But whoever he may be, my most beloved Fabio, if you have any esteem for me at all I pray that it please you to reveal to me the reason why this man's fate causes you such bitter anguish; I ask this in order that it be granted me, as your loving and faithful companion, to grieve along with you not just for the pain that you feel, but also for the cause of the pain. Since I love you so very deeply, you know well that there can be no pain in you that does not cause pain and distress in me; just as any joy that you feel brings great contentment to me as well."

The loving Emilia's sweet words soon won over Urania. It was some time before she regained the power of speech, but as soon as she could, she answered Emilia thus: "Lady Emilia, my honored mistress, it is not news to me to hear how excessively you love me, even though this love comes about solely through your kindness, and I am completely undeserving of it. Because of this, of all the things which make me sad, I suffer not least from the awareness that in all the days of my life I will never be deserving, even in a small part, of this love of yours. The greatest misery which this causes in me lies in seeing how this wretched life, however little it may be worth, is not even mine; and for that reason I cannot even give you what little it does have of value, in order to satisfy my debt to you. If once I was prevented from doing this because that part of me belonged to Love, now I cannot because it belongs to death, and thus it is denied me to offer you anything whatsoever of myself. In order to let you know the reason, which you desire to hear, why I have decided to end both this pain and my unhappy life, I will tell you this: it is essential that you know that this Fabio, who at present finds himself under such an unusual sentence of death, is not conjoined to me by blood, but by love, and to such a degree that you would find it difficult to imagine. My lady, this Fabio is the brother of my beloved Urania, and there is nothing in the world which she loves, esteems and appreciates more than him. Moreover, I

puto dubitar si debbe, che s'avien ch'egli muoia, ch'ella parimente non muoia ancora; et s'ella morisse non vi pensate che io dopo la morte sua una sola hora potesse più vivere; hor potete Signora Emilia, conoscere quanto la vita et la morte di costui a me importi, et quanto di dolermi io habbia giusta cagione."

Udendo la bella Emilia con molto affanno dir queste parole al suo amato Fabio, quantunque apertamente conoscesse non esser di quell'amore amata da lui, del quale ella desiava ch'egli la amasse, non però potea rimanere di non ardentissimamente amarlo, et di non desiderarli più tosto il suo, che'l proprio contento; et perciò con gli occhi piangenti così gli disse. "Deh Fabio mio, maladetto sia quell'empio destino, il quale ti sforza a seguir chi non t'ama, et chi forse al fin ti potrebbe esser cagione di morte; et ti fa fuggire cui più della propria vita ti pregia; et con la quale tutti que' commodi, et piaceri, i quali si ponno qua giù in questo basso mondo desiderare, abondantissimamente potresti havere. Nondimeno poi che alla tua, et mia sorte piace che ciascuno di noi debba sempre il suo peggio seguire, ho deliberato, poi che per farti mio non vaglio, di farti almeno conoscere di quanto valor sia l'amor, che io ti porto; et voglio tentar s'io posso, basciando la Salvatica Femina, questo tuo Fabio liberare, acciò che non potendo io di te alcun mio contento ottenere, tu almeno per mezzo mio ottenghi il tuo; imperciò che se m'aviene, che con lusinghe, come io penso di saper fare, io possi dalla Salvatica Femina havere un bascio, per lo quale io harrò Fabio scampato da morte, la prima cosa, che io gli dirò sarà il pregarlo, ch'egli sia contento che la Urania divenghi tua sposa; et così havendo tu co'l mezzo mio ottenuto il tuo intento, non ti sarà in dispiacere, s'io facendo cambio della mia Firenze, co'l tuo Salerno, poi che non ti è stato in piacere come tua sposa amarmi, almeno come carissima cognata tenermi."

Non piacquero molto queste ultime parole alla Urania; imperciò che non le piaceva, che altra donna, che lei sopra il suo amantissimo Fabio facesse disegno; et perciò co'l viso turbato così le rispose. "Non piaccia a Dio, Signora Emilia, che altri che me medesimo sia, che al fratello della mia dolcissima Urania rendi la vita; che quantunque per esser io huomo non sia buona l'opera mia per salvarlo co'l mezzo della Salvatica Femina, non perciò mi si torrà, che tra il mio ingegno, et Amore, che in ciò mi darà aiuto, qualche altra via io non scuopra, per la quale io potrò anco salvarlo. Et poi troppo gran peccato sarebbe, quando questa vostra sì bella faccia poneste a pericolo, che da quel bruttissimo mostro fosse squarciata. Nondimeno piacendovi voglio che andiamo in palagio a vedere quello, che circa questo fatto si dice."

"Fabio dolcissimo," rispose la Emilia, "io dissi quelle parole solamente con intentione di giovarti, et non per farti ingiuria, come per la tua altera risposta par

believe that it cannot be doubted that if he happens to die, she will die as well; and if she were to die, do not think that after her death I would be able to live a single hour. Now you know, Lady Emilia, how important the life and death of that man are to me, and how justified I am in my sadness."

Even though she clearly knew that the love Fabio felt for her was not of the sort that she wished he felt, the lovely Emilia was much distressed to hear his words, and could not refrain from loving him most passionately, and from desiring his contentment over and above her own. Therefore, with weeping eyes, she spoke. "O my Fabio, cursed be that cruel destiny which forces you to pursue one who does not love you, one who in the end may be the cause of your death! Moreover, this woman makes you flee from another who values you more than her life, and with whom you could have in abundance all the comforts and pleasures that are possible to have down here in this sublunar world. Nonetheless, since it pleases both your fate and mine that each of us must always seek the worst for ourselves, and seeing how I am not worth enough in and of myself to make you mine, I have decided at least to let you see the stuff of which this love I bear you is made. I wish to attempt, if I can, to free this Fabio of yours by kissing the Wild Woman. In this way, even if I cannot have my heart's desire from you, you at least will have yours through my efforts. Therefore, if I am able to get a kiss from the Wild Woman through flattery, as I believe I know how to do, and thus save Fabio from death, the first thing which I will do will be to plead that he allow Urania to marry you. Once I have obtained your desire through my own abilities, you will not object to my exchanging my Florence with your Salerno; for if it has not been pleasing to you to love me as your wife, at least you will deign to have me for your dearest sister-in-law."

Urania did not find Emilia's last words entirely pleasing, for she did not like the idea that another woman might have designs on her beloved Fabio. "Let it not please God, Lady Emilia, that anyone other than I trade my life for the brother of my sweetest Urania," she answered with a troubled look. "For even though I am a man and my efforts would not suffice to save him by means of the Wild Woman, this will not keep me from finding some other way to help him, with the aid of Love and my own cleverness. In any case it would be too great a shame for you to place this lovely face of yours in danger, and have it torn to shreds by that hideous monster. Nevertheless, if it please you, I want us to go to the palace to find out what people are saying about this affair."

"My sweet Fabio," answered Emilia, "I said those words with the sole intention of helping you, and not to offend you, even though it seems by your haughty

che tu accenni d'haverle ingiuriosamente pigliate. Fa pur, Fabio mio, di questa, et d'ogni altra cosa come ti piace; imperciò che tutto quello a me piace, il quale esser di tuo contento conosco."

La Urania a cui maggior cura premeva il cuore, che non facevano le parole, che costei le diceva; sanza darle altra risposta ritirossi con l'hoste, et fece tanto, ch'egli le ritrovò una certa veste come di masnadieri, la quale unta, et bisunta, per molto sudore stranamente putiva; et pigliata che l'hebbe, con quella parte più unta si fregò d'avantaggio il collo, la faccia, et le mani, di maniera che sè, di sè stessa stomacata si stava. Et indi ritrovato similmente un vil capellaccio, che a similitudine della veste era bene unto, et che quasi tutta la faccia coprivale, in capo se lo pose; et similmente la unta veste si mise intorno. Et così bene addobata ritornò dalla bella Emilia, alla qual disse essersi così vestita acciò da alcuno riconosciuto non fosse.

Et indi ambe due andate in palagio, la Femina Salvatica ritrovarono che era in tanto furore per una giovane che poco inanzi l'havea per basciarla tentata, che a riguardarla poneva terrore in ciascuno. Ma come la Emilia, che tutta delicatissima era, vide quell'horribile aspetto tanto spavento le prese, che ritiratasi presso la Urania in tal modo le disse. "Deh Fabio mio, io ti prego che tosto di qui si partiamo, che io ti giuro per lo amor ch'io ti porto, che tanta è la paura, la quale nel veder questa bruttissima bestia l'anima, et il cuor mi circonda, che non che di aiutar Fabio, come io mi ti haveva offerta mi son svogliata, ma di più dicoti che se padre et madre in pericolo di morte mi ritrovasse havere, et che solamente avicinandomele salvar gli potesse gli lasciarei più tosto tutti morire, che pur un poco all'horribile mostro accostarmi; et perciò caro mio Fabio io ti prego che tostamente di quinci partiamo, che altro mezzo men pericoloso non ti mancherà per poterti la tua cara Urania acquistare."

Sorrise alquanto a questo suo dire la Urania et poscia così le disse. "Ditemi Signora Emilia vi prego di gratia, se io fosse quello, il quale come Fabio in quello istesso pericolo di morte mi ritrovasse, hor che la horribilità della faccia di questa Salvatica Femina havete veduta, tentareste voi almeno di basciarla, per farmi vostro, et salvarmi? O pure sgomentata dalla grande paura, come hora sète, mi lasciareste morire?"

"Fabio mio," rispose la Emilia, "per dirti il vero, io non so me medesima quello che in cotal caso io mi facessi; così fuor di misura al presente spaventata mi veggio. Ma ben ti so dir questo, che per farti mio, overamente per liberarti di un simil pericolo io soffrirei passar per mezzo un grandissimo foco; nè fuggirei il pericolo d'un rapidissimo torrente. Ma a dire il vero questo mostro è pur fuor d'ogni humana stima spaventevole, et brutto; et io ti giuro Fabio mio, che così da

response that you show signs of having been offended. You may do with this, as with anything else, just as you like, my Fabio, for I know that everything I find pleasing makes you content as well."

Urania, whose heart was heavy with greater worries than those caused by Emilia's words, went off with the innkeeper without saying anything else to her. From the innkeeper she was able to get a suit of clothes such as a brigand would wear, which was very greasy and smelled oddly from the great quantity of sweat it held. Once she had it, she rubbed the greasy parts on her neck, her face, and her hands to such an extent that she found herself sickening. After that she likewise found a ragged hat, which was greasy like the outfit and covered almost her entire face. She put this on her head, and put the filthy outfit on as well. Now suitably attired, she returned to the lovely Emilia and told her she had dressed in this way in order not to be recognized by anyone.

Thereupon the two went to the palace, where they found the Wild Woman in a state of great fury because a young woman had just tried to kiss her. Just to look at her was enough to strike terror into anyone. When Emilia, who was quite delicate, saw the horrible apparition she was overcome by so much fear that she shrank back against Urania. "O my Fabio," she said. "I pray you let us leave this place quickly. I swear to you by the love I bear you, the fear that envelops my heart and soul at the sight of this hideous beast is so great that I have lost all desire to help Fabio, as I first offered. Even if I were to find that my father and mother were in danger of death, and that I could save them just by getting close to her, I would rather let them die than approach the horrible monster. Therefore I beg you, my dear Fabio, let us get away from here immediately, for there must be some other less dangerous means for you to win your dear Urania."

Urania smiled a little upon hearing this. "Pray tell me, Lady Emilia," she said. "If I were to find myself in the same mortal danger as Fabio, would you at least try to kiss the Wild Woman to save my life and make me yours, now that you have seen how horrible her face is? Or would you let me die, undone even as you are now by your great fear?"

"My Fabio," answered Emilia. "To tell the truth, I do not know what I would do in such a case, so extraordinarily terrified do I find myself at the moment. This much I can tell you: to make you mine, or to free you from a similar menace, I would pass through a very hot fire; or, if faced with the danger of a swift torrent of water, I would not flee. But in truth this monster is frightening beyond all human comprehension, and ugly to boot. I swear to you, my Fabio, even as far away

lei lontana, come mi vedi, mi sento per la grande paura di modo battere il cuore, et arricciarmisi i capelli, che io non dubito punto che poco più che io le mi avicinassi morirei di certo."

Udendo la Urania cotai parole dire alla Emilia, mandando uno ardentissimo sospiro dal suo petto, così le disse. "Eh Signora Emilia, molti son quelli, che amano; ma pochi sono quelli, che si possano dir veri amanti. Et infiniti ancora poi sono quelli, i quali si dicono esser soggetti d'Amore; ma pochissimi si trovano de quelli, che sapino bene amare; o per dir meglio, che vogliano quelle vere dimostrationi, et affettuali operationi fare, nelle quali si ricerca che sempre si esserciti un vero amante. Credete a me certo che quello, over quella, ch'esser Amante si mostra, fugge, non dirò con lo haver suo di soccorrer al bisogno, over pericolo di quella cosa, che ama; imperciò che io non reputo così smisurato segno d'amore, se chi ama cerca con suoi haveri di farsi grato alla cosa amata; quando tutto il giorno vediamo a molti mal regolati appetiti, per cosa di pochissimo valore; anzi più volte per cosa, la quale danno, et vergogna gli recca, struggere, et discipar di molti tesori. Credete dico, che quello over quella, che con la propria vita fugge di salvar la vita over l'honor di cui ama, non ama da dovero, ma finge; et se pur ama, superficiale è quello amore, et da non farne gran stima: nè dovrebbe la cosa amata di tale amante molto fidarsi.

"Già so ben io, Signora Emilia, che al presente vi pare, che dall'acqua et dal foco non fuggireste per farmi vostro, o per scamparmi da morte. Nondimeno io credo poi anco, che quando così vicina vi ritrovaste al foco, che abbruscia, et all'acqua, che soffoca, come a questa Salvatica Femina vi ritrovate; che così, et forse più, spaventata vi dilongareste da quelli, come al presente da questa dilongarvi cercate. Ma so ben quello, che io per acquistarmi quella cosa, che amo io farei; et forse di questo palagio hoggi non partiremo, che grande isperienza ne potreste vedere. Ma prima voglio provar se io potessi questa Femina Salvatica tanto humiliare, ch'ella poi stesse cheta, se per aventura qualche altra donzella per basciarla sopragiongesse; perchè io so ch'ella fuor di misura de gli huomini si compiace."

"Deh Fabio mio," disse la Emilia, "poi che l'opera tua non è buona con costei per scampar quell'altro Fabio da morte, lasciala star ti prego, et non mi dar tanto cordoglio, come mi sarà il vederti molto a quella brutta bestia vicino; chè se bene hai fermo nel tuo pensiero, che io quanto più si possa amar non ti ami, il tuo ingannarti non scema però punto il grande amor, ch'io ti porto; nè fa minor in me quel timore, il quale cotanto par che di perderti hoggi più che mai facesse mi prema il cuore."

Urania: The Story of a Young Woman's Love

from her as I am now, I feel my hair standing on end, and my heart beating so much from terror that I do not doubt that I would die if I were to approach her any more closely."

When Urania heard Emilia say such things, she gave a heavy sigh. "Eh, Lady Emilia," she said. "Many are those who love, but few are those who can call themselves true lovers. In addition, there are infinite numbers of people who say they are the servants of Love, but of these, very few really know how to love. Or to put it another way, there are not many who want to do those loving deeds and make those sacrifices which are always required of a true lover. Believe me, the man or woman who merely pretends to be a lover will run away to avoid giving aid to his or her beloved who might be in need, or in danger. Such a putative lover might well offer material assistance; however, I do not consider it a very great sign of love if a lover seeks to ingratiate himself or herself to the beloved through the offering of material possessions. We continually see people who cannot restrain their appetites for things of little value, or in many cases, for things which bring them injury or shame, or which ruin or squander one's hoarded wealth. Believe me when I say that the man or woman who runs away from saving the life or honor of his or her beloved, in order to preserve life and limb, does not truly love, but is only pretending. Or, if such a person does love, that love is superficial, and not worth much; so the object of these affections ought not to put much trust in lovers of this sort.

"Now I know full well, Lady Emilia, that at present you imagine that you would not flee from water or fire in order to win me, or save me from death. Nonetheless I am convinced that if you were to find yourself as close to a fire that might burn you or a flood that might drown you as you are to this Wild Woman, you would flee from those things just as you now wish to flee from this one; and you would be just as terrified, if not more so. But I know well what I would do in order to gain the thing I love: and perhaps you will have great proof of this today, before we leave this palace. But first I want to see if I can calm this Wild Woman to such an extent that she will quiet down, in case another maid comes who will attempt to kiss her. I know that she has an extraordinary fondness for men."

"O my Fabio," said Emilia. "Please abandon this plan, since it will serve no purpose with the monster as far as saving Fabio's life is concerned. Spare me the anxiety I will feel when I see you get so close to that hideous beast! Even though you have this fixed notion that I do not love you more than it is possible to love anyone, your misconception about me does not in any way diminish my feelings for you, nor does it reduce the fear which oppresses my heart now at the thought of losing you."

"Non vi dubitate di perdermi hoggi Signora," rispose la Urania, "che io vi assicuro che non mi perderete, che prima voi, et io saremo, come cosa conforme; et quasi l'uno all'altra simile da ciascun conosciuti; pure non mi negate ch'io possa fare per questo sol giorno tutto quello, che io ho voglia di fare."

"Altro da te non desidero," rispose la Emilia, "eccetto che ambi noi siamo da ciascuno conosciuti conformi. Il che se così sarà, non dubito che tosto non mi divenghi marito; et perciò fa come hai detto, per questo giorno tutto quello, che ti piace di fare."

Mentre ch'ella così diceva, s'andava la Urania pian piano accostando alla Salvatica Femina, et mille vezzi facevale; ma quando che le fu più vicina sì che la Femina puote quel gran puzzo della bisunta veste, ch'ella havea in dosso sentire, parendo a quella, che quel fosse il proprio et naturale odore dell'huomo, del quale ella così fortemente si dilettava, incominciò quella sua ferina faccia quanto più poteva a rasserenare, et a cennare la Urania, che più vicina le si facesse; la qual cosa ella vedendo un grandissimo conforto, et speranza ne prese; et confidandosi nella sviscerata fede, et amore, con i quali ella si movea per dare aiuto al suo Fabio, sanza più alcuna cosa temere, fattasi a lei più vicina, sopra una di quelle sue pilose gotaccie un gran bascio le diede. Ma lei, che per cagion dell'odor della veste credevasi che la Urania fosse huomo; nè restando sodisfatta per un sol bascio, anzi essendo per quello desto in lei l'appetito, con ambe le braccia, et con tal furor la si strinse al suo petto, che poco vi mancò che quel ferino furore, facendola per la gran stretta scoppiare, non privasse Salerno di una, la quale doveva da gli habitatori di quello esser non poco prezzata. Et tanti, et tanti salvatichi, anzi ferini basci le dava, che più volte la Urania si ritrovò in strano pensiero di non dover viva uscirle di mano.

Eravi molte genti, nobili, et non nobili in quel loco concorsi, i quali sì dal tumulto tratti, che facevano i circostanti per lo pericolo, nel quale la Urania vedevano, che uno assai leggiero giovine, per essersi fuor di proposito posto in un tal pericolo, esser stimavano; et sì ancora per lo acerbissimo pianto, il quale la bella Emilia faceva; la quale quando vide il suo tanto amato Fabio, da quella a lei sì odiosa Femina così al parer suo, mal trattare; parve che a lei medesima le fosse schiantato il cuore, et perciò fortemente piangendo, con quanta maggior voce haveva, "Aiuto, aiuto!" gridava. Ma non si ritrovava chi aiutar la infelice Urania volesse; imperciò che ciascuno diceva, "S'egli è pazzo lascianlo fare, che forse così della pazzia guarirà."

Poi che per buona pezza hebbe la Salvatica Femina a suo senno basciata la Urania, più stanca che satolla quando a Dio piacque, per riposarse la lasciò pure

Urania: The Story of a Young Woman's Love

"Do not be afraid of losing me today, my lady," answered Urania. "I assure you that you will never lose me until such a time as we have become the very same thing, appearing to resemble each other completely in the eyes of everyone. So do not deny me the chance to do everything I wish to do, just for today."

"I desire nothing more from you," Emilia responded, "than this: that we indeed appear to be in complete accordance in the eyes of everyone. For as soon as that is the case, I do not doubt that you will quickly become my husband. Therefore, on this day you may do everything you desire, just as you have requested."

While she was saying this, Urania was very quietly approaching the Wild Woman, saying gentle words over and over. When she got close the Wild Woman could smell the great stench of the filthy outfit that Urania was wearing, which seemed to her to be exactly like the natural odor of the Wild Man who had once delighted her so much. Her bestial face became as calm as could be, and she gestured to Urania to come nearer. At this, Urania was much comforted, and she felt hopeful. Trusting in the boundless faith and love which had moved her to bring aid to her Fabio, all her fear left her and she came right up to the Wild Woman, planting a big kiss on one of her hideous hairy cheeks. But the Wild Woman was convinced that Urania was a man, from the smell of her clothing. She was not satisfied with a single kiss; indeed, it merely kindled a desire within her for more. Using both arms, she crushed Urania against her bosom with great force, so that her savage passion squeezed her until she nearly burst; and thus Salerno came close to losing a woman whom its citizens had cause to regard with the highest esteem. The Wild Woman then gave her so many savage, even bestial kisses, that more than once the bizarre notion came over Urania that she would never get out of her arms alive.

Many people, both noble and common, had come into that place, drawn by the tumult produced by the onlookers who saw Urania in such danger. They imagined Urania to be a very heedless youth for risking his life in so outrageous a fashion. They also came in response to the mournful cries of the lovely Emilia, who thought her heart would break to see her beloved Fabio abused (as it appeared to her) by the woman she found so odious. Weeping loudly, she shouted "Help, help!" with all the voice she had; but no one there would dare go to the aid of the unhappy Urania. The people all said, "If he is crazy leave him be, for perhaps in this way he will be cured of his craziness."

When the Wild Woman had kissed Urania as much as she wanted, as God willed she released her hold on her a bit in order to rest, more tired than satisfied.

alquanto. Perchè pigliando la Urania il tempo opportuno, molto destramente dalle man se le tolse, quantunque si ritrovasse assai lassa, et mal concia. Ma come la bella Emilia vide il suo caro Fabio fuori di tanto pericolo, li si gettò al collo da soverchia allegrezza piangendo; et tutti quelli, che ivi erano, parte di loro la riprendevano, et parte la deleggiavano ancora; dicendoli che pur era stata grande la sua sciocchezza; poi che sanza alcuna necessitade sè medesimo haveva posto in discrettione di quella rabbia ferina.

Ond'ella, che poco di quel loro dire curavasi così gli rispose. "Perchè più oltre voi non sapete, perciò havete detto quel, che vi pare; nondimeno se alcuno di voi volesse condurmi dinanzi al Prencipe, al quale vorrei supplicare, che in piacere gli fosse, che io alla sua presenza dicesse alquante parole allo sventurato Fabio per commissione di una donzella, la quale lo ha amato ardentissimamente; io vi farei in perpetuo obligato."

Non vi mancorono molti, i quali sperando che questa qualche buona nova fosse per Fabio, subitamente lo condussero al Prencipe. Et come dinanzi gli furono, dopo fattagli riverenza così la Urania gli disse. "Eccellente Signore, quantunque non venisse a me data comissione, che io dovesse a Vostra Eccellenza presentarmi, anzi solamente io fui pregato da una donzella, la quale per quanto mi parve, non credo che altra donna, o donzella fosse più di lei innamorata giammai; fui pregato da lei dico, che io fosse contento, per suo amore qui in Salerno condurmi; et che io dovesse dire alquante parole in nome suo ad un suo amante, che Fabio si chiama; il quale per quello ne ho qui inteso egli si ritrova in pregione, et da Vostra Eccellenza sentenziato alla morte; onde non potendo quale io haveva commissione, quella nova, che io li porto, darli secretamente, Vostra Eccellenza sarà contenta, che qui alla vostra presenza quale si può glie la manifesti."

Il Prencipe, che un troppo grande affanno sentiva, vedendosi serrata ogni via (volendo non esser men che giusto tenuto) di poter da morte liberar Fabio; perciò sperando, che forse questa qualche nova potrebbe essere, alla quale egli appigliandosi potrebbe facilmente, se non scamparlo da morte, almeno prolongarli la vita. Et perciò alla Urania disse che contentissimo era che quanto, et di quello più gli piacea li parlasse; et pregava Iddio che tale fosse la novella, che gli portava, che potesse darli cagione di por la mano ad aiutarlo; perchè altro maggior contento non potrebbe nel mondo havere come sarebbe di poter liberarlo a fatto.

Et così detto fece incontanente ivi a sua presenza Fabio condure; il quale vedendo che hoggimai quasi era sera; nè ancora la Urania, come era per la visione entrato in speranza, nè veruno altro aiuto per lui compareva, quasi che più di mezza la speranza perduta malissimo contento nella pregione si stava. Ma hora

Urania: The Story of a Young Woman's Love

Seeing her chance, Urania deftly slipped out of her arms, even though she was quite exhausted and knocked about. But when the lovely Emilia saw her dear Fabio free of so much danger, she threw her arms around his neck, weeping from great joy. Of those who were present, some admonished Urania and some mocked her, saying that she had been extremely foolish to place herself in the power of such a savage wrath, to no useful purpose.

Urania was little bothered by their comments. "You speak in this careless fashion because you do not know the full story," she said to them. "However, if one of you would deign to conduct me to the Prince, I would be eternally grateful. I would like to ask the Prince's leave to say a few words to the unfortunate Fabio, in the Prince's presence, on behalf of a certain maid who once loved Fabio most passionately."

Most of the people there hoped that this meant good news for Fabio, and so there was no shortage of them who were willing to bring Urania immediately to the Prince. When they were in his presence, Urania bowed to him, and spoke: "Excellent Lord, I have not been charged to seek an audience with you. Indeed, I was only bidden by a maid, one who seemed more in love than any other maid or worldly woman who ever lived, to make my way to Salerno where I was to say a few words on her behalf to a lover of hers, a certain Fabio. According to what I have heard here, he is in prison, condemned by Your Excellency to death. Since on this account I cannot fulfil my duty and give him the news I bear in secret, Your Excellency must be willing to allow me to make it known to him in your presence."

As long as the Prince wished to be seen as supremely just, every means of freeing Fabio from death had remained blocked to him, and because of this he had been in great distress. Therefore, hoping that this news might perhaps give him at least an excuse to prolong Fabio's life, if not save him from death, he said that he was content to allow Urania to say whatever she liked to Fabio, and for as long as she liked. Moreover he prayed to God that the news that this man brought would give him cause to help Fabio, for nothing in the world would make him happier than to be able to set the young man free.

Having said this, he commanded that Fabio be brought before him immediately. Fabio was lying miserably in prison, nearly deprived of all hope. He saw that by now it was nearly evening, yet Urania, who had given him such hope in her vision, had not appeared; nor was any other succor forthcoming. But now he

intendendo come un giovine per nome d'una donzella cercava parlarli, et che perciò lo facea il Prencipe trar di pregione, alquanto da nova speranza racconfortato, un poco più lieto dinanzi dal Prencipe si condusse.

Ma come la Urania, la quale al partir suo di Salerno tutto gioioso, et bellissimo l'haveva lasciato, et che al presente così melanconico, et di tristissima aria lo vide, tanto le si strinse il cuore, che ben poco vi mancò che prima con gli effetti che con le parole non manifestasse cui ella era, pur con lo suo grande valore fece forza a sè stessa; dissimulando la acerbissima amaritudine, nella quale tutta sentivasi struggere. Hora il cortesissimo Prencipe, il quale come vide Fabio, anch'egli tutto si commosse in sè stesso; ma facendo (come la Urania havea fatto) buon viso, così a lei disse. "Tratti innanzi buon giovine, se tu voi con Fabio alcuna cosa ragionare." Ond'ella alquanto avicinandosi a Fabio, et contrafacendo la voce così gli disse. "Nobilissimo Giovine, quanto della mia sorte mi dolga, di dover esser io quello, che trista novella vi apporti, come medesimamente mi dolse quando con questi miei occhi fui astretto a veder la cagione di tal novella Iddio lo sa; che essendomi certificato subito ch'entrai in questa vostra cittad, delle rare, anzi singolari qualitadi vostre; et insieme havendo la vostra disaventura intesa, di dover esser lo apportator di tal rea novella doppiamente mi dolgo; ma poi che così ho promesso, per non mancar di mia fede, sarò pur nondimeno contra mia voglia necessitato a dir quanto io so.

"Voi dovete dunque sapere come io sono un giovine figliuolo d'uno assai commodo mercatante bolognese; che essendo mandato da mio padre (come spesse volte suol fare) a ispedire per conto della mercatantia alcuni negotij a Vinegia; et havendo quelli ispediti, vennemi voglia, non per acqua come era costumato di fare, ma per terra (per più cose vedere) di ritornarmi in Bologna. Et così per le contrade della Euganea passando, mentre lungo un fiume cavalcavo, il quale con la Brenta si unisce; et creggiomi che Bacchiglione si chiama, passando dico un giorno di là, mi percosse gli orecchi una assai lamentevole voce; et come è quasi universal desiderio de tutti, ma particolare de' giovani di voler di ciascuna dubbia cosa certificarsi; venne così a me un desiderio infinito di sapere chi fosse quello, che così fortemente si lamentava; perciò fuori della dritta strada levandomi, che assai dalla strada discosto parevami che la voce venisse; et dietro alla voce

URANIA: THE STORY OF A YOUNG WOMAN'S LOVE

heard that a young man was seeking to speak to him, on behalf of a maiden, and to this end the Prince was having him brought out of prison. Somewhat comforted by this new hope, and a little bit happier, he went before the Prince.

Upon leaving Salerno, Urania had known Fabio to be a very cheerful and handsome young man. When she saw him as he was now, so melancholy and sad, she felt such compassion in her heart that she felt quite tempted to make a gesture to reveal her identity to him, instead of waiting to do it with words. Yet so great was her inner strength that she forced herself to hide the sharp bitterness that came over her. At this moment the most courtly Prince also felt great emotion deep inside, but like Urania he made an outward show of calm. "Step forward, good youth, if you wish to say something to Fabio," he told her; whereupon Urania approached Fabio and spoke, disguising her voice. "Most noble youth, God knows how much it grieves me to have to bring you sad news, just as I was grieved when I had to look upon the source of this news with my own eyes. As soon as I arrived in this city I was told of your rare, indeed unique qualities, and when I was also told of your great misfortune, I felt doubly sad at having to be the bearer of such bad news. But since I have promised to do this, in order to keep my word it is necessary that I reveal to you what I know, against my will.

"Therefore you must know that I am a young son of a very wealthy merchant of Bologna, who sent me, as he often does, to expedite certain business affairs in Venice. When I had finished this task a desire came over me to return to Bologna by land, in order to enjoy the sights, instead of going by water as I was accustomed to do. Thus it was that I passed through the region of the Euganean Hills,[65] and one day while I was riding beside a river that joins up with the Brenta, which I believe is called the Bacchiglione, a very mournful voice suddenly came to my ears. The desire to investigate mysteries may be almost universal, but it is particularly strong in young people; and so it was that I really wanted to know who this person was, the one lamenting so loudly. Therefore I got off the road, for it seemed that the voice was coming from a considerable distance away

---

[65] The Euganean Hills rise a few miles south of Padua, and also serve as the locale for the frame story of "Giulia Camposanpiero." This is the only setting in either of Bigolina's stories which reflects any precise geographical knowledge; indeed, Bigolina is indifferent to the fact that her character Urania never ventures far enough north to see this place, and yet somehow is able to describe it. Bigolina likely has in mind the setting of the Villa Bigolin, which still stands at the edge of the town of Selvazzano, within sight of the banks of the Bacchiglione (Mancini, *La Villa Bigolin*, 53-84).

cavalcando non feci lungo camino, che in un verdeggiante prato entrai nel mezzo del quale vi era un piacevol laghetto; et sopra la riva di quello sedeva tutto solo un giovine, che tenendo gli occhi fissi nel lago, un pietosissimo lamento faceva. Ond'io mosso a pietade me gli feci vicino; et lo incominciai dolcemente a pregare ch'egli fosse contento se si poteva sapere di scoprirmi la cagione per la quale a pianger amaramente s'haveva condotto.

"Il Giovine, che di me accorto non s'era, come m'udì parlare, subitamente levando la vista di ove fissata l'haveva, così mi disse. 'Deh giovine per Dio vi prego, che se la habitatione vostra non è propriamente qui in questo loco, che siate contento di seguire il vostro viaggio, et non più quinci fermarvi; imperciò che a voi poco, anzi nulla può giovare lo intender la mia sciagura; et a me infinitamente noce lo intratenervi più in questo loco, nel quale ho già deliberato di por fine a' miei guai, et che questo lago a me sia sepoltura: et perciò partitevi di qui tosto vi prego.'

"Parvemi tanto strana cosa questa da udire, che io harrei piu tosto voluto morire, che con ogni mio sapere non ingegnarmi di levar quel giovine d'un così fero proponimento, come era di voler da sè stesso darsi la morte; et perciò disceso ch'io fui da cavallo, et fattomegli più vicino, con tutte quelle più amorevoli, et dolci parole, che io seppi usare, et seco per compassione piangendo lo supplicai, et lo astrinsi a dovermi tutta la cagion, che a voler così disperatamente morire lo induceva, manifestare. Onde egli, che per dire il vero gentilissimo era così mi rispose.

"'Cortesissimo giovine, poi che'l Cielo cotanto pietoso et cortese vi fece; et me così arrendevole alle cortesi dimande parve di fare, sarò dunque forzato a tanto dirvi di me quanto a voi medesimo sarà in piacer di sapere. Ma ben vi prego, poi che così cortese sète, che vi piaccia promettermi un dono; il che se mi promettete, vi giuro, che havendo io in ogni modo deliberato di volere hoggi in questo loco morire, tanto contento andarò di là, quanto forse di qui per alcun tempo io sia stato.'

"Io, che in quell'hora altro maggior desiderio non mi ritrovavo havere, come era di poter quello afflitto giovine compiacere, me gli offersi co'l cuore di far a suo beneficio tutto quello, a me fosse possibil di fare; et perciò lo pregai che sanza alcun rispetto gli piacesse di comandarmi; et poi che io così gli hebbi detto, egli incominciò così a dirmi: 'Non dubito cortese giovine, che voi non crediate, che come voi sète io sia huomo; ma per farvi tutto l'esser mio manifesto, voi dovete sapere, come io non sono huomo, ma donna; et sono una giovane d'assai nobile sangue nata in Salerno; che per la grandissima crudeltate usatami da un nobilissimo giovine, il quale io assai più che la istessa anima mia havea caro, et amava; et al

Urania: The Story of a Young Woman's Love

from it. Riding along and following the voice, I did not have to go far before I entered a lush meadow, in the middle of which was a pleasant little lake. On the bank there sat a young man all alone, who kept his eyes fixed on the water and sobbed most pitifully. Moved to pity, I approached him, and began to ask him gently if he would be so kind as to tell me why he had come to this place in order to weep so bitterly.

"The youth had not realized I was there. When he heard me speak, he immediately raised his eyes from the spot at which he had been staring. 'Ah, young man,' he said, 'in the name of God, unless your dwelling place is in this immediate area, I beg you to kindly go on your way and stay here no longer. You would gain little or nothing from hearing my tale of woe, and it distresses me greatly to make conversation in this place, where I have decided to put an end to my troubles. This lake will be my grave, so please leave quickly.'

"All this seemed very strange to me, and I would sooner have wanted to die myself than fail to employ all my wits to find some way to dissuade the youth from his cruel plan to commit suicide. Therefore I got off my horse and went up to him, saying all the sweet and loving words I could think of. I wept along with him, out of compassion, and begged him, compelled him even, to reveal to me the reason why he so desperately wished to die. Whereupon he, who truly was of gentle birth, answered me thus.

"'Most courteous youth, heaven made you both compassionate and polite, while forming me with an inclination to respond to questions put to me in a genteel manner. On this account I am forced to tell you as much about myself as you might wish to know. But I pray you to promise me something in return, since you are so courteous. If you accede to this, I swear to you that even though I have decided in any case to take my life today in this place, I will go to the other world as content as I once may have been, albeit briefly, in this one.'

"I had no other desire in that moment but to please that tormented youth. Therefore I made a heartfelt offer to do whatever I could to help him, and begged him to command me in any way he pleased, without hesitation. 'I do not doubt, O courteous youth, that you believe that I am a man just as you are,' he began. 'But in order to reveal everything about myself, I must tell you that I am not a man, but a woman; a young woman of very high degree, born in Salerno. However, on account of the great cruelty shown me by a most noble young man, a man whom I once held dear and loved more than my own soul, and to whom I had shown innumerable favors, I have been wandering about here and there for

quale innumerabili favori havea fatti, così da uno anno in qua ne vado dispersa, et al presente a miserabilissimo fine io son giunta. La gratia, che io da voi vorrei è questa, cioè che vi fosse in piacere, per mia estrema sodisfattione, poi che a compiacermi così pronto vi veggio, di condurvi sino in Salerno, et ivi ritrovar questo crudele mio amante; del quale hora vi parlo, che Fabio si chiama; et dirli come quella Urania, la quale già tanto sviceratamente l'ha amato; et che per lui tanto fece, et disse; per lui medesimamente, anzi per la sua crudeltate al doloroso fine, quale prima che di qui partiate far mi vederete, è condotta. Et s'egli queste cose di me creder non vi volesse, questo annello, il quale hebbi amorevolmente in dono da lui nel tempo a me felicissimo tanto gli darete, in segno che il vero direte.'

"Et così l'annello mi porse, il quale io medesimamente per ubidirla a voi Fabio lo porgo; et indi tutti i successi amorosi diportamenti tra voi et ella con gran spargimento di lagrime di parte in parte narromi. Le quali parole io vi giuro che non sanza mia gran doglia ascoltai; ma non hebbe ella a pena fornite queste parole, che non me ne avedendo, d'un pugnale ch'ella havea seco nel petto si diede; dicendo, 'Non piaccia a Dio, che sanza te Fabio mio, più lungamente in vita io mi serba.' Onde io di ciò avedendomi piangendo, et gridando per rimoverla dall'empio atto nello destro braccio la presi; et ella quantunque già quasi vicina fosse alla morte, pur con fiocca voce così mi disse. 'Deh caro fratello, se gli è vero che (come dimostrate d'havere) in voi pietà si ritrovi, pregovi che siate contento di non più homai molestarmi; ma come mi havete promesso ponetevi hor hora per Salerno in viaggio.' Vedendo io, che tale era il suo desiderio, et che più alla sua vita non poteva porgere aiuto, mi disposi in ogni modo di contentarla; et subitamente, non poco turbato nel cuore, per venir qui mi posi in camino; dove essendo hoggi arrivato ho inteso quello, che per dirvi il vero di doppia doglia mi tormenta; et mi affige."

Ma non potendo la infelice Urania, al dir di queste parole quasi più le lagrime ritenere si tacque. Fabio, il quale per lo innanzi, solamente del proprio danno si haveva affannato, et hora da quest'altro novello vedendosi sopragiunto, il quale conosceva tutto da lui solo procedere, perciò con un tale acerbo dolore, quale altro maggiore human cuore più possi sentire, verso il Prencipe volgendo la faccia così gli disse. "Deh pietoso, et giusto Signore, io vi supplico, et prego che vi piaccia dar opera, che la giusta vostra sentenza sopra di me sanza alcuno intervallo sia essequita; che se ciò prestamente farete io vi giuro Signore, che non meno sarete meco giudicato pietoso donandomi presta morte, di quello, che togliendomi la indegna vita possiate esser giusto tenuto; et ben vi dico che hoggimai io confesso esser degno di ogni crudelissima morte, poi che io infelice son stato cagione di morte a cui non meritava morire."

nearly a year, and now find myself reduced to this most wretched point. Since I find you so disposed to please me, the boon which I ask of you, for my final satisfaction, is this: that you be willing to go to Salerno and find there this cruel lover of mine, the one of whom I have just spoken. His name is Fabio. Tell him how Urania, who once loved him so passionately, and who did and said so much for him, has been led by him, indeed by his very cruelty, to such a miserable end (as you yourself will see before you leave here). If he does not wish to believe what you say, give him this ring, which he lovingly gave to me as a gift in my happiest time, as a sign that you speak the truth.'

"She gave me the ring, which I will now give to you, Fabio, in obedience to her. Then, shedding many tears, she recounted to me point by point all of the loving acts which had transpired between you two. I swear I felt no little sadness as I heard her words. But no sooner had she finished her account than she stabbed herself in the breast with a dagger that I did not realize she had, saying 'Let it not please God that I remain alive any longer without you, my Fabio!' Weeping and shouting, I seized her right arm once I was aware of what she was about, to try to prevent her from committing this impious act. As close as she was to death, she still managed to speak with a weak voice: 'O dear brother, if it is true, as indeed you have shown, that pity resides in you, I pray that it be your will to cease hindering me. Instead, set out right away for Salerno, as you have promised.' Seeing that this was her desire, and realizing that I could do nothing to save her life, I resolved at least to make her happy. With troubled heart I began my journey here immediately, and upon arriving today I heard of the present state of affairs, which to tell the truth has left me doubly grieved and afflicted."

As she said these words the unhappy Urania fell silent, scarcely able to restrain her tears. Fabio, who had previously been anxious only about his own fate, now saw that he alone was responsible for everything that had just been reported. Consumed by a pain as bitter as any a human heart could bear, he turned toward the Prince. "O merciful and just lord," he said, "I beseech and pray that you be willing to have your just sentence against me carried out without delay. If you will do this quickly I swear to you, my lord, that you will be judged no less merciful in giving me such a death, than righteous for taking my unworthy life. Let me tell you, at this point I confess that the cruelest sort of death is fitting for me, since in my wretchedness I have caused the death of one who did not deserve to die."

Era stato il Prencipe sino a quell'hora, come fuor di sè stesso; che non havendo per innanzi alcuna vera cagione potuta intendere, per la quale la Urania s'era nascosamente di Salerno partita; et perciò mosso da compassione sì per l'una, come per l'altra parte, quasi piangendo così a Fabio disse. "Deh Fabio, è possibile che da te sia la cagion proceduta, per la quale, la da noi tanto prezzata Urania ci ha come ciechi lasciati? Et per la quale poi, come questo giovine afferma esser vero, ella si sia a disperata morte condotta? Tu pur solevi esser (et questo io lo so certo) tutto benigno, tutto cortese, et gentile. Per la qual cosa come ti sia accaduto, che solamente verso di lei t'habbi discortese, et crudel dimostrato, non lo mi so imaginare. Et perciò io ti prego (perchè sommamente ho desiderato di saper la cagione, che così repentinamente a partirsi la mosse) che ti piaccia dirmi s'ella qualche cagione ti diede, per la quale essendoti verso lei incrudelito, ella poi così disperata ne gisse. Et non meno voglioti ancora pregare, che così questo tuo affanno, et cordoglio debbi temprare, che da te ogni sorte di disperatione fugga lontana; la quale come tu sai, non già con li generosi, et gagliardi; ma solamente con gli vili, et deboli animi s'accompagna; et perciò non temer tanto ti prego, che non sai ancora quello, che'l Cielo in un punto di soccorso ti potrebbe mandare; il che più grato assai mi sarebbe, che se un'altro stato presso questo mi vedesse aggiunto. Et Iddio lo sa, benchè dir no'l devrei, che quando questa crudele sentenza fu da me fatta (nella quale per tua, et mia sciagura hora ti veggio caduto) io credevo, anzi come cosa certa io tennevo, che quella trista Clorina non Menandro, ma te per marito addimandarmi dovesse. Ma la cosa è molto diversamente passata da quello, che io tra me divisato m'haveva; chè havendo io per suoi mali vezzi molto odio posto addosso a Menandro; et havendo te (perchè lo meriti) forse più caro di qualche altro giovine di questa città io m'havessi, pensavami te salvare, et lui sanza mia infamia da gli occhi levarmi.

"Onde io voglio credere che Dio per castigarmi et acciò che io mai più non ardisca di far sentenza se del tutto l'animo mio non si trova da ciascuna passion ignudo, et sincero, habbia permesso che questa mala ventura sul capo mi si riversci. Nè d'altra cosa mi doglio eccetto che di non esser solo io (che solo il merito) il castigato; et non tu meco che meritato non l'hai. Nè ti creder Fabio ti prego, che s'avien che tu muoia (che Iddio non lo permetta) per ben che io in vita rimanga, che minore habbia ad esser il mio, di quello, che fia il tuo castigo; imperciò che se d'una subita, et non meritata morte ti sarò stato procuratore, a me un perpetuo, et eterno discontento harrò procacciato."

"Signor mio benignissimo," rispose gli Fabio, "queste vostre parole cotanto dolci, benigne, et amorevoli sono, ch'elle mi faranno assai men dura la morte, di

Urania: The Story of a Young Woman's Love

Until this point the Prince had appeared to be a man overwhelmed by grief. Never before had he heard any true explanation as to why Urania had secretly fled Salerno. Now moved by compassion for both Urania and Fabio, he turned to the latter almost in tears. "O Fabio, is it possible that you were the reason our much esteemed Urania went away, leaving us blinded, as if in darkness? And were you also the cause that brought her to so desperate a death, as this young man affirms to be true? You used to be so gentle, so courtly and polite; and this I know with certainty. How it happened that you became discourteous and cruel towards her I cannot imagine. I have always greatly desired to know the reason why she left so abruptly; therefore I pray you, tell us if she gave you any cause for acting so cruelly towards her, so that she left in so desperate a state. Moreover, I would like you to temper your anxiety and distress, and banish any desperate thoughts. As you know, desperation is no friend to generous and vigorous souls, only to souls which are weak and vile; therefore I beg you not to be so fearful, for you do not know yet what heaven might send you by way of succor. I would be so very grateful if some new condition could be added to change the situation. Even though I should not say it, God knows that when I imposed this cruel sentence and brought you low, to your misfortune and mine, I believed (and indeed was quite certain) that the wicked Clorina would ask to marry not Menandro, but rather you. But things went very differently from what I had planned. Since I had come to hate Menandro so much for his wicked vices, and since I held you dearer perhaps than any other young man of this city (and you deserve no less), I thought I was saving you, and getting Menandro out of my sight, without risk to my honor.

"Thus I believe that God has permitted this evil to fall upon my head in order to punish me, so that I will never again dare to pass judgment on a person at a time when my soul is not completely sincere, and deprived of all passion. I am not sad for any reason save that I am not the only one being punished; for only I deserve it, and you, who do not, should not be punished along with me. Please do not believe, Fabio, that (God forbid!) should you die, my own punishment will be any less than yours, for as long as I live. For you I will be the provider of a quick, though undeserved death; whereas for myself I will be creating a state of endless, eternal misery."

"My most benign lord," answered Fabio, "your words are so kind, sweet, and loving that they will serve to render my death less harsh than I would like it to

quello vorei ch'ella mi paresse; imperciò che quando io considero haver disubedito, et ingiuriato così benigno, et amorevole Signore, al quale più tosto che un sol punto mancare io dovea mille volte morire, et havere offesa et oltraggiata donna, la quale per lo suo valore, et lo smisurato amor ch'ella mi portava, ma molto più per gl'infiniti favori da lei ricevuti era meritevole, che in tutti i miei giorni io la dovessi amare, et giovarle, parmi rispetto alla grande punitione ch'io merito, che una sol morte non possa esser bastevole a castigare un tanto mio errore. Gli è vero, amorevolissimo Signor mio, che mentre questa mia breve vita si starà meco, che brevissima in ogni modo ella ha da esser, che mai farò fine di lodare, et benedire la tanta vostra verso di me usata benignità. Et se di la mi sarà conceduto il poter per la salute vostra pregare, come di qui mentre questa poca vita mi dura non mi è negato il potervi continovamente lodare; credete certo Signor mio, che così caldamente porgerò la su per voi le mie preci, che assai meglio (ritrovandomi di là) de' segnali del mio vero amore v'accorgerete, che mentre io son stato di quà, di quelli di mia fede accorto vi sète.

"Ma poi che vi sarebbe in piacere di saper la cagione, per la quale la Urania già mia meco alterata da Salerno s'hebbe a partire; quantunque Signor mio, non molto io la sappia; pur quello, che io mi imagino che fosse, tutto lo vi dirò, benchè per dire il vero, io non hebbi animo di ingiuriarla giamai; anzi io havea fisso il pensiero, fin che io vivevo d'honorarla, et amarla sempre. Dico adunque Signor mio, che havendo io per un, benchè picciol, tempo assai amata la Urania, nel qual tempo ella giamai manco di usarmi tutte quelle cortesie et favori de quali, come sapete, ella ne era assai buona maestra; et io all'incontro per quel breve tempo assai buon cambio rendevale.

"Ma come suole avenire, non già perchè ella a fatto mi fosse uscita del cuore, mi posi ad amare questa maladetta Clorina, la quale impresa non così tosto incominciai a seguire, come la Urania se ne fu accorta; della qual cosa hor in carte, hora in voce spesse volte di cuore dolevasi meco; ma io il tutto con buon viso negavale. Ma essendo io per cagion del novello amore, assai meno osservatore del suo divenuto, et consequentemente essendo più rade, et meno ferventi divenute le visitationi mie verso lei, pensomi che non dandole forse il cuore di poter sofferir di veder per donna di minor pregio di lei esser in parte scemato quel grande amor, che io le soleva portare, così si disponesse partire. La onde, poi che una sua lettera m'hebbe mandata, la quale una tigre harrebbe mossa ad amarla, sanza altrimenti aspettar mia risposta, vestita da huomo da noi dileguossi.

"Et ben vi giuro Signore, che così fortemente per lo valore di quella lettera mi commossi nel cuore, che s'ella pur tanto s'indugiava a partire, che io havesse potuto, subito c'hebbi vedute le lettere sue rimediarli, che di modo ogni occasione

Urania: The Story of a Young Woman's Love

be. For when I consider that I have disobeyed and offended so kind and loving a lord (rather than wrong you in the slightest, I should have died a thousand deaths!); and when I consider that I have offended and insulted a woman who was worthy of being loved and supported by me for all the days of my life (and not just for her merits and for the boundless love she bore me, but even more for her infinite favors), it seems to me that one death is not enough to punish me for so great an error, and I deserve something worse. My most loving lord, I will truly never cease to praise and thank you for the kindness you have shown me, as long as my brief life shall last; and no matter what occurs, it will surely be brief. And if after death it will be granted to me to be able to pray for your health, just as it is not denied me to praise you continually in these fleeting moments while I still live, you may certainly believe, my lord, that I will offer you in heaven my most heartfelt prayers. Once I am up there, you will be much more clearly aware of the signs of my true love than you ever were of my faithfulness while I was here on earth.

"My lord, even though you would like to know the reason why Urania, who once was mine but then changed her feelings toward me, ever left Salerno, I do not really know. Nonetheless I will tell you what I imagine is the reason, although to tell the truth I never intended to hurt her. Indeed I had a firm notion to honor and love her for the rest of my life. So I say, my lord, that I loved Urania passionately for a time, regrettably brief, and during that time she never failed to show me those courtesies and favors of which she provided so fine an example, as you know. For my part, in that short period I paid her back quite respectably, in kind.

"But as it often happens, even though Urania had not gone out of my heart at all, I began to love this cursed Clorina, and no sooner had I begun this undertaking than Urania became aware of it. She often lamented about it to me both in writing and in speech; but I denied everything with a straight face. But interest in my new love had caused me to pay less attention to Urania, and as a consequence my visits to her became rarer and less heartfelt. I believe that she decided to leave perhaps because she could not bear to see the great love I had felt for her diminished on account of a woman who was less excellent than she. Therefore, after she had sent me a letter that would have moved a wild beast to love her, she dressed herself as a man and disappeared without awaiting any response from me.

"But I swear to you, my lord, so moved was my heart by the power of that letter that had she delayed her departure, I would have had the opportunity to make things right as soon as I had seen her words. I would have taken away every

di più partirsi levata le harrei, che mai più di me non harrebbe havuta cagion di dolersi. Ma ahimè misero infelice, che più mi può al presente alcun mio buon volere giovare, poi ch'ella meschina assai più di me fedele, non potendo più sanza lo amor mio vivere, si ha data la morte? Et io di lei traditore, le ne ho dato cagione? Adunque necessario è che io muoia; et se molto tarderà la giustizia nel darmi quella morte alla quale io fui sententiato da Vostra Eccellenza non sarà tarda la mia mano nel darmi quella convenevole, della quale la mia impietà verso la infelice Urania usata, meritevol mi ha fatto."

Vedendo la Urania che'l suo Fabio cotanto amaramente del suo acerbo caso dolevasi, non potendo più sofferire ch'egli più s'affliggesse, gettato a terra quel vil capellaccio, et correndo ad abbracciarlo così con dolcissimi accenti gli disse. "Ecco Fabio mio desideratissimo, come quella amata tua Urania, che tu piangi per morta, non è morta, ma vive; nè ancora solamente pur vive, ma con la sua vita ha insieme salvata la tua! Nè ti creder Fabio mio dolcissimo, che per null'altra cagione m'habbino i Cieli, mal grado di me medesima da mille morti fuggendomi, in vita serbata; se non acciò che questa mia humile vita giovasse per salvar la tua sopra ogn'altra valorosa, et gentile; et acciò che la sincera, et inviolabil mia fede manifesta si ti facesse."

Et come così hebbe detto, levando le braccia dal collo a lui, che fuor di sè medesimo, et quasi come morto si stava; così verso il Prencipe rivolse il suo dire. "Eccellentissimo Signore, non dubito, quando a una parte considero, che vi dovete maravigliare, come sia stato tanto ardire in donzella, che bastevole fosse a tanto chiuder gli occhi alla ragione, che ella le consentissi, che vestita di huomo della propria casa partendosi, per diverse parti del mondo errando n'andasse; et che, dopo che isconosciuta ritornando, et dinanzi al suo proprio Signore appresentatasi, non habbia havuto rispetto di abbracciare alla sua presenza colui, il quale ella per suo idolo nel suo cuor si ha formato. Ma quando all'altra parte io considero, non dubito poi che cotale vostra maraviglia non habbia tosto a mancare; che sapendo (come so che sapete) quanto possono ne' cuori humani le forze d'Amore, son sicurissima che non che accusata nè ripresa di cotale atto, ma da Vostra Eccellenza ne sarò difesa, et lodata.

"Creggiomi Signor mio, che habbiate gia conosciuto, che io sono la Urania, et che quella io sono, che da estrema disperation tratta, parendomi che quanto io meritava, o forse per dir meglio, quanto era il mio desiderio, non fosse dal mio dolcissimo Fabio amata, con fermo proposito di non più mai riveder queste parti di qui mi hebbi a levare. Ma come ciò sia accaduto non lo so, ma ben crederò io sempre, che voler divino sia stato, poi che nello estremo bisogno di salvar la vita

URANIA: THE STORY OF A YOUNG WOMAN'S LOVE

reason for her to leave, and never more would she have suffered on my account. But alas, I am an unhappy wretch! Of what use is all my good will now, since that the poor woman, far more faithful than I and unable to go on living without my love, has killed herself? And did I not give her a good reason, having betrayed her? Thus it is necessary that I die, and if justice delays too long in giving me that death to which I was sentenced by Your Excellency, my hand will not wait in giving me another that is most fitting, given my cruelty towards the unhappy Urania."

When Urania saw her Fabio bemoaning his miserable fate in such a bitter fashion, she could no longer bear to witness such self-torment. Throwing her vile hat on the floor, she ran to embrace him. "Look, my most beloved Fabio!" she said in her sweetest voice. "Your Urania, whom you love so much and mourn as dead, is not dead; she lives! And not only does she live, but she has saved your life along with her own. O my sweetest Fabio, you must believe that the heavens kept me alive and preserved me from a thousand deaths, despite my own efforts, for no other reason than to permit that my humble life could serve to save yours, more noble and valorous than any other; and also to allow me to demonstrate to you my sincere and undying faith."

When she had said this, she removed her arms from his neck. Fabio was in such shock that he seemed almost a dead man. Urania turned to the Prince. "Most excellent lord, when I first think about it, I do not doubt that you must be amazed that a maid could have so dared to close her eyes to reason that she left her home dressed as a man, in order to wander through the various parts of the world; and then, having returned unrecognized, she would dare appear before her own lord and have the nerve to embrace the man whom she has made an idol in her heart. But on the other hand, when I consider further, I imagine that your amazement must not be so very great, for you know (and I know well that you know) what the power of Love is capable of in human hearts. Therefore I am quite certain that Your Excellency will neither blame nor reproach me for such an act, but rather will defend me, and give me praise.

"My lord, I think you have already understood that I myself am Urania; and that I am the woman who, driven by desperation, came to believe I was not loved by my sweet Fabio as much as I deserved, or to put it better perhaps, as much I wished. I am the one who departed from this place with the firm resolution never to see it again. How it happened I do not know, but I will always believe that it was through divine will that I found myself here at an hour of extreme need, in

a colui, la cui vita a reviver nova vita m'invita, a tempo mi son ritrovata. Onde Signor mio dico che se la legge fatta per Vostra Eccellenza della liberatione di Fabio, può così a me, come all'altre donzelle harrebbe potuto giovare, che non pure l'ho campato da morte, ma ancor ch'io l'ho fatto mio posso dire, havendo io, come ho, non un solo, ma mille, et più basci dalla Femina Salvatica liberamente ottenuti; come quanti si ritrovano qui presenti ponno per me giustificare." Alle cui parole tutti confirmarono, con somma allegrezza esser vero.

Il Prencipe, che da cotali variati accidenti era quasi fuori di sè medesimo uscito, quando, dopo alquanto che fu stato sopra di sè, hebbe il primo suo valore ricuperato, di tanta allegrezza si sentì riempire il cuore in un punto, che lasciando ogni rispetto da un canto, amorevolmente abbraccio la Urania, e così le disse. "Benedetta sei tu Urania, et benedetto lo strale, che tanto a dentro per Fabio ti punse il cuore; benedetta la fedelissima tua perseveranza, et benedetti siano tutti gli stratij, disagi, pene, et tormenti, che per lui hai sofferti, poi che per lo valor di quelli doveva manifestarsi un cotanto utile, et lodevole effetto, che tutto il tribolato Salerno ritornerà più che mai fosse allegro, et gioioso, bene è giusta cosa amantissima Urania, che'l tuo tanto diletto Fabio ti sia libero restituito; et giustissima cosa è poi ancora, ch'egli come tuo riscatto di sè medesimo a te faccia amorevolissimo dono."

Et così detto prese Fabio per l'un de' bracci, il quale ancora attonito, et fuori di sè sanza alcuna cosa dire si stava, et avicinatolo bene alla Urania fece sì, che ritornando in sè stesso, et strettamente abbracciandola, tante, et così amorevoli, et dolci parole le disse, che troppo gran carico sarebbe a chi volesse s'una, in una tutte narrarle. Ma tra tutti gli altri, che ammirati, di tal novità si trovavano; la bella Emilia era quella, che tanto estremamente in quel punto si ritrovava confusa, che non sapeva ella stessa se veghiando sognava, o se dormendo, quello che vedeva, et udiva fosse vero. Ma la cortese Urania, che del suo grande horrore già s'era accorta, et di ciò dolendolene assai deliberò di volere in quel punto a lei porgere aiuto, et sè medesima di quel sospetto liberare; nel qual sarebbe il suo Fabio con tutti gli altri caduto quando in quella credenza gli havesse lasciati, che quel sì bel giovine, con lo quale era venuta in Salerno fosse huomo, et non donna come era. Et perciò dopo che alle molte, grate, et dolci accoglienze ch'ella a Fabio, et che egli a lei fece hebbe pur dato fine; et che con accorto, et bellissimo modo le convenevoli gratie al cortesissimo Prencipe hebbe rendute, in cotal guisa novellamente soggiunse.

"Nobilissimo Signore, et tu mio gentil Fabio, poi che la Fortuna meco riconciliata mi ha condotta, et riposta in loco dove giamai più sperava di ricondurmi,

URANIA: THE STORY OF A YOUNG WOMAN'S LOVE

time to save the life of this man, whose survival inspires me to live anew. Therefore, my lord, if the decree pronounced by Your Excellency regarding the liberation of Fabio applies to me, just as it would have applied to the other maidens, then not only have I saved him from death, but I may also say that I have made him mine; for I have quite freely received not only one, but a thousand or more kisses from the Wild Woman, as all those present here can confirm." At these words everyone did very joyfully pronounce this to be true.

When the Prince, who had been almost dazed by these various events, recovered his wits again, he felt his heart so suddenly full of emotion that he set aside his princely dignity and gave Urania a loving embrace. "Blessed are you, Urania," he said, "and blessed is the Cupid's dart that so deeply pierced your heart, and made you love Fabio. Blessed is your most dogged perseverance, and also all the pains, sufferings, discomforts, and torments that you have undergone for him.[66] Out of these tribulations has come a useful and marvelous result, so that long-suffering Salerno can become happier and more joyful than she has ever been. It certainly is right, most loving Urania, that your beloved Fabio be set free and restored to you, and it is even more right that he give himself to you as a recompense."

So saying, he took the still dazed Fabio by the arm and, without saying anything more, led him to Urania and got him to return to his senses. Then Fabio held her close and said so many sweet and loving words to her that it would be too great a task to recount each one. But among the many people who stood there marveling at these strange events, the lovely Emilia was the one who found herself so confused that she could not tell if she was dreaming while awake, or else hearing and seeing things that were true while asleep. But the kindly Urania was aware of how upset she was, and decided at this moment to come to her assistance. She also needed to free herself of the suspicion that her Fabio and all the others would have if she were to leave them with the impression that the young person who had accompanied her to Salerno was a man, and not the woman she actually was. Therefore once she and Fabio had concluded their sweet and pleasant welcomings, and once she had rendered proper thanks to the most courtly Prince, she spoke up once again.

"Most noble lord, and my gentle Fabio," she said, "now that Fortune has reconciled herself to me and brought me back to a place which I had never hoped

---

[66] This passage contains clear echoes of Petrarch's sonnet 61 ("Benedetto sia 'l giorno, e 'l mese, et l'anno").

voglio per esser cosa molto necessaria, et opportuna narrar sucintamente qual fosse il mio viaggio quando di qui feci partita, acciochè insieme venghi a manifestarvi quale sia la compagnia, con la quale io mi son qui ricondotta; dico adunque, che poi c'hebbi quella lettera nelle mani del mio servo consegnata, la qual tu Fabio mio hai confessato di haver ricevuta, subito vestita da huomo, et sola uscì di Salerno, con intentione di mai più in vita mia ritornare a riveder queste parti; et di non mai in verun loco fermarmi, ma sempre errando per tutto il mondo discorrere. Et con tal deliberatione come disperata per Napoli sanza arrestarmi punto passando, feci il simigliante di terra, in terra, sin che quasi ne i confini della bella Toscana pervenni, dove tanto un giorno dalla acerbissima passione mi lasciai vincere, che disperata del tutto, mi disposi di volermi lasciar di fame morire.

"Et come il mio destino permesse, in una grande, et deserta campagna entrai, al fine della quale non giunsi, che per dire il vero spaventata dalla horribilità di quella morte che già parevami dinanzi da gli occhi scolpita vedermi, mi pentì di più voler così miserabilmente la mia vita finire, quantunque assai poco grata l'havesse; et per tal cagione assai più che dianzi non facevo affrettando i passi, come a Dio piacque col finir del giorno parimente al fine della lunga campagna mi avidi esser giunta; et insieme al fine di quella una assai commoda hosteria vi trovai. Perchè non picciolo conforto pigliando; che pensando certo di dovermi ritrovar in tal loco (come suol'esser de gli hostieri costume) più che volontieri raccolta, mi ritrovai del creder mio molto tosto ingannata; imperciò che all'uscio dell'hosteria, ch'era chiuso picchiando, et chiedendoli alloggiamento, mi fu data tanto contraria risposta da quel ch'io credevo, che la memoria di così amara risposta mi fa ancora il sangue agghiacciar nelle vene. Perchè havendo come io dissi picchiata la porta, et da alloggiar dimandato, mi fu dall'hoste risposto, che più non si poteva in quel loco per alcun modo verun'altro alloggiarsi, per haver una nobilissima giovane, gentildonna fiorentina, et vidua per sè, et per la sua compagnia tutti gli alloggiamenti ingombrati; la qual gentildonna per sodisfar alcuni suoi voti n'andava a Loretto.

"Onde io udendo una cotal nemica risposta, diffidandomi di più mai poter cosa ritrovare, che giovar mi potesse, da tanto estremo affanno mi si strinse il cuore, che sanza dir parola giù del cavallo in terra cadei tramortita, et credo che così morta vi sarrei. Imperciò che quel cane hostieri più non si curava in tanto mio bisogno porgermi aiuto di quello, che harrebbe fatto quando io fosse stata uno animal brutto. Ma essendo andata la nova di così strano accidente alla gentil Signora, che Emilia si chiama, perchè è benigna in estremo, assai tosto dove io simile a morta in terra giacea, si condusse. Et vedendo come ciascuno abbandonata

Urania: The Story of a Young Woman's Love

to visit again, I think it is very necessary and proper that I recount precisely the details of my voyage since I left here, so that I can reveal to you who has accompanied me during my return. I say therefore, that once I had placed the letter in the hands of my servant, the letter that you, Fabio, said you received, I immediately left Salerno alone and dressed as a man, with the intention of never returning to see this area again. I also planned never to stop in a single place, but to wander without ceasing through the whole world. Following this plan I passed through Naples in a desperate state without stopping at all, and then did the same in one land after the other until one day, as I approached the border of lovely Tuscany. There I let my bitter emotions overcome me, and I became so completely desperate that I decided to let myself die of starvation.

"As my destiny willed, I began crossing a wide, deserted region. But before I could reach the end of it I became so truly terrified by the prospect of this horrible death, a death I seemed to see already graven before my eyes, that I regretted my desire to end my life so miserably, no matter how unpleasant it had become. On this account I picked up my pace, going more swiftly than before, and as it pleased God I saw that I had reached the end of the long stretch of countryside just as the day was ending; and in that place I found a very comfortable inn. I took no small comfort in this, for I was certain I would be more than gladly received there (one expects this sort of behavior from innkeepers). But I had deceived myself; for when I knocked at the door and asked for lodging I was given a response completely contrary to what I had hoped, and the memory of this harsh answer still makes my blood freeze in my veins. For after I had knocked and asked for lodging the innkeeper told me no more lodgers could be accepted because all of the rooms had been taken by a young noblewoman of high degree, a Florentine widow, along with her entourage. He said this noblewoman was going to Loreto to fulfill her vows.

"When I heard this unfriendly response, I doubted I would ever find any other place where I could receive help. My heart was so overcome by distress that I fell off my horse in a swoon, without a word. And I believe I might have died there, since that dog of an innkeeper did not offer me even the kind of assistance that he would have given a brute beast. But the news of this odd incident had reached the gentlewoman, whose name was Emilia; and since she is a very compassionate person, she came quickly over to where I was lying as if dead. Seeing that I had been

m'havea, quel suo gentilissimo cuore verso di me le si mosse a pietade; nè essendole honore, perchè huomo mi giudicava, il pormi ella medesima le mani addosso, fece perciò, che una sua assai attempata cameriera con acqua fresca, et altri rimedij gli smarriti miei spiriti dopo gran pezza ritornomi.

"Et poi che la cortese Signora ritornata in assai buon esser mi vide prima che di là si partisse chiamati alquanti suoi servi, sotto pena della sua disgratia gl'impose, che dovessero per quella notte haver di me buona cura. Ma io volendo più tosto morire, che dalle mani di quella vil gentaglia vedermi pur e' panni toccare, parvemi perciò il meglio di dovermi quale io era con questa gentil Signora scoprire; et così supplicatola che più vicina mi si facesse, che io era Donna; et in gran parte la conditione mia le scopersi. La qual cosa ella intendendo, et certificatasi quanto io diceva esser vero, tanto dimostrò havermi grata, che a pena se una sua carnal sorella le si fosse alhor presentata non credo che maggior dimostrationi di cortesia et amorevolezza, di quello che meco fece, havesse seco potuto fare; imperciò che subitamente presami ella medesima per l'un de' bracci, et la sua cameriera per l'altro amorevolmente nella camera per lei preparata mi condussero, et sopra il suo letto mi corricorono; dove volle la cortese Signora, che ogni mio esser le raccontasse. Et vi giuro che così per compassione delle mie miserie meco la vidi piangere, come se a lei parte de' miei danni pervenuti fossero; et poi c'hebbi fornito di dire, con tanta amorevolezza, et ornato parlar racconfortommi, che in gran parte l'acerbissima passione m'hebbe a scemare; chè in fine non giova d'altro tempo tanto lo amico, come fa quando la disperatione, del lume della ragione ci ha privi; et indi soggiunse dicendo, che per amorevole sorella mi accettava, et che mai acconsentir non voleva, che io più da lei mi partisse; et tante cortesi et amorevoli proferte mi fece, che chi tutte raccontar le volesse, troppo lungo sarebbe a dirlo.

"Ma vedendo poi come questo mio habito di huomo sanza alcuno utile, gran vergogna arrecar le poteva mi pregò dolcemente che io fosse contenta de gli habiti feminili, più a me convenevoli rivestirmi, che così facendo sarei stata a me di maggior commodo, et a lei di maggior contento cagione. Onde io conoscendo quanto le ero obligata, et come la sua dimanda era giusta, da quell'hora in dietro ogni mia operatione ad ogni suo piacer dedicai. Et per conchiuderla, seco me ne andai honorevolmente trattata a Loretto; et dopo a Firenze seco ancora mi ricondussi; dove nè più, nè men d'ella medesima da ciascuno honorata, et ben veduta mi ritrovavo.

"Ma perchè quella piaga, Fabio mio, qual per te Amore primieramente mi fece, era trapassata sino alle radici del cuore, per la qual cosa incurabile era già fatta, perciò vie più sempre in me il suo incendio crescendo, nè havendo tanto

abandoned by everyone, her kind heart was moved to pity for me. As she thought me a man, she felt it would be dishonorable to touch me herself, so she told her elderly serving woman to revive my diminished spirits with cool water and other remedies.

"When the courteous lady saw that I was myself again, she called several of her servants while still in my presence, and ordered that they take good care of me that night if they wished to avoid suffering her wrath. However, since I would rather have died than let those ignoble commoners see me or even touch my clothing, I decided it was better that I reveal who I was to the gentle lady. Asking her to come close to me, I told her that I was a woman, and revealed much of my situation to her. When she had heard this, and verified it to be true, she showed herself to be so kindly disposed to me that I do not believe she could have shown more courtesy or affection to a sister of her own flesh and blood than she did to me. She fondly took me by one arm, the old serving woman took the other, and they led me into the room that had been prepared for the noblewoman herself, where they laid me on her bed. At that point the gentle lady asked me to tell her my whole story, and I swear to you that I saw her weep as much for the sufferings I had undergone as she would have had she experienced part of them herself. When I had told her everything, she comforted me with such affection and such dignified words that I felt much of my bitter sadness ebb away; and indeed we never need a friend more than when desperation has deprived us of the light of reason. She told me she would accept me as her loving sister, and that she would never be willing to let me leave her. In fact, it would take too long to recount the many kindnesses and courtesies she offered me.

"But seeing that my man's clothing might be a hindrance to her, and might even bring shame upon her, she sweetly asked me if I would be willing to dress as a woman, as was more appropriate; for if I did this, I would be more comfortable, and she would be happier. Recognizing how obliged I was to her, and how proper was her request to me, from that moment on I dedicated all my efforts to pleasing her; and to this end I went to Loreto with her as an honored guest. After that I returned to Florence with her, where I was as well received and honored as she was.

"But the wound which Love had first made in my heart for you, my Fabio, had passed to the very depths, and thus had become quite incurable, burning ever more intensely within me. Neither distance from you, nor my exposure to the

potere lo starti lontana, et il continovo udire alla castissima lingua della mia Signora Emilia molto vituperosamente dannare chiunque si lascia accendere di qualunque sorte di insano foco d'Amore; chè fosse bastevole almen a por freno a quello ardentissimo desiderio, che dì, et notte di rivedere te mio caro Fabio struggevami, feci deliberatione al fine non potendo più con alcuna ragione ostare al gran desiderio, che di rivederti il cuore mi ardeva, di ritornarmi pur vestita da huomo in Salerno, ben con fermo proponimento come una sol volta ti havesse veduto, di ritornarmene in dietro.

"Fatta c'hebbi adunque alla Signora Emilia questa mia deliberation manifesta, udì farmi da lei una molto acra, et ragionevole riprensione. Ma vedendo poi come sue riprensioni, o persuasioni niente meco valevano; et che io pur sempre più mi stabilivo di ritornarmi a vedere il mio caro Fabio, come m'hebbe assai detto, et ridetto, mi soggiunse che poi che io ero così sciocca, ch'io havevo deliberato di ritornare a cercar la cagion della mia morte, ch'ella per lo amor grande che mi portava non harrebbe sofferto mai che sanza lei questo mio viaggio io facessi; perchè ella ritrovandosi meco, mi sarebbe freno alla vita; et all'honore. Assai io feci, et dissi, acciò che si contentasse di rimanere, ma in fine niente il mio dire mi valse, ch'ella pur al tutto meco vestita da huomo volle venire. Et così havendo un cotale ordine fermato tra noi, molto tosto di honorevoli panni vestitesi, et sopra due buoni roncini cavalcando, in camino ambedue, et da un solo fidato servo accompagnate si ponessimo. Et hoggi come a Dio ha piacciuto tanto ad hora, per bel punto qui in Salerno giungessimo, che a far la miglior opera, che mai più alcuno nel mondo facesse ci è stata bastevole.

"Hor dunque, Signor mio amorevolissimo, et tu sopra ogn'altra cosa da me amato Fabio, dovete sapere, che questa, che è meco, et che forse sia un giovine havete giudicato è donna come sono io, la quale tanto accostumata ne i gesti; et di valoroso, et gentil animo praticandola vi si farà conoscere, come bella mirandola la potete vedere."

La gentil Emilia, quantunque strana cosa le paresse il ritrovarsi al parer suo quasi come dalla Urania aggabata, pur conoscendo che alle cose passate alcun rimedio non ci era; et vedendo quanto ingeniosamente ella le haveva ogni vergogna levata, anzi tanto havea con bel ordine accomodato il suo dire che quello, che udendone il vero ogn'uno le harrebbe attribuito a vergogna in somma lode le riusciva, et nome di pietosa le ne acquistava. Perciò perchè era assai accorta non potendo far altro, si dispose d'accommodarsi col tempo; et fattasi al Prencipe più vicina gran riverenza gli fece. Ma egli, che come altre volte si ha detto, cortesissimo era, con grande amorevolezza abbracciandola le disse; "Siate, valorosissima

chaste words of my lady Emilia, who kept on harshly berating anyone who gave in to the insane flames of Love in any of its forms, were enough to impede my most ardent desire to see you again; and this desire consumed me day and night, my dear Fabio. Finally I made up my mind that I could no longer employ rational arguments to block this great desire to see you again, and decided to return to Salerno dressed as a man. However, it was also my firm intention to make my way back to Florence after having seen you but a single time.

"When I made this plan known to Lady Emilia, I heard her reproach me in quite harsh and rational terms. But soon she saw that neither her reproaches nor her persuasive arguments had any effect on me, and that I was ever more intent on going back to see my dear Fabio. When she had done with haranguing me time and again, she said that if I was so foolish that I had decided to return to seek the cause of my death, then she would never permit me to make this journey alone, on account of the great love she bore me. She also said her presence would help to preserve my honor and my life. I said and did all I could to get her to agree to stay home, but in the end nothing I said worked, for she still wished to come with me dressed as a man. So we agreed on this, and shortly thereafter donned very proper men's clothing and set out on our journey together on a pair of fine horses, accompanied by only a single faithful servant. As it has pleased God, we arrived in Salerno today with just enough time to accomplish as worthy a deed as anyone in the world has done.

"And now my most kind lord, and beloved Fabio, you must both be informed that this person with me is a woman just as I am, even though you have imagined she was a young man. When you have gotten to know her you will find her manners genteel and her spirit strong and compassionate, just as you can already tell that she is lovely by looking at her."

Even though the noble Emilia thought it strange to hear Urania describe her in terms she found practically mocking, she realized nothing could be done to change past events. She saw moreover how cleverly Urania had removed all sense of impropriety from her actions; indeed Urania had phrased her speech in such a way that all of Emilia's deeds now seemed worthy of the highest praise, even though they would have seemed shameful to anyone who knew the truth. Because of Urania, Emilia had now acquired a reputation for compassion. She was wise and knew nothing could be done about it, so she resolved to make the best of the situation. Going up to the Prince, she showed him all due reverence; but he, who as I have often said was most gracious, embraced her with great affection.

giovane, per mille volte la ben venuta; et Iddio sia quello, che vi meriti il tanto beneficio che tutti noi habbiamo da voi ricevuto serbando in vita costei, la quale a noi doveva arrecar vita, et contento; chè io per me confesso non valer tanto, che a gran parte io potessi a tanto debito sodisfare." Et a queste così cortesi parole del Prencipe, vi raggiunse con altretante, et più delle sue cortesi et amorevolissime, Fabio; a i quali amendue la gentile Emila, con grato et accorto dire gratie convenevoli rese.

Et il Prencipe, ch'altro non desiderava, che di veder compiuta allegrezza nella sua corte, voltatosi a Fabio così disse. "Poi che questa sì savia giovane è sanza marito, io desidererei grandemente che qui in Salerno maritandosi con essi noi sempre si rimanesse; et sarebbe buono, quando a lei fosse in piacere, il che a me di sommo contento sarebbe, che Hortensio tuo fratello, il quale è giovine assai vago et gentile, la si pigliasse per moglie. Et così ella et Urania, di fedelissime compagne che sin hora son state, amantissime cognate viverebbono sempre."

Piacque sommamente a Fabio questo aviso del Prencipe; et perciò volle intender da lei se di ciò volea contentarsi. Et ella, che di meglio alhora non vedeva di poter fare, rispose che pur che dalla amata sua Urania scompagnata non fosse, harrebbe fatto tutto quello che al Prencipe, et a lui fosse in piacere. Et così tra cotali parole sopragiunsero tutti gli parenti di Fabio, da uno infinito numero d'altri gentilhuomini accompagnati, a i quali era la buona novella della liberatione sua pervenuta a gli orecchi. Nè a pena questi comparsero, che dalla madre della Urania, et da molti suoi parenti furono sopragiunti, i quali come intesero, che la loro parente era stata quella, che Fabio havea liberato da morte, con somma allegrezza per rivederla, et seco rallegrarsi vi concorsero tutti. Hor se quivi sì dall'una, qual dall'altra parte de gli abbracciamenti, et delle amorevoli accoglienze furono fatte, non è chi raccontar lo potesse a pieno.

Ma facendosi homai sera, il cortese Prencipe per dimostrar quanto delle loro allegrezze egli medesimamente si rallegrava, volle in quella sera, che seco cenassero tutti; et di più ordinò che le nozze di tutti nel suo palagio, et a spese sue si facessero. Et così facendosi da casa sua alcune sue assai belle vesti, et gioie portar la Urania per sè stessa, et per la bella Emilia, ambe due da donna si rivestirono, et con infinito contento l'una, et l'altra quella sera passarono. Imperciò che havendo la Emilia veduto il giovine Hortensio fratello di Fabio, et perchè era assai bello, essendole sommamente piacciuto, tanto di dovere haver così bello et leggiadro marito era allegra, che quasi non capiva in sè stessa.

Ma volendo il buon Prencipe raddoppiare in sè, et ne gli altri il piacere, chiamò il seguente mattino quel vecchio della Duchessa consigliero, il quale la vaga

Urania: The Story of a Young Woman's Love

"May you be a thousand times welcome here, most worthy young lady," he said. "May God reward you for the great service you have done us in saving the life of that young woman, who was so important to us as a source of vitality and well-being. For my part, I do not believe I am worthy enough to pay our debt to you in any sufficient way." To the Prince's courteous words Fabio added as many or more that were even more courteous and fond, and the kind Emilia gave grateful and eloquent thanks to both of them.

The Prince, who desired nothing more than to see consummate joy in his court, turned to Fabio: "Since this wise young woman is without a husband, I would very much like her to marry here in Salerno and stay with us always. If she is agreeable, it would be a good thing, and quite pleasing to me, if your brother Hortensio were to take her as his wife, for he is a very handsome and noble young man. In this way she and Urania, who have been most faithful companions up to now, will ever live together as most loving sisters-in-law."

The Prince's recommendation was highly pleasing to Fabio, so he wanted to know if Emilia would willingly accede to it. She, who could not think of any better course of action, answered that she would do anything the Prince and Fabio wanted, provided that she would not be separated from her beloved Urania. As she was saying this all of Fabio's relatives appeared, accompanied by a great many other gentlemen; for the good news of Fabio's salvation had reached them. And no sooner had all these arrived, than Urania's mother and many of her relatives joined them. They had heard how their own relative had been the one to rescue Fabio from death, and thus all came running in a state of great happiness to rejoice with her. No one could ever adequately describe all of the embraces and fond greetings that were exchanged at this moment.

By now evening was coming on, and the Prince, in order to demonstrate how much he himself rejoiced to see everyone so happy, wished that they all join him in a feast. He also decreed that the weddings would take place in his palace, and at his own expense. Urania had some beautiful clothes and jewels brought from her household for herself and Emilia, and when both had dressed themselves as women once more, they spent that evening in a state of infinite contentment. Emilia had seen the young Hortensio, Fabio's brother, and finding him quite good-looking and pleasing, she could scarcely contain herself for joy at the thought of having so handsome and charming a husband.

Now the Prince wanted to heighten even further his own pleasure and that of the others, so the next morning he summoned the Duchess's old counselor, the

ghirlanda delle rose, di tanto mal cagione, gli haveva donata; et dissegli; "Padre mio, gli passati travagli m'hanno impedito che io non ho potuto sino a quest'hora farvi veder quello, che io sommamente desiderava, cioè il degno, et nobil soggetto, al quale ho destinata la bella ghirlanda, che donata m'havete. Ma hora che con lo aiuto di chi l'ha potuto fare, le cose sono riuscite a miglior termine assai di quello, che io da me medesimo harrei saputo desiderare, andiamo felicemente, et allegri a dar fine al giustissimo mio desiderio."

Et havendo ciò detto, chiamò seco il pittore, Fabio, et altri gentilhuomini assai; et facendo portar seco la bella ghirlanda, alla casa della savia damigella si condusse, la quale era in que' giorni da Napoli ritornata; et ritrovando il Padre di lei su l'uscio, il quale ancora non era uscito di casa, gli richiese egli medesimo la sua figliuola per moglie; la qual cosa quanto paresse nova, et maravigliosa a quel Conte da udire non è chi dir lo potesse. Onde con un smisurato piacere, et con riverenza rispose al suo Signore, che essendo egli, con quanto possedeva, di sua Eccellenza, poteva del tutto a suo modo disporre; et a queste molte altre honorevoli parole vi aggiunse. Il che udendo il Prencipe, con grande amorevolezza come padre abbracciandolo, seco colà dove era la savia damigella si condusero; alla qual giunto, dimandò il Prencipe s'ella si contentava d'esser sua sposa; et ella d'infinita gioia ripiena rispose sè esser parata a dover far tutto quello che al suo Signor fosse in piacere. Ond'egli, ch'altra risposta non aspettava abbracciandola strettamente, et basciandola la bella ghirlanda su'l capo le pose dicendo: "Et io, mia savia, et amantissima damigella, per diletta sposa vi accetto."

Et così detto verso il vecchio consiglieri rivolgendosi, disse. "Parvi, padre mio honorato, che'l mio giudicio nello eleggermi bella, et valorosa sposa sia stato tale che alcuno non è, il quale opporre mi possa? Hovvi mo' fatto vedere come il soggetto, al quale io ho donata la vaga ghirlanda a maraviglia è degno, et pregiato? Dite quello che ve ne pare adunque, vi prego."

Il buon vecchio a cui con verità pareva, che tanto alla sua bellissima Signora uguagliar si potesse costei, come le stelle alla luna, o come la luna al sole si ponno. Perciò, non meno d'amaro sdegno, che di maraviglia ritrovandosi a un punto pieno, avenga che'l tutto dissimulasse, così gli rispose. "Signor mio, a dire il vero, io non credo che chi tutto 'l mondo intorno, intorno cercasse un'altro simile a voi in giudicio potesse ritrovare. Nè meno so conoscere alcuno, che di cotale vostro giudicio opporvi potesse. Et perciò io prego il Signor nostro Iddio, che tanto a questo vostro aventuroso congiungimento doni felicità, et contento, quanto a punto il mio cuor vi desidera."

one who had given him the lovely rose garland that had been the cause of so much mischief. "Good father," he said to him, "our recent trials have kept me from doing something I greatly desired to do, that is, reveal to you the worthy and noble recipient upon whom I will bestow the lovely garland that you gave me. But now that things have been resolved far more happily than I myself ever hoped, with the aid of the one person who could bring about such a resolution, let us go forth in joy and contentment, to fulfill this desire of mine in a most proper fashion."

Having said this, he called into his presence the painter, Fabio, and many other gentlemen. Then, having the garland fetched forth as well, he betook himself to the house of the wise maiden, who had just returned from Naples. There he found her father, who had not yet left the house, in the doorway; right then and there the Prince asked him personally for his daughter's hand in marriage. It would be impossible to describe how strange and marvelous this act seemed to the count! With the greatest pleasure and with a bow he answered his lord, saying that he and everything he possessed belonged to His Excellency, and he could dispose of all these things as he wished; he said many other honorable things besides. Hearing this, the Prince embraced him with great affection, as if he were his father; then the two of them went straight to the wise maiden. When they found her, the Prince asked if she was content to have him as her husband; whereupon she, transported by joy, said she was prepared to do whatever her lord wished. The Prince did not expect any other answer. Holding her tightly in his arms and kissing her, he placed the lovely garland on her head. "And I accept you, O wise and most loving maid, as my beloved bride," he told her.

The Prince turned toward the old counselor. "Does it not seem to you, my honored father," he said, "that I have judged so well in choosing a beautiful and talented bride that no one could possibly object to my choice? Have I not shown you now that the person to whom I have given the lovely garland is marvellously worthy and estimable? Please speak openly, and say whatever you wish."

In truth it seemed to the old man that this maid could compare to his most lovely mistress only as the stars compared to the moon, or the moon to the sun; and therefore he found himself full of both bitter disdain and wonder all at once, even though he kept it hidden. "My lord," he answered, "to tell the truth, I do not think that one could search the world over and find someone who is as able a judge as you; nor could one find anyone who could object to your judgment. Therefore I pray to the Lord our God that He bestow as much happiness and contentment on this fortunate union as I desire for you in my heart."

Et poi che così hebbe detto accennò il pittore, et insieme levatisi di quello a loro odiosissimo loco sanza far motto ad alcuno, di Salerno partirono. Ma quando si ritrovorono in parte dove potevano sanza rispetto il loro ferissimo sdegno sfocare, in tante, et così dishonorevoli parole, in vituperio di quel buon Prencipe le loro lingue sciolsero, che ne sarebbe venuto pietade a chiunque uditi gli havesse; et quel povero Prencipe di poco giudicio, di animo vile, et d'ingratitudine sanza alcuna ragione accusavano; et ciò tutto aveniva, perch'egli nel mirar quelle bellissime membra della Duchessa lor Signora, non haveva a fatto estinto quel foco che di vive fiamme per la sua savia damigella gli abbrusciava il cuore; et nello amor della loro bella Signora non s'haveva tutto acceso in un punto; come se l'amor col quale l'huomo la donna, et la donna ama l'huomo fosse a similitudine di quello col quale un bel cavallo, una bella gioia, et una buona possessione si amano; chè di più belle, o di megliori vedendone, facilmente dalle men belle, et men buone si può tutto lo amore levarne, et nelle migliori riporlo. Sciocca opinione per certo; chè non considerano come quella materia, la quale ha già presa la forma, non così facilmente in un'altra si può trasformare, come medesimamente un panno in un ben tinto colore, a gran fatica in altro novo colore s'appiglia.

Ma poi c'hebbero a lor seno quel povero Prencipe con le lor lingue oltraggiato, incominciarono a consigliarsi tra loro di quello che alla loro sventurata Signora dovessero dire sì, che questo grande ricevuto oltraggio con men affanno passase. Et dopo che hor quella, et hor quell'altra ragione hebbero da parte lasciata, al fine conchiusero, che il meglio sarebbe finger che havendo molti vitij in quel gentilissimo Signore compresi, non gli vollero dar la ghirlanda, acciò ch'ella non fosse poi stata astretta a dover divenire d'un così vitioso Prencipe moglie; et che poi loro in dispregio havevano la bella ghirlanda gettata nel mare.

Et così giunti che furono co'l debito tempo dalla infelice Duchessa, la quale con un troppo affettuoso desiderio gli aspettava, con suo infinito discontento si affaticarono in farle creder la favola, che composta s'havevano. Ma lei, che assai era savia, et accorta, quantunque fingesse di crederli il tutto, troppo s'avisò che, perchè quel Signore dovea havere il suo cuore in altra parte riposto, poco di sue rare bellezze si sarebbe curato. Et che loro le havevano così detto pensando con que' biasmi che loro gli davano, così potere a lei levarlo del cuore, come le molte lode di lui udite, porlovi puote. Ma ben dimostravano d'haver assai poca isperienza de gli effetti d'Amore; il quale è di tal natura, che quanto più ode biasmare la cosa amata,

URANIA: THE STORY OF A YOUNG WOMAN'S LOVE

With that, he made a sign to the painter, and together the two of them left that place, which had become most hateful to them, without a word to anyone; and soon thereafter they left Salerno as well. But when they found themselves in an area where they could give vent to their vehement disdain without fear of being overheard, they loosened their tongues and poured forth so many dishonorable words against the good Prince that anyone who heard them would have felt sorry for them. They complained, quite unfairly, that the unfortunate Prince was a man of poor judgment, mean-spirited, and ungrateful. All of this occurred, they said, because when the Prince looked upon the beautiful body of their lady the Duchess, he had not yet extinguished the living fire of love for the wise maiden that burned in his heart. That was why he had not suddenly burned with love for their beautiful lady. They spoke as if the love of a man for a woman, or a woman for a man, was the same as the love people feel for a fine horse, a lovely jewel, or some worthy possession; that is, a love which can be easily shifted from something that is less beautiful or of lesser quality to something more beautiful or more excellent, as soon as such an object comes into view. This is surely a foolish opinion, for such people do not consider how material that has already taken one form cannot easily transform itself into another, just as a piece of cloth that has been properly dyed one color takes a new color only with great difficulty.

But when they had exercised their tongues in insulting the poor Prince as much as they were able, they began to confer together about how they should break the news to their unfortunate lady without causing her so much distress, considering how greatly offended she would surely be. After they had rejected first this plan, then that, they ended up deciding that the best course would be to pretend that they had detected so many vices in that noble lord that they had chosen not to give him the garland, so that their mistress would not have to become the wife of so depraved a Prince. They would then say that they had contemptuously thrown the garland into the sea.

And thus, when the usual time necessary for the journey had passed and they presented themselves to the Duchess, who had been waiting for them with great impatience, they worked hard to make her believe the fable they had made up. But even though she pretended to believe them, she was too wise and clever not to realize that the Prince had his heart set on someone else, and cared little for her rare beauty. She also realized that the two men had said all those bad things about the Prince in order to remove him from her heart, just as they had been able to put him there by praising him so much. But in so doing they showed too well how little experience they had had of the effects of Love; for the nature of Love

tanto in lui vie più cresce l'amore; che non parendoli che possi esser vero che quella, ch'egli ama habbia in sè alcun difetto, tutto in un punto odia colui al quale ne sente dir male; et movendosi verso la amata a pietade, in sè raddoppia l'amore; et così questa mal aventurata Duchessa, non potendo sopportare che quelli del suo amato Prencipe tanto male dicessero, sanza cosa veruna crederli, un sommo odio addosso gli pose. Et tanto in lei crebbe in poche hore l'amore, et l'affanno, che considerando, come con poco suo utile havea fatto mostra dello ignudo suo bellissimo corpo, tanto dico crebbe in lei l'affanno, et l'amore, che non havendo ardire di scoprir con alcuno la amarissima pena, che'l cuor le struggeva, dal quale forse qualche conforto harrebbe potuto havere, in pochi giorni finì la infelice sua vita. Et così aviene a chiunque dietro lo obliquo guado d'Amore tanto a dentro dal solo proprio desiderio si lascia scorgere;[67] chè bisognando poi ritornare non sa da qual parte incominciasse il camino.

Ma lasciamo homai questo dire; et al gentil Prencipe ritorniamo in Salerno. Il quale più allegro, et gioioso che più alli suoi giorni si ritrovasse, fece così honorevoli nozze preparare, che ad ogni gran Re, anzi ad uno Imperatore bastevoli sarebbon state. Et volle il cortesissimo Prencipe che tutti in un giorno, egli la savia sua damigella, Fabio la valorosa Urania, et Hortensio la bella Emilia sposasse. Et per far la festa maggiore, et per più dimostrar la grande cortesia sua manifesta volle medesimamente che rimettendo ciascuno tutte le ingiurie fosse in quel giorno novellamente la Clorina dal suo Menandro sposata.

Ma nel più bel delle nozze accorgendosi il Prencipe, come il vecchio dalla ghirlanda, et il pittore non si trovavano, di tal mancamento assai se ne dolse. Ma sapendo poi come ciò non era incontrato per discortesia alcuna, che da lui havessero ricevuto, quasi che si indovinò la cosa come era, et perciò celando in sè stesso il tutto, et poco curandosene allegro, et content le belle nozze, et la sua amata sposa godeva.

Ma dopo che passato alcun mese, furono tutte le feste fornite, et che venne in Salerno la nova come quella bellissima Duchessa da non so quale non conosciuta passione assalita, haveva in pochi giorni perduta la vita, tanto ne increbbe al Prencipe, persuadendosi certo che cotale strano caso le fosse per amor, che a lui portava incontrato, che assai ne patì nel suo cuore. Pur vedendo come rimediare

---

[67] *Scorgere* should be read here according to the archaic meaning "to guide," or "to direct."

URANIA: THE STORY OF A YOUNG WOMAN'S LOVE

is such that the more a lover hears his beloved censured, the more his love grows within him. Since he cannot believe that the woman he loves could possibly have any defect, he at once despises the man whom he hears speak ill of her, while at the same time he feels pity for his beloved, which redoubles his love. So it was for the ill-fated Duchess: she could not stand hearing those two say so many bad things about her beloved Prince, so she began to hate them fiercely, without believing a word they said. At the same time her love grew all the more in just a brief time, and also her distress at the thought that she had put her beautiful nude body on display for no good purpose. So much did this emotional torment mixed with amorous yearning grow that her heart was consumed with it, especially since she did not dare reveal to anyone the bitter pain she felt. She might have derived some comfort from this, but as it was, her unhappy life came to an end in the space of just a few days. And so it always happens to anyone who tries to cross the sinister waters of Love, and then follows a yearning to act as his or her own guide, thus getting immersed too deeply: for when it becomes necessary to retrace one's steps, the starting point can no longer be found.

But let us leave this story, and return to the kindly Prince in Salerno. Now that he found himself happier and more joyful than he had ever been in all his days, he arranged for a wedding so lavish that it would have been adequate for any great king, indeed for an emperor. This most courtly Prince desired that they would all be married in a single day: he to his wise maiden, Fabio to the courageous Urania, Hortensio to the lovely Emilia. To make the party even bigger, and to show his great courtliness even more plainly while at the same time banishing all the hard feelings of the past, he commanded that Clorina and her Menandro be married yet again, on that same day.

At the height of the festivities the Prince became aware that the old man of the garland and the painter were not there, and their absence saddened him greatly. But then he realized that this was not the result of any discourtesy that they might have received from him; and indeed he could almost guess the reason they were not there. Therefore he kept the matter to himself, and scarcely thought any more about it, devoting himself in his joy and contentment to the party, and to his beloved bride.

But later, after some months had passed and all the festivities were over, news reached Salerno that the beautiful Duchess had been overcome by some strange passion, losing her life in the space of a few days. The Prince was very sorry to hear this, and became convinced that this bizarre turn of events could only be due to love, a love which she must have felt for him; and this caused him to be very sick at heart. But then he realized that he could do nothing to remedy an unfor-

al mal ch'era occorso non si poteva, non scoprendo questa cosa, eccetto che con Fabio, con verun'altro, come savio attenendosi al rimanente si diede pace; et così da indi in dietro egli con la savia sua Damigella; Fabio con la Urania; Hortensio con la Emilia; et Menandro con la sua Clorina lungamente, et felicemente vissero.

tunate occurrence that was over and done with. He told no one about this matter save Fabio, and like the wise man he was he concerned himself with his future heir, and thus found inner peace. From that day on he lived a long and happy life together with his wise lady, as did Fabio with Urania, Hortensio with Emilia, and Menandro with Clorina.

The Novella of Giulia Camposanpiero and Thesibaldo Vitaliani

NOVELLA DI GIULIA CAMPOSANPIERO, ET DI THESIBALDO VITALIANI RACCONTATA NELLO AMENISSIMO LUOGO DI MIRABELLO DA UNA NOBILISSIMA GENTILDONNA PADOVANA

Sì come è bella, ma difficile oltre modo, l'impresa che m'è imposta dalla Signora Cavaliera Conte nostra Reina, nobilissime donne et valorosi huomini, così potess'io bene sperare di condurla a quel debito fine che ricerca la sua grandezza. Meravigliosa per avventura mi darebbe l'animo di far' apparere la novella di Giulia Camposanpiero[1], la quale mi commette la Reina che io racconti; novella della quale indarno chi spera di udire nè la più bella nè la più adorna. Ma che debbo far'io? Certo se alli comandamenti della cavaliera tenterò di far resistenza, haverà giusta ragione ogn'uno di voi di concludere che io sola di tanti sia stata ardita di contravenire a i dolci solazzi di così soave compagnia; cosa della quale non potrebbe succedere altra che mi travagliasse maggiormente hora et sempre.

Dove debito officio mio è di far prova se con la debolezza del mio ingegno foss'io bastevole di metter' insieme questa non novella ma historia; il che se piacerà a Dio, che succeda sarà anche per aventura da me se non illustrata almanco adombrata la sua grandezza: se veramente, (come temo) non risponderà alla sua altezza, et alla vostra espettatione; quello che di quella dirò, sarò io reputata ufficiosa, et non disobediente.

Piacciavi donche gratiose donne; poi che in così delettevol luogo com'è questo di Mirabello, ne ha condotto il giuditio meraviglioso della Reina nostra, et poi,

---

[1] This name is spelled "campo san piero" or "campi san piero" throughout BP 1451 VIII.

THE STORY OF GIULIA CAMPOSANPIERO AND THESIBALDO VITALIANI RECOUNTED BY A VERY NOBLE PADUAN LADY, IN THE MOST PLEASANT SURROUNDINGS OF MIRABELLO

Noble ladies and valorous gentlemen, since the task assigned to me by our Queen, the Lady Cavaliera Conte, is pleasing and yet exceedingly difficult, I can only hope that I may bring it to the worthy conclusion its marvelous greatness requires. By chance, this greatness might give me the courage to bring to life the novella of Giulia Camposanpiero, which the Queen entrusts me to recount; and indeed anyone who hopes to hear a novella more beautiful and polished than this one hopes in vain. But what am I to do? Certainly if I try to disobey the commands of the Cavaliera, each one of you will be justified in concluding that I alone, out of so many in this charming company, have dared to break our rules of pleasant entertainment; and nothing could ever occur that would disturb me more, now or at any other time.

It is my right and proper duty to see if I am able, given the weakness of my faculties, to piece this together, this thing which is not just a novella, but an historical account. If it please God, perchance I shall at least be able to hint at the tale's greatness, if not reveal it in full. But if what I will say about this story will not (as I fear) truly measure up to it, and to your expectations, I will at least be seen as obliging, instead of disobedient.

Then let this be pleasing to you, gracious ladies, inasmuch as the marvelous judgment of our Queen has brought us to so delightful a place as this Mirabello.

che così grave soma sopra sta l'imbecille mie forze, di far sì che io, donna mal'usa a questo, senta dal vostro favorirmi da ogn'una di voi ricevere tal giovamento che ove manca l'ingegno suplisca il vostro favore nel quale confidata facile per aventura mi potrà riuscire sì difficile impresa.

§

Fu donche già dugento et più anni nella città nostra di Padova a tempo che sollevata dalla stragge d'Eccelino, et non pervenuta anchora alle mani de' Carraresi, ella si governava a Republica signoreggiando molti castelli et alcune città circumvicine con molta sua gloria, et satisfaction di tuttj, un giovene della nobil famiglia de' Vitaliani chiamato Thesibaldo; al quale si come Iddio et la fortuna erano stati sommamente favorevoli et nel farlo nascere il più bello, et gratioso giovene che fosse giamai stato per avanti veduto, et si potesse sperare forsi di vedere per l'avenire, così haveva egli con si meraviglioso artificio atteso, et alla cognition delle littere, et all'instruction dell'armi un' et l'altra sommamente convenevoli alla vita cittadinesca, che era riputato di gran lunga avanzare gli altri tutti. Da tutti queste sue rare bellezze congiunte a così chiare doti de animo procedeva, ch'era non pur stimato et honorato da tutti i cittadini ma era singolarmente amato da ogni conditione di donne, ma da quelle principalmente che erano da marito, ogn'una delle quali riputava sè felice oltre modo se havesse potuto ardire di sperare la grazia di così aventuroso giovene. Accompagnava egli la bellezza et dottrina con sì ammirabil arte, che furno molti che dubitorno che più tosto fosse celeste che humana creatura; et come sempre rimaneva superiore in qualunque delle più ardue disputationi, che molte et frequenti haveva nelle schole et nelle deliberationi della Republica, nelle quali haveva sempre honorato luogo così in danzare, in giostrare, in lottare, non era alcuno che più ardisse di seco contrastare, però, che era altretanto destro, agile, forte et gagliardo, quanto dotto, arguto, et ingegnoso. Havea fatto egli fermo propponimento di non maritarsi giamai, benchè fosse et solo et richissimo, però fece lungamente resistenza grande a qualunque donna, che per marito

"The Novella"

May it please you as well that so weighty an undertaking overcomes my foolish resistance, so that I, a woman little accustomed to such things, may find assistance in the favor shown me by each of you; and wherever my wit is found lacking, I may be confident that your favor will compensate. Perhaps in this way I will easily be able to accomplish so difficult a task.

§

More than two hundred years ago, during the time when our city of Padua had been rescued from the massacres of Ezzelino but had not yet fallen into the hands of the Carrara family, she was governed as a republic, and to her great glory and the satisfaction of all she held sway over many castles and certain nearby cities. At this time there lived in the city a young man named Thesibaldo, of the noble Vitaliani family, to whom God and fortune had shown great favor by making him the most handsome and graceful youth that had ever been seen, or that one could ever hope to see.[2] Moreover, Thesibaldo had applied himself with such marvelous diligence to the study of letters and to training in arms, those highly appropriate skills for city life, that he was held to be far superior to all others in such pursuits. As a consequence of this combination of rare good looks and outstanding gifts of intelligence, Thesibaldo was not only esteemed and honored by all citizens, but he was also greatly loved by every sort of woman, especially by those who were marriageable. Each one of them imagined she would be happy beyond measure if she could dare hope for the favor of such a remarkable youth. His beauty and learning were conjoined with such admirable abilities that there were many who wondered if he were a celestial creature instead of human. Just as he always had the upper hand in any of the many rigorous debates which were often held in the schools and councils of the Republic, and wherein he always had a place of honor, so too in dancing, jousting, and wrestling there was no one who dared to compete with him, since he was as dexterous, agile, strong, and vigorous as he was learned, sharp, and clever. Having solemnly sworn never to get married, even though he was free and exceedingly wealthy, for a long time he resisted mightily any woman

---

[2] For Ezzelino see *Urania*, 153 n. 42. On the history of the Vitaliani family in Padua, see A. De Marchi, "Storia dei Camposanpiero," in *Cenni storici*, 306–22. De Marchi describes a number of distinguished members of this family, but none of them bears the name Thesibaldo. De Marchi makes much of the close connection between the Vitaliani and Borromeo families, which might explain Anton Maria Borromeo's motivation in first publishing this story in 1794.

lo ricercava: anzi essendo da molte vie de continuo combattuto di lasciarsi almeno amare, dimostrò sempre di non haver cosa alcuna che maggiormente lo travagliasse di questo.

Et in questo suo fermo parer fermato visse qualche anno lontano da sì gran travaglio, avvenne pure che vinti e superati i Scaligeri dalla Republica Padovana, in quella memorabil sempre et sempre, et sempre gloriosa guerra[3], giudicorno i Padri della Republica (seguendo in questo le vestigie de' passati) che fosse ben fatto, di far publiche feste et di bandire honorate giostre in segno di così grande allegrezza della città. Però dato buon' ordine alle feste, che sempre se[4] hanno fatte grandi et honorevoli per la special gratia che ha havuta questa città di haver sempre copia grande di belle donne, fecero di più bandire per il primo giorno di maggio una publica giostra, il prezzo della quale fu una pezza di panno d'oro foderata tutta d'ermellini, con una colomba d'oro in cima, che haveva in bocha una rama d'olivo carica di smeraldi. Alla grandezza di questa giostra concorsero molti et honorati principi et cavalieri di molte parti.

Fra tanto non restavano i giovani a questo deputati di fare honorevoli feste in corte delli signori a una delle quali danzando Thesibaldo a caso con Giulia Camposanpiero unica figliuola al Cavalier Thiso non manco bella che artificiosa, avenne che hora mirandola fissa; quando raggionando con lei che parlava accortamente s'avide Giulia ch'era mutato in parte il molto rigore di Thesibaldo. Però divenuta animosa hebbe ardito di dirli che per suo amore fosse contento di dimostrare il suo valore nella giostra. A questo non hebbe vive ragioni di contravenire il Vitaliano; anzi convinto et violentato promise di sodisfare al disiderio di lei alla quale affirmava d'haver obligo di sodisfare in maggior cosa[5]. Contenta Giulia di questa promessa, et finito il ballo giudicò esser benissimo fatto di sollecitar l'amor suo.

Thesibaldo veramente quando combatendo con i studii della filosofia procurava di resistere alle fiamme di amore hora contemplando le bellezze di Giulia,

---

[3] In Borromeo's edition (*Notizia di Novellieri italiani*): "... in quella memorabil sempre, e sempre gloriosa guerra ..." (122).

[4] This pronoun does not appear in Borromeo's text (*Notizia*, 123), so that the construction changes from *si* impersonal to the active voice, in keeping with the use of the auxiliary *avere*.

[5] In Borromeo "... anzi convinto e violentato promise di sodisfare in maggior cosa," with eleven words from the manuscript text missing (*Notizia*, 123). Either Borromeo or his editor confused one *sodisfare* with the other.

who sought him for a husband. Indeed, he was continuously assailed from all sides by requests that he at least permit himself to fall in love, yet he always made it plain that nothing was more distressing to him than this.

Firmly adhering to this course, he lived for some years far from such concerns. Then, after the Scaligers had been defeated by the Republic of Padua in that ever-memorable and ever-glorious war, it happened that the elders of the Republic decided it was right and proper, and in keeping with past custom, that they hold public celebrations and jousts for honor in recognition of the city's great joy. Once they had organized the celebrations, which have always been grand and venerable in this city because it is especially blessed with great numbers of lovely women, the elders proclaimed a public joust for the first of May. The prize for this joust was to be a piece of cloth of gold all lined with ermine and surmounted with a golden dove bearing in its beak an olive branch laden with emeralds. Many honorable princes and knights, from far and wide, assembled for this grand joust.

Meanwhile the young people appointed to hold honorable parties in the courts of the noble lords were quite busy at their task. At one of these parties Thesibaldo happened to dance with Giulia Camposanpiero, the Cavalier Thiso's only daughter, who was no less beautiful than she was clever.[6] He fixed his eyes upon her while they conversed, and Giulia, who was speaking very eloquently, noted that Thesibaldo's stern attitude had softened a bit. Therefore she became bold, and ventured to tell him that he should consent to show his skill at the joust on her behalf. Vitaliano had no keen reason to refuse her. Indeed, persuaded by her arguments and overwhelmed, he promised to satisfy her desire, and affirmed that he owed her satisfaction in even greater matters. Giulia was content with this promise, and at the end of the dance she judged that he had quite reached the point where she could request his love.

Thesibaldo had truly struggled in his philosophical studies to resist the flames of love. Now, as he contemplated Giulia's beauty, a beauty that was conjoined

---

[6] On the Camposanpiero family, which had a long and important history in Padua, see Scardeone, *Historiae*, 329–34; Zwinger, *Methodus Apodemica*, 278–79; and Calza, *Cronica di Padova*, fol. 8v. A great many Camposanpiero scions throughout the centuries bore the name Tiso (Thiso), along with such variations as Tisone and Tisolino. The most famous was the one whom Scardeone calls "Tisonus Magnus," renowned for his opposition to Ezzelino's tyranny; however, he died in 1269, before the historical period depicted in this story. His son Tiso Novello, who died in 1312, fits more ideally within Bigolina's rather muddled chronology; however, no names of any of his daughters are provided in the histories (Scardeone, *Historiae*, 331–32; De Marchi, "Storia dei Camposanpiero," genealogical table 11).

ch'haveano[7] accompagnata alle bellezze[8] una viril dispostezza, si fermava in propponimento d'amarla; hora riducendosi a memoria la vita sua passata, deliberava de rimoversi dalla sua promessa, hora considerando l'efficacia della fede data di dover giostrare. Giudicava d'esser' astretto a farlo, di maniera, che combattendo da questi dui così gravi pensieri, et stando nel fare, che questo cedesse a quello, finalmente mirando in quella dubietà gli occhi di Giulia, conobbe nel vivo raggio di quelli esser descritto; "Donche manchar tu tratti di quel che sei obligato?"

Et però risoltosi et d'amarla et di dover giostrare hebbe ricorso da M. Daulo di Dotti[9] suo strettissimo parente, col mezzo del quale fatta secretissima provisione di cavalli et armadure hebbe commodità di apparechiarsi alla giostra che già era principiata; et nella quale per giorni tre continui fu da ogn'uno riputato vincitore Lucio Orsino Gentiluomo Romano col quale horamai non compariva alcuno che ardisse di contrastare. Poco prima che al fine de' giorni tre compariva finalmente Thesibaldo, tutto armato d'armi bianche, con una sopraveste di raso medesimamente bianco riccamate tutte d'oro con l'elmo ch'haveva una man d'avorio con un motto che diceva TU SOLA PUOI. Fu così subito all'apparire conosciuto da Giulia, come dal resto della città fu reputato cavaliere incognito.

Hora dati i segni della tromba, si vennero l'Orsino et Vitaliano ad incontrare con le grosse lance di tal maniera che rotte quelle in mille pezzi alfine fu astretto di cadere in terra l'Orsino. Per la caduta del quale subentrò Thesibaldo nell'obligo di mantenere la sbarra et quella sera istessa molti abbattete[10] da cavallo et fece il

---

[7] In Borromeo this verb is in the third person singular ("ch'avea"), thereby making "Giulia" the subject, not "le bellezze" (124).

[8] In Borromeo "alla bellezza" (124).

[9] In Borromeo "... hebbe ricorso a M. Daulo de' Dotti ..." (124).

[10] In Borromeo "abbattette" (125).

with a manly disposition, there were times when he firmly proposed to love her. In other moments he remembered his former ways, and resolved to break his promise, reconsidering the force of his pledge to participate in the joust. He finally decided that he was bound to do it, for while he was in his confused state, with these two weighty choices warring within him, one giving ground to the other, he finally looked within Giulia's eyes and read these words in their vivid gleam: "So, are you thinking of breaking your promise?"

Having resolved that he not only loved her, but also was compelled to joust, he turned to his very close relative Messer Daulo de' Dotti.[11] With his help, all in secret, he was able to procure horses and arms, and thus prepare himself for the joust which was already under way. For three days without a break the Roman nobleman Lucio Orsino had been considered by everyone to be the winner, and by now no one came forth who would dare take him on.[12] Just before the three days were up Thesibaldo finally appeared in white armor, with a white satin surcoat all embroidered in gold. He also bore a helmet adorned with an ivory hand, upon which was written the motto YOU ALONE ARE ABLE. Thus he was immediately recognized by Giulia as soon as he came out, while the rest of the city considered him an unknown knight.[13]

Now the trumpet gave the signal. Orsino and Vitaliano came at each other with huge lances, striking with such force that the lances were shattered into a thousand pieces and Orsino was thrown to the ground. His fall compelled Thesibaldo to defend himself as the new champion, and that very evening he unhorsed

---

[11] On the Daulo de' Dotti (or Dotti de' Dauli) family see Scardeone, *Historiae*, 342–46; C. Malfatti, *Cronichetta*, fol. 10r; and V. Badoer, "Daulo de' Dotti," in *Cenni storici*, 57–62. Bigolina does not appear to have any specific figure in mind.

[12] The Orsini were one of the most important Roman families during the Middle Ages and Renaissance. It would seem that the name, conjoined with the classical given name Lucio (Lucius), is meant to evoke a "typical Roman" and not some specific historical figure.

[13] Bigolina seems to model her description of Thesibaldo's appearance at the joust on a similar scene in Straparola's *Le piacevoli notti* (*favola* 3.4): "Fortunio adunque il giorno seguente, guarnito di rilucenti armi coperte di una sopraveste di raso bianco, di finissimo oro e sottilissimi intagli ricamata . . ." ["Then the following day Fortunio, equipped with shining arms covered with a white satin surcoat embroidered with very pure gold and very fine intaglios . . ." (1: 224)]. Fortunio also jousts incognito, and ultimately defeats the knight who has bested all others, in order to win the hand of the Princess Doralice. For the topos of the unknown and unbeatable white knight see also Ariosto, *Orlando Furioso* 1. 60–64 (1: 27–28).

simigliante il seguente giorno, di modo che fu ragionevolmente publicato vincitore della giostra; per la qual publicatione avenne, che conosciuto da tutta la città fu senza fine allegra quella vittoria sì per le conditioni del Vitaliano, come per honore universale. Ma come fu di contento questa vittoria a tutti così fu disturbo et dolore all'Orsino; il quale fra sè medesimo conclude di non lasciar mai senza vendetta quella caduta.

Vittorioso adonque Thesibaldo della giostra; ma vinto dallo amor di Giulia. Hebbe poco di poi comodità di esser in casa di lei, ove fatte secrete nozze secretamente anche la fece de donzella donna. Ma mentre che spesso frequentavano questi novelli amanti et sposi questi reiteramenti amorosi; venne nuova alla Republica che Sigismondo Imperadore era giunto a Bologna da Eugenio Quarto et per coronarsi et per dar ordine a molti loro importanti negozij. Giudicorno però convenevol cosa i Padri della Republica di fare elettion di questo ambasciadori i quali subito andassero, et a quella coronatione et a fare ufficio con Sigismondo di rallegrarsi dello imperio poco prima caduto nella sua persona. Furno perciò eletti M. Giacomo Dotto, M. Giovanni Francesco Capodilista[14], M. Rubertho Trapolin, uomini gravi et vechij, et a loro fu aggiunto Thesibaldo per compagno a' quali fu dato ordine espresso di partirsi subito. Dispiaque questa elettione a Giulia sopra modo, ma con la certezza che presto dovesse ritornare si consolò molto.

Hora fatta provision presta et honorata dalli oratori se inviorno a Bologna, ove giunti hebbe carico Thesibaldo di satisfare al disiderio della Republica. Per ciò

---

[14] This name is spelled "capo di lista" in BP 1451 VIII (fol. 5v).

"THE NOVELLA"

many men. The next day he did the same, so that he was quite properly proclaimed the victor of the joust. On account of that proclamation the whole city found out who he was, and rejoiced greatly in his victory, not only for Vitaliano, but also for the general honor of all. Yet even though everyone else found contentment in this victory, it brought grief and anguish to Orsino, who told himself that he could not let that fall go unavenged.

In this way Thesibaldo, victorious in the joust, was in turn conquered by the love of Giulia. Shortly afterwards he found the opportunity to come to her house, where they were secretly married, and where just as secretly he changed her from a maiden to a woman.[15] But while these two lovers and newlyweds were engaged in their amorous meetings, news came to the Republic that the Emperor Sigismund had arrived in Bologna to meet Pope Eugenius IV, so that he could be crowned and the two of them could put several important affairs in order.[16] The elders of the Republic decided that it would be most proper to elect ambassadors who would immediately go to the coronation and be received by Sigismund, in order to congratulate him for the imperial power so recently bestowed upon him. To this end Messer Giacomo Dotto, Messer Giovanni Francesco Capo di Lista, and Messer Rubertho Trapolin, all old and grave men, were elected; and to them Thesibaldo was added as a companion.[17] An express order was given to them to leave at once. Giulia was extremely displeased by this election, but she found much consolation in the certainty that Thesibaldo would return quite soon.

As soon as the ambassadors had been arrayed by the orators in a prompt and honorable fashion, they set out for Bologna. Upon their arrival Thesibaldo was

---

[15] Cfr. Bandello's novella 2.27, which describes the consummation of a secret marriage in similar terms: "E così il buon Aleramo la sua Adelasia di pulcella fece donna" ["and thus the good Aleramo changed his Adelasia from a maid to a woman"], *Tutte le opere*, 1: 946.

[16] Emperor Sigismund was actually crowned in Rome in May of 1433 (see "Sigismund" in *Encyclopaedia Britannica* 20: 638). Thus neither he nor Henry VII was crowned in Bologna (see Introduction, 47–48).

[17] Although the name Giacomo sometimes appears in Badoer's history of the de' Dauli family, it is not clear to whom Bigolina is referring here. Giovanni Francesco Capodilista is a much more specific figure, belonging to the time of Sigismund and Eugenius IV; he was a famous jurist who was sent to the Council of Basel in 1433, where he served both Sigismund and Eugenius, drawing up the former's will at the time of his death (Scardeone, *Historiae*, 199–200; A. D'Acqua, "Transalgardi, Forzatè, Capodilista, Picavra," in *Cenni storici*, 21–22). According to Cappelletti, he was also sent as an ambassador to Bologna in 1428 (*Storia di Padova*, 2: 30). For the Trapolin family see Scardeone, *Historiae*, 350 and Malfatti, *Cronichetta*, fol. 22r; however, no one named Roberto is mentioned therein.

messa insieme una eloquente oratione in lingua latina in publica audienza alla presentia di Eugenio et di tutta la cità fece di tal maniera che fu giudicato, com'era, huomo superiore a tutti, nel parlare eloquentemente; et piacque sì l'uffizio che fece, et ad Eugenio et a Sigismondo; che da quello indutti l'uno et l'altro; più che dall'honorevolezza dell'ambasciaria (che era per il vero sommamente honorevole) et per i vestimenti delli ambasciadori et di tutta la loro corte, et per tutti gli accidenti come di cavali muli et argentarie; con molti privilegij. Venne a Padova la fama di così egregio portamento di Thesibaldo et insieme la certezza della cortesia che infinita lo[18] usava l'Imperadore, di modo ch' havendo finito l'officio suo, l'oratore che seguitava ordinario di continuo lo Imperatore elessero in suo luogo Thesibaldo, et subito li destinorno[19] comandamento che dovesse seguir l'Imperadore.

Fu di travaglio questa nuova a Thesibaldo; ma di crucio infinito a Giulia. Questo si doleva che disiderava di ritornare a Padova a dar compimento a' suoi studij, questa si cruciava che morto il Cavalier Thiso suo padre, intendeva di publicar le nozze. Ma astretto dalla viva forza de' comandamenti della sua Republica d'animo assai composto ritornò con l'imperadore a Vienna et accasato appresso il Palazzo Imperiale faceva sempre orationi degne di lui; nè cosa alcuna mai dimandò in nome de' suoi signori all'Imperadore che più ampla molto non la ottenesse.

Sigismondo, parte per le sue[20] virtù, parte perchè era graziosissimo Thesibaldo, sempre quando li occorreva di ragionar di lui, con vive et vere ragioni concludeva che fosse impossibile, che si truovasse vivente alcuno che di gran lunga se li potesse pareggiare. Udì questi raggionamenti più volte Odolarica sua figliuola, che era a quei tempi la più bella et più gratiosa giovene che si potesse ritrovare et senza haverlo pur veduto s'accese talmente, che reputò sè beata se poteva acquistare l'amore di sì lodato giovene, però diliberata di volerlo vedere, avenne che il seguente giorno andando Thesibaldo all'Imperadore fu non pur visto da Odolarica; ma riputato angelo di cielo, di modo che accese maggiormente le fiamme d'amore, tentò di haver commodità di vederlo quando lei voleva in casa sua, nella quale

---

[18] In Borromeo "gli" (127).

[19] The first two syllables of this word are difficult to read in BP 1451 VIII (fol. 4r). Borromeo changes it to "fu fatto" (127) and avoids the third person plural construction (even though the ending in the manuscript is plainly visible as "-norno"). I am indebted to Franca Petrucci Nardelli for her help in reading this passage.

[20] In Borromeo "la sua" (128).

charged with satisfying the Republic's wishes. To accomplish this he composed an eloquent oration in Latin which he delivered in public, with Eugenius and all of the city present. He did this so well that he was judged a man superior to all others in eloquent speaking; as indeed he was. He discharged his duties in a fashion that was so pleasing to both Eugenius and Sigismund that they were more impressed by his words than by the dignity of the ambassadorial entourage, which was indeed quite dignified, on account of the clothing of the ambassadors and all of their courtiers, as well as the many distinctive qualities of such details as their horses, mules, and silver accouterments. The news of Thesibaldo's excellent work spread to Padua, along with reliable accounts of the infinite courtesies which the Emperor had shown to him. Because of this, once Thesibaldo had finished his task they elected him to replace the Emperor's permanent staff orator, and immediately he was given the order to follow the Emperor.

If this news was disturbing to Thesibaldo, it was infinitely distressing to Giulia. While he was lamenting because he wished to return to Padua to finish his studies, she felt anguish because she had intended to publicly reveal their marriage, as soon as her father the Cavalier Thiso was dead. However, since he was compelled by the great authority of his Republic's commandment, Thesibaldo returned with the Emperor to Vienna in a very calm frame of mind. Taking up residence near the Imperial Palace, he delivered continuous orations that were worthy of him; nor did he ever ask the Emperor for anything, in the name of his superiors, that was not granted many times over.

Sigismund, in part because of his virtue and in part because Thesibaldo was so very gracious, could not talk about him without reaching the vehement and heartfelt conclusion that it would be impossible to find any living man who might come close to equaling Thesibaldo. The Emperor's daughter Odolarica, who at that time was the most beautiful and graceful young woman one could find, heard these opinions many times, with the result that she fell in love with Thesibaldo without having ever seen him, and decided she would attain a state of bliss if she could gain the love of so praiseworthy a young man.[21] Therefore she determined that she would see him. It happened that the following day Thesibaldo went to call on the Emperor, and not only did Odolarica see him, but she decided he must be an angel from heaven. With the flames of her love flaring up all the more, she took the opportunity to look upon him in his own house whenever she wanted,

---

[21] The name Odolarica is clearly fictional. Sigismund had only one daughter, his heiress Elisabeth, who married the Emperor Albrecht II of Hapsburg (Stieber, *Pope Eugenius IV*, 205 n. 7).

certe finestre del palazzo potevano guardare commodamente. Era usato Thesibaldo dipoi i suoi studij di attendere a molti honorevoli esercitij, quando giocava a saltare quando ballava, ora maneggiava cavalli, et mentre che ciò operava senza punto avedersene, era non pur veduto, ma amirato da Odolarica.

Fra tanto sendo sparsa per tutto il mondo la fama delle sopra humane bellezze di Odolarica et pervenuto all'orechie dell'Orsino riputò sè felicissimo se poteva haver luogo di donzello appresso di lei. Fulli in questo molto favorevole la fortuna, però che con lettere semplici di Eugenio fu non pur accettato; ma raccomandato dallo Imperadore ad Odolarica.

Era costume dello Imperadore di far molte et solenne feste a consolation di Odolarica; perhò facendone una sera una più solenne delle altre, a quella invitato Thesibaldo, ma tardando egli a venire con molto dolore di Odolarica, fu lei astretta di comettere all'Orsino suo nuovo donzello, che andasse a levarlo, il quale contento per il comandamento ma dolente per l'odio, che portava a Thesibaldo andò di subito a levarlo et fece si indusse[22] Thesibaldo ad andarli, che per aventura puoco si curava.

Comparse alla festa Thesibaldo, a lume di torce, con la sua corte avanti che era fornita di fioriti giovani, vestito alla italiana di calce rosse coperte di veluto richamato d'oro con uno robbone di sopra pur di veluto cremesino foderato di lupi cervieri, et haveva in testa un cappelleto di pello guarnito di seta e d'oro. Al comparire del quale le donne tutte che più non l'haveano veduto, conclusero che mai più fosse stato il più bello et il più gratioso giovene il comun parlar delle quali sentendo Odolarica, maggiormente si confermava, et accendeva nel suo amore, hora principiato il ballo, al quale e lecito alle donne di levare un huomo, piacque all'Imperadore et al resto de' principi, che facesse Odolarica questo favore allo ambasciador padovano, di danzar seco; la quale non aspettando d'esser molto astretta con riverente inchino presentossi a Thesibaldo et lo invitò a ballare; ma cortese egli levato, di subito principiò in germana lingua, da lui benissimo appresa a ringratiare la signora Odolarica di sì gran favore; la grandezza del quale affermava di riconoscere, et dalla cortesia di sua signoria et dal representar egli così honorata Republica come quella di Padova.

Da queste parole prese ardire Odolarica, et subito soggiunse, "Anzi al vostro valore et alle vostre bellezze dovete voi questo obligo dalle quali accesa il primo giorno che vi vidi, il primo giorno medesimo me vi donai tutta, et non mi pentisco hora di haverlo fatto anzi tanto più son contenta, quanto che vedo il mio

---

[22] In Borromeo "... fece sì che indusse ..." (*Notizia*, 129).

from certain windows of the palace which could provide a convenient vantage point. After his studies it was Thesibaldo's custom to perform many worthy exercises, sometimes practicing leaps for dancing, sometimes putting horses through their paces; and while he was about this, quite unaware, he was being not only observed but also admired by Odolarica.

Meanwhile, the fame of Odolarica's superhuman beauty was spreading throughout the world. Once it reached Orsino's ears he imagined that he would be extremely happy if he found a position as a manservant in her service. Fortune favored him greatly in this, for on the basis of nothing more than letters from Eugenius the Emperor not only accepted him, but recommended him to Odolarica.

It was the Emperor's custom to hold many formal parties for Odolarica's entertainment. One evening he gave one that was more formal than most, to which Thesibaldo was invited; but since he was very slow to arrive, Odolarica became quite upset, and was forced to send her new manservant Orsino to fetch him. Orsino, who was happy to do her bidding, yet also upset on account of the hatred that he bore for Thesibaldo, went immediately to do this, and was able to convince Thesibaldo to come. As it happened, Thesibaldo did not particularly care to go.

Thesibaldo arrived at the party by torchlight, his entourage of men in the flower of youth arrayed before him. He was dressed in the Italian fashion, with red leggings covered with velvet embroidered in gold. Over these he wore an academic robe, also of crimson velvet, lined with lynx fur. On his head he wore a fur hat adorned with silk and gold. At his appearance all the women who had never seen him before concluded that there had never existed a more handsome and graceful youth, and when she heard the crowd speak thus, Odolarica felt more firm in her purpose, and she burned with love. Now the dance in which women are permitted to choose a man as a partner had begun, and it pleased the Emperor and the rest of the princes that Odolarica bestow this favor on the Paduan ambassador. She, not waiting for further urging, presented herself to Thesibaldo with a reverent curtsey, and invited him to dance. He rose politely and immediately began to thank the Lady Odolarica in the German tongue, which he had learned very well, for such a great favor. He affirmed that he recognized that the greatness of the favor was due both to his ladyship's courtesy and to the fact that he represented a Republic as honored as that of Padua.

At these words Odolarica became bold, and quickly remarked, "On the contrary, you owe this to your valor and your handsome appearance, which caused me to burn with love from the first day I saw you. On that very first day I gave myself to you entirely, and I do not regret having done this now; indeed, I am even more content when I see that my judgment concurs not only with that of

giuditio conforme non pure a quello dello Imperadore mio padre che vi ha concluso superiore a tutti in lettere; ma a quello di queste signore che vi concludeno voi di bellezza contrastare con qual si voglia angelo del cielo. Però, honorato signore, piaccia a voi di esser contento ch'io vi servi, et d'accetarmi per vostra."

A queste parole mutossi Thesibaldo et più volte dubitò, che da altri non fussero state intese, havendo lei parlato altretanto liberamente, quanto arditamente; pure aveduto, che non erano state udite, principiò egli a rispondere in tal materia. "Grave offesa fate signora alla vostra altezza a ricercare che io per mia accetti vostra signoria alla quale son indegno di servire, et ben mostrate esser disiderosa di favorirmi maggiormente, poi che scherzando meco, prendete gioco di darmi ad intendere; che quello diciate col core che con le parole esprimete."

Soggiunse alhora Odolarica interrompendo il parlar di Thesibaldo, "Piacesse a Dio, che come parlo io da dovero, così foss'io da voi esaudita che questa notte non tardarebbono ad haver fine i miei tormenti anzi hora sareste voi mio."

Non sopportò l'accorto ambasciadore che più continuasse Odolarica a parlarli in questa materia, anzi li affermò che ad ogni altra cosa pensasse, che a questa, però che a lei nasciuta aventurosamente figliuola di sì grande Imperadore, conveniva pensare di haver signore, et marito conforme alla sua grandezza. Finì fra tanto il ballo, et rimase da questa conclusione sopra modo dolente Odolarica pensando hora una cosa hora un'altra, tentò varij mezi, i giorni sequenti per indurre al suo volere Thesibaldo, ma furno tutti indarno, però che ad Emilia figliuola del Duca d'Alba che di queste cose li parlò molte volte efficacemente, li diede risposta[23] tale che intese, che quando fusse egli più di ciò sollecitato, lo proppalerebbe al signor suo Imperadore.

Avenne poi che Odolarica soprapresa da molta manenconia gravemente infermò, nè truovandosi medicina che la potesse sanare, anzi facendoli ogni cosa nocimento, Lucio Orsino, che dell'amor suo s'era benissimo accorto, giudico questa opportuna occasione et di acquistare la signora Odolarica, et di vendicarsi col Vitaliano. Però fatto un giorno animoso, et condotto al letto d'Odolarica con

---

[23] Borromeo modernizes the indirect object pronouns here: "... di queste cose le parlò molte volte efficacemente, le diede risposta ..." (*Notizia*, 132).

the Emperor my father, who has concluded that you are superior to all others in letters, but also with the opinion of these ladies who consider that you rival any angel in heaven when it comes to beauty. Therefore, honored lord, let it please you to be content with my service to you, and to accept me as yours."

Thesibaldo changed his demeanor at these words, greatly worried that they had been overheard by others, since she had spoken in a manner that was as free as it was bold. Once he had determined that her words had not been overheard, he began to respond in this manner: "You commit a grave offence against your high station by requesting that I accept you as my own, when I am unfit even to serve your Ladyship. You also show a willingness to favor me even more, since by joking with me, you amuse yourself by pretending that the words you pronounce express what is in your heart."

At this point Odolarica interrupted Thesibaldo's words. "Let it please God, since I am speaking truthfully, that this very night you might grant my wish. In this way my torment would not be slow to reach its end, and indeed you would be mine right now."

The wise ambassador did not allow Odolarica to continue to speak to him in this fashion. Instead he insisted that she think about something else, anything but this; and since fate had decreed that she be born the daughter of so great an Emperor, it was proper that she consider having a lord and husband equal to her in rank. Meanwhile the dance ended, and Odolarica remained extremely distressed at this outcome. Planning first one thing and then another, she tried various means over the next few days to bend Thesibaldo to her will, but to no avail. He replied to Emilia, the daughter of the Duke of Alba, who spoke with him about these things many times quite clearly, and made her understand that if he were harassed any further concerning this he would tell his lord the Emperor about it.[24]

It happened then that Odolarica, overcome by much melancholy, fell gravely ill. No medicine could be found to cure her, and indeed everything made her worse. Lucio Orsino, who was very aware of her love, decided that this provided him with an opportune moment both to win the Lady Odolarica and to take vengeance on Vitaliano. Therefore he emboldened himself one day, and had himself

---

[24] With this reference to the Duke of Alba, Bigolina is more likely reflecting an interest in the events of her own time than in any earlier historical figure. Fernando Alvarez de Toledo, Duke of Alba (1507–1582), was one of the most famous generals of the Holy Roman Empire throughout Bigolina's lifetime. His campaigns took him to Italy during much of the 1550s: see W. S. Maltby, *Alba* (Berkeley: University of California Press, 1983), 86–109.

queste parole cominciò a parlarli, "Sacra Corona, mal si ponno celare le forze de amore alle piaghe del quale non si trova remedio che basti. So io et me ne sono accorto che il mal vostro procede da molto amore che portate al Signor Orator Padovano; nè me ne maraviglio punto, che voi savia, et accorta donna non l'amiate anzi mi maravigliarei se così non fusse; sendo egli tale qual'è. A questo amore pensando io, pietade molte volte m'ha astretto a fare questo ufficio, il quale prego vostra altezza, che non giudichi prosontuoso, perchè spinto da solo disiderio di servirla mi son mosso a farlo. Voi donque amate? Il mal vostro è amore? A questo poss'io darvi quel solo rimedio, ch'è bastante di sanarvi, se così vi piace. Però ditemi liberamente se così volete, et del resto lasciate a me il pensiero."

Piacque ad Odolarica l'accorto parlamento dell'Orsino et disiderosissima di ajiuto non solo accettò le sue proferte, ma lo pregò grandemente, che facessesi che suo diventasse Thesibaldo, che in ricompenso di questo li prometteva la signora Emilia figliuola del Duca d'Alba per moglie. Lucio rispose che attendesse lei a guarire, che quanto prima a lei bastasse l'animo di venire di notte alla finestra, che guarda sopra una corte, all'hora gli darebbe l'animo di dare Thesibaldo in suo potere. Rimase di questa promessa talmente consolata Odolarica, che da lì a pochi giorni, non solo risanata, ma ritornata al pristino stato di bellezza fece intendere all'Orsino, che facesse quanto havea detto di dover fare.

Contento l'Orsino fuori di modo, havuto fra tanto l'habito medesimo, col quale comparse quella sera Thesibaldo alla festa, per via d'un cameriero, di quello vestito, la notte medesima, secondo l'ordine dato andò a ritruovare Odolarica, la quale credendo che fosse veramente Thesibaldo, non solamente riceveste in camera allegramente; ma allegramente lo lasciò diventar possessore, et patrone della sua persona, et così senza punto avedersene continuò più volte, una delle quali veduto pure a sallire quelle schalle con lo habito conosciuto da tutti di Thesibaldo, fu la sequente matina detto all'Imperadore il quale non potendo ciò credere per le condittioni di Thesibaldo, si risolse di volere intendere se ciò vero fusse da Odolarica. All'appartamento delle camere della quale andò et seco principiò a trattare di darli per marito Odoardo figliuolo del Re d'Ungheria, il quale per aventura, per questa occasione havea mandati suoi ambasciadori a Viena.

Rispose a queste parole Odolarica, "Indarno tenta Vostra Maestà di darmi marito alcuno; però che quale m'è stato conceduto da Iddio, tale l'ho havuto io prima che hora et bene che io sappia, che vi debb'esser molesta cosa d'intendere; pure io vi faccio sapere che Thesibaldo è mio signore et marito, et con lui ho celebrato secrete nozze."

brought to Odolarica's bed, where he began to speak to her with these words: "Sacred Crown, it is hard to hide the powers of Love, for whose wounds no sufficient remedy can be found. I am aware that your illness derives from the great love you bear the Paduan orator, and I am scarcely surprised that you, a wise and clever woman, are in love with him, seeing what he is like; and indeed I would be surprised if you were not. When I have considered this love, I have often felt urged by pity to offer to do you this service, which I pray Your Highness will not judge to be presumptuous, since nothing more than desire to serve you has moved me to do it. So you are in love? Love is your malady? For this I can give you that single remedy which is required to cure you, if it please you. Just tell me freely if you want this, and leave the rest to me."

Odolarica liked Orsino's clever speech, and since she wanted help very much, not only did she accept his offer, but she begged him earnestly to win Thesibaldo's love for her, and in recompense for this she offered him Lady Emilia, the Duke of Alba's daughter, for a wife. Lucio answered that she should see to getting well, and as soon as she might be inclined to come by night to the window that overlooked a courtyard, he would find a way to put Thesibaldo into her hands. Odolarica was so consoled by this promise that in only a few days she not only got better, but returned to her original state of beauty, whereupon she let Orsino know that he could do what he had said he would do.

Orsino was extremely content. With the help of a servant, he had in the meantime gotten hold of the very suit of clothes that Thesibaldo had worn at the party. Dressed in this, and following the plan, he went that same night to visit Odolarica. She, thinking he really was Thesibaldo, not only received him joyfully in her chamber, but joyfully allowed him to become the possessor and master of her body. And, without realizing her mistake, she did this many more times, until one night he was seen climbing the ladder wearing the suit that everyone knew was Thesibaldo's. The following morning the matter was reported to the Emperor, and even though he could not believe it because he knew what kind of man Thesibaldo was, he resolved to hear whether or not this was true from Odolarica. He went to her suite of rooms and began to discuss with her the possibility that she might have Odoardo, the son of the King of Hungary, as a husband; by chance this king had sent his ambassadors to Vienna to propose this.

To these words Odolarica responded, "Your Majesty attempts in vain to give me any husband whatsoever, since as God has allowed, I have already acquired one, even though I know that this must be a disturbing thing for you to hear. Nonetheless, I tell you that Thesibaldo is my lord and husband, and with him I have celebrated a secret marriage."

Travagliorno queste parole lo Imperadore talmente, che fu più volte per incrudelire contra Odolarica, ma più vinto dalla raggione comandò di subito che secretamente fosse lei posta in fondo di torre, il che fu fatto. Ma non si dolse lei tanto di questo, che non si dolesse maggiormente di quello, che dubitava che accascasse a Thesibaldo, a casa del quale andò per comandamento dell'Imperadore di subito il governadore della città, et senza difesa lo ritenne che a punto studiava, et lo custodite[25] in horribil prigione. Si meravigliò Thesibaldo assai di questa retentione, nè sapendosi imaginar la causa, stando in molto affanno fulli portata nuova, che piaceva alla Maestà dell'Imperadore che fusse publicamente non pur morto ma arso; dolente di questa nuova ma consolato nella sua innocentia, procurò ma mai puote ottenere gratia, di parlare allo Imperadore anzi quanto più procurava tanto più era repulsato.

Dovendosi donque dar' esequutione[26] a questa imperial sentenzia, una matina dapoi molto contrasto delli consiglieri cesarei prevalse finalmente il parer d'uno, che affermò non potersi di raggione far morire uno oratore se prima il principe da lui rapresentato, non intendeva la causa, però ottennuto questo parere sospesa l'esecutione furno subito rinviati a' capi della Republica padovana doi oratori, con lettere impirialj nelle quali era dato pieno aviso, non pure dell'eccesso dell'oratore; ma della capital condennatione, alla quale piacciuto allo Imperadore di condannarlo.

Giunti questi oratori a Padoa, et inteso così horribil mancamento dallj capi della Republica fu non pur commendata la condannation cesarea, ma fatta delliberation di eleggere oratori, che suplicassero l'Imperadore et a dare a Thesibaldo maggior pena, et a credere fermamente che la Republica havesse di questa ingiuria conferita oltre ogni sua espettatione, dolore infinito fatta perciò questa cosa palese nella città, et pervenuta con molto ramaricho all'orecchie di Giulia (benchè se sentisse ella offesa grandamente da Thesibaldo per questa imputatione) argumentando però et concludendo che potesse esser che fosse Thesibaldo inocente di questa colpa, subito si risolse comunicato questo suo parere con doi sui cugini della medesima famiglia de' Campisanpiero de andar a Viena vestita da huomo, concludendo se felice oltre modo se dalle mani di quei, che conducevano a morir Thesibaldo fosse lei prima morta.

Però fatta provisione secreta d'ogni cosa necessaria et principalmente d'arme et di denari andò a Viena, aggiungere alla quale non tardarono molto gli oratori eletti.

---

[25] In Borromeo "custodì" (*Notizia*, 135).
[26] This bizarre spelling is an apparent anomaly; four lines down the same word appears more conventionally as "esecutione."

"The Novella"

These words so outraged the Emperor that several times he came close to committing violence against Odolarica. But reason won out, and he commanded immediately that she be placed in the tower cellar, which was done. She did not grieve for her own state anywhere near as much as she grieved for what might happen to Thesibaldo. By the Emperor's command, the governor of the city went immediately to Thesibaldo's house and seized him without resistance while he was studying, then locked him in a horrible prison. Thesibaldo wondered greatly at this custody, and while he suffered great anxiety, not being able to imagine the cause, news was brought to him that it pleased His Majesty the Emperor that he be publicly executed, indeed burned at the stake. Grieving at this news but serene in his innocence, he tried but could not obtain permission to speak to the Emperor. The more he sought a hearing, the more he was refused.

With this imperial sentence pending, one morning after much debate with the imperial counselors the opinion of one of them prevailed; he said that one could not execute an orator without first informing the prince whom he represented of the case against him. This judgment was accepted, and the execution was suspended. Two orators were sent to the leaders of the Paduan Republic with imperial letters which told fully not only of the orator's excesses, but of the capital sentence which it pleased the Emperor to pass upon him.

When these orators arrived in Padua, and the leaders of the Republic heard about this most horrible crime, they not only commended the imperial sentence, but also decided to elect orators who would appeal to the Emperor to give Thesibaldo an even worse punishment. Moreover, they would beseech the Emperor to believe that this offence had brought them pain beyond all expectation. Since this affair had become known throughout the city, it reached Giulia's ears, causing her much grief (even though she felt greatly offended by Thesibaldo for this charge). However, thinking it over and concluding that Thesibaldo might be innocent of this crime, she communicated this opinion to two of her cousins in the Camposanpiero family, then resolved immediately to go to Vienna dressed as a man. She decided that she would be happy beyond measure if she were to die before Thesibaldo did, at the hands of those who were leading him to his execution.

Therefore, having secretly provided herself with everything necessary, especially arms and money, she went to Vienna, which the orators themselves also

Ma giunti subito pregorno in publico sua Maestà et ad incrudelire maggiormente contro il Vittaliano et a perdonare alla signora Odolarica la colpa della quale haveano commissione et d'alleggerire et d'attribuire tutto al troppo ardire di Thesibaldo. Havendo donche questi oratorj eseguito questa commessione potero bene dall'Imperadore otenner la condennation di Thesibaldo, ma non già l'assolution d'Odolarica, contra la quale havea di già publicata la medesima sententia, cioè che fosse insieme arsa.

Questa sententia quella matina medesima fu dato ordine, che fusse esequita. Però condotta al luogo solito in mezo la piazza Odolarica vestita di panni neri ardita et affermando di haver ciò comesso che l'era opposto ma negando di haver fallato fu da tutti comunemente pianta, et tanto maggiormente quanto che in lei si vedeva grandissima constantia. Condotta al luogo del fuoco Odolarica et portata la corte per condurvi medesimamente Thesibaldo acciò che legati tutti dui ad un medesimo pallo, un fuoco medesimo ardesse et abruciasse.

Giulia non pentita del suo propponimento anzi fatta maggiormente animosa, vestita pur da huomo non sì tosto vide fuori delle prigioni il suo signore tutto languido et afflitto, che subito messa mano alla spada cominciò quando a ferire un'officiale quando ad amazzarne un'altro; di maniera che se non venivano altri in aiuto lei sola et abandonata da' suoi cugini havea liberato lo innocentissimo suo consorte dalle mani di venti et più ufficiali; ma corsi altri, non solo impedirono la sua liberatione ma la ritennero, et in quella prigion medesima la condussero della quale haveano puoco prima tirato fuori Thesibaldo, il qual condotto al luogo medesimo ove era Odolarica; et dovendosi alhora dar'esecutione alla sententia; corse uno ufficiale a comandare che si soprasedesse.

Fra tanto meravigliandosi Thesibaldo più di vedere nel medesimo travaglio Odolarica che sè medesimo cominciò Odolarica a così dire. "Mio signore sarebbe a me questo tormento se non dolce, almeno manco noioso, se in questo non vedessi voi anchora mio unico contento. Ma poi che così piace allo imperadore mio signore et padre, che noi quali havea congiunti insieme il voler di Dio, insieme corriamo, un medesimo tormento, nel morire, consolatevi et siate securo, che io più compassiono voi, che me stessa."

Da queste parole comprese Thesibaldo che qualche falsa demonstratione, intorno ad Odolarica, havea mosso l'Imperadore ad incrudelire così atrocemente et così ingiustamente. Però a lei rivolto, così disse. "Fin qui certo signora mi ha doluto non pure il morire, et il modo del morire, ma anco il non sapere per qual caggione habbi lo Imperadore contra di voi et me publicata così atroce sententia; se per non haver lo voluto assentire alle vostre preghiere, ciò è accaduto, mi con-

reached without much delay. As soon as they arrived they publicly requested that His Majesty use extreme cruelty against Vitaliano, while pardoning Odolarica and showing her leniency for the crime which they had committed, all of which should all be attributed to Thesibaldo's excessive lust. After the orators had discharged this duty, they were able to obtain the Emperor's condemnation of Thesibaldo, but not Odolarica's absolution, since the same sentence had already been proclaimed upon her, that is, that she be burned together with him.

It was commanded that this sentence be carried out that very morning. As she was being led to the usual place of execution in the square, the courageous Odolarica, dressed in black clothing, declared that she had indeed done what she had been accused of, but denied that she had done anything wrong. Everyone wept for her, the more so when they saw such great constancy in her. Odolarica was taken to the place of burning, and the court officials went off to bring Thesibaldo there as well, so that, with both of them bound to a single stake, a single fire would burn them.

Giulia did not regret her decision; indeed, she became even bolder. She was still dressed as a man, and no sooner did she see her lord outside the prison, weak and dejected, than she drew her sword and began to attack, wounding a guard here and killing one there, so that had others not come to their aid she would have freed her most innocent consort from the hands of twenty or more guards, alone and abandoned by her cousins as she was. But others ran up, and not only did they prevent Thesibaldo's liberation, but they also seized Giulia, and led her into the same prison from which they had removed him just a little while earlier. Thesibaldo was led to the same place where Odolarica was, and just as they were about to execute the sentence, an officer ran over and commanded that it be delayed.

Meanwhile Thesibaldo was more amazed to see Odolarica in this terrible situation than he was to see himself. Odolarica began to speak thus: "My lord, this torment would be sweet to me, or at least less troublesome, if I did not see you, my only happiness, in these conditions. But since it pleases my lord and father the Emperor that we, who were joined together by the will of God, in dying undergo a single torment together, be consoled and rest assured that I feel more compassion for you than I do for myself."

By these words Thesibaldo understood that some false evidence regarding Odolarica had inflamed the Emperor and made him behave so cruelly and unjustly towards him. Therefore he turned towards her and said, "Lady, up to now I have surely been aggrieved not only by my death, and by the method of my death, but also by not knowing the reason why the Emperor proclaimed so atrocious a sentence against you and me both. If this has occurred because I did not wish to

tento di quello che piace a sua altezza se veramente perchè habbi havuta qualche sinistra informatione di me et di voi, questo mi travaglia più del morire, et del modo del morire."

Rispose Odolarica, "Non accade mio signore che neghiate quello, che è fatto palese a tutto 'l mondo per mia causa, anzi confessiate come confesso io che non merita il nostro amore così crudel fine; et così confessando, siate securo d'esser maggiormente compassionato da tutti."

A queste parole rispose Thesibaldo arditamente; et afermava che li piaceva il morire; ma che li dispiaceva che restasse impressione nell'animo degli huomini che havesse egli usato tal viltade, quale sarebbe stata di domesticarsi con la signora Odolarica sua signora, et sperava che Dio haveria dimostrato miracolo di questa sua innocentia; ma in tanto che con efficace parole, se affatichava l'innocentissimo et eloquentissimo oratore di persuadere questo a tutti.

All'hora uno padre di San Francesco, huomo di molta religione, affermò alla Maestà dello Imperadore che havendo confessato quella stessa matina, l'Orsino subito poi venuto a morte della infermità guadagnata per le molte fatiche fatte con Odolarica, havea egli et palesemente detto a lui, et publicato a tutti l'horribil tradimento fatto ad Odolarica et a Thesibaldo, comprobando la verità di questo tradimento, et con l'habito di Thesibaldo, che si ritrovava haver'anchora in casa et con molte cose le quali erano successe tra Odolarica et lui: inteso questo dallo Imperadore et certificato et da altri, et da haver[27] ritruovato l'habito istesso, comandò subito che fossero non pure liberati, ma condotti l'uno et l'altro alla sua presenza.

Giunti i quali cominciò l'Imperadore non pure col escusarsi con Thesibaldo, ma a dimandarli perdono havendo egli creduto, che ciò che diceva la figliuola fosse vero. Thesibaldo, veramente veduti i duo oratorj da lui benissimo conosciuti, cominciò in tal guisa a parlare. "Sacra Maestà, quello che possa Dio sopra di noi, ho apertamente conosciuto, in questo affare; nel quale ha piacciuto a sua Divina Maestà, ad un medesimo tempo, et di fare prova della mia constanza, et di mostrarmi la sua pietade, non mi lasciando morire con tal calonnia. Ringratio donque sua Divina Maestà et all'altezza vostra afermo che non accade che meco si scusi di questo, che ha piacciuto ad Iddio di provare di me. Ben mi duole che innocentemente habbi non pur patito, ma la signore Odolarica insieme."

---

[27] In Borromeo "dall'aver" (*Notizia*, 140).

grant your desire, I will be content with whatever pleases Your Highness. If on the other hand this has occurred because the Emperor has acquired some suspicious information regarding me, and you, this distresses me more than dying, and the manner of my death."

Odolarica replied, "It is not right, my lord, that you deny what has been revealed to all the world through me. Instead you should solemnly declare, as I do, that our love does not deserve so cruel an end; and in so doing, you may rest assured that everyone will show you even greater compassion."

Thesibaldo replied forthrightly to these words, announcing that he was happy to die, but it disturbed him that the impression would remain in people's minds that he had committed such villainy as to become too familiar with his mistress, the Lady Odolarica. He hoped that God would reveal his innocence through a miracle; but in the meantime this most innocent and eloquent orator endeavored mightily with effective words to persuade everyone of this.

At this point a Franciscan friar, a very pious man, declared to His Majesty the Emperor that he had heard the confession that very morning of Orsino, who had died immediately thereafter of the infirmity he had acquired from his excessive exertions with Odolarica.[28] Orsino had openly told the friar, and made a public declaration to all, of the horrible betrayal he had committed against Odolarica and Thesibaldo, proving the truth of this with Thesibaldo's suit which he was found to still have in his house, and with his account of many things which had occurred between him and Odolarica. When the Emperor had heard this and had it confirmed both by others and by the discovery of the suit itself, he commanded immediately that both of them be not only freed, but also brought before him.

When they had arrived the Emperor began not only to justify himself, but also to ask Thesibaldo's forgiveness for having believed that what his daughter had told him was true. Thesibaldo, surely having seen the two orators whom he knew quite well, began to speak in this fashion: "Holy Majesty, in this affair I have clearly come to know what power God has over us. In one stroke it has pleased His Divine Majesty both to give proof of my constancy and to show me His mercy by not letting me die in such dishonor. Therefore I thank His Divine Majesty, and to Your Highness I declare that it is not necessary that you apologize to me for what it has pleased God to reveal about me. It truly grieves me that not only I have suffered innocently, but also the Lady Odolarica together with me."

---

[28] For the notion in Bigolina's time that death could result from excessive copulation see Leone Ebreo, *Dialoghi*, 1.49.

Anzi soggiunse l'Imperadore, "Voi solo altretanto a torto foste da me condannato, quanto che giustamente Odolarica; la quale però rimarrà condannata grandemente quando che ella intenda, che credendo d'esser stata vostra, sappi et conoschi esser di Lucio Orsino, come a voi Odolarica figliuola, non pure affermo, ma con mio grave dolore attesto."

Il che inteso da Odolarica, et sendosi di ciò certificata a varij segni, de' quali ne parlò tra tanto il frate; fu talmente dolente, che manco dolente era prima; ma l'accorto Imperadore trattò di consolarla, dicendoli pubblicamente, "Odolarica, poi che così a voi son piacciute et piacciono tuttavia le bellezze et conditioni di Thesibaldo; io che sono a voi padre et amorevole mi contento (se così a lui piace) che voi, che sète rimasa miracolosamente vedova, siate sua moglie."

A questo rispose Odolarica ringratiandolo grandemente, ma diversa fu la risposta di Thesibaldo, perciò che disse che non era in termine di accettare così gran cortesia, sendo obligata la sua fede a donna, la quale seben non era da aguagliarsi alla signora Odolarica; meritava però per le degne sue conditioni di non esser ingannata. Dispiacque questa risposta a tutti, ma ad Odolarica più d'ogni uno.

Haveano fra tanto i consiglieri cesarei comandato che quello che havea non pur violentato, ma ferito et amazzato alcuni ufficiali, fusse publicamente decapitato, quando che trattandosi di esequire questa sentenza, intese Giulia mentre, che era condotta al luogo destinato, che erano fatti liberi et Thesibaldo, et Odolarica, dalla pena del fuoco, per la innocentia di Thesibaldo, et perciò suplicò lei, che fussero contenti quei ministri di fare intendere all'Imperadore che avanti morisse intendeva di palesarli importantissima cosa.

Fu ciò referto all'Imperadore il quale si contentò, et condotta alla sua presentia Giulia, et di tutti i circonstanti et benissimo conosciuto Thesibaldo, cominciò a così dire, "Sacra Maestà, sono io non huomo, ma donna, et quella donna alla quale sola ha concesso Iddio si meraviglioso signore et marito com'è Thesibaldo; viva forza d'amore congiunta ad una certezza che havea della sua innocentia m'ha indotta a far questo che ho io fatto. Pregovi donque o che mi escusiate o, ciò recusando il rigore delle vostre leggi, che almanco soprastiate a questa sentenza per tre giorni sin tanto che io dia alcuni ordini al mio signore consorte."

Non puotero lo Imperadore et gli altri circonstanti tutti astenersi alle lagrime, quando conobbero esser quella Giulia Camposanpiero. Ma sopratutti Thesibaldo,

"The Novella"

But the Emperor replied, "Only you were wrongly condemned by me, as wrongly as Odolarica was rightly condemned. She will remain condemned, especially when she comes to know, and realizes fully, that she had actually been possessed by Lucio Orsino when she believed she was yours. Not only do I declare this to you, Odolarica my daughter, but I vouch for the truth of it, with deep sadness."

When Odolarica had heard this, and when it had been confirmed to her through various indications, concerning which the friar spoke at length, she was so miserable that it seemed she scarcely could have been called miserable before. But the wise Emperor tried to console her, saying to her in front of everyone, "Odolarica, since you have found, and continue to find, Thesibaldo's charms and condition pleasing, as your loving father I will allow you to be his wife (as long as he is willing), seeing that you have been miraculously left a widow."

Odolarica responded to this by thanking him profusely; but Thesibaldo's response was different, for he said that he was not in a position to accept such a great courtesy because he had pledged his faith to a woman who, even if she could not compare to the Lady Odolarica, did not deserve to be deceived, given her respectable circumstances. No one liked this response, but Odolarica liked it least of all.

Meanwhile the imperial counselors had commanded that the man who had not only attacked, but had also wounded and killed several guards, be publicly beheaded. When it came time to carry this sentence out, and while she was being conducted to the designated place, Giulia heard that Thesibaldo and Odolarica had been freed from the sentence of burning on account of Thesibaldo's innocence. Whereupon she pleaded with the officials to agree to inform the Emperor that she, before dying, wanted to reveal something of prime importance to him.

This was communicated to the Emperor, who acquiesced. When Giulia had been led before him and all the onlookers, among whom she recognized Thesibaldo quite plainly, she began to speak thus: "Holy Majesty, I am not a man, but a woman, the only woman to whom God has granted as lord and husband the marvellous Thesibaldo. The strong power of love, conjoined with the conviction I held of his innocence, have led me to do what I have done. Therefore I pray you to exonerate me; or at least, if the severity of your laws does not allow this, I pray that you defer this sentence for three days so that I may make certain arrangements with my lord consort."

The Emperor and the others present could not hold back their tears, when they learned that this woman was Giulia Camposanpiero. But none wept more

il quale corso a lei, con licentia dello imperadore non pure la liberò, ma condotta in camera della signora Odolarica, et vestitala da donna, la ricondusse di fuori, ove l'Imperadore non pure l'assolse; ma la comendò grandemente; et dipoi dato buono ordine fece per questo solennissime feste. Et volendo pur tutti dui ritornare a Padoa[29] non solo gli ornò loro et suoi descendenti di molti privilegij facendoli conti; ma li donò molte gioie et alcuni castelli.

Per il che non pur ritornorno tutti dui a Padova, felici et gloriosi, ma furno a quei tempi et dipoi altretanto ornamento et splendore di questa città, come amplissimo testimonio della nobiltà delli animi padovani. Odolarica veramente visse il restante del tempo assai gloriosamente in un monasterio di venerande monache.

Questa è quella novella anzi quella historia, gratiose donne et valorosi huomini la quale ho pur io tentato di raccontarvi; se tale non è riuscita, et quale voi speravate, et quale si richiedeva alla sua grandezza; imputate la Reina nostra, che ha commesso sì grave impresa a me, che mal son atta a fornir compitamente simil uffici. Ma so nel raccontar questa novella; ho io mancato, come conosco, et confesso apertamente, che debbo dubitare, che mi avvenirà se sarò io così ardita che tenti di dire all'improviso in sonetto, un enigma, il quale si possi in parte uguagliare a quelli che dopo le savie novelle sono stati detti da ogn'una di voi. Chiaramente bisogna ch'io concludi che haverete voi giusta raggione di concludere che ardir grande sia stato et il mio et del mio signor consorte, a metterci con sì ellevati ingegni, come sono i vostri tutti. Ma dirò pure un'enigma; et sebene lo giudicherete voi indegno, come, che sarà, di contrastare con i vostri, sarò io di questo altretanto contenta quanto gloriosa, se l'acutezza d'ogni un di voi non penetrerà nella sua acutezza come che mi giova di sperare. Uditelo donque con viso allegro, et da niuna parte turbato:

---

[29] This is the Paduan dialect form of the city's name, followed just three lines down by the standard Italian form.

than Thesibaldo, who ran to her. He released her with the Emperor's permission and led her to Lady Odolarica's chamber. After he had had her dressed in woman's clothes, he led her out again where the Emperor did more than merely exonerate her; he also commended her greatly. Then the Emperor gave the proper orders and arranged very grand parties in honor of this event. Afterwards, since the two of them wished to return to Padua, the Emperor not only bestowed numerous privileges upon them and their descendants, making them counts, but he also gave them many jewels and several castles.

On account of this the two of them did not simply return to Padua in joy and glory; they also became the adornment and splendor of this city, in those days and thenceforth, providing a very fine example of the nobility of the Paduan spirit. To tell the truth, Odolarica lived the rest of her days quite gloriously, in a convent of venerable nuns.

Gracious women and valorous men, this is the novella, or rather the historical account, which I have attempted to recount to you. If the result has not been what you hoped, nor what the story's greatness demands, blame our Queen who has assigned this heavy task to me, a person poorly equipped to undertake duties of this nature in a competent fashion. But I know that in recounting this novella I have been found wanting, just as I know and openly confess that I must be afraid of what might happen to me if I should be so bold as to attempt to improvise a sonnet, a riddle which might be as good as the ones which have been recited by each one of you at the conclusion of your wise novellas. It is clearly necessary that I conclude that you will have every right to decide that both my husband and I have shown great audacity in joining with such high intellects as all of you have. Nonetheless, I will tell a riddle, and even though you will judge it to be unworthy to compete with yours, as indeed it will be, I will be no less pleased than basking in glory, if, as I like to hope, the keen wit that each of you possesses succeeds in penetrating the mystery of the riddle. So listen to it with joyful countenance, untouched by cares of any sort:

Giulia Bigolina

ENIGMA

Io nasco padre, e meco nasce anchora
moglie, e cinque figliuoli in un'instante
e tutti sempre stiam cohabitante
nè dall'altro si parte l'un tal'hora.

Diversi son gli uffici, ma all'hora
riposa l'uno, quando l'altro avante
stanco d'operare cose sante[30],
manco riposo chiede che d'un'hora.

Ma grand disgratia di sì nati figli
chè se da me avien che si diparte
mia moglie, che fu madre a tutti quigli

rimangono in tutte le sue parte
senza vita, et lei insieme con egli;
disgratia la maggior che s'oda in carte.

Ma avanti che io mi parta
so che la Reina nostra ella ch'ha ingegno
indovinerà ciò per sì gran pegno

se non fatte voi segno
d'esser sì dotti questi versi sciorre
com'i vostri sapeste ben esporre.

---

[30] In Borromeo "stanco già di operare cose sante"; the "già" was probably added by the editor to create a complete hendecasyllabic verse (*Notizia*, 145).

"The Novella"

RIDDLE[31]

I am born a father, and with me too are born
a wife and five children all in an instant;
we all always live together,
nor does one ever abandon another.

Diverse are our tasks, but whenever
one rests, another comes forth,
weary of doing his blessed deeds;
no one asks even an hour's rest.

But the great misfortune of children so born
comes if it happens that from me departs
my wife, who was mother to all of them;

they remain in every one of their parts
without life, and she together with them;
the greatest misfortune ever heard of in books.

But before I take my leave,
I know that our Queen, who has the talent,
will guess this, for so great a pledge:

if not, you should indicate
that you are learned enough to solve these lines,
just as you knew enough to expound your own.

---

[31] Bigolina's riddle, a *sonetto caudato* of twenty lines (with the actual riddle appearing in the first fourteen), follows a typical pattern for sixteenth-century Italian literary riddles, one established early in the century by Angiolo Cenni (De Filippis, *The Literary Riddle in Italy*, 8–12). It does not resemble as closely the riddles included in Straparola's *Le piacevoli notti*, which are in octaves and do not usually include lines addressed to the reader or listener. For an explanation of this riddle (father=arm, mother=hand, children=fingers) see De Filippis, *The Literary Riddle in Italy*, 88.

Works Cited

PRIMARY SOURCES

A. Manuscript Sources
Bassano del Grappa, Biblioteca Civica. *Epistolario Remondini* 1166–1182. Vol. 6.
Bassano del Grappa, Biblioteca Civica. *Novellieri, materiali bibliografici.* Vol. 4. Manoscritti autografi di Bartolommeo Gamba. 5 vols.
Besançon, Bibliothèque Municipale. MS. 597. Mario Melechini, *A ragionar d'amore.*
Milan, Biblioteca Trivulziana. Trivulziana 88. Giulia Bigolina, *Urania.*
Padua, Archivio di Stato di Padova. Archivio Notarile vols. 829, 4830, 4839, 5208, 5216.
Padua, Archivio di Stato di Padova. *Estimo 1518.* Polizze della città, busta 34.
Padua, Biblioteca Civica. MS. BP 1451 VIII. Giulia Bigolina, *La novella di Giulia Camposanpiero et di Thesibaldo Vitaliani.*
Padua, Biblioteca Civica. MS. 2134. Marcantonio Calza, *Cronica di Padova con l'origine di tutte le notabili famiglie che in quella al presente s'attrovano, 1556.*
Padua, Biblioteca Civica. MS. 1239 XV. Cesare Malfatti, *Cronichetta ovvero epitome delle famiglie che ora sono nella città di Padoa, composta nel 1538.*
Paris, Bibliothèque Nationale de France. Fonds Latin 7218. *Lettere Missive scritte da diversi à Francesco Barozzi.*
Vatican City, Biblioteca Apostolica Vaticana. Patetta 358. Giulia Bigolina, *Urania.*

B. Printed Sources
Alberti, Leon Battista. *On Painting and Sculpture.* Ed. and trans. Cecil Grayson. London: Phaidon, 1972.
The Apocrypha of the Old Testament. Ed. Bruce M. Metzger. New York: Oxford University Press, 1977.
Aretino, Pietro. *Lettere.* Ed. Paolo Procaccioli. 6 vols. Edizione nazionale delle opere di Pietro Aretino 4. Rome: Salerno Editrice, 1997–2002.

Works Cited

Ariosto, Ludovico. *Orlando furioso*. Ed. Marcello Turchi. 2 vols. Milan: Garzanti, 1984.

Aristotle. *De Anima*. Ed. and trans. R. D. Hicks. Amsterdam: Hakkert, 1965.

Assarino, Luca. *Raguagli del regno d'amore Cipro di Luca Assarino*. Venice: Turrini, 1646.

Bandello, Matteo. *Tutte le opere di Matteo Bandello*. Ed. Francesco Flora. 2 vols. Milan: Mondadori, 1966.

Bembo, Pietro. *Prose e rime*. Ed. Carlo Dionisotti. Turin: Unione tipografico-editrice torinese, 1960.

Betussi, Giuseppe. *Il Raverta*. *La Leonora*. In *Trattati d'amore del Cinquecento*, ed. Giuseppe Zonta, 3–150; 307–50. Bari: Laterza, 1912.

Bigolina, Giulia. *Urania*. Ed. Valeria Finucci. Biblioteca del Cinquecento 104. Rome: Bulzoni, 2002.

Boccaccio, Giovanni. *Decameron*. 2 vols. Ed. Vittore Branca. Einaudi tascabili, classici 99. Turin: Einaudi, 1992.

———. *Famous Women (De Claris Mulieribus)*. Ed. and trans. Virginia Brown. The I Tatti Renaissance Library 1. Cambridge, MA: Harvard University Press, 2001.

———. *The Fates of Illustrious Men (De Casibus Virorum Illustrium)*. Ed. and trans. Louis Brewer Hall. New York: Frederick Ungar, 1965.

———. *Filocolo*. Ed. Antonio Enzo Quaglio. Milan: Mondadori, 1967.

Boethius. *The Consolation of Philosophy*. Ed. and trans. V. E. Watts. New York: Penguin, 1981.

Borromeo, Anton Maria, ed. *Notizia di Novellieri italiani posseduti dal conte Anton Maria Borromeo, gentiluomo padovano, con alcune novelle inedite*. Bassano: Remondini, 1794.

Castiglione, Baldassare. *Opere di Baldassare Castiglione, Giovanni della Casa, Benvenuto Cellini*. Ed. Carlo Cordié. Milan: Ricciardi, 1960.

Caviceo, Iacopo. *Il Peregrino*. Ed. Luigi Vignali. Rome: La Fenice Edizioni, 1993.

Chrétien de Troyes. *The Complete Romances of Chrétien de Troyes*. Trans. and ed. David Staines. Bloomington: Indiana University Press, 1990.

Colonna, Francesco. *Hypnerotomachia Poliphili*, 1499. Reprint, New York: Garland, 1976.

Corfino, Ludovico. *Istoria di Phileto veronese*. Ed. Giuseppe Biadego. Livorno: Giusti, 1899.

Dante. *Convivio*. Ed. Piero Cudini. Milan: Garzanti, 1980.

———. *Inferno*. Ed. Natalino Sapegno. Florence: La Nuova Italia, 1984.

———. *Purgatorio*. Ed. Natalino Sapegno. Florence: La Nuova Italia, 1975.

Works Cited

D'Aragona, Tullia. *Dialogo dell'infinità d'amore*. *Trattati d'amore del Cinquecento*. Ed. Giuseppe Zonta. Bari: Laterza, 1912.

Ficino, Marsilio. *Commentary on Plato's Symposium on Love*. Trans. Sears Jayne. 2nd rev. ed. Dallas: Spring Publications, 1985.

———. *Five Questions Concerning the Mind*. Trans. Josephine L. Burroughs. In *The Renaissance Philosophy of Man*, ed. Ernst Cassirer, Paul Oskar Kristeller, and John Herman Randall, Jr., 193–212. Chicago: University of Chicago Press, 1948.

Franco, Niccolò. *La Philena di M. Nicolo Franco. Historia amorosa ultimamente composta*. Mantua: Ruffinelli, 1547.

Homer. *The Odyssey*. Trans. A. T. Murray. 2 vols. Cambridge, MA: Harvard University Press, 1995.

Leone Ebreo. *Dialoghi d'amore*. Ed. Santino Caramella. Bari: Laterza, 1929.

Leonico, Angelo. *L'amore di Troilio, et Griseida, ove si tratta in buona parte la guerra di Troia*. Venice: Gerardo, 1553.

Livy. *Ab urbe condita*. Ed. Robert Seymour Conway. Oxford: Oxford University Press, 1964.

Macrobius. *Commentary on the Dream of Scipio*. Ed. and trans. William Harris Stahl. Records of Civilization, Sources and Studies 48. New York: Columbia University Press, 1966,

Marguerite de Navarre. *Heptaméron*. Ed. Michel François. Paris: Garnier, 1967.

Masenetti, Giovanni Maria. *Il divino oracolo in lode dei nuovi sposi del 1548 e di tutte le belle gentildonne padovane*. Venice: n.p., 1548.

Masuccio Salernitano. *Il Novellino*. Ed. Salvatore S. Nigro. Universale Laterza 530. Bari: Laterza, 1979.

Ovid. *Heroides and Amores*. Trans. Grant Showerman. Cambridge, MA: Harvard University Press, 1958.

———. *Metamorphoses*. Trans. Frank Justus Miller. 2 vols. Cambridge, MA: Harvard University Press, 1960.

Orosius, Paulus. *The Seven Books of History Against the Pagans*. Trans. Roy J. Deferrari. Washington: Catholic University of America Press, 1964.

Parabosco, Girolamo. *I Diporti*. Ed. Giuseppe Gigli. Bari: Laterza, 1912.

Passero, Felice. *Urania, overo la costante donna*. Napoli: Roncagliolo, 1616.

Petrarca, Francesco. *Canzoniere*. Ed. Gianfranco Contini. Turin: Einaudi, 1964.

Pizan, Christine de. *The Book of the City of Ladies*. Trans. Rosalind Brown-Grant. London: Penguin, 1999.

Pliny. *Natural History*. Trans. H. Rackham. 10 vols. Cambridge, MA: Harvard University Press, 1952.

WORKS CITED

Plutarch. *Makers of Rome: Nine Lives by Plutarch.* Trans. Ian Scott-Kilvert. Baltimore: Penguin, 1965.

———. *Fall of the Roman Republic: Six Lives by Plutarch.* Trans. Rex Warner. Harmondsworth: Penguin, 1958.

Poliziano, Angelo (Politian). *Le stanze per la giostra del magnifico Giuliano di Piero de' Medici.* In *Poesie italiane*, ed. Saverio Orlando, 35–105. Milano: Rizzoli, 1976.

Pomponazzi, Pietro. *On the Immortality of the Soul.* Trans. William Henry Hay II. In *The Renaissance Philosophy of Man*, ed. Ernst Cassirer, Paul Oskar Kristeller, and John Herman Randall, Jr., 280–381. Chicago: University of Chicago Press, 1948.

The Recognitions of Clement. Trans. Thomas Smith. In *The Ante-Nicene Fathers, Translations of the Fathers down to A.D. 325*, ed. Alexander Roberts and James Donaldson, 10 vols., 8: 75–211. Grand Rapids, MI: Eerdmans, 1951.

Le roman de Tristan en prose. Ed. Renée L. Curtis. 3 vols. Cambridge: D.S. Brewer, 1985.

Ruzante (Angelo Beolco). *L'Anconitana: The Woman from Ancona.* Ed. and trans. Nancy Dersofi. Berkeley: University of California Press, 1994.

Sacchetti, Franco. *Il Trecentonovelle.* Ed. Antonio Lanza. Florence: Sansoni, 1984.

Sercambi, Giovanni. *Il Novelliere.* Ed. Luciano Rossi. 3 vols. I novellieri italiani 9. Rome: Salerno Editrice, 1974.

Straparola, Giovan Francesco. *Le piacevoli notti.* Ed. Donato Pirovano. 2 vols. I novellieri italiani 29. Rome: Salerno Editrice, 2000.

Suetonius. *The Twelve Caesars.* Trans. Robert Graves. Harmondsworth: Penguin, 1979.

Virgil. *The Aeneid of Virgil: A Verse Translation.* Trans. Allen Mandelbaum. Berkeley and Los Angeles: University of California Press, 1981.

Wroth, Mary. *The First Part of the Countess of Montgomery's Urania.* MRTS 140. Binghamton, NY: Medieval and Renaissance Texts and Studies, 1995.

SECONDARY SOURCES

Albertazzi, Adolfo. *Romanzieri e romanzi del cinquecento e del seicento.* Bologna: Zanichelli, 1891.

Auzzas, Ginetta. "La narrativa veneta nella prima metà del cinquecento." In *Storia della cultura veneta*, ed. Girolamo Arnaldi and Manlio Pastore Stocchi, 6 vols., 3: 99–138. Vicenza: Neri Pozza, 1976–1986.

Badoer, Vincenzo. "Daulo de' Dotti." In *Cenni storici sulle famiglie di Padova e sui monumenti dell'università*, 57–62. Padua: Minerva, 1842.

Works Cited

Baldini, Ugo. "Clavius, Christopher." In *Encyclopedia of the Renaissance*, ed. Paul F. Grendler, 6 vols., 2: 17–18. New York: Charles Scribner's Sons, 1999.

Baratto, Matteo. *Realtà e stile nel Decameron*. Rome: Riuniti, 1984.

"Barozzi, Francesco." *Dizionario biografico degli italiani*. 56 vols. to date. Rome: Istituto della Enciclopedia Italiana fondata da Giovanni Treccani. Vol. 6 (1964): 495–99.

Bartra, Roger. *The Artificial Savage: Modern Myths of the Wild Man*. Trans. Christopher Follett. Ann Arbor: University of Michigan Press, 1997.

Bassanese, Fiora A. "Selling the Self; or, the Epistolary Production of Renaissance Courtesans." In *Italian Women Writers from the Renaissance to the Present: Revising the Canon*, ed. Maria Ornella Marotti, 69–82. University Park, PA: Pennsylvania State University Press, 1996.

Bettella, Patrizia. "Corpo di parti: Ambiguità e frammentarietà nella rappresentazione della bellezza femminile nei trattati di Trissino e Firenzuola." *Forum Italicum* 33 (1999): 319–35.

Boerio, Giuseppe. *Dizionario del dialetto veneto*. 1856. Reprint, Milan: Martello, 1971.

Brumble, H. David. *Classical Myths and Legends in the Middle Ages and Renaissance*. Westport, CT: Greenwood Press, 1998.

Bruni, Francesco. *Boccaccio. L'invenzione della letteratura mezzana*. Bologna: Il Mulino, 1990.

Buranello, Robert. "Figura meretricis: Tullia d'Aragona in Sperone Speroni's *Dialogo d'amore*." *Spunti e ricerche* 15 (2000): 53–67.

Buti, Maria Bandini. *Poetesse e scritrici. Enciclopedia biografica e bibliografica italiana*. Rome: Tosi, 1941.

Cappelletti, Giuseppe. *Storia di Padova dalla sua origine sino al presente*. 2 vols. Padua: Premiata Tipografica Editrice F. Sacchetto, 1874.

Carucci, Carlo. *D. Ferrante Sanseverino, Principe di Salerno*. Salerno: Stabilimento Tipografico Nazionale, 1899.

Castan, Auguste. *Catalogue Général des Manuscrits des Bibliothèques Publiques de France*, vol. 32: *Besançon*. Paris: Plon, 1897.

Cesarotti, Melchiorre. *Opere*. 40 vols. Pisa: Capurro, 1813.

Ciccuto, Marcello, ed. *Novelle italiane. Il cinquecento*. Milan: Garzanti, 1982.

Clark, Gillian. *Women in Late Antiquity: Pagan and Christian Life-Styles*. Oxford: Clarendon Press, 1993.

Clements, Robert J., and Joseph Gibaldi. *Anatomy of the Novella. The European Tale Collection from Boccaccio and Chaucer to Cervantes*. New York: New York University Press, 1977.

Cleugh, James. *The Divine Aretino*. New York: Stein and Day, 1966.

Works Cited

Colapietra, Raffaele. *I Sanseverino di Salerno. Mito e realtà del barone ribelle*. Salerno: Laveglio, 1985.

Contarino, Luigi. *Il vago e dilettevole giardino*. Vicenza: Perin Libraro, 1589.

Cottino-Jones, Marga. "The Pen and the Brush: Woman Portraiture in the Renaissance." In *Da una riva all'altra. Studi in onore di Antonio D'Andrea*, ed. Dante della Terza, 229–32. Florence: Cadmo, 1995.

Cox, Virginia. "Fiction, 1560–1650." In *A History of Women's Writing in Italy*, ed. Letizia Panizza and Sharon Wood, 52–64. Cambridge: Cambridge University Press, 2000.

Cropper, Elizabeth. "The Beauty of Woman: Problems in the Rhetoric of Renaissance Portraiture." In *Rewriting the Renaissance: The Discourses of Sexual Difference in Early Modern Europe*, ed. Margaret W. Ferguson, Maureen Quilligan, and Nancy J. Vickers, 175–90. Chicago: University of Chicago Press, 1986.

D'Acqua, A. "Transalgardi, Forzatè, Capodilista, Picacavra." In *Cenni storici sulle famiglie di Padova*, 1–22.

Davies, Norman. *God's Playground: A History of Poland*. 2 vols. New York: Columbia University Press, 1982.

De Filippis, Michele. *The Literary Riddle in Italy to the End of the Sixteenth Century*. Berkeley and Los Angeles: University of California Press, 1948.

Degli Erri, Luigi-Ignazio Grotto. "Conti, Maltraversi, Da Carturo, Cittadella." In *Cenni storici sulle famiglie di Padova*, 25–55.

Della Chiesa, Francesco. *Theatro delle donne letterate. Con un breve discorso della preminenza, e perfettione del sesso donnesco*. Mondovì: Gislandi, 1620.

De Marchi, Alessandro. "Storia dei Camposampiero." In *Cenni storici sulle famiglie di Padova*, 473–526.

Douglas, Andrew Halliday. *The Philosophy and Psychology of Pietro Pomponazzi*. Hildesheim: Olms, 1962.

Duvernoy, Charles. *Notice sur les maisons de Granvelle et de St. Mauris-Montbarrey, dans le comté de Bourgogne*. Besançon: Proudhon, 1839.

Esposito, Enzo. Introduction to Ser Giovanni Fiorentino, *Il Pecorone*, vii–xxxiii. Classici italiani minori 1. Ravenna: Longo Editore, 1974.

Fassini, Antonio. "Vitaliani e Borromeo." In *Cenni storici sulle famiglie di Padova*, 306–22.

Ferri, Pietro Leopoldo. *Biblioteca femminile italiana*. Padua: Crescini, 1842.

Forin, Elda Martelozzo, ed. *Acta Graduum Academicorum Gymnasii Patavini. Ab anno 1501 ad annum 1550*. Padua: Antenore, 1982.

Frati, Ludovico. "Un'egloga rusticale del 1508." *Giornale storico della letteratura italiana* 20 (1892): 186–204.

WORKS CITED

Freedman, Luba. *Titian's Portraits Through Aretino's Lens*. University Park, PA: Pennsylvania State University Press, 1995.

Gamba, Bartolommeo. *Delle novelle italiane in prosa. Bibliografia di Bartolommeo Gamba bassanese*. Florence: Tipografia all'insegna di Dante, 1835.

Gilbert, Creighton E. *Italian Art 1400–1500: Sources and Documents*. Englewood Cliffs, NJ: Prentice-Hall, 1980.

Gillett, H. M. "Loreto." In *New Catholic Encyclopedia*, ed. William J. McDonald, 15 vols., 8: 993–94. New York: McGraw-Hill, 1967.

Ginzburg, Carlo. "Titian, Ovid and Sixteenth-Century Codes for Erotic Illustration." In *Titian's Venus of Urbino*, ed. Rona Goffen, 23–36. Cambridge: Cambridge University Press, 1997.

Goffen, Rona. "The Problematic Patronage of Titian's *Venus of Urbino*." *Journal of Medieval and Renaissance Studies* 14 (1993): 301–29.

———. "Titian's *Sacred and Profane Love and Marriage*." In *The Expanding Discourse, Feminism and Art History*, ed. Norma Broude and Mary D. Garrard, 110–25. New York: IconEditions, 1992.

Guglielmi, Guido. "Una novella non esemplare del *Decameron*." *Forum Italicum* 14 (1980): 32–55.

Guglielminetti, Marziano. Introduction to *Il tesoro della novella italiana. I secoli XIII–XVII*, ix–xlii. Milan: Mondadori, 1986.

Heijkant, Marie-José. "Tristan pilosus: La folie de l'héros dans le Tristano Panciatichiano." Trans. Sabine Raaijmakers Costa. In *Tristan-Tristant. Mélanges en l'honneur de Danielle Buschinger à l'occasion de son 60ème anniversaire*, ed. André Crépin and Wolfgang Spiewok, 231–42. Wodan 66. Greifswald: Reineke, 1996.

Hotchkiss, Valerie R. *Clothes Make the Man: Female Cross-Dressing in Medieval Europe*. The New Middle Ages 1. New York: Garland, 1996.

Junkerman, Anne Christine. "The Lady and the Laurel: Gender and Meaning in Giorgione's Laura." *Oxford Art Journal* 16 (1993): 49–58.

Keller, W. "Granvelle, Antoine Perrenot de." In *New Catholic Encyclopedia*. 6: 695–96.

Kristeller, Paul Oskar. *The Philosophy of Marsilio Ficino*. Trans. Virginia Conant. Gloucester, MA: P. Smith, 1964.

Loi, Maria Rosa, and Mario Pozzi. Introduction to Sperone Speroni, *Lettere familiari*, 2 vols., 1: 5–29. Alessandria: Edizioni dell'Orso, 1993–1994.

Lovarini, Emilio. *Studi sul Ruzzante e la letteratura pavana*. Padua: Antenore, 1965.

Maltby, William S. *Alba: A Biography of Fernando Alvarez de Toledo, Third Duke of Alba*. Berkeley and Los Angeles: University of California Press, 1983.

Mancini, Vincenzo. *Lambert Sustris a Padova. La villa Bigolin a Selvazzano*. Qua-

derni di storia locale 5. Selvazzano (PD): Comune di Selvazzano/Biblioteca Comunale/Centro Culturale, 1993.

Marescotti, Hercole. *Dell'eccellenza della donna*. Fermo: Sertorio de' Monti, 1589.

Mazzuchelli, Giammaria. *Gli scrittori d'Italia*. 6 vols. Brescia: Bossini, 1753–1763.

Milani, Marisa. Introduction to Angelo Leonico, *Il soldato*, 7–28. Quaderni veneti 13. Ravenna: Longo Editore, 1991.

Nissen, Christopher. "The Motif of the Woman in Male Disguise from Boccaccio to Bigolina." In *The Italian Novella*, ed. Gloria Allaire, 201–17. New York: Routledge, 2003.

———. "Subjects, Objects, Authors: The Portraiture of Women in Giulia Bigolina's *Urania*." *Italian Culture* 18 (2000): 15–31.

Park, Katherine. "The Organic Soul." In *The Cambridge History of Renaissance Philosophy*, ed. Charles B. Schmitt, 464–84. Cambridge: Cambridge University Press, 1988.

Passano, Giambattista. *Novellieri italiani in prosa*. 2nd ed. 2 vols. Turin: Paravia, 1878.

Perry, Ben Edwin. *The Ancient Romances*. Berkeley and Los Angeles: University of California Press, 1967.

Pietrucci, Napoleone. *Delle illustri donne padovane*. Padua: Bianchi, 1853.

Piovan, Francesco. "La condotta allo Studio di Salerno di Matteo Macigni e Paolo da Lion (1543)." *Quaderni per la storia dell'Università di Padova* 32 (1999): 99–111.

Piranesi, Pietro, ed. *Novelle tratte dai più celebri Autori antichi e moderni*. Paris: Barrois, 1823.

———, ed. *Nuova scelta di Novelle, tratte dai più celebri autori antichi e moderni*. Paris: Baudry, 1852.

Porcelli, Bruno. *La novella del Cinquecento*. Letteratura italiana Laterza 22. Bari: Laterza, 1973.

Porro, Giulio, ed. *Trivulziana. Catalogo dei Codici Manoscritti*. Turin: Paravia, 1884.

Procaccioli, Paolo. Index to Pietro Aretino, *Lettere*, 2 vols., 2: 1089–1214. Milan: Rizzoli, 1991.

Quadrio, Francesco Saverio. *Della storia e della ragion di ogni poesia*. 2 vols. Milan: Pisarri, 1741.

Raya, Gino. *Storia dei generi letterari italiani: Il romanzo*. Milano: Vallardi, 1950.

Ribera, Pietro Paulo. *Le glorie immortali apologetiche de' trionfi et heroiche imprese d'ottocento quarantacinque Donne Illustre antiche, & moderne, dotate di varie scienze, e conditioni segnalate*. Venice: Deuchino, 1609.

Richardson, Francis L. *Andrea Schiavone*. Oxford: Clarendon, 1980.

Works Cited

Rogers, Mary. "The Decorum of Women's Beauty: Trissino, Firenzuola, Luigini and the Representation of Women in Sixteenth-Century Painting." *Renaissance Studies* 2 (1988): 47–75.

Rohlfs, Gerhard. *Grammatica storica della lingua italiana e dei suoi dialetti*. 3 vols. Turin: Einaudi, 1968.

Rua, Giuseppe. "Intorno alle Piacevoli notti dello Straparola." *Giornale storico della letteratura italiana* 15 (1890): 111–51.

Saggiori, Giovanni. *Padova nella storia delle sue strade*. Padua: Piazzon, 1972.

Scardeone, Bernardino. *Historiae de Urbis Patavii*, 1560. Reprint, Bologna: Forni, 1979.

"Sigismund." In *Encyclopaedia Britannica*, 1965 ed. 20: 637–38.

Smoller, Laura Ackerman. *History, Prophecy, and the Stars: The Christian Astrology of Pierre d'Ailly, 1350–1420*. Princeton: Princeton University Press, 1994.

Stieber, Joachim W. *Pope Eugenius IV, the Council of Basel and the Secular and Ecclesiastical Authorities in the Empire: The Conflict over Supreme Authority and Power in the Church*. Leiden: E. J. Brill, 1978.

Toffanin, Giuseppe, Jr. Introduction to Carlo Leoni, *Cronaca segreta de' miei tempi 1845–1874*, 4–6. Padua: Rebellato, 1976.

———. *Le strade di Padova*. Rome: Newton e Compton, 1998.

Tomasini, Iacopo. *Bibliothecae Patavinae Manuscriptae* ... Udine: Schirotto, 1639.

Vedova, Giuseppe. *Biografia degli scrittori padovani*. 2 vols. Padua: Minerva, 1832.

Veronese, Emilia, and Elisabetta Dalla Francesca, ed. *Acta Graduum Academicorum Gymnasii Patavini ab anno 1551 ad annum 1561*. Fonti per la storia dell'Università di Padova 16. Rome: Antenore, 2001.

Vitullo, Juliann. *The Chivalric Epic in Medieval Italy*. Gainesville: University Press of Florida, 2000.

Wiel Marin, Giovanni. "Antiche vicende di Santa Croce Bigolina." *Padova e la sua provincia* 2 (1969): 2–4.

Zwinger, Theodor. *Methodus Apodemica in eorum Gratiam, qui cum fructu in quocumque tandem vite genere peregrinari cupiunt*. Argentinae (Strasbourg): apud Zetznerum, 1594.

Zumthor, Paul. *Toward a Medieval Poetics*. Trans. Philip Bennett. Minneapolis: University of Minnesota Press, 1992.

Index

Achilles Tatius, 32
Ahasuerus, 150–51
Albertazzi, Adolfo, 32nn
Alberti, Leon Battista, 201n
Albrecht II of Hapsburg (emperor), 303n
Aleramo and Adelasia (in Bandello, *Novelle* 2.27), 301n
Alfonso II (King of Naples), 197n, 209n
Amazons, 143n
Ambrosiana Library, 22, 27
"Antione," 142–43, 143n
Antiope, 143n
Apelles, 98–99, 99n, 198–99
Aragonese Kings of Naples, 185n
Archivio di Stato di Padova, 4n, 5, 5n, 29n
Aretino, Pietro, 8, 9–14, 15, 20, 22, 24, 27–29
Ariosto, Ludovico, 16, 39, 40n, 143n, 299n
Aristotle, 71n
Arnaldo (papal legate), 48
Asolo, 21
Assarino, Luca, 21–22
Athens, 143
Auzzas, Ginetta, 29, 30n, 32n

Bacchiglione River, 260–61, 261n
Badoer, Vincenzo, 299n, 301n

Baldini, Ugo, 15n
Bandello, Matteo, 29, 34, 34n, 207n, 301n
Baratto, Mario, 31n
Barbo, Ludovico (Abbot of Santa Giustina and Bishop of Treviso), 48
Barozzi, Francesco, 14–16, 20
Bartra, Roger, 40n
Bassanese, Fiora, 45, 45n
Battifero, Laura, 3
beauty, 72–75, 92–99, 97n, 156–57
Bembo
    Benedetto, 15
    Pietro, 18, 21, 39, 44, 65n, 97n
Besançon, 17
Bettella, Patrizia, 201n
Betussi, Giuseppe, 37n, 97n
Biblioteca Civica (Padua), 42
Biblioteca Municipale, Bassano del Grappa, 44–45, 45n
Bigolin
    Alessandro, 4n
    Dioclide, 8, 42n
    Gerolamo, 4, 27
Bigolina
    Gerolama, 8–9
    Giulia:
        Aretino's letters to, 9–14
        as author of "Giulia Camposanpiero," 42–45

INDEX

as author of *Urania*, 34–35
biography derived from archival documents, 4–5
in Borromeo's *Notizia di Novellieri italiani*, 23–25
champions women's participation in arts and sciences, 41, 116–17
conception of frame story, "Giulia Camposanpiero," 45–47
desires to be remembered after death, 41, 58–59, 82–83
holographic will of, 5–8
interest in male disguise, 39–41
interest in motif of female audacity, 48–50
interest in Prince of Salerno, 19–20
knowledge of Veneto geography, 261n
in Leonico's poem, 16–17
letter to Barozzi, 14–16
love doctrine of, 38–39
in Masenetti's poem, 8–9
in Melechini's dialogue, 17–19
nineteenth-century critical references to, 25–26
problems as historian, 47–48
Quadrio's and Mazzuchelli's assessment of, 22–23
relation to sixteenth-century narrative prose, 29–34
Scardeone's assessment of, 3–4
seventeenth-century critical references to, 20–22
sixteenth-century critical references to, 1–3
twentieth-century critical references to, 27–29

Maria, 7
Bigolini (family), 3, 4, 4n
Boccaccio, Giovanni:
   Decameron, 1, 3, 30–31, 35, 44
   Elegia di Madonna Fiammetta, 31, 33, 35
   Famous Women, 35, 143nn, 146n, 149n, 153n, 201n
   Fates of Illustrious Men, 35
   Filocolo, 31, 32, 35
   Filostrato, 49
Boerio, Giuseppe, 178n
Boethius, 35, 35n, 105n
Bologna, 47–48, 260–61, 300–1, 301n
Borromeo, Anton Maria, 23–26, 27, 29, 30, 42, 42n, 44, 44–45n, 47n, 51, 240n, 295n, 296n, 306n, 320n
BP 1451 VIII (MS), 42, 42n, 53–54, 302n
Bradamante (in Ariosto's *Orlando Furioso*), 40n
Bragantini, Renzo, 41n
Brazola, Laura Sperona, 18
Brenta River, 260–61
Brumble, H. D., 37n
Bruni, Francesco, 3n
Buranello, Robert, 18
Buti, Maria Bandini, 27

Calabria, 184–85, 188–89
Calza, Marcantonio, 297n
Campiglia, Maddalena, 22
Camposanpiero (family), 297n
Camposanpiero, Giulia, 38, 48–50, 54, 296–303, 310–13, 316–19
Can Grande della Scala, 47
Capodilista, Giovanni Francesco, 300–1, 301n

INDEX

Cappelletti, Giuseppe, 47, 47n, 153n, 301n
captatio benevolentiae, 45
Carmenta (Carmentis), 142–43, 143n
Carrara (family), 47, 47n, 294–95
Carucci, Carlo, 19, 19n, 20, 85n
Cassola, Luigi, 37n
Castan, Auguste, 17n
Castiglione, Baldassare, 44, 97n
Cavaliera Conte (character in "Giulia Camposanpiero"), 30, 43–46, 292–93
Caviceo, Iacopo, 31–34, 34n, 39n, 83n
Celotti, Alvise, 51
Cenni, Angiolo, 43, 321n
Cesarotti, Melchiorre, 25, 28
Chariton, 32
Charles of Bourbon, Duke, 97n
Charles V (emperor), 19
Chrétien de Troyes, 39
Ciccuto, Mario, 35
Circe, 146–47, 147n
Clark, Gillian, 141n
Clavius, Christopher, 15
Clements, Robert J. and Joseph Gibaldi, 34n
Cleugh, James, 11n
Clorina (character in *Urania*), 38–39, 51, 180–83, 217–33, 236–37, 240–41, 244–47, 266–69, 286–88
cognition (functions of senses), 70–73, 94–97, 97n
Colapietra, Raffaele, 19n, 20, 85n
Colonna
    Francesco, 31–32
    Vittoria, 2
confraternities (*fraglie*), 7–8
Contarini, Luigi, 2–3, 20
Conte (family), 43–44

Conte
    Alberto, 43–44
    Bianca, 43
    Lucietta, 43–44
    Paolo de', 43
Coraro, Antonio, 17–19
Coriolanus, 150–51, 153n
Cottino-Jones, Marga, 207n
Council of Basel, 48, 301n
counselor (character in *Urania*), 33, 184–85, 190–99, 280–87
Cox, Virginia, 4n, 22n
Crema, 5
Cropper, Elizabeth, 207n
Cupid, 65n, 204–5, 272–73
Cyprus, 21

D'Acqua, A., 301n
Dante Alighieri, 65n, 103n, 153n
Da Porto, Luigi, 35
D'Aragona
    Alfonso (Duke of Calabria), 185n
    Ippolita (Duchess of Calabria), 185n
    Tullia, 18n, 97n
Davies, Norman, 197n
De' Dauli (family), 301n
De' Dotti, Daulo, 298–99, 299n
De Filippis, Michele, 27, 43, 321n
Della Chiesa, Francesco Agostino, 21
De Marchi, Alessandro, 295n, 297n
Doralice (Straparola, *Le piacevoli notti* 3.4), 299n
Dotto, Giacomo, 300–1, 301n
Douglas, Andrew Halliday, 73n
dreams (romance motif), 32–34, 241–45, 245n
Duchess of Bourbon (character in *Urania*), 194–95, 197n, 200–1

INDEX

Duchess of Calabria (character in *Urania*), 33, 37–38, 184–215, 282–87
Duke of Alba (character in "Giulia Camposanpiero"), 306–9, 307n
Duke of Alba (Fernando Alvarez de Toledo), 307n
Dukes of Calabria, 184–85, 185n, 197n, 208–9, 209n
Duvernoy, Charles, 17n

Elisabeth (daughter of Emperor Sigismund), 303n
Emilia (character in "Giulia Camposanpiero"), 306–9
Emilia (character in *Urania*), 38, 164–81, 246–59, 272–81, 286–88
Eremitani (church in Padua), 6–8
Esposito, Enzo, 2n
Esther, 36, 150–51, 151n
Euganean Hills, 43, 260–61, 261n
Eugenius IV (pope), 47–48, 300–3, 301n
Ezekiel, 65n
Ezzelino da Romano, 47, 47n, 152–53, 153n, 294–95, 295n, 297n

Fabio (character in *Urania*), 36, 39–41, 49, 82–83
    attempts to steal garland, 218–21
    begs Prince for death and recognizes Urania as the best of women, 264–71
    fights Menandro and is arrested, 220–23
    first in love with Urania, 86–87
    has allegorical dream, 33, 240–45
    hears Clorina's challenge to steal garland, 216–19
    laments his rejection of Urania, 236–41
    marries Urania, 286–88
    rejected by Clorina, 228–33
    rejects Urania for a more beautiful woman, 87–89
    woos Clorina, 180–83
fairy (character in *Urania*), 33–34, 210–13
Fassini, Antonio, 48
faun (character in *Urania*), 242–45
Faverney (abbey), 17
Fernandez, Enrique, 143n
Ferri, Pietro Leopoldo, 25
Ficino, Marsilio, 37n, 71n, 73nn, 95n
Finucci, Valeria, 27n
Floire and Blanchefleur, 35
Florence, 166–69, 276–77
Forin, Elda Martelozzo, 5n
Fortune, 102–5
Fortunio (Straparola, *Le piacevoli notti* 3.4), 299n
Franco, Niccolò, 33–34, 99n
François, Michel, 45n
Frati, Ludovico, 26
Frederick, Duke of Calabria (character in *Urania*), 184–85, 196–201, 208–9, 209n
Freedman, Luba, 187n
Fregoso (family), 16

Gallerani, Cecilia, 207n
Gamba, Bartolommeo, 25, 25n, 30, 50
Gambara, Veronica, 3
Genesis, 65n
Gilbert, Creighton, 189n
Gillett, H. M., 165n
Ginevra (character in Caviceo's *Libro del Peregrino*), 32
Ginzburg, Carlo, 207n
Giolito, Gabriele, 51
Giovanni Fiorentino, Ser, 2n

INDEX

Giovio, Paolo, 187n
Goffen, Rona, 207n
Gregory XIII (pope), 15
Grotto degli Erri, Luigi Ignazio, 44
Guglielminetti, Marziano, 29n
Guglielmo, Guido, 31n

Heijkant, Marie-José, 40nn
Helen of Troy, 148–49, 149n, 201n
Henry VII (emperor), 47–48, 301n
Hippolytus, 49, 50n
Hircan (Henri d'Albret, in *Heptaméron*), 45
Holofernes, 150–51
Holy Roman Empire, 307n
Homer, 147n
Horace, 80–81
Hortensia, 142–43, 143n
Hortensio (character in *Urania*), 280–81, 287–88
Hotchkiss, Valerie, 165n

Idea (in neo-Platonic process of cognition), 94–95, 95n
idleness, 66–67, 158–59
Innsbruck, 19
Isaiah, 65n
Iulio (character in Politian's *Stanze*), 49–50

Jagiełłonka, Katarzyna, 197n
Jesus Christ, 53
Judgment (allegory in *Urania*), 36, 38, 60–83
Judgment of Paris (painting), 37, 37n, 194–205, 197n
Judith, 36, 150–51, 151n
Junkerman, Anne Christine, 207n
Juno, 194–95, 197n, 200–3

Jupiter, 51

Keller, W., 18n
King of Sweden, 197n
Kristeller, Paul Oskar, 73nn

Lando, Pietro, 15
Lazara
  Giovanni de, 42, 42n
  Giulia de, 42n
Lendinara, 42
Leone Ebreo, 18, 65n, 97n, 315n
Leoni
  Carlo, 29n
  Iacopo, 29n
Leonico, Angelo, 16–17, 17n, 20
Livy, 151n, 153n
Loi, Maria Rosa, and Mario Pozzi, 17n, 43–44
Longus, 32
Loreto, 162, 165, 165n, 168–69, 274–75
Lovarini, Emilio, 26
Love (invoked or personified), 86–87, 108–9, 116–17, 182–83, 186–87, 194–95, 204–7, 248–49, 254–55, 284–87
love sickness (romance motif), 190–93, 306–9
Luke, 65n, 111n

Macassola, Francesco, 11–12
Machiavelli, Niccolò, 35
Macrobius, 245n
Malfatti, Cesare, 299n, 301n
Maltby, William S., 307n
Mancini, Vincenzo, 4n, 8–9, 12n, 42n, 197n, 261n
Manutius, Aldus, 31
Marescotti, Ercole, 2, 20

INDEX

Marguerite de Navarre, 45
Marius, 152–53, 153n
Masenetti, Giovanni Maria, 8–9, 20, 43–44
Masuccio Salernitano, 29, 185n, 209n
Matthew, 65n, 111n
Mazzuchelli, Giammaria, 22–23, 27, 51
Medea, 146–47, 147n
Medici, Catherine de', 16
Melechini, Mario, 17–19, 20, 22
Menandro (character in *Urania*), 39, 51, 182–83, 216–33, 236–37, 244–45, 266–67, 286–89
Mezentius, 152–53, 153n
Michelangelo Buonarotti, 99n
Milani, Marisa, 16
Mirabello, 30, 43, 45, 53, 292–93
Mongibello (Mount Etna), 212–13
Montpensier, Louise de (Duchess of Bourbon), 197n
Mussato, Albertino, 47

Naples, 19, 21, 36, 108–9, 131–32, 206–7, 209n, 274–75, 282–83
Nardelli, Franca Petrucci, 302n
Nature, 68–71, 76–77, 92–93, 98–99, 104–5, 134–35, 144–45, 174–75, 188–89, 204–5
neo-Platonism, 73n, 95n
Neptune, 51
Nero, 152–53, 153n
Nissen, Christopher, 36n, 40n, 115n
novella:
    as comedy, 2n
    different from prose romance, 30, 34–35
    different from *Urania*, 30–31
    as opposed to history, 47–48, 292–93, 318–19
    orality in, 34–35
    popularity in Veneto, 29, 29n
    role of women in, 3
    "The Novella of Giulia Camposanpiero and Thesibaldo Vitaliani," 23–27, 29–30, 33n, 38, 42–50, 53–54, 153n, 197n, 261n, 292–93
nudity, 60–65, 65n, 196–99, 197n, 198–207, 207n

Odoardo (character in "Giulia Camposanpiero"), 308–9
Odolarica (character in "Giulia Camposanpiero"), 38, 49, 302–3, 303n, 304–19
Orlando (in Ariosto's *Orlando Furioso*), 39–40
Orosius, Paulus, 143n, 153n
Orsini (family), 299n
Orsino, Lucio (character in "Giulia Camposanpiero"), 298–1, 306–9, 314–17
Ovid, 147nn, 149n, 191n, 197n

Padua, 17, 18, 19–20, 26, 28, 47–49, 73n, 153n, 294–97, 302–5, 310–11, 318–19
Padua, University of, 5, 12, 15, 18n, 19–20, 19n, 73n
Paduan (or Veneto) dialect, 53–54, 62n, 178n
painter (character in *Urania*), 186–89, 195–205, 208–9, 214–15, 282–287
Paleotto, Camillo, 15
Pallas (Minerva), 1, 2n, 18, 195–96, 197n, 200–3
"Panfilo" (novella), 23–25, 29–30, 44

INDEX

Papafava (family), 17n
Parabosco, Girolamo, 30
Park, Katherine, 73n
Paris (Trojan prince), 37, 148–51, 194–95, 198–99, 200–3
Parlemente (Marguerite de Navarre, in *Heptaméron*), 45
Passano, Giambattista, 25–26
Passero, Felice, 37n
Patetta 358 (MS), 51
Penthesilea, 142–43, 143n
Peregrino (character in Caviceo's *Libro del Peregrino*), 32
Perrenot de Granvelle
    Antoine, 17, 17n
    Charles (Carlo Perenotto), 17–19, 19n, 20
Perry, Ben Edwin, 31n
Petrarch (Francesco Petrarca), 35, 39, 51, 205n, 273n
Phaedra, 49
Phalaris, Tyrant of Acragras, 152–53, 153n
Phidias, 204–5, 205n
Philena (character in Franco's *Philena*), 99n
Philip II (king), 17
Pietrucci, Napoleone, 25, 27
Piovan, Francesco, 19n
Piranesi, Pietro, 26n
Pirovano, Donato, 29
Pizan, Christine de, 35–36, 35n, 65n, 143nn, 149n, 151nn, 153n
Plato, 80–81
Pliny, 99n, 107n, 205n
Plutarch, 153n
Poccianti, Michele, 2n
Policlitus, 204–5, 205n

Politian (Angelo Poliziano), 49–50
Pomponazzi, Pietro, 73nn
Porcelli, Bruno, 34n
Porro, Giulio, 25–26, 27, 30, 50
portraits in private collections, 186–87, 187n
portraiture, 36–37, 41, 60–61, 68–71, 82–83, 88–89, 96–99, 186–91, 194–205, 208–9
Prince of Salerno (Giufredi, character in *Urania*), 20, 34, 38–39, 39n, 41, 84–85, 85n, 182–83, 186–95, 198–217, 222–33, 236–37, 258–61, 264–68, 270–73, 278–88
Princess Costanza (Straparola, *Le piacevoli notti* 4.1), 40n
Princess of Poland (character in *Urania*), 194–97, 197n, 200–1
Procaccioli, Paolo, 27–28
Procne, 146–47, 147n
Pseudo-Dionysius, 103n
Pygmalion, 190–91, 191n

Quadrio, Francesco Saverio, 22–23, 27

Raya, Gino, 32n
Reason:
    as allegory in Christine de Pizan, 65n
    as faculty in *Urania*, 70–71
The Recognitions of Clement, 235n
Remondini, Giuseppe, 44–45n
Ribera, Pietro Paolo di, 20–21
Richardson, Francis L., 197n
riddle (at end of "Giulia Camposanpiero"), 27, 42–43, 320–21, 321n
Rogers, Mary, 97n, 201n
Rohlfs, Gerhard, 238n
romance (literary mode), 30–35, 165n

Index

verisimilitude in, 33–34
love madness in, 39–40
Rome, 108–9, 150–51, 197n, 198–99, 299n, 301n
rose garland, in *Urania*, 33–34, 208–9, 212–25, 282–85
Rua, Giuseppe, 26–27
Ruggiero (in Ariosto's *Orlando Furioso*), 40n
Ruzante (Angelo Beolco), 26, 40n

Sabine women, 36, 150–51, 151n
Sacchetti, Franco, 34
Saggiori, Giovanni, 28
Saibante, Giambattista, 51
Saibante Library, Verona, 23–24, 27
Salerno, 19, 39, 40, 84–85, 108–9, 166–67, 174–75, 178–81, 186–87, 198–99, 208–89, 212–19, 224–25, 230–31, 236–39, 224–47, 256–69, 272–75, 278–82, 284–85
Salvatico, Bartolomeo, 12, 12n, 20, 25–26, 29, 30, 41n, 50–51, 57–58, 68–71, 82–83
San Bernardino (church in Padua), 6–8
Sannazaro, Iacopo, 31–32
Sanseverino, Ferrante (Prince of Salerno), 19–20, 20n, 21, 23–24, 29, 85n
Sappho, 142–43, 143n
Sarpi, Paolo, 15
Scaligers, 296–97
Scardeone, Bernardino, 1–4, 4nn, 11, 12n, 20–21, 24, 27, 30, 47, 297n, 299n, 301n
Scipio's ghost (in Caviceo's *Il Peregrino*), 83n
Semele, 51
Seraphim, 103, 103n
Sercambi, Giovanni, 34

Sforza
    Bona, 197n
    Ludovico, 207n
Shakespeare, William, 153n
sibyls, 142–43, 143n
Sigismund (emperor, character in "Giulia Camposanpiero"), 47–48, 300–3, 301n, 303n, 304–19
Sigismund I (King of Poland), 197n
Simonetta (in Politian's *Stanze*), 50
Sinope, Queen of the Scythians, 143n
Smoller, Laura Ackerman, 111n
Socrates, 80–81
Sogno Faceto sopra le Scarpe di Aldo Manuzio, 22, 27
Soncin
    Alvisa Barbo, 4–5
    Antonio Maria, 12, 12n
Spain, 198–99, 202–3
Sperona
    Diamante, 17n, 18
    Giulia, 43–44
    Lucietta, 17n
Speroni, Sperone, 17n, 18, 18n, 43–44
Stampa, Gaspara, 25, 28
Stieber, Joachim W., 303n
Straparola, Giovan Francesco, 26–27, 30, 33–34, 40n, 42–43, 43n, 197n, 233n, 299n, 321n
Strozzi (family), 16
Suetonius, 153n
Sulla, 152–53, 153n
Sustris, Lambert, 41n, 197n

Tamyris (Tomyris), Queen of Scythia, 142–43, 143n
Temple of Peace, 106–7, 107n
Terracina, Laura, 3

Index

Theseus, 49, 143n
Titian (Tiziano Vecellio), 9, 11, 99n
Toffanin, Giuseppe, jr., 28–29, 29n
Toledo, Pedro de, 19
Tomasini, Jacopo Filippo, 21, 23–25, 29
Torelli Benedetti, Barbara, 22
Torreglia, 43
Trapolin (family), 301n
Trapolin, Rubertho, 300–1
Tristan, 39, 39n
Tristano Panciatichiano, 39–40nn
Troy, 37, 144–45, 148–51
Trivulziana 88 (MS), 42, 50–52, 54
Trivulziana Library, 25–27, 50–51
Trivulzio, Marchese, 51
Tuscany, 162–63, 274–75

Urania (character):
    approaches Wild Woman, 256–59
    arrives at Salerno with Emilia, 246–49
    as alter-ego of Bigolina, 17
    asks to see Fabio, 258–261
    as authority on love, 18
    Bigolina's conception and naming of, 36–41, 37n
    converses with Emilia, 164–69
    creation of, 82–83
    declares need to rescue Fabio to Emilia, 248–53
    invents story to preserve Emilia's honor, 272–79
    laments to Fabio, 109–11
    lectures to Emilia on true love, 252–57
    lectures to five men in defense of women, 132–61
    lectures to five women on love, 111–29
    letter to Fabio, 90–107
    marries Fabio, 286–88
    referred to with masculine pronouns, 115n
    resolves to flee in male disguise, 88–89
    reveals identity to Fabio and Prince's court, 270–73
    rides to Tuscan inn, 162–65
    sees mother and resumes woman's clothing, 280–81
    tells court of her own death 260–65
Urania, 6, 12
    critical views of, 29–30
    defined as *operetta*, 23–25, 30, 82–83
    defined as romance, 30–31, 33–34
    innovations and novella characteristics in, 35–36
    manuscripts and translation, 50–52
    references to Salerno in, 19–20
    spontaneous conception of, 82–83
    structure and themes of, 36–41
    works of same name by Cassola, Wroth and Passero, 37n

Vatican Library, 51
Vedova, Giuseppe, 12n, 25, 26n
Vendramina (Bigolina's servant), 7
Venice, 9, 16, 19, 21, 260–61
Venus (or Aphrodite), 8, 21, 37, 49, 65n, 190–91, 196–97, 197n, 198–99, 200–3
Verona, 25, 27
Veronese, Emilia, and Elisabetta dalla Francesca, 20n
Veturia, 36, 150–51, 153n
Vicomercato
    Bartolomeo, 4–5, 12, 29n

Index

Gabriela, 6–7
Ottavio, 6–8
Silvio, 5–6
Vienna, 302–3, 308–11
Vignali, Luigi, 32n
Villa Bigolin (Selvazzano), 8, 41n, 197n, 261n
Virgil, 80–81, 153n
Vitaliani (family), 294–95, 295n
Vitaliani
    Palamede de', 48
    Thesibaldo, 42, 47–50, 53–54, 294–319
    Thiso (Cavalier), 296–97, 297n, 302–3
Vitullo, Juliann, 40n
Volumnia, 153n

Weil Marin, Giovanni, 4n
Wild Man (Huomo Salvatico), 40–41, 41n, 232–35, 233n, 256–57
Wild Woman (Femina Salvatica), 40, 40–41n, 226–27, 230–37, 250–59, 272–73

wise maiden (la savia damigella), 38, 204–5, 208–9, 214–18, 282–88
women:
    contrasting moral types, 38
    defense of, 35–36, 138–55
    disguised as men, 40–41
    as inappropriate subject for sculpture, 60–61, 61n
    love crisis for, 39–40
    roles in novella, 3–4
    social risks of posing for portraits, 36–38, 207n
    as unaccustomed to recounting historical narratives, 45–47, 294–95, 318–19
Wroth, Lady Mary, 37n

Yvain, 39

Zeuxis, 98–99, 99n, 198–201, 201n
Zumthor, Paul, 31n
Zwinger, Theodor (Teodoro Zuingero), 3, 20, 24, 297n